HAV

"I was captured by the book's pace and the voices of the narrators. Jaida Jones and Danielle Bennett have written a really pleasurable book, and I look forward to reading a second one from them."
—CHARLAINE HARRIS,
New York Times bestselling author

"Delicious! The characters are unique, entrancing and believable: dinner-party guests you never want to see go home. I will gladly walk again in this city, now that I know my way around."
—ELLEN KUSHNER,
author of *The Privilege of the Sword*

"A dazzling cast of memorable characters! *Havemercy* is a wonderful debut from two talented new authors."
—LYNN FLEWELLING, author of *Shadows Return*

"Warning: the dragons in this remarkable first novel are wickedly innovative creations. Once they take flight in your imagination, they may supplant your childhood memories of their fairy-tale cousins. I, for one, will never think of dragons again without hearing the roar of these metallic monsters."

—Drew Bowling,
author of *The Tower of Shadows*

"Debut coauthors Jones and Bennett have created a freshly imagined fantasy universe with magically powered metal dragons, a hard-living, tough-talking crew of dragon riders, and tales of hidden identities, long-kept secrets, and loves that prove stronger than magic."

—*Library Journal*

"Jones and Bennett vividly convey the testosterone-saturated world of fantasy fighter pilots in this fast-paced debut."

—*Publishers Weekly*

"These ladies write like a house on fire, delivering fantasy's most pleasant surprise since Temeraire himself took wing in 2006. Jones and Bennett have reinvented dragons yet again, this time in a steampunk context. But the bulk of their story is driven by some of the most sensitive and authentic attention to character you're likely to see this side of Westeros. . . . *Havemercy* works beautifully as a rich and rewarding stand-alone adventure. It's an

impressive debut for its twenty-year-old creators and one of the few truly notable titles of 2008."
—SFReviews.net

"Each protagonist has a distinctive voice, from Royston's catty sarcasm to Rook's unrestrained anger, and each undergoes sensitive and realistic changes because of their relationships. The few flaws are minor compared to the strengths of this fantasy that satisfyingly concludes within the same volume in which it started."
—*Booklist*

"Dragons, like elves, are so common in fantasy literature that the palate can get tired of them. They can be used in new, interesting ways . . . but often they aren't. *Havemercy* is one of the interesting ones. . . . The world they've created is one I want to know more about and their characters are interesting."
—SFSite.com

Also by Jaida Jones and Danielle Bennett

SHADOW MAGIC
DRAGON SOUL
STEELHANDS

HAVEMERCY

JAIDA JONES AND DANIELLE BENNETT

BALLANTINE BOOKS • NEW YORK

Havemercy is a work of fiction. Names, characters, places, and incidents either are the product of the author's imagination or are used fictitiously. Any resemblance to actual persons, living or dead, events, or locales is entirely coincidental.

2009 Spectra Mass Market Edition

Copyright © 2008 by Jaida Jones and Danielle Bennett

Published in the United States by Spectra, an imprint of The Random House Publishing Group, a division of Random House, Inc., New York.

SPECTRA and the portrayal of a boxed "s" are trademarks of Random House, Inc.

Originally published in hardcover in the United States by Spectra, an imprint of The Random House Publishing Group, a division of Random House, Inc., in 2008.

Map by Neil Gower
Cover art by Stephen Youll
Cover design by Jamie S. Warren

ISBN 978-0-553-59137-8

Printed in the United States of America

www.ballantinebooks.com

9 8 7 6 5 4

To Uncle David, for all the walking and talking
Jaida

To Andrew, for not laughing when I said "metal dragons"
Dani

And to Ellen, without whom this book would
never have been a book at all
J & D

If it takes a village to raise a child, then it takes an army to write a book, and we couldn't have done this without our army. To those who were brave enough to read this in its earliest stages—Susan, Natasha, Yi Liu, Tashina, Sara, Laura, Justine, Mom, Uncle David, Grandma Fay and Grandpa Terry—thank you for being swift and merciless with your feedback. Many thanks, of course, to our tireless agent, Tamar Rydzinski, to Anne Groell, our editor at Bantam Spectra, for taking a chance on Rook, Thom, Royston, Hal and all the metal dragons, as well as to our copy editor, Sara Schwager, and Joshua Pasternak, who was always kind enough to tell us "Don't panic." Thanks to both our dads for the straight-talkin'; to John Jurgensen at the *Wall Street Journal* for including Jaida in his article, "Rewriting the Rules of Fiction," which somehow landed us on this path in the first place; to the society of Nitpicky Babes for their sound advice and witty repartee; to Cassie and Holly, for being our first inspirations; to Claudia and all the fine ladies at Java City, for keeping the coffee coming; to Jonah, for the soundtrack; and to those in our lives who put the right books in our hands when we were the right age. Finally, thanks to the boxers: You know who you are, and where would we be without you?

❧❧❧

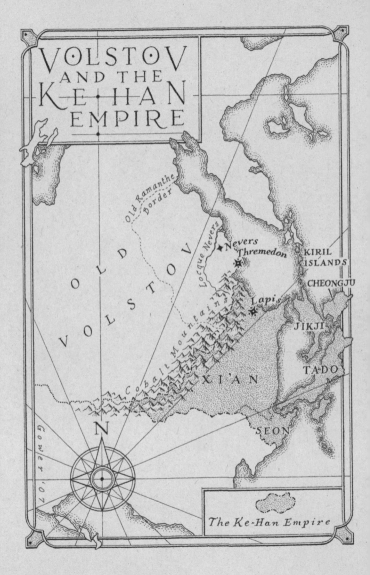

VOLSTOV
AND THE
KE·HAN
EMPIRE

Old Ramanthe Border

Locque Nevers

★ Nevers
Thremedon

KIRIL
ISLANDS

CHEONGJU

O
L
D

V
O
L
S
T
O
V

Lapis

Cobalt Mountains

JIKJI

TA·DO

XI'AN

SEON

Gowler '07

N

The Ke·Han Empire

CHAPTER ONE

ROYSTON

That morning, I awaited my arrest in Our Lady of a Thousand Fans. I wasn't alone, but it seemed I might as well have been, for the young man in the bed next to me was asleep. He had no particular reason not to be—after all, it wasn't *his* future upon which fell the shadow of impending arrest—and though I found that I could not look at him, neither did I begrudge him the repose.

It was rather a curious situation in which I'd found myself. Truth be told, I'd considered myself clever enough to avoid such entanglements altogether. Yet the problem with doing foolish things was that it was quite often impossible to tell what was foolish and what wasn't until you'd swum too far out to turn back again. After that point, it was either carry on or drown.

Of course, you were hanged either way if another man stood up to accuse you of doing all manner of things you were relatively sure you hadn't.

And *that* was the thing about men: They could so easily change their minds, become frightened of what might happen to them, and throw you to the wolves. If you were very, very unlucky, they might even do all three.

At least—if you were more than passably wealthy—you might be able to go out in style.

I was waiting that morning for the footfalls I knew were coming. They were neither the trained, delicate rhythms of Our Lady's skilled professionals nor the uneven steps of sated patrons, but rather those that held all the surety and sharpness of a man of the law. The man who was coming for me was one who did not need to hunt his quarry because he knew very well where it would be. Though my offense was by all accounts a serious one, the way in which it must be handled would demand a touch of finesse. Most political matters did, though it was a philosophy lost on some men.

Despite my assumptions, I couldn't have said quite what I was expecting, but it certainly wasn't the Provost of the city himself, leaning in the doorframe as though he hadn't a care in the world.

There was a large mirror hanging on the wall opposite the bed—for people who liked that sort of thing, I supposed—ornately framed in dark cherrywood. So I saw the scene as it must have appeared to him: the lines forming thin and faint at the corners of my eyes, gray hairs glinting at my temples more obviously than I'd have liked in the late-morning sun. I thought ruefully of how little I deserved those marks of age, and how well I had won them, for a man just past thirty-five years of age. Next to me the young man slept on, his tanned shoulders smooth, his mouth open and vulnerable. I tilted my head, fingers measuring the dark unkempt edges of the beard creeping over my cheeks and under my chin.

I'd not had the time to shave before—and after, it had seemed like something of a trifle. After my betrayal by Erik, many things had seemed a trifle.

"Margrave Royston," said the Provost. "You're a hard man to track down."

"Not particularly," I said.

His nose wrinkled at the smell of burnt cloves that permeated the air, and I could sense how very badly he wished to tell me to stop smoking. His excellent comportment prevented him from doing so; or perhaps it was his keen attention to protocol. Nevertheless, there were those who believed the Esar had made a grievous error in letting a commoner enforce his laws. The Provost was a man of the Charlotte district, center-born and center-bred. The people liked him because he didn't put on airs, and everyone else liked him because he minded his own business—with the exception, of course, of those rare occasions when the noblesse went out of their way to do something exceedingly imprudent or alarming; and then his intervention was required.

There was a bowl carved from black stone on the nightstand, in anticipation of the possibility that the wealthy patrons of Our Lady might need a place to put their cuff links or jewelry. I myself had adopted it as an ashtray, a purpose for which I felt it was peculiarly suited.

"You'd better get dressed," the Provost continued, removing a round, gold watch from his pocket. "There's a ruling to be had."

"So soon?" I didn't know myself whether the surprise in my voice was feigned or genuine. I decided on the third option, which was trousers, and got out of bed. "Dmitri, I must say the efficiency of this nation in condemning a man is simply astounding."

The Provost continued to examine his pocket watch with somewhat forced interest. "Your duties within the Basquiat will be assumed by another, in accordance with the sentencing."

"Sentencing?" I caught a glimpse of myself again in the mirror, hair dark and sleep-wild, half-dressed, white shirt voluminous and untucked, my nose stark and sharp and the new lines tight around my eyes and mouth. I'd lost my cuff links under a mound of ash. I looked exactly as I felt: a man thrown off center.

"Oh. There's no official trial," Dmitri said quickly, casting a glance upward. Finding me more or less decent, he nodded and tucked the watch away into some invisible pocket. "We just thought it might be time for a little, ah, chat."

His attitude confirmed my worst fears.

We stepped outside together, and I looked about at the city I loved.

Our Lady of a Thousand Fans was situated in the heart of Miranda. Most will tell you it's the palace, or even the Basquiat, that's the real center of the city's uppermost district. In truth, it all depends on where you're coming from, or what attracts you most.

You can tell a lot about people by the details they choose to employ when describing Volstov's capital.

If you ask anybody who's anybody, though, they'll tell you that if you wish to get through the city and *not* end up hopelessly lost, it isn't at the palace or Our Lady that you want to begin. Leaving from the Basquiat is actually easiest, taking the Whitstone Road, which leads in a counterclockwise direction through 'Versity Stretch, past the Rue d'St. Difference and its countless milliners—elaborate hats being very much in fashion this season, the sort with lace veils, wide brims, and feathers—along with all the other shops. The Rue is just on the edge between lower Miranda and upper Charlotte, so once you're past the merchants' quarter you're smack in the middle of Charlotte herself, teeming and fat-voweled and cocky. No one much cares what you do in Charlotte so long as you're not doing it to a friend or member of the family. Once you accustom yourself to Charlotte's indifference, she will adopt you as her son or daughter, so long as you look after yourself and don't stray too close to Mollyedge.

It was a principle that could be applied to any of the three sister districts, for each had its own boundaries, as well as its own consequences for dealing with those who strayed too close to them.

The Provost's hansom had windows, at least, and for that I was thankful. I had the odd idea in my head—pervasive no matter how I tried to distract myself—that this might be the last time I got to examine the city I so loved with such reverent attention. I'd had the same feeling with Erik the last occasion I'd met with him, though at the time I hadn't paid my misgivings much mind.

In the end I didn't blame Erik. Volstov was accepting of such dalliances, while Arlemagne took the opposite approach. And Erik was an Arlemagne prince. He was under edict, and he did no credit to his royal family nor to the time-honored tradition of diplomacy for which Arlemagne was famous. On top of all that, we hadn't exactly been careful—a fact for which I blamed myself—making eyes at one another in broad daylight, in the streets, in the middle of the Basquiat. My only surprise was that no one had noticed us sooner.

If I were being ruthless in my honesty, I would admit that it was not the *only* surprise I had felt over the matter, but I had told myself it was pointless to wrestle with such thoughts beyond what good they could do me. Arlemagne had no understanding of Talents: a magician's particular aptitude within a given field. The same man who could pull a stream from its bed could not create enough heat to boil water unless he did it the same as the rest of us, with a stove, or by building a fire with his own two hands.

Likewise, a man whose skills lay chiefly with combustion would have to rely on his own considerable charm, rather than his Talent, to seduce any sort of prince.

Erik had capitalized on the ignorance of his countrymen and saved himself a great deal of grief in doing so. Really, it should not have surprised me. He was boundlessly clever; one almost wanted to admire him.

Now, in the absence of what regret I'd not yet allowed myself to feel, I felt an overwhelming sense of loss concerning Thremedon City herself, her twisting uneven skyline and its gentle sloping toward the sea.

We jostled around a corner, the Provost staring at his watch with the keen interest of a man determined not to be late or one who was extremely uncomfortable with the situation at hand. From the fervor he was devoting to the task, I had to assume that, wherever we were heading, it was certain to be a room full of self-important men, waiting to decide my fate. I normally had nothing against self-importance, but the idea that, at this moment, someone could be settling a sentence upon my head was both disquieting and invasive, as though the private events of my life had all too quickly become public.

I might have considered this fact before involving myself with Arlemagne's heir, but I have always been much cleverer in retrospect.

There were certain freedoms allowed to men of the Basquiat—men of privilege and wealth. I wondered if this would help my case. But there were *some* limits to that freedom for which one couldn't be pardoned. I'd never been at the center of an international incident before. On the periphery, perhaps—skirting around the edges like the proper young madames keen on avoiding puddles in the street—but this time was different. Displease the wrong people, and even your connections can't save you. Displease the wrong *country,* and—well, I would find out shortly.

I refused to blame Erik. Panic was a natural reaction; it could make you stupid, selfish. I'd seen it often enough. It was a rare man who had the natural proclivity to do the right thing when the wrong one might save him a share in the punishment or blame. Erik had been young. In his place and at that age, I might well have done the same.

This was a lie—I knew even as I thought it—but it was a lie that gave me some comfort.

Our carriage halted in front of the Esar's palace: a long, low-ceilinged building of cream and gold. The Provost got out before me and held the carriage door, so I knew that things couldn't be so dire as all that. Still, it was with a sense of slow, settling disaster that I stepped onto the Palace Walk.

For the first time in a long while I felt utterly powerless to shape my surroundings.

"It's this way," said the Provost. He tapped me once on the shoulder, then took the lead. I followed him, for I could go no other way.

ROOK

The only reason we got punished the way we did was 'cause th'Esar was spitting mad for too many reasons that had nothing to do with *me* and what *I'd* done. All of a sudden and out of nowhere, we were getting slapped with a ruler on the wrist, only there was a whole lot more of a ruckus about it, and it was th'Esar himself instead of some prissy-pants schoolma'am doing the slapping. I mean, we were *all* called in—me and the rest of the boys—and lined up on these uncomfortable chairs that smelled of old velvet and dust, and made to wait in this place Balfour (his voice reminding us he'd been raised with all the privileges of a thoroughbred bitch) said was Punishment's Antechamber. And even I had to admit it: That seemed about right. Nobody said anything to us, just gave us a couple of dark looks before making us wait, no doubt so we could think long and hard about what we'd done. They were scowling at me in particular, seeing as how I'd been the one to do it, and everyone knew.

I wasn't sorry. None of the boys were, either—I could see it in the way they were scowling right back. Th'Esar was just pissed and looking for someone to blame it all on. Because we were having enough trouble with Arlemagne without all this on top of the rest, Ghislain'd said, and Adamo'd just shook his head like maybe he wished he'd been a part of it and maybe he was real glad he hadn't been, and maybe it didn't matter either way since he was called in for it with the rest of us.

The thing was, I didn't *know* she was married.

She wasn't so fine and so sweet-curved as I couldn't've found somebody else—and better—to tickle that night. But she was married to a diplomat, which was what made it so bad, so when I tried to pay her like she was a common whore, she got wild as a wet cat on me, screaming and throwing things and breaking vases. I thought she *was* a whore, the way she'd tarted herself up, but apparently that was just an Arlemagne's way: powder on everything and too many undergarments, the kind of teasing frippery you only see in Our Lady and which I normally don't have time for. Her breasts were incredible, though—big and round and soft and warm—and I spent a lot of time letting her know how incredible I thought they were. Even if I did think it was a commercial exchange, she might've been grateful instead of screaming rape all over, like that's what you can do if you're a woman when things go sour and you feel a slight.

She called me all kinds of things in her raw-edged Arlemagne voice, all kinds of incredible things I passed on afterward to Magoughin, who collected that kind of talk. But then all of a sudden there was a diplomat with some ridiculous mustache knocking down our door like he was going to kill us, and I almost had my knife in him, all the boys laughing and whooping it up, when Adamo got his arms round me and dragged me off, both of us cursing up a storm.

Which led us to where we were, too early for my tastes, ready to take our lumps from th'Esar—which is what they call him in the streets, on account of there being one too many e's in the title otherwise—and nobody happy about it, except me, since at least I'd seen some action and was feeling pretty good despite the situation.

"So what about this fuck-up with the little Cindy?" I asked, 'cause I knew I could fish it out of Jeannot, who loved gossiping about the noblesse better than the noblesse did themselves.

Jeannot sighed. "Rook," he began.

"Fine," I said, amending. "The *Margrave,* then. Biting the pillow with one of Arlemagne's princes? Everyone's talking about it. I just figured you'd know the sordids."

"Heir apparent," Jeannot replied. "He was 'biting the pillow' with Arlemagne's heir apparent."

"*Fuck,*" I said, and whistled.

Balfour gave me a look like I'd offended him something awful, which was ridiculous, seeing as he'd been one of us long enough that no man could call him rookie. Besides which, I'd found better names for him since, and he knew what to expect from me.

"It won't be anything serious," said Ace, who never thought anything was serious unless he was in the air, and even then he was keeping score. But I didn't know whether he'd been listening to us or whether he was trying to reassure himself about the punishment that was waiting for us just on the other side of th'Esar's door.

Evariste took it as the second meaning, and didn't bother answering. He was only ever half-listening to anything anyone ever said, anyway. "They never punish the Margraves."

"They never punished *us* before, either," I pointed out. "Where the fuck is fucking Niall?"

The ninth of our company had talked his way past the guards, pleading a weak bladder, but I didn't think it'd have worked for anyone else. Niall came from soldiering blood; they recognized their own and favored him as such. Unfair fucking world, but Niall was tight in a pinch, especially when the pinch required sweet-talking. Even now he was probably reading the rags on one of th'Esar's own porcelains or, better yet, milking information from a maid somewhere with his hand right on the teat.

Besides the boys, there wasn't much to look at in the Antechamber, just blank walls painted the same puke tan every which way you stared. Raphael said it was supposed to be calming, the color, so as to soothe the wild psychopath within, but Raphael talked like that all the fucking time, like he'd read one too many fancy books as a kid and the words had left him addlepated. Anyway, I figured the men that designed the room wanted anyone waiting to think long and hard on what they'd done, instead of letting them relax by filling the place with fancy picnic scenes so they could sit and think "What a lovely painting" and not "If Merritt goes on tapping his foot like that, I'll kill him."

"She did have amazing breasts," Ace said finally, before he kicked Merritt in the shin, at least solving that problem.

His topic was a pleasing one, though it always set me on edge to be agreeing with anything Ace had to say. But I guess even disagreeable men could come together over a nice pair of breasts.

I smiled, fierce and smug. Along the line of chairs, one or two bodies shifted like they had something important to say but couldn't see their way toward saying it. I crossed my arms and dared them to go on and get it off their chests, but anyone who wanted to protest at being called in on my account had missed his chance when it'd first happened. 'Course, they may've been discouraged by my knife and my temper at the time, but that just meant they were prudent.

Had to be prudent to fly with the Dragon Corps.

Niall came skidding back into the room, looked relieved and then disappointed that we were all sitting exactly where he'd left us. He took the empty seat, fussing with the high collar of our uniform. "Esar's tied up in some big to-do a ways down. Very top secret. Something to do with a Margrave and the prince of Arlemagne?"

"Heir apparent," I told him, in a foul mood now because this was no news, and I hated hearing the same rumors twice. "Seems he's bent as a—"

"Rook," Adamo cut in, calm as ever, but with a promise in his tone for anyone who took that calm as anything like weakness.

"Friend of yours?" I asked, and then I closed my mouth. Adamo'd always said I had more guts than good sense. Why anyone'd want or need the latter, I couldn't imagine, but Adamo was too big for arguing with.

"As a matter of fact, he is," said Adamo, like he knew I'd just been mouthing off and hadn't been expecting that.

Before it could get nasty, or interesting—or both—the heavy doors at the end of the room gave way. The kid who'd opened them looked barely thicker than the doors themselves, but he wore the frip and cut of a man in the service of th'Esar.

"We're ready for you," he said.

Compagnon snorted, triggering a ripple of amusement through the rest of us as we stood, ranged more or less shoulder to shoulder with the exception of our punier members.

No one was ever ready for us, I thought. Not even th'Esar himself.

HAL

The story began the way all the old legends began:

This is only a story. Whether there is some truth to it is for the discerning reader to decide.

Many years ago, in a distant land, there was born a most extraordinary young man to two entirely mundane parents. With his parents being such simple country creatures, it came as no surprise that young Tycho was born without any magical powers to speak of, let alone a Talent of his own. Perhaps it was this absence that caused his behavior, queer and brash at once, as though he did not understand that he too was meant for a common life, and wished to rail against the stars that had ordained his purpose.

Tycho was many things before he was the Brave. Just short of twenty years, he lost his nose while outmatched in a duel with a magician. It is said that the lady they fought over was so impressed with his foolhardy courage that she implored her father—a silversmith—to craft the young Tycho a nose of precious metals to wear instead.

She was a beautiful lady, unmarried and kindhearted. Therefore she was precisely the sort of lady any man would start a duel over, and even a man so peculiar as Tycho was not immune to her charms.

What happened next was unclear; whether the lady held Tycho's favor for the good she'd done him, or whether he had so indisputably impressed her that night. Whatever the case, it is certain that they made an impression on each other, for they came to be engaged over the course of the next year. Tycho visited his lady's house to ask after the progression of his fine new nose, and soon he grew accustomed to taking her walking in the gardens or through the streets of the city.

"We should be married in a garden," he would say to his lady.

"Yes," said the lady, for that was what she always said.

They might have been married the very next month, for the lady's father had finished his work on Tycho's fine nose, and there was no reason for any further delay. However, the magician who had taken Tycho's nose in the first place had a delicate sense of honor, which had been dealt a frightful hurt over losing the lady when he'd won the duel.

He came to Tycho's wedding, dressed all in black velvets with a splash of white lace at his throat. There he placed a curse on the bride, that before the year's end harvest she would fall ill and become a lady entirely of stone.

"Your body will become as cold as your heart!" the magician cried, and he disappeared before any member of her family could reach his rapier in time.

The lady was most distressed over this news. She fretted all through the reception and would take no cake, nor drink any wine.

"I will take care of this," Tycho said, for her father had many books, and he himself was incredibly learned.

"Yes," said the lady, for that was what she always said.

They enjoyed no honeymoon, and the newly married couple went to none of the fine summer festivals that year. Tycho spent his days locked away in the study of their small home, poring over his vast library for any spell that might counter what the magician had done. His lady wife interviewed hundreds of magicians in their parlor, asking them each what might be done about the curse placed upon her, and if there was anything that might be done to keep a lady's body flesh and blood the way it was meant to be.

Every day, the magicians shook their heads and left the house regretful. Every night, Tycho would unlock the window casement in his study and climb to the roof of their house to sit with his wife and gaze at the stars.

"The harvest comes soon," Tycho said, stretching his fingers to trace the shape of a horse's head in the sky.

"Yes," said his lady, for that was what she always said.

The summer ended, and it came time for the year's end harvest. Magicians from all four corners of the world visited Tycho's house, but none of them was able to offer a single suggestion that could offset the magician's curse. The lady's mother came to stay at their house and to look after her daughter, while Tycho expanded the time he spent with his books, reading through them like a man caught up in some terrible fever.

"There must be something," he said to his lady's mother.

"A pity you had no children," replied the old woman.

The harvest came. The men and women on their farms scythed their fields and reaped their wheat, and one morning Tycho woke to find his lady wife a gray weight beside him, stony and silent.

A great heaviness settled over his own heart that day, as though some part of him had turned to stone as well. He set his lady in the garden, where they had taken their first walks and spoken their first vows. Then he locked the doors to the house they had shared and left the village where he had been born and raised.

The events of those years are not well documented. It is said that Tycho was searching for the magician who had cursed his wife, or that he was searching only to forget his wife entirely. Some accounts insist that Tycho encountered a dwarf and took to keeping him as a kind of jester, to lift his spirits. Others say that he took to riding a moose, stating that it traveled much faster than even the swiftest of horses.

Of the many differing accounts of these years, it may be argued that the most true is the very first: that he sought to take his revenge on the magician who had so cruelly stolen his lady wife.

No one knows how many years it took for Tycho to find the magician. The only certainty can be that he did, one dark, chill night very far from home. Night was when the magician traveled best, since his clothes were black and his horse a fine black gelding.

The magician saw only a flash of silver—Tycho's nose in the dark—before he was dragged from his horse and the rapier plunged into his chest.

"This is for my wife," said Tycho the Brave.

The magician in black said nothing at all.

Tycho the Brave took the magician's horse, and spurred him toward his old home. Who can say why he decided to return? Perhaps it was the notion of spring in the air, and the promise of rain in the clouds. All around, the land spoke of new beginnings, and the ground was green and fertile when at last he arrived.

Tycho the Brave brought the horse around to stable it in the back, and stopped in wonderment at what he beheld. The stone statue was gone from the garden, and there was a woman singing in the kitchen, sweet-faced and dark-haired.

It was his own lady.

She came running out of the house when she saw him, and stretched her hands out to clasp his own.

"You broke the curse," his lady said.

"I killed the magician," Tycho the Brave countered. While possessed of a curious befuddlement at this turn of events, he was nonetheless thrilled beyond the telling. "Is that what's done it?"

"Yes," said his lady, for that was what she always said. She took him by his hands, and led him back into their home, where they celebrated his return in a manner as befits a husband and wife, and they were very happy until the end of their days.

The stories I read to my young cousins always ended the same way, just as they always began the same way, and sometimes I wondered about them. Was it really possible to be simply happy until you died of gout, or old age, or some kind of nefarious poisoning? It seemed to me that a man like Tycho the Brave—more peculiar than brave, to my own private thinking—would have had a very difficult time staying out of trouble entirely. There were other tales about him, romans filled with them in the library, so I could only assume he hadn't.

Perhaps his wife didn't mind it so much. She must have been a very different woman from the chatelain's wife, my adoptive mother, who would have run screaming in the opposite direction from even so much as a whisper of magician's curses. She didn't approve of my reading romans.

The Margrave Royston was related to me very distantly through marriage, because he was the chatelain's brother. And this was why he came to stay with us of all people, in the middle of Nevers—between Nevers and Nowheres, as most liked to call it.

As far as my place in Castle Nevers was concerned, there was some business of third cousins and thrice removals, but no one could keep it straight, not even the chatelain himself. Most of the time we figured it didn't matter, and the little lords and lady of the house called me no less than Cousin, while the chatelain and the Mme addressed me by name when they addressed me at all.

We had barely three days' notice of the Margrave's arrival.

Upon receiving the news, the entire house was thrown into a whirlwind of excitement, Mme going into fainting spells every two minutes about how we'd never be ready in time, and all the servants bearing the brunt of the real business. The chatelain wasn't pleased for a number of reasons, not the least of which being the cause of his brother the Margrave's sudden imposition. The scullery maids were all whispering about it, but everyone quieted before I ever had a chance to sort this troublesome business out. Instead, I made a point of keeping out of sight and out of mind, since I was in the middle of a new roman about the Basquiat itself and wanted to read in peace.

Eventually, the chatelain found me.

"Damn it, boy, what are you doing *there*?" he called up to me, arms folded, standing beneath my tree. I nearly fell off the branch and only managed to catch myself just in time. I wasn't keen on falling, not again, since the first time I had I'd done considerable damage to my wrist.

"Oh, well," I said. "Didn't want to be in the way." Then, I realized it was very awkward talking to the chatelain this way, and clambered down the trunk.

The chatelain looked at me with some bafflement—a big man, broad-shouldered, good-natured but often red in the face about something or other. I was quite fond of him, though there were a rather large number of people who found themselves put off by his bellowing.

"Well," he said. "Hal, you've a leaf in your hair."

So I had. I combed it out as quickly as I could with my fingers, book tucked under my arm and threatening to slip all the while. "Sorry," I said.

"At your age," said the chatelain, "you've no business still reading in trees. Well, no matter. We have something to discuss."

I walked beside him on the bank of Locque Nevers for a time while he said nothing and worked his large jaw. The upset with his brother had unsettled him. I was unsure of what to do or say, and so did and said absolutely nothing, which seemed the best option.

At last, the chatelain took a deep breath, clasped his hands together, and said, "The Mme and I will be trusting you to take care of him."

I didn't have to ask who. "Oh," I said, and without thinking, "in— Well, *how*?"

"You may have noticed that your room is situated very close to the guest's chamber," the chatelain explained. "My brother is . . . not impressed by country life, nor was he crafted as a person to respect or uphold any of our . . . country values."

"Ah," I said, when it appeared I needed to confirm I was listening.

"He thinks they're damn backward," the chatelain clarified. "Already, there is some suspicion among the servants concerning members of the Basquiat. Besides which, my brother is by no means an inconspicuous man. It is this decided lack of inconspicuousness that has returned him to us in the first place, and will no doubt cause a considerable volume of misunderstandings in the coming weeks until he is once again . . . accustomed to our lifestyle here."

"Ah," I said again. I was coming to understand this better, though he was speaking as if were uncomfortable, and therefore without his usual brusque clarity. At its simplest, I realized the chatelain wanted me to treat the Margrave as I would have treated his sons and daughters: half-schooling and half-nannying.

I didn't think this was the best of plans, but it wasn't my place to air these concerns.

"Yes," said the chatelain, even though he'd agreed to his own statement and nothing more. Perhaps he'd seen the understanding on my face, for Mme often commented I was as easy to read as a book. Though I was uncertain as to whether my adoptive patroness could read at all, and couldn't keep from wondering whenever she used this expression.

Still, I didn't think the Margrave would appreciate being treated as a child by one not so long departed from that state himself. This was not my observation to make, and yet I couldn't help but hope that the chatelain would realize this for himself.

All I knew about the man—save that he was the chatelain's brother—was that he was a Margrave, which meant that he was a magician who'd done great service for the Esar in one way or another. The title was usually awarded to a man who had distinguished himself in the war. What I'd read about the Basquiat offered little help, for I felt that any man sensational enough to be a member of the city's elite assembly of magicians would find no amusement in the country. Many people referred to the Basquiat as the heart of Volstov—to the Esar's displeasure—as their meeting place stood second only to the palace in scale and architectural marvel.

How anyone could leave all that excitement for a place as simple as Nevers, I didn't know.

Then I remembered that it had not been his choice to begin with, and a dark cloud settled over my heart as swiftly as the weather can change on a summer's day. Dealing with the Margrave would be far worse than even dealing with William, the chatelain's middle son.

Wind stirred my hair, in want of a cutting, and made little eddies and ripples on the lake's smooth surface. The chatelain had been standing silent for some time now. I found myself wondering after his thoughts. I'd never had a brother myself, and so I had nothing to be used for comparison. He seemed agitated, which was usually left to the Mme, and what was more, he had nothing to say for himself, which I thought terribly strange.

"He'll likely be rude," the chatelain said at last. He too was studying the lake, as though it might offer some helpful wisdom to deal with what I was privately beginning to view as the coming storm, throwing our little household into disarray.

I nodded, to show that I'd heard him.

"He's a good man," he continued, with a conviction that assured me he believed at least this about his brother. "A good man. Not as good as some, and certainly not as sensible, but his heart's in the right place."

I was relieved to hear this, as there had been a section in the roman about the very early founders of the Basquiat, two of them with their hearts removed entirely and stored elsewhere for safekeeping.

"I'll look after him," I said, with more courage than I felt. There were some days, after all, when I felt that I was inadequate to bear the responsibility of the chatelain's sons and daughter. His brother, some small rebellious part of me insisted, was asking too much. I'd already decided the Margrave would see straight to my purpose and would hate me on sight.

But I've always found that it's best to prepare for the worst possible eventuality in any given scenario. Then you can only be pleasantly surprised.

Three days went by faster than I could possibly have imagined, with the servants shooing me out of every room I could find in which to take refuge, even the ones we never used. The children were the only ones who seemed pleased, referring to the Margrave as Uncle Roy. To the children, he was preceded only by his reputation for lavish gifts. Mme, on the other hand, developed a tight look about her mouth whenever he was mentioned, and the lines only grew deeper as the days went on.

Breakfast on the fourth day was one of the most awkward meals I'd ever had at the table, rivaling the time Alexander had eaten too much ice cream and been sick all over me and his birthday cake.

The Margrave would be arriving by carriage, we'd been told, and the letter had held a date but no specific time.

The chatelain fiddled absently with his silver coffee spoon.

From the drawing room, where the windows were wide and the view was best, we at last heard a small shriek and the patter of shoes as Emilie went running to the front door in a manner unbefitting a lady, exactly the way Mme had warned her against.

There was a short silence. Then, chaos broke loose in a clamor of scraping wood, chairs being pushed back from the table so the three boys could follow their sister in a most undignified rabble. I hoped that it did not reflect on my own influence in any way. At least I wasn't yet their tutor.

"Well," said the chatelain, wiping his mouth with a linen napkin. "I suppose we should go and ensure my brother's well-being in the face of the young herd of elephants I've apparently raised."

I nodded and got up from the table too quickly, almost knocking over my chair.

The lines around Mme's mouth looked as deep and permanent as if they'd been carved with a chisel, but she rose with enviable grace. Together, the three of us stepped into the hall and made our way to the front door, where the Margrave was waiting for us.

ROYSTON

The terrible thing about the country—and this was why I'd left in the first place—is that you can't spit sideways without hitting a sheep. They're smelly, cruel creatures, malevolent and unclean. They clog the roadways, chew their cud, and clutter the landscape, abundant as the grass—gray and misshapen and utterly depressing. My brother's castle in Nevers was exactly like every country castle on the continent, and I was jostled by the country roads, nauseated by the country smells, and assaulted by the country architecture, so that I arrived late with a headache sharp between my eyes.

My brother's men were waiting to greet me, suspicious eyes sidelong and unwelcoming, though they were dressed as if they did indeed know what civilization was. Then all at once my brother's children, two of whom I'd met when they were on holiday in Miranda some years earlier, were piling out the door into the sunlight, shrieking my name and kicking up dust.

"Have you *brought* anything for us?" the girl asked. She was the youngest; I hadn't met her before, though I had sent her a tiger rug once, much to the distress of my brother's simple wife. I tried to remember her name, but I found I could not.

"I might have done," I replied, stepping back to avoid letting her clamber up my leg as if it were a tree trunk.

"Emilie!" I knew before lifting my head that this was the wife come out to greet me. I procured my pocket watch for the eldest of my nephews to examine, while Emilie jumped away from me and smoothed out her skirts, her cheeks bright red.

"It's no trouble," I said.

"She must behave as befits her," the wife sniffed, keeping her distance. "I know standards are . . . different in the city, but in the country a young lady's upbringing is a serious matter."

"Naturally," I replied.

The house was ugly but large, with a sloping shingled roof over the old castle walls and windows like gaping eyes. I shuddered to think what it would be like inside during the winter, when the snow was deep and the wind sharp. The courtyard was neatly kept, the stable far enough from the house that at least the smell of animals would not invade our living quarters except in the height of summer, and nearby I could hear the Locque Nevers rushing desperately onward. I felt a momentary kinship with the river, as if we were both aching yet helpless to escape, bound each in our own way to our eternal, shackling paths. But I was no poet, nor was I a river, and at some point I presumed the waters of Locque Nevers would reach the sea—whereas I was here indefinitely, with no similar prospects of escape.

One of the younger boys, William, was busy trying to break and not to break my pocket watch all at once. My brother had gone to see to the horses, which I'd expected of him, and I was glad he remained the same as ever. Too much change isn't good for a man. It troubles him and hinders him from digesting his meals properly. However, it left the wife, the children, the servants, and me alone together, and not one of us able to speak.

"Well," the wife said at length, though it seemed every word she spoke pained her, "these are the children."

"Yes," I agreed. "They are indeed."

"Alexander is the eldest," said a new voice, warm and uncertain. "William is about to break your pocket watch."

I refocused my attention just over the wife's shoulder and noticed someone unfamiliar hanging back not as a servant would, but neither like a true member of the family. I decided right away that he must have been no more than a distant cousin, which was why no one had seen fit to trim his hair.

"Then there are Etienne and Emilie," he went on, shifting a poorly bound roman from under his left arm to under his right.

"Emilie and I have already met," I said.

"Etienne is shy," the young man explained, shrugging. He had a strange sort of grace about him, the unusual and post-adolescent combination of complete self-consciousness and blissful distraction. He bore it well despite the hair.

"Which we will very soon break him of," the wife added sharply. She seemed to be on the verge of having the vapors.

"Like a horse, I presume," I replied, and then added smoothly, coming up to take her hand and press it against my lips in my most formal of bows, "I am your servant, Mme, in all things. Your hospitality overwhelms me. I shall repay it any way I can."

"Oh, well," she said, fluttering like a poor man's peacock—a rooster with too much tail for its own good but a rooster nonetheless. "You're family, of course."

I was, for good or for ill. "And who is this?" I asked, gesturing to the young man. I realized now the dreamy air that hung about him—like dust motes in a shaft of light—must have been a reflection of the great and secret desire he was harboring even now: that he wished to be elsewhere, reading his book, completely unbothered by our posturing.

"Who? Oh, Hal," the wife said. "He's to be Alexander and William's tutor, when Alexander comes of age."

"Next summer," Alexander said proudly.

"Very good," I replied, distracted. The tutor-to-be was pale but freckled along the bridge of his nose, and he was neither awkward nor shy but acutely polite. I shook his hand. "What are you reading?"

"This? Nothing," he said, and endeavored to hide it from me.

"Hal very much enjoys his romans," the wife said. She was sniffing again.

I thought about offering her a handkerchief, then discarded the notion. It would not do to offend my brother's wife all at once. There would be no sport left for later on, and now that I was in the country, I needed to ration my amusements as meagerly as I could.

Instead, I offered the youth a thin smile, taking advantage of his preoccupied state to lift the badly concealed volume from his hands. It was uncouth of me, but I did not expect to be reprimanded by the lady of the house, who had already made it quite evident that Hal was not among her chief priorities.

"Oh," he said, not sounding distressed but merely surprised.

The roman was a familiar one, though not the most widely respected or circulated collection of information on the Basquiat. The author had taken several creative liberties with the origins of the thing, for one, and there was scarcely even a mention of the Well. It skirted the matter of its overzealous guardians entirely, save a small notation that they called themselves the Brothers and Sisters of Regina. Yet I raised an eyebrow, surprised in turn, for I hadn't expected to find any touchstone to the city here.

"Are you interested in the Basquiat, boy?" I smoothed my fingers down the roman's spine, judging how long it would be before the pages began to fall out. Cheap books were a terrible shame, and no doubt a result of spending all your money on sheep.

"No," he said. "Well, yes, that is—I do like to read."

My brother's wife made a soft, clucking sound, the rooster emerging again in quiet disapproval.

"When I'm not studying, of course," Hal corrected himself before he smiled openly and unself-consciously. "I have a lot to learn before next summer. I'm sorry about your pocket watch."

"William!"

I'd scarcely had the time to turn around before I heard the faint wrench of machinery. Minute pieces of clockwork sprang out in every direction, raining down on the steps and over my young nephew's shoes. If I closed my eyes, it was almost a musical sound, like the chimes some magicians hung in their windows to ward off bad luck.

When I opened them, I was still in the country.

"That's all right," I said, as the boy in question raised round saucer eyes to his mother, then me. This one I had met before, though it seemed in the passing years he'd grown wild. There was an unhappy set to his mouth, halfway between rebellion and a fit of sulking. I felt an instant kinship with him and ruffled his hair where a handshake might have done. "Never mind," I said, and in my own selfish way it might have been to keep Mme my sister-in-law from punishing him, as she seemed so keen on doing. "I have others for you to break."

When he smiled, I saw that he was missing a tooth.

"Ah, Roy." My brother's voice sounded bell-clear across the grounds. I turned to greet him as he came striding toward us. The chatelain, my estranged country blood, had grown a little wider over the years, spread, settled into his skin. His face was red as it had ever been, suggesting either a very good constitution or a very poor one. Or perhaps it was sunburn.

I wondered if, living in the country, my face would grow as red. I would have to kill myself, I decided; I would take death before growing to resemble something so round and red as a tomato. I said none of this, however, and merely held out a hand for my brother to shake. There had been too many years and too many miles between us to foster an embrace, and even with our kinship it seemed a folly to pretend otherwise.

"I've come to be a burden," I said, the jest falling flat as it left my lips.

My brother's broad face creased with uneasiness. I struck his shoulder genially, in keeping with the ancient custom of male bonding that I abhor and was quite content to leave behind at seventeen. "I've just been introduced to your lovely children, brother. You've been very productive."

"Yes," he said, looking around at my impromptu welcoming committee as though gathering his bearings. I could almost see the workings of his mind, laid bare as my broken watch. Then he offered a smile, though it came less easily than either Hal's or William's. "Welcome to Castle Nevers."

I tried to keep the disdain from my face as I examined the house in a broad sweep once again. Surely the house could only be called a castle in the loosest sense of the word. It had been a castle once, but now it resembled its former self about as closely as I resembled a member of the Basquiat—which is to say, not at all.

"Well," my brother continued, anxious to be elsewhere. "We were just in the middle of breakfast. We'll have someone show you to your room."

As if reminded suddenly of some hidden cue, the tutor—Hal—nodded and smiled at me again. I didn't know how anyone could smile so often, especially at a complete stranger who'd stolen his book. Perhaps he was simple.

I trusted my brother not to leave me, much less his children, in the hands of anyone incapable, however. He knew the limits of my patience as far as fools went, and I couldn't see my sister-in-law trusting her precious ducklings to anyone she deemed unfit.

They filed inside in a staggered line, the girl holding hands with her brother, Etienne-whom-I-had-not-met, with William stepping determinedly upon the backs of Alexander's shoes.

This left me alone on the steps with Hal, not quite a tutor, not quite a relation. He moved past me and crouched to examine the remains of my pocket watch.

"That was very kind of you," he said, carefully sweeping the pieces of the watch into a neat little pile on the path. "Not to be cross with William."

I eyed him. "You have servants for that, do you not?"

"Oh," he shrugged, as though it weren't important. "That's all right, I've almost finished. William makes so much mess throughout the day, I hate to burden them with extra work if I don't have to."

I nodded after a moment, as though this made sense, which it didn't. "Would you like your book back?"

"Please," he said, looking up in surprise as if the idea hadn't occurred to him.

"I suppose the country can't be so very terrible," I said insolently. "Is there at least a library in the house?"

"Oh," said Hal. "No." He must have been frightened by what my face did then—quite of its own accord—for he added quickly, "But your brother, the chatelain, has bought a good many books for my education, and for Alexander's."

I shielded my eyes against the glare of sunlight, looking

out into the trees. There was a dreadfully large number of them, and like the sheep they were everywhere.

Our esteemed Esar had phrased my exile thus: that it would be relaxing, that it would be a quiet place to consider my actions, and that—were I lucky enough to be called back one day—I would return from it as I would from a jaunt to the islands, refreshed and with a revised perspective on my country and my duties as a citizen. The particular tone of his voice implied that I would not be so lucky as to be called back anytime soon, if at all. Thus, here I was, trapped as if I were jailed, my only recourse children and children's books, a woman I hated, and a brother I barely knew. The truth was evident. I'd never felt so indulgently sorry for myself, not even when I was much younger.

At least, in those days, I hadn't known what it was like *not* to feel helpless.

ROOK

"So he says, 'I wouldn't touch *that* with a ten-foot pole,' and the whore says, 'Which one, my lord?'" The usual chorus of halfhearted laughter greeted Magoughin's conclusion—the sound of Compagnon's just shy of a giggle, I always thought, and rising above the rest because as soon as you said the word "whore" he was off, no matter whether the joke was funny or not, and Luvander slapping his leg like he hadn't heard that one three times already. I didn't care a minute for any of it, because Ace and I were playing darts, and you can't let Magoughin's whore jokes or *nothing* distract you when you're playing darts with Ace, seeing as how distraction leads to almost taking one of Ivory's eyes out with a throw gone sour.

The truth was, nobody wanted to do any thinking about what was in store for us, and nobody wanted to do any thinking about how we hadn't been up in the air since the cold front hit. Or, to be more precise, since we wiped out the Blue Horde just outside of Lapis and left the whole Ke-Han licking their wounds like the dirty bitches they were. They'd taken back the Kiril Islands after that, and it'd set th'Esar *roaring* mad, but there wasn't a thing we could do since the Islands were so far out seaward that there was hardly any chance of getting out there, let alone there *and* back all in one flight. Anyway, the Kiril Islands had changed hands more times than good coin in a whorehouse, so it wasn't like we wouldn't be getting them back one of these days. The Dragon Corps couldn't fight all of Volstov's battles for her, but if we could've, there wouldn't have been a dispute over the Kirils in the first place. Leastways, not any kind of dispute that could be backed up with solid firepower. Simple truth was, the Ke-Han didn't have an air force at all, much less one as fucking precise as ours, as fucking deadly. And so th'Esar and all of Volstov needed us real special—but they didn't need us if we weren't fighting, and since we weren't fighting, everyone was edgy, like we were all balanced on the blade of the knife and if anyone moved for certain one way or the other, we were all screwed at both ends.

I wasn't worried. Just because the Ke-Han were quiet since Lapis didn't mean they weren't going to get loud again, and soon. They always bounced back, neat as you like, and th'Esar knew that, too. He wouldn't squander his surest bet; he wasn't going to send us into exile like old Mary Margrave, which was what they were calling the Cindy down around Mollyedge, where they could get away with it, and I was all for the nick-name seeing as how he was queerer than a three-chevronet. The corps was a different matter. We were needed in the city with our dragons polished and ready to respond like always, in case anything came up real sudden, so like I said, I wasn't worried about horseshit like *that*.

But it all still kept me guessing, same as the rest, what th'Esar *was* going to do about us, since the Arlemagnes were pissed off already due to the incident with their cindy-prince and the Margrave. Maybe I shouldn't have slapped the diplomat's wife on the ass in public and maybe I shouldn't have tried to pay her after the sex, but the point was: She was asking for it, wearing a dress like that, and so how was I supposed to know who she was? You don't wear a dress like that and *not* expect to get all kinds of attention, and none of it from your husband. You buy a dress like that to make it happen, and she knew it same as I did. Th'Esar knew it, too.

"Shit," Ace said, because he'd missed the mark. It was worrying Ace, too, which was where the line between us was drawn. Ace got worried; I didn't. Sometimes it didn't make a difference, but by my count I was three points ahead of him, and it was only on bad days that went below two. Worrying was why: Ace doing it and me not.

"What if we *are* exiled?" Balfour was asking Jeannot. Balfour was also fiddling with his gloves, taking them off and putting them back on again, and if I hadn't been busy aiming for bull's-eye, I would've aimed at his head.

It was true that the diplomat—who had a name, only I preferred to call him Mr. Mustache—was kicking up a real fuss, and wouldn't be satisfied until he thought his honor avenged. I'd offered a duel so he could win it back, but he didn't seem too keen on that option, and th'Esar was still talking things over with the bastion and some of the members of the Basquiat he actually trusted.

Jeannot took Balfour's gloves away. It wasn't a permanent solution, not as permanent as I'd have gone for, but it's been said I have less patience than most. "They won't exile us," he said, for maybe the eight thousandth time.

"Yeah, it's not like we all slept with her," said Ghislain, laughing wickedly and ducking swift as a shadow to miss my dart as it ricocheted off the wall where his head had been.

"That counts as your shot," said Ace.

"Like hell," I said, and marched over to find where it had landed.

Evariste hissed for quiet, sounding for all the world like someone's grandmother, or an angry goose, or both. I didn't know why he bothered; no one could ever beat Adamo at chess, even if he gave you the first three checks and a fair head start. I didn't know what for he was kicking up such a fuss, his defeat hanging so obvious around him the way it was. See it often enough and defeat gets a certain look to it, a certain smell; gets so that you can predict it as easy as the old coots in lower Charlotte predict the weather. Anyway, no winning man tears at his hair so. Evariste would like as not be bald by thirty if he kept that up, a fact I took upon myself to remind him of as often as possible.

"I'm not waiting forever," Ace piped up.

"*Talk* about waiting forever," Raphael snarled, too out of sorts even to come up with something appropriately cindy to say about the great hands of time and men wasting away to nothing. Ghislain toed my dart across the floor. I picked it up.

We weren't made to wait, the fourteen of us. Th'Esar knew it, had us trained all but a few from the age when most milk-suckers are still firmly attached to their mama's teat. Keeping us pent-up—and even worse, keeping us on the ground—was like lighting the fuse to a powder keg. Eventually something was going to blow up, and when it did, it wasn't going to be pretty.

"Maybe he's forgotten about us," said Merritt, counting out beats against his jiggling knee, then scribbling on a sheet of paper.

"He won't really exile us," said Balfour *again* to Jeannot, not a question, but like he needed to say it.

Some years back, when the war was real bad, we'd seen a lot of fugees—people with no place to go, no homes, just mowed right down by the Ke-Han. Probably it was because we hadn't been the *only* country to go to war with the Ke-Han, just the only one able to hold out worth a damn. That was just what happened when you ended up sharing a border with crazed, greedy bastards who didn't know they'd got enough land once they had it and were always peekin' their damned heads over the mountains to see what else there was. Never mind if there were other people living there. The Ke-Han'd done well enough in building themselves a big blue empire, or whatever the fuck it was they were after until they ran up against us. The people they'd displaced repeated themselves a hell of a lot when they talked though, like they needed to hear something more than once for reassurance. Now, Balfour was no fucking shell-shocked fugee but occasionally he did this, like we'd traumatized him or something.

No one ever listened to my clever theory that he was really a girl in disguise. I even took his pants off once to prove it, but it just pissed Adamo off.

Jeannot only handed his gloves back, like he had access to some infinite well of patience—maybe that fairy-story Well the magicians were always on about. "He won't. We're still at war, even though things have quieted down for now. If word got out that th'Esar had done away with Volstov's dragons, I can't imagine what the people would do."

I could. It's not every man who can say a riot's been held on their account, but if th'Esar was somehow persuaded into doing something so damn foolish as to send us all packing, then I knew at least fourteen who could and would. No one took care of business like we did, and no one could fly those dragons like we could. The Basquiat had seen to that, and now they were paying for it. Good. Let them pay. We went down to the wire for our country when they needed us, and now some prissy little diplomat wanted to tell me what ass I could or couldn't slap?

It was in these low years, the lulls between open conflict, that th'Esar was hardest on us. We'd been fighting for longer than I'd been around, and longer even than Adamo'd been flying. As far back as I cared to know, the war had started when Volstov had moved in on the Ramanthines without taking any of their outstanding grudges into account. Fucking lousy sort of thing to inherit, this war with the Ke-Han, but th'Esar's family was inbred as any right-proper nobility, and it wasn't out of bounds to assume his great-great-granddaddy had been more insane than cunning. Plus, the dirty Ke-Han bastards had gone in and taken the Kiril Islands while Volstov'd been busy with the Ramanthines, which kind of sidestepped any issue of peace between the two of us. It was kind of convenient, seeing as without the war, there wouldn't have been any Dragon Corps to begin with. It was just these quiet patches that got us into trouble, when the Ke-Han lay low planning their next attack and acted like they'd leave us alone to do it. I knew as soon as the Ke-Han came crawling like vermin over the Cobalt Mountains, th'Esar'd come back to us with his tail between his legs, kissing ass like that Margrave he banished.

"I should have just killed her husband," I said to no one in particular, shouldering Ace out of the way to line up my shot.

"Because murder's better than adultery?"

"It's only adultery if you're the one who's married, Niall."

"Wouldn't be anyone to complain about it though, would there?" Compagnon often thought he was speaking softer than he actually was. It got him into more than a few fistfights.

"Dunno," said Magoughin, with characteristic and therefore irritating amusement. "She seemed pretty vocal."

Didn't matter what country they came from, the upper class were always screamers.

"Bull's-eye!"

Ace had the gall to look surprised. He examined the board carefully, as though there were any doubt where my aim was concerned. People could and did shout bloody murder about my comportment and la-de-da, but the skills were never in question.

"Best out of three?"

THOM

The lay of Thremedon City—a shortening and bastardization of Three Maidens, which is what it was in the old Ramanthe—is a difficult one for foreigners in the Volstov to accustom themselves to. It often startles the new wave of foreign exchange studying alongside me at the 'Versity each year that there are some who live their entire lives without cause to go past Mollyedge, either out or in. More than once, while giving a tour, I've explained that the reason for this is the powerful force of segregation and old customs, and that the prejudices at work on us today are far stronger even than those of class. They have had well over a hundred years to steep, after all, from the year when Volstov pressed its considerable advantage in hitting the already-exhausted Ramanthine forces from behind. Their victory was absolutely guaranteed, since whatever powers the Ramanthines would have called upon to defend themselves had already been spent on their own bitter struggles with Xi'an—the mother country of what was now commonly known as the Ke-Han Empire.

From a strictly militaristic viewpoint, it was a brilliant move by the man who was then th'Esar, since there was little loss on the Volstovic side of things. From the viewpoint of the Ramanthines, and those who still considered themselves direct descendents, it was an act of aggression that remained unforgivable some hundred-odd years later. When we were renamed Thremedon by the Volstov more than a hundred years ago, those who still called themselves Ramanthine were the poor and penniless citizens of Molly, who had nothing to lose through the claim.

Most living below the Mollyedge referred to the leader of Volstov as th'Esar, cutting out the extra vowel for what they considered a simplification of speech. This was usually accompanied by a derisive hawking of spit onto the ground, or the floor, or wherever you happened to be standing at the time. As a general rule, in Molly, it made little difference. Things were much better along the 'Versity Stretch—cleaner for one, though the people there still referred to him as th'Esar, and I'd never learned anything different. To be honest, I'd never imagined it would matter. I certainly hadn't thought, when Marius said "Thom, sit down, I think I've found you the project of a lifetime," that I'd be heading anywhere near the palace.

This is what comes of befriending magicians.

When th'Esar wanted something done, he wanted it done *now,* and though there were members of the Basquiat he'd listen to, I imagined it took an awful lot of convincing to get him to accept that a student in the university could be the solution to his problems.

What had happened was, I was up late working on a paper when Marius walked in. Normally he knocked, so the way he slipped in and shut the door behind him coupled with the look he wore told me something was wrong. Something was up, they'd have said down in Molly, but I'd spent a lot of time getting the slang and the slur out of my voice—and when it comes to relearning everything you know, you couldn't slip up, not even inside your own head.

"Evening, Thom," said Marius.

"Good evening," I said, and stood quickly. There was only one chair. In terms of seniority, talent, and pretty much everything, that chair was rightfully Marius's.

"No, Thom," Marius said. "Actually, I think you'd better sit."

"It's not the scholarship," I said, feeling my heart sink like lead somewhere deep into my stomach. I thought I'd earned the renewal—Marius said it was as good as signed, sealed, and delivered to my doorstep—but sometimes when you were dealing with scholarship officials, signed and sealed occasionally did *not* deliver, no matter how much of a sure thing it was.

"What? No, Thom. That's not what I've come here to talk about."

Ah, I realized, getting a closer look at his face; and then I *did* sit down, because I knew I had to. "What's happened?"

"You're aware of the . . . incident," he began.

Because it was peacetime—or as close to peacetime as we'd seen in a hundred years—there'd been more incidents lately than I could count on the fingers of one hand, and possibly on the fingers of two; I'd been too busy to keep track of them all. It was end of term, and my research nearly done. Such was the life of the able-bodied and able-minded student, and besides which, I'd never stepped inside the palace, nor seen the noblesse any closer than out a window or by accident in shops when Marius was kind enough to take me along, and let me look, and advise me not to touch.

In other words, I knew there had been incidents, a significant number of them, because no one had anything else to worry about. For the life of me, however, I couldn't fathom to *which* incident my mentor was referring.

He must have read as much on my face: bewilderment, confusion, apology. He sighed and waved his hand. "The most famous one," he said. "The Dragon Corps. Surely you *have* heard—"

"Oh, yes," I said. "The diplomat's wife."

"Arlemagnes," Marius groaned, and heaved a weary sigh. "I've been in damn talks for the past forty-eight hours. The man wants their heads."

"Well we can't give him that," I said, and felt stupid almost immediately after.

"They're the only thing standing between us and the Ke-Han," Marius confirmed. "Well, the corps and the magicians, of course, but the Ke-Han *also* have magicians. The corps is vital. Everyone knows it. We're in a bind, Thom."

I paused. "But what—"

"Does this have to do with you?" Marius drew both hands through his hair, looking tired. I realized, shamed, that I hadn't offered him anything to drink or eat, but from the worry drawn in sharp lines about his mouth, I knew he wouldn't have accepted anything. It was often—though luckily not always—business first, with Marius; business before anything else. "A good question. Yes. Well."

I waited for it, saying nothing.

Marius coughed, swallowed, and looked for a moment very sorry himself. "You're an incredibly clever young man, Thom," he began carefully. "And with the right initiative—or if someone else saw the opportunity you yourself had no way to see, if they *saw* it, right there, before them, waiting to be taken—" He broke off and shook his head, clearly angry at himself. "No," he said, changing tacks. "Thom, I've volunteered you."

"For what?"

"To rehabilitate the corps," he said. "It's your thesis, isn't it?"

"Well," I attempted, "not *exactly*."

"The Esar, his esteemed and *incredibly* wealthy highness, will give you more funding than you could ever have dreamed of," Marius said evenly, his dark eyes bright. He was on the younger side of very old, but he looked in that moment as vital and powerful as any of the younger magicians, despite the gray streaking his hair and beard. "You will never have to bank on scholarships again. If you can do this—*if* you can do this—you will be a national hero, and the Esar ecstatic, and the Arlemagnes less damn loud, and the corps more diplomatic, and everyone so happy their jaws ache with grinning."

"And if," I said, swallowing hard, "I don't do this?"

"That's not an option," Marius said. "I'm sorry. It's an opportunity, Thom. The best you'll ever get."

"Oh," I replied. "That's why it's so terrifying."

And then, quick as that, Marius had me in his hansom, and was hurrying me through the carpeted halls, everything gilded or real gold. And then we were in private audience with th'Esar—*the Esar*—himself.

It was all like a dream, really. Or perhaps a nightmare. I was uncertain as to which this could possibly be.

The foreign diplomat from Arlemagne said things mostly in his own unfamiliar language. He was angry, though on a topic much more personal than that of his sovereign's dalliances. He frequently burst into tirades in a broken tongue I could barely understand (though I'd been trained in both Arlemagnes' tongue and old Ramanthe), hurling threats and the occasional writing implement around the unexpectedly small bastion room.

I was trying as hard as I possibly could not to stare at my surroundings, or to look around the room any more than was strictly necessary. We'd studied the bastion in school, of course, though I'd never thought that I would be lucky enough to chance on ever entering. It was one of the oldest buildings in Thremedon, and one of the only original Ramanthine edifices that had been permitted to remain instead of being destroyed like the rest.

The reasoning behind this was quite simple. The bastion was built to be a fortress. In the unsteady years when Volstov's rule was yet settling in, there had been countless rebellions, men and women fighting for Ramanthe in the streets of the city itself. The then-Esar had needed a place to put them all, and the bastion was just as good at keeping people in as it was at keeping people out. It was the largest and most famous prison we had. It had housed more historical figures than I could count. It was a piece of *history*.

At least the diplomat wasn't throwing anything that could cause any true damage, I comforted myself.

I got the sense that almost everyone in that room wanted to tell the man with the mustache to calm down, only they were afraid of triggering some unstoppable upset that would send our country tumbling into war with not only the Ke-Han but with all of Arlemagne as well.

All I could think, in my inimitable intelligence, was: *But they're supposed to be our allies come spring.*

Opinion differed on whether we truly needed allies at all. We had been at relative peace for so long now that the prevalent attitude in the city was that we would win the war within the year. Among the most common—and least charitable—sentiments was the idea that Arlemagne was only joining with us now that it was clear who the victor would be in our seemingly unending conflict.

I was glad Marius had not sent me in alone. Politics were his affair, and despite a glowing recommendation, I felt certain that, without his presence, I would not have been allowed a foot in the door.

At last, the cuckolded diplomat ceased his ranting, his face bright red and his shoulders heaving, and all eyes in the room turned to me.

"I'm told," said th'Esar, whose face before this I'd only ever seen on coins and miniatures, "that you might have a solution?"

I bowed lower than I'd ever bowed before in my life and nodded weakly. Of course, you cannot say no to a king.

CHAPTER TWO

HAL

The chatelain's brother wasn't eating.

I didn't really think it was my place to coax him to accept food like a sick cat, but leaving plates by the door wasn't advisable either because one of the dogs was bound to eat the food before Margrave Royston—Uncle Roy to the children—ever deigned to touch it.

The situation didn't seem about to get better, and I didn't seem about to get any smarter. I had a bowl of the Mme's favorite stew in one hand, a book tucked under my arm, and a closed door right in front of my face. I had to shift things a little and nearly dropped the bowl, but after a minute of awkward struggling, I managed to knock against the door with my right elbow.

From within, I heard the Margrave sigh. This was not a good sign. The week before he'd been possessed of energy and defiance enough to swear, but since he'd begun to boycott food he'd graduated to sighing only, and the chatelain spent most of his time shouting at everyone he could because, I suspected, he was worried the same as I was.

"Dinner," I said, because I couldn't think of anything else, and then, "if you wouldn't mind. If it's not too much trouble, I mean."

He seemed to know what I was talking about before I could even get it out, which was as unsettling as it ever was. Margrave Royston often gave the impression that he was reading my mind, though I knew he wasn't. Even in my books, it said the ability to draw another's thoughts into your consciousness was a rare gift—what was known as a quiet Talent—and those who were mind readers even went by a special name: *velikaia*. Most went mad from it, and those who *did* have the Talent were required to wear a badge that declared them and gave people fair warning. No; likely it was that the Margrave was just so enormously clever and I so lacking in pretense.

The door creaked as it opened and I slipped inside before I could spill or drop anything.

The room the chatelain had given his brother was one of our largest, with windows overlooking the Locque Nevers, a large desk against one wall, and a bed against the other. The curtains were drawn, though the days were long enough yet that the sun hadn't set, and I got the uncomfortable feeling they hadn't been opened all day. A thin shaft of purple evening light split the drapes in two, illuminating the dust swirling around the room and little else. Last week I'd not been bold enough to make any changes to the Margrave's room. Today, borne by some strange fit of audacity, I set the bowl of stew on the desk along with my book and crossed the room to throw the curtains wide.

There was another sigh, from behind me this time, and I turned aside from the dusty folds of fabric. Margrave Royston was kneeling on the ground, sifting through an enormous black trunk with silver fastenings. Next to the trunk was a stack of romans in all range of shapes and sizes. He seemed to be looking for something.

"Have your orders extended to staying and making sure I eat?"

I blinked, feeling immediately guilty as though I'd been caught staring—which in a way I had. At least his irritability was a comfort, for if he still had it in him to snap at me, then I could at least feel assured he hadn't given up entirely.

"No," I said honestly, remembering the stew. It wasn't my place to judge Mme's cooking, but she could put together a mean dinner when she had a mind to—or when she was required, on days when our cook fell ill.

I went to fetch the meal I'd brought. The Margrave dropped another roman on top of his unsteady pile in response.

"It's better warm," I persisted. There wasn't anyplace to set the bowl near the Margrave that I could see, so I kept ahold of it.

Finally, he looked up. I was still having trouble seeing the resemblance between Margrave Royston and the chatelain. They were brothers, of course, and I knew that, but I'd been looking for some small signifier, any sign at all that this man shared a relation to the kindly, blustering man I'd come to appreciate as my patron. They had the same nose, I decided, and perhaps they once might have had the same mouth, but then the chatelain didn't have dark eyes that pinned me as surely as a beetle on a card. And their voices were so different it was hard to imagine them both men, much less relatives.

"You aren't going to leave until I've eaten, are you?" The Margrave's questions lately had been resigned, tinged with acquiescence, as though he didn't really need to ask at all.

"No," I said, surprising myself. I sat on the floor a good distance from the books in case any drops from the bowl should escape. "What are you looking for?"

"Poison," the Margrave answered sourly, reaching across the distance between us to take the dish from my hands.

I didn't know what to say to that.

He ate a spoonful of the stew—more than I'd seen him eat the entire previous day. Then his eyes found me again.

When I'd first come to the chatelain's family, we'd gone to the lakeside country, where the waters were deep and wide. Here I felt again as if I was young, on a tiny boat in the middle of a deep lake, staring into the depths of water that had no sign of a bottom. It confounded me some, that I could spend so long gaining years and experience only to have them stripped away in a matter of seconds. If this was what everyone in the city was like, I decided it was a good thing I'd never been to the Volstov capital.

"So," the Margrave said at last, rolling the word around in his mouth as though he were tasting it, like the stew. "What are you reading?"

I'd been staring at the romans again.

"It's about the Ke-Han," I answered, eager to have something to talk about. "Is it true they really have magicians like ours?"

"They do." He swallowed another spoonful of the stew. The chatelain had been the proud owner of a beard for a little over a month, and he'd ended up with more food caught in it than his mouth. The Margrave did not share his brother's problem. "They aren't . . . exactly like ours, but they're magicians, true enough."

"How—How are they different?" The query was out before I could stop it. The chatelain had instructed his children not to pester their uncle with questions, and I had to assume the same rules were meant to apply with me as well—more strictly, in fact, than to the others.

He answered me, though, in the weary voice I'd come to recognize so well. "No one knows their source."

"Oh," I said. And then, hating myself for my own ignorance, "You mean like the Well?"

"Like our Well, yes." He nodded, stirring his dinner in precise, careful motions. I watched his hands, imagination lending a paleness to them that could not have been real; he'd not been shut up in his room that long. Even so, I'd never before felt so inadequate, not even when I was new to the castle and constantly getting in the way of my adoptive family.

There were no simple rules to learn that would help me accustom myself to Margrave Royston.

"I've never understood everything about the Well," I said before I could stop myself. "I mean, some of the books say that there was a time when men could drink from it directly, but there are others that say that such a straight dose of power would kill a man."

The Margrave looked at me over the dinner I'd brought him, and I thought that I saw a glimmer of something like interest in his expression.

"It wasn't guarded to begin with," he said, "if that's what you mean. The Ramanthines had a very different idea of how to go about things. They were much freer with who might be granted great power and who might not be. Our Esar likes things to be far more controlled—far more institutionalized, you might say—and he likes to know just how many magicians there are with pure Talents. By which I mean, those who haven't bred with the common folk, or diluted their power by marrying someone with a completely different Talent from their own." He paused to see if I was following, then carried on. "The Well water gets into your very blood, and it operates like a pedigree. Most magicians view dilution as an inevitability, that our powers will dwindle over the course of years, now that the Esar has his zealots to guard the Well and there's no one drinking from it directly. Of course, every assembly of individuals has its recalcitrants. There are those who are very reluctant to lose their power, and who believe that it is of the utmost importance to keep their bloodline pure. Never mind that there are only so many times one can reproduce within similar categories before you're marrying your own cousin. *That's* how you get inbred but extremely useful lunatics like young Caius Greylace—from families too keen to preserve the purity of their Talents, and without the good sense it would take to fill a thimble."

"And it's guarded?" I asked, almost breathless. Hearing the Margrave speak was better even than reading the most thrilling of romans. And, even better, what the Margrave told me was true; the history of Thremedon, the story of the Well.

"By the Brothers and Sisters of Regina," the Margrave said, "yes. Theirs is a story you don't find in every history book. They're devotees of a young Volstov woman who died for her country. Regina was tortured for information, but she never spoke a word. In honor of her, the Brothers and Sisters often sew up their mouths. So you can see why they are perfect for the task of guarding one of Volstov's best-kept secrets."

"Oh," I said, trying not to look as painfully foolish and eager for knowledge as I felt. It wasn't just that this was the most that Margrave Royston had spoken to me in all the time since he'd come to stay at Castle Nevers. It was that this was the first time anyone had answered a question of mine with more than a cursory reply, and a brusque warning not to spend all my time thinking of such nonsense.

"I doubt such knowledge will do you much good here," the

Margrave said after my silence, no doubt mistaking my lack of further response for a lack of interest. I could see it the moment the interest faded from his eyes.

"I'm sorry," I said suddenly. "I don't mean to bother you." The chatelain had warned me of the possibility that his brother might be rude in his displeasure, but I'd not been prepared for the slow, unsettling misery that hung around the Margrave like a heavy fog, obscuring whatever precarious attachments he had grounding him to this room, to the countryside, and perhaps even to the world.

To my dismay, he lowered the bowl and placed it on the floor. He took a moment to adjust his cuffs, then reached back into the trunk, rustling softly as he searched for something that I hoped wasn't poison.

Luck was with me, as what he drew out of the trunk was nothing more suspect than yet another roman, bound in red leather, title and author embossed in gold plating. I had to sit on my hands to keep them from reaching for it of their own accord.

"Would you like to read something besides histories, Hal?" He held the volume out to me without a care, as though it were not an item worth more than my own life—something which I was almost certain it *was*.

This civility from the Margrave was somehow worse than his previous defiance.

I took the roman, fingers hesitating over the pages before I could bring myself to open it. It fell open as easily as a door fitted with the right key, with no crack of stiffness from the spine. A story often read, then. I cleared my throat. Occasion sometimes called for me to soothe the children to sleep by reading to them, and though Margrave Royston was no child, I'd been charged with caring for him all the same.

Even if I hadn't been, I felt a little sorry for this man, whose misery marked everything he touched.

There was a chair at the desk, and a perfectly serviceable bed, but the Margrave made no move to rise from the floor, so neither did I. He only closed his trunk and leaned his long arms against it, watching me with an unexpected patience, as though he had all the time in the world. Such exclusive attention made me nervous.

My fingers stilled against the first page.

"This is about Tycho the Brave," I said, recognizing the words all at once.

The Margrave stirred with what I thought might be annoyance, but when I looked at him, his expression hadn't changed any. He'd only lifted his head to speak.

"Yes."

It was much thicker than my own volume. I found myself turning the pages ahead, to the place that I knew best: *And they were very happy until the end of their days.* There was a full roman's length again after those words.

In fact, my finger was placed solidly in the middle of the book.

"Oh," I said again, back to feeling foolish. "There's so much more *left* to this one."

The Margrave cleared his throat, and though I looked up too late to catch it, I thought he might have been smiling.

"Yes," he said again. "You'll find in this next part that he is quite unfortunate enough to have been struck by lightning."

All at once I felt a curious reverence overtake me, the way I felt when I encountered a new and particularly wonderful story. There was no time to examine it, however, since the Margrave had been kind enough to entrust me with one of his books. He was waiting for me to start reading. With a prickle of excitement I could scarcely contain, I concentrated hard on the unfamiliar words in front of me, reading aloud until there was no longer any light to see the words by.

THOM

My thesis was of a different nature from Marius's particular field, despite the considerable and fortuitous overlap. He specialized in politics, while I'd been studying the various peculiarities of a society raised exclusively on war. When Marius had said, then, that my time with the Dragon Corps would help me to write my thesis, he hadn't been entirely incorrect. He'd helped me a great deal over the years by being a fount of knowledge and encouragement, but most of my studies had become independent once I'd refined my own field. That year was to mark my last as a student; Marius had promised to recommend me at the least as an assistant professor before I was found a supporter, either in the bastion or the Basquiat, to fund my work so that I might turn my treatise into a proper volume.

These were dreams: small and unassuming, but nevertheless mine. I set a considerable store by them.

"Think of it this way," Marius said. He'd come earlier to take me to see the dragon compound, the Airman, and I was grateful for the company, though he would not be able to escort me to that first crucial meeting with the corps at th'Esar's palace. "You can have an entire chapter devoted to the peculiar and fraternal behavior of the members of the Dragon Corps, raised not on mother's milk but rather the innate knowledge of their own vital importance—who are allowed to do as they please without fear of any repercussion, and who think so highly of themselves that they are able, without pause, to call a diplomat's wife from Arlemagne a hapenny whore in the middle of Miranda, in broad daylight."

I'd done my research for this particular test as I did my research for all other exams. I was well-read, up-to-date, and completely prepared. That wasn't to say I didn't feel a sick kind of nervousness churning and clenching in my stomach, because I did, and had for the past twenty-four hours, only two of which had approximated sleep.

"Well, you're not getting the chop," Marius reasoned with me gently, tugging at his beard. "Thom, I *do* think you can pull this off."

His trust meant a great deal to me. I knew that if I failed, it would reflect very poorly on his standing in the Basquiat and in th'Esar's bastion both. And after all Marius's support, I didn't want to let *him* down, either. "Don't worry," I said, then, lying through my teeth, "I'm not. Worried, I mean."

"Thom," he said, "you're green."

I didn't look in the mirror to corroborate this assessment. I was almost certain he must be right, since I certainly felt green enough. "Do you think they'll notice?" I asked instead.

"Yes," Marius said. "They smell fear. They're trained to."

There was very little information about the corps accessible to the public. Margraves from the Basquiat bound me to secrecy about the preparatory knowledge I was given, as well as the knowledge I would come to gather in my own, personal experiences dealing with the dragons and their pilots. My thesis would have to deal with the corps' psychology alone, and not even approach the many secrets hidden behind the Airman's doors. I'd only ever seen dragons from the ground, wheeling overhead in the sky on their way to deployment: great, metalline, sleek. Copper and silver and steel, catching the sunlight along the glint and arc of their spiny wings. They were as mythical as they were man-made. I was out-of-my-mind terrified, and the members of the corps would sense that as soon as they looked at me—if they even bothered to look.

Luckily, I had very little to pack, and therefore little time to consider my fate.

"Again," Marius said, tapping his foot on the carriage floor.

I drew in a deep breath. "Chief Master Sergeant Adamo is their superior," I said patiently. "I'm to direct all questions, plans, purposes, grievances to his desk, and report only to him. Anything else will be seen as an act of insubordination and, once I've lost his support, I'll have no more luck than a fish on a hook." That last bit was Marius's personal elaboration, but I found thinking about it in those terms, while admittedly chilling, did help keep me focused.

"And the others?" Marius was exacting, but I'd no cause to be resentful of his precision as an instructor. In fact, it had only ever served me well.

"I've devised a mnemonic device for the others," I said. "By Night, I'll Always Remember My Effective and Judicious Lecturer Marius's Companionable Guidance."

"Very kind," said Marius. "Well?"

"Balfour, Niall, Ivory, Ace, Raphael, Merritt, Evariste,

Jeannot, Luvander, Magoughin, Compagnon, and Ghislain."
It was a mouthful, and I'd forgotten to breathe.

"You're missing one," Marius informed me.

I frowned. "I am?"

"Rook, I believe," Marius said. "He's Havemercy's pilot.
He's also the one who caused this mess in the first place."

The strangest detail about the dragons was that each magician who designed and built them named them like they were
his or her own children. Some were named after lovers, famous battles, lost children. One of the scientists—widely
considered the most talented architect in all of Volstov—was
something of a zealot, and the three dragons he'd designed
were all named after prayers: Thoushalt, Compassus, and his
most recent triumph, Havemercy, the scourge of the skies.
Havemercy was the latest of the dragons and arguably the
most famous. They said she was as black as onyx or obsidian
laced with platinum—an experimental and alchemic metal-
lurgy that had the Basquiat up in arms no more than fifteen
years ago—and she'd been exceedingly picky about choosing
her pilot. Marius had already shared with me his opinion as to
why: that, though the science was not perfected yet at the time
of Havemercy's forging, the technology still depended upon
individual Talents, and the result was a capriciousness in
which machines should never be allowed to indulge. That,
and the question of their capacity for fuel, made up the only
two flaws that any man, scholar or magician, could pick out in
the crafting of the dragons. Even the largest of them couldn't
hold enough to carry it into the heart of Lapis, the capital city
of Xi'an where the Ke-Han magicians made their home. Or at
least, not enough to mount a serious attack on the city, then
carry them back, as well. No one knew what the dragons ran
on, since it was meant to be kept a secret, but I'd heard several
clever theories that speculated their fuel was a diluted solution of water from the Well itself.

"I don't have room for another R," I said cheekily. "I'll
have to remember him as the one I forgot."

Marius clapped me on the shoulder. "Well, then, Thom,"
he said. "Are you ready?"

"Yes," I said.

But I wasn't.

ROYSTON

The tutor, Hal, took to reading to me near the end of my second week in exile. And, when I offered no immediate protest, the practice became first habit, then ritual. Resignation, boredom, the sheep, the incessant and constant proliferation of uninspiring trees, the coming of cold weather, my own idiocy and self-pity, my shame and loss—all these factors conspired against me until I was helpless against any external forces, incapable of making any choice or decision. I allowed Hal to do as he pleased when it pleased him, and while part of me grudgingly anticipated his arrival each evening to coax me toward food and conversation, I knew my brother had put him up to the task. Still, it was a break in the monotony of my day that interested me—even if this was only a vague interest, in that it was not expressly *disinterest*. I felt enveloped not in a blizzard but in a fog; I could barely muster the enthusiasm to roll out of bed in the morning, leave my dust-settled room, and roam the blocky, uninspired hallway.

I recognized the signs: This was depression, in its purest and most clinical form. Despite my self-awareness, I was incapable of warding off its advance—perhaps because I no longer cared if it swallowed me whole. It was quite possible I hadn't noticed its first stages and was already long lost to its grip.

Then, one evening, in the middle of a passage on Ifchrist the Barbarous, Hal looked up, and said, "It's going to get very cold soon."

"That's not part of the story," I replied, too tired to be perplexed by this interjection.

"I only thought," Hal said, struggling visibly, "that perhaps—if you wanted to go for a walk—you might do better to start now, before the rains come."

"I wasn't aware I'd expressed an interest in walks," I said. Though I tried to keep the measured, humorless judgment from my voice, I saw him flinch and knew I hadn't succeeded. Such self-loathing is cruel to others, though it's cruelest to the self. "What I mean to say is," I amended, "it's already the rainy season."

"Well, there are good spots of sunshine," Hal went on bravely. "Noon is often very nice for walking by the Locque Nevers."

"Is it," I said. "Well. I see."

"And I thought you might enjoy the fresh air," Hal finished. "It's dreadful in here—stuffy, dust everywhere. I don't know how you stand it."

"If it's that unpleasant," I replied, "you needn't spend hours here every day."

He colored at that, cheeks and ears pink and the freckles on his nose suffused with the blush, and I knew I'd been cruel to him again. I cast about for an apology, but before I could find something suitable he was speaking again. "I just—I just thought," he said, "that you might like it. There aren't *so* many mosquitoes. It isn't *so* bad, not on the bank of the Nevers in any case, and on the weekends some of the boys from upriver have paper-boat races."

I felt numb all over, with no more feeling than a boat folded out of paper and submitted to the whims and fancies of children. I rolled over in my bed and faced the wall, trying to gather my composure. "When do you suggest?" I said, at length.

Hal's voice was warm. "*Oh,*" he said, as if he'd expected me to put up much more of a fight. "Well— Tomorrow after lunchtime, I think."

I nodded slowly to the wall, then realized he couldn't see it. "All right, then."

"I think," he insisted, "I think that it'll do you good."

I didn't need to turn in order to know that he was smiling. As though all my cruelty had washed away to reveal clearer skies, like these so-called spots of sunshine he claimed existed.

I hoped he was not going to try anything like a picnic to trick me into eating.

It was a rare day in the country that I rose in time for lunch at all. Already my clothes were beginning to hang where they had once fit in perfectly cut lines—what happened, I knew, when you had to be cajoled into eating your requisite one meal a day by a young man barely out of adolescence. It was for the best, really. Dressing as I'd dressed in the city left me with a querulous helplessness, serving only to magnify my alien presence in the house. My tall boots were made to sound smartly against cobblestones, paved streets, or the marble floors of the Basquiat, not to slog through cow pastures.

After a moment of hopeful silence, Hal went back to his reading, voice surer with the written word than he was in conversation. It was evident even to me, mired as I was in my own private misery, that the young man held a natural proclivity for learning. It was rare to find in country lads at that age—or any age, really, I thought disparagingly, as most seemed more inclined to riding, and hunting, and thwacking at one another with large sticks, if my brother and his friends had been anything to go by. If Hal had been born in the city, he might have found a considerable peer group at the 'Versity, in time.

If Hal had been born in the city, I'd have had no one to read to me at all.

In a state less self-absorbed than my own, I might have taken more recognition, more of an interest in his obvious hunger for knowledge. Members of the Basquiat often took on assistants from the 'Versity in order to pass along their learning. It was often easier than apprenticing another magician, whose Talent might be so antithetical to your own that you ended up like Shrike the Bellows, buried in an avalanche by his own Talent of blasting sound in conjunction with his young apprentice's capacity for exploding rock.

At my very best, all I could offer him were my romans, some of which were quite illegal—these being volumes written in the old Ramanthe, and several anthologies of Ke-Han verse that I'd picked up during my service toward the war—stacked in an undignified heap at the foot of my bed like corpses for the burning. Volstov was decidedly liberal when it came to what romans traveled beyond the pale, but since the call for the burning of all Ramanthine novels, one had to be careful to keep one's library under lock and key.

As Hal read, I drifted in and out of a conscious state, turning the words over in my head to discern another meaning if I could. It was an old game, made for common rooms and peers. One of the things they taught you in the Basquiat was that nothing had only one use, one meaning, one state of being.

Magicians understood this, and thus were better able to change the realities around them. Of course, the true and greater source of our power was the closely guarded Well. But, as youths, the ideologies of our professors had ignited some whimsical spark within us, and many a night was spent reading passages and trying to understand not what was, but what *could be*.

In the war, such thinking saved my life, as not even allies can say what they mean—or mean what they say—in every instance.

Of course, such duality couldn't be mistaken for malicious intent. As a soldier, one had to understand that there was a great deal that couldn't come guaranteed, and that a man's word was more like his intent. I had experienced such a dichotomy firsthand when the troops I'd been traveling with had been stranded in the mountains for nearly a month before there was any need for us. Of course our captain hadn't intended it that way, and *certainly* the Esar would never intentionally doom any of his men to potential death and frostbite in the Cobalts, but that was what had happened nonetheless. There were men who were not as forgiving as I.

Silence settled over the room like an additional layer of dust, and I could hear Hal getting up to leave with quiet, uncertain movements. Halfway there already, I decided to feign sleep so as not to prolong this visit any more than was strictly necessary. He was only with me as per request, after all, and

I was not so old that I couldn't remember what it was like to have no time to call my own.

The door closed behind him with a soft but nevertheless grating creak. Everything in the country made noise, but it was never the right sort of noise. In the city everything was boisterous, vibrant, chasing you at the heels so that you had to step lively every second to survive.

In the country, everything sighed like a dying man.

I thought about what Hal had said, about the coming cold, and how I would possibly weather out the season trapped inside this house like a prisoner with a family I'd made a point of never visiting. Surely, I would sink as if to the bottom of a lake, slow and certain.

When I dreamed, it was of another cold, another time. The war crept often enough into my dreams; there was nothing I could do about it.

It had been a foul season in the mountains, frigid and unwelcoming when last the war had been at its peak, the Ke-Han magicians performing whatever barbaric rituals they needed to harness the wind. Blue was considered the color of our enemy, but it was also the color of the mountains, dark and deep as purest steel. The Cobalts bordered Volstov to the east and were our first defense against any attack.

It had been nearly a three-week wait, our fingers as blue as the Ke-Han's coats, before we saw any action. Such things happened—we'd heard of them—but the years had given me a patience and understanding that I didn't have in the dream. I hadn't had it there in the mountains either. In the end we'd come across an enemy battalion simply by chance of remaining in one place for long enough that the Ke-Han had run into us.

The battle started very quickly. At that time, the fighting in the mountains was often a swift and violent business, ending when one side brought the rocky hills down onto the other. We were lucky enough to have come out victorious in that particular battle, leaving enough enemy magicians alive so that we could question them about their operations. The cold often aided such things, as the snow clotted the blood, so that we had a long time to question them. One of my fellows lost a hand in those hills.

I have hated the cold ever since.

THOM

I'd changed my shirt twice in the morning. I was not so foolish as to think it would make a difference one way or the other with men trained to sniff out fear the way most of us were trained to speak, but it made me feel a little calmer, and so I allowed myself the indulgence.

I was no longer quite so uneasy about my current project. As with anything—applying for the scholarship, taking the nation's exams, et cetera—I found most of the worrying was spent in preparation for the event. When the event itself came, however, I was merely afflicted with the same fatalistic numbness that I'd heard afflicted soldiers during the war.

What would come would come, and I'd deal with it to the best of my abilities, using the knowledge I'd gained. Laid out like that, it didn't seem so overwhelming.

Besides, I thought it rather unlikely that anyone would be taking it upon himself to slap *my* ass and call *me* Nellie. So it seemed I already had at least one advantage over the Arlemagne diplomat's wife.

Navigating the palace would take some getting used to, though. More than once I wished I'd taken Marius's offer of company for my first day.

"You're more nervous than I am," I'd accused him, after ensuring my materials were all in order.

"No, I'm not," he'd said, tugging at his beard all the while— which meant that he *was* nervous and trying not to show it, and was failing miserably.

"Marius," I'd said, familiarity and exhaustion both creeping up to make me rather more impertinent than usual. "Leave. It's late, and I still cherish the idea that I may yet get some sleep."

"Yes," he'd said, but still had made no effort to get up, so that in the end I'd had to be quite firm with him, fairly ejecting him from the 'Versity at an hour that most decent people were abed anyway, so that the pair of us might get some rest.

It was a left, then a right, or a right, then a left. I breathed deeply to calm myself, feeling nerves disappear in a quick rush of annoyance. It wouldn't do to begin my day by cursing the architect of the palace, but I quite felt like it by the time I'd passed that same statue of the current Esar for the sixth time, bronzed and brave and quite twenty years younger than he was now.

"*Bastion,*" I said heatedly, coming upon his courageous brow once more.

"Oh," said a voice from behind me. "Are you lost?"

I turned and was surprised to see someone of about my own age. He had the dark hair and pale complexion of a nobleman and was fiddling absently with a pair of gloves. He was also, I realized a moment later, wearing a coat with large brass buttons and a high Cheongju collar, and I recognized the colors immediately. He was a member of the Dragon Corps.

I made to bow, before it occurred to me that teachers did not bow to their students—that bowing might be considered a sign of weakness—and then I didn't know what to do, so I held out my hand.

He took it with a bemused smile, and shook it. He was most genteel.

"I'm Balfour," he added helpfully, after a spell.

The newest member, my brain provided from the notes I'd made and committed to memory. Also, it pointed out, I'd not introduced myself yet.

I cleared my throat loudly, to cover up for the rather obvious breach in etiquette I'd just made, and hoped this wouldn't make it back to the Chief Sergeant before I'd even had the chance to meet him. "Thomas," I said. "From the 'Versity. I believe I'm supposed to be meeting your . . . the rest of the corps in the atrium, only I can't seem to . . . that is . . ." I looked to th'Esar, large and bronzed, as though this were all his fault. And in a way it was—his and the airman Rook's, and I blamed them both equally.

"*Oh,*" said Balfour, with a rush of gladness that threw me off. "I thought I was late! Merritt stole my alarm clock, see, to fish the bells out of it. Come along, then. It's this way."

He set off ahead of me, chattering still, so that I could only assume I was meant to keep up.

The atrium had walls of glass and a black-and-white-tiled floor that resembled a giant game board. I felt like an expendable and very small plebe piece in a round of Knights and Margraves, but it did me no good to indulge in thoughts like that.

It would be very warm in the atrium in the full flush of summer, I thought, but today was suitably overcast so as not to turn the room into a giant greenhouse. The sound of raucous laughter echoed from just around the corner.

I held my nerves in check as firmly as a horse's reins and stepped after Balfour to meet the Dragon Corps.

Right away, I could see being outnumbered fourteen to one would make this no simple task. Once Balfour joined them in the row of graceful, gold-backed chairs, I found myself alone on a dais. Fourteen pairs of eyes pinned me. My throat was very dry.

"Well if it isn't himself," said one all the way on the end, whose coat was unbuttoned and whose boots were tall but slouched. He had the lazy, self-satisfied grace of a cat, and I was certain—though I shouldn't have been so quick to judge—that this was Rook in all his infamy. The smug expression he wore, remorseless and amused, lit his cold blue eyes as if they were trapped behind stained glass. His mouth was unrepentant, almost cruel, his blond hair in knotted braids in the Ke-Han style, streaks of royal blue at his temple.

I disliked him, and I was frightened of him yet oddly intrigued by him as well.

"Come to teach us all to talk and act like the noblesse and keep our fucking private-like?" he went on, leaning forward and making a lewd Molly gesture between his legs. "'Cause we've been waitin' on you. And I've heard it's considered *rude,* in some places, to leave esteemed guests *waitin'.*"

"Rook," said the eldest—a heavyset man with an even

heavier brow and a square jaw like a nutcracker's—in a voice that suffered no insubordination. "Sit the fuck back and shut the fuck up. Your pardon," the man went on, giving me a once-over.

"You must be Chief Sergeant Adamo," I said.

"Yeah," said Adamo. "That's right."

"Well," said Rook, who'd managed the art of sitting back but not, apparently, of shutting the fuck up, "when's the sensitivity start?" The airman next to him giggled—at least I thought it might be a giggle—and I swallowed as hard as I could to prevent my own tongue from choking me.

This wasn't simply going to be difficult. This was going to be suicide.

Of the fourteen men lined up and sitting before me like princes, there was only one kind face to be seen, which the rest soon shamed out of its kindness. I didn't blame Balfour for falling in step with the others. I'd seen such behavior during my worst days at the 'Versity—but those young men had always fallen by the wayside quickly enough, as the 'Versity was an institution of learning, not a catchall house for fraternities and (to put it like a boy raised on the Mollyedge strip) fuck-ups.

Here, it seemed that such stupendously cruel hierarchical systems were encouraged rather than torn down before they could form.

"I thought we might first introduce ourselves," I said, buying myself time. I had notes—files, papers, years of behavioral research—behind me, and yet I didn't want to scrabble at odds and ends, nor seem as young as I felt. Not in front of these men. I thought of Marius's reminder—that they could smell fear—and swallowed down my intimidation as best I could.

"You thought we might?" asked Rook. "How fucking old *are* you?"

"Rook," said Adamo. Balfour made a high, disapproving noise.

"It's just he looks fucking *twelve,* is what I'm sayin'," Rook said.

"Rook," Adamo repeated.

"And I don't want to be taught fucking *anything* by a fucking *twelve*-year-old," Rook finished, then shut his mouth easy as you please, as if he were a choirboy at week's end and his parents were looking up at him from the pews.

I dug my fingernails into my right palm. *Steady, Thom,* I told myself. *Steady.* I thought of distant, soothing things: of the strength of my dead brother, of Ilsa on Hapenny Lane who always was kind to me, of Marius's gentle laughter. In the face of what I'd lost and what I'd accomplished, a handful of self-important men were nothing I couldn't handle. "We're going to start by introducing ourselves," I said. "Now. Who wants to begin?"

Silence was my only reply, and the sound of the wind against the glass walls. I saw Balfour look nervously about at his fellow airmen, as if he wanted to volunteer but knew he couldn't. And then at last, as if it were being drawn out of him by the screws, Adamo cleared his throat.

"Thank you," I said, and meant it with all my heart.

"Tell us how it's done," Adamo said, a little grudgingly, as if he knew as well as I did that I didn't have a clue what I was doing; that I was green as the grass, and that I was going to mess all of this up.

I licked my lower lip. "We're going to say our names, which dragon we fly—well, that's not for me to say, obviously, but for the rest of you—and something the others have never known about you."

"Something private?" said the giggler.

"*How* private?" Balfour asked nervously.

"It can be anything," I said. "Anything at all."

"Right," said Chief Sergeant Adamo. "Well, I'm Chief Sergeant Adamo. Proudmouth's my girl, and if another one of you little shits brings up 'Mary' Margrave again, it's dog rations for you for a month afterward."

Another silence followed. The giggler was gaping; Balfour had pulled off both his gloves and was worrying them in his fingers as if he sought to tear them to shreds. Rook's smile had turned outright nasty, twisted down at the corner.

"I'm not sure that entirely constitutes a private detail," I said at length.

"Doesn't it?" Adamo asked, lifting one heavy brow at me.

"You're not some fucking pillow-biter," Rook said sullenly, crossing his arms over his chest.

"I don't believe that's exactly what I said," Adamo said, like any Margrave or professor I'd ever met for diction, but with an edge to it, and showing more teeth than was necessary. "He's an acquaintance of mine."

"I'm just saying," Rook began, but before this came to blows, I knew I had to cut him off.

"Thank you for volunteering to go second, Rook," I said.

He turned his eyes to me, colder than glass but more indifferent than ice, blue and sharp in his lean face. On the whole, he was simply a sharp-looking man, and admittedly almost painfully handsome, but it was a statue's beauty he possessed, a bit roughed up around the edges—for his nose was broken, and there was a scar along his left cheekbone like a half-moon, crescented, just under his eye. And, like some artists' portrayals of beauty, there was too much spite and malice in him; one could hardly bear to look at him for long.

"You already know my name," he said. "Don't you?"

He said it like a challenge; I knew I couldn't back down, though I felt cornered and trapped and on the verge of complete humiliation.

"For the others, then," I said patiently.

"They know my name, too."

"Yes," said the giggler. "It's Rook."

"The other part," I insisted, refusing to be bested.

"I fly Havemercy," Rook said. "She's pretty famous. You might even have heard of her."

"And the last?" I prompted. It wouldn't do to let him get away with anything, no matter how minor.

"Oh, that." Rook bit his thumbnail, looking up at the ceiling, putting on an excellent show of being in deep thought. Finally, he said, "I sure like fucking women."

"That's not exactly news," Balfour said, somewhat darkly.

"Yeah, well, it's true," Rook went on, relishing every second of it. "I like to grab 'em around the waist and shove their legs wide open and make 'em beg for it, 'cause you know—"

"My name's Balfour," Balfour said very quickly. "I fly Anastasia. We met in the hallway. I . . . I'm very fond of certain philosophical treatises."

At that moment, I was more grateful to Balfour than to anyone else in my entire life. I couldn't show favoritism, but I knew my expression revealed the wealth of my gratitude, for he responded with a halfway sort of grin—as if it were no trouble at all, and he was in fact glad for the excuse to get the better of his fellow airman.

"You know, a lot of fucking pillow-biters like philosophy," Rook said.

"Oh, yes," said the giggler, giggling again. "And d'you know where they like it?" Adamo gave him a look then like melting steel, and he cleared his throat. "By which I mean to say, I'm Compagnon. I ride Spiridon, and I own the most thorough collection of indecent imprints in the entire city."

"It's true," said a swarthy man with a hook nose and impossibly white teeth. He sighed fondly.

"And your name, please?" I asked.

He shrugged broad, graceful shoulders. "Ghislain," he said. "Compassus. My great-great-grandfather died for th'Ramanthe."

I was surprised, though I knew I shouldn't have been. Many families had originated as Ramanthe supporters, as once there had been no one else to support. Ghislain had the dark eyes and the burnt-sugar coloring of someone from an old Ramanthine family—one that had declined to interbreed with the Volstovic invaders from the west. It was a rare thing to see in a man of our generation, unless he was a part of the nobility.

Not even Rook could think of a clever way to make what he had said into an insult, though, so I put my curiosity aside and took the opportunity to move along down the line.

There was a man with a chin sharp and pointed as an arrow seated next to Ghislain. He looked bored, his legs stretched out in front of him, and paused midway through a yawn when he realized I was looking at him.

"I think you're up." Ghislain elbowed him harder than seemed necessary, and he straightened in the chair.

"I'm Ace." He had bright red hair and a sleep-thick voice, as though he'd only just woken up. "Thoushalt's mine. When I was little my mam caught me tryin' to take a swan dive off our terrace; ever since I've wanted to be up in the air."

"That's a load of horseshit," said Rook. "What is that, a fucking poem? You sound like Raphael."

"Yes, and I so love it when you insult me where I can *hear* you, Rook."

There were so *many* of them, screamed a panicky voice in my head. I quelled it quickly, gaze flicking over to a man with black, curly hair. He'd leaned halfway out of his chair to shout down the line.

"You must be Raphael," I said bravely, attempting to regain the thread of what I'd started.

He looked at me as though he'd forgotten I was in the room at all. I nodded encouragingly.

"Oh," he leaned back in his chair and crossed his legs with a fluid motion. "I'm sorry, I didn't realize we'd reached my place in line yet."

I couldn't tell from his tone whether that was meant as a jibe at me or an honest apology. My money was on the former, but before I could decide, he was speaking again.

"I am Raphael," he said with an illustrative wave of his hand. "I've been blessed with flying Natalia, the beauty. Truth be told, I was getting very bored with the monotony of our days with hardly any battles to fight. Perhaps this will prove interesting."

"Thank you, Raphael," I said quickly, over a loud and disbelieving sound from Rook down at the far end. I was beginning, I felt, to get the hang of this. The key was to speak quickly, before Rook could get his comments in and set off the others. "Next," I said, a little too sharply and a little *too* closely to the way one of my least favorite professors had, but I couldn't afford to wince.

Mercifully, there was only a short silence this time, as those who'd introduced themselves glared at the stragglers.

"I'm Jeannot," said another man with the dark hair and eyes of a Ramanthine, which meant that his family too must have been very old or very inbred. His nose was thin, like the blade of a knife. "I'm on Al Atan, and I've never seen the ocean at anything closer than a dragon's height."

"Oh," said Balfour, from whom I hadn't expected an outburst. He looked as though he'd just heard something very sad. "Sorry," he said, by way of realizing he'd interrupted. "Only, I didn't know that."

"I *told* you he was a girl," said Rook with savage triumph. "Got feminine parts between his legs, airman's honor."

I bit my tongue and counted slowly to five. Balfour put his gloves back on and stared down at his hands.

"Merritt, I swear by the bastion, if you don't sit still I am going to lynch you in the showers."

At the opposite end of the line, a man entirely too freckly for his own good scowled in hurt dignity. His companion, the one who'd spoken, turned in his chair to face me.

"This training, will it make Merritt less irritating?"

"Well," I began.

"Fuck *off*, Evariste." The freckled one crossed his arms across his chest, then his legs at the ankle, like a sullen child who'd been scolded.

"Ah," I tried again. "It's not exactly—why don't the pair of you tell us something about yourselves." This was progress, I told myself. Real progress.

And if not, it would make for excellent research material once I'd picked the shattered fragments of my dignity up from off the black-and-white floor.

The one who'd complained—Evariste—chewed at his lip. His hair stood at ends, like he'd often tugged at it in thought. "I fly Illarion. What about me, what about me . . . oh yes! Once I ate a pound of butter."

The giggler—Compagnon; I drilled it into my memory—started up again.

I had a feeling I didn't want to ask after the story that went with that anecdote. If anything, I could save it for a later exercise.

Merritt's cheeks were stained bright red with either anger or embarrassment, I couldn't tell which, though it made me wonder how many of the airmen were happy being tied together in such an intimate way. Several of them seemed as though they'd function best as individuals and not smaller parts of a greater whole.

"I'm Merritt," he said gruffly. "I've got Vachir. My sister got married last month."

"And you didn't invite us to the wedding?" A man who'd turned his chair the wrong way around, seemingly for the sole purpose of leaning his arms across the back, turned his head to leer at Merritt. "Might have liked the opportunity of seeing your sister again."

Adamo cleared his throat from the center of the room, as though he was growing short of patience. I was grateful, even if his impatience was sure to be directed toward me in due time.

"Oops," said the man in the backward chair. His mouth would have looked distinctly feminine on anyone else, round and full as it was. He flashed a careless smile. "Niall. I fly Erdeni. I've found the perfect place to nap in th'Esar's orchard, and I'm not telling a man of you where it is."

"*Fuck*, Magoughin told us that joke last week," Rook pounded his fist against the chair. Then, he smiled like a cat having helped himself not only to the canary, but to the entire Esarian aviary of birds. "It's th'Esarina's lap."

Someone laughed, broad-faced and friendly. He waved his one enormous shovel-pan hand in the air like a child at school eager for recognition.

"Magoughin?" I asked, even though I was fairly certain of the response.

"Chastity's mine. And I collect jokes, of a sort," he replied.

I nodded, though presumably this was not a private piece of information. I would have to bend a little, I'd realized, in order to get anywhere successfully with the Dragon Corps. They no longer seemed as one, a wall of intimidation stark against me, but rather like a mob of jackdaws, pecking at each other, and cawing, and preening their own feathers. I could manage this. I *would*.

"He's Ivory," Magoughin added helpfully, nodding to the man at his left, so blond and pale that he looked almost unreal.

"They call me that because I'm good at the piano," he said, in a voice as dry as sandpaper. "Not because of my skin, so don't even bother asking. Oh, and I ride Cassiopeia."

"I—I wasn't going to," I assured him, quickly stifling the sudden, insistent notion that I should and could have been taking notes this entire time. They may have seemed like trivial bits of information, but anything additional I could learn about this merry band of lunatics might very well help me in the future. You never knew what was going to be important, as Marius was often fond of pointing out when my patience with studies had worn thin. Jokes, the piano, the giggling—even Merritt's tapping and Balfour's gloves—there was something to be gleaned from all of this, if I were to treat them as individuals.

Divide and conquer—it was an old adage.

"Luvander," the final voice piped up, and I forced myself to acknowledge him politely instead of slumping to the floor with relief. He wore dark hair tied back from his face, and his coat was unbuttoned. "I fly Yesfir, though I like to think it's more as how she deigns to let me hop on once in a while. In any case, I really *hate* going last."

"Ah," I said, most cleverly. And then, when no one jumped in immediately to comment, I straightened my shoulders and allowed the success of the moment to buoy my spirits, however briefly. "Well. Thank you, everyone. I appreciate the . . . enthusiasm some of you exhibited in sharing."

"Whoa there just a second, 'Versity boy." Rook had leaned forward in his chair again, eyes like twin chips of bright ice. "Where's your introduction?"

Ah, yes, I thought. I'd forgotten that. I'd prepared something in advance—something clever and noncommittal, something which wouldn't prove fuel for the fires—but at the moment my energy was sapped, my nerves jangling, Rook's eyes skewering me like I was the board in a game of darts. I knew immediately that I'd forgotten all of it—my introduction and my speech, my purpose in neat and precise order; everything I'd prepared and memorized.

I looked out over the group, all fourteen of them against the one of me. They were only men, I thought; they flew great steel beasts that were quirky and capricious, but these were only men, and all men had some human tenderness.

"Well, as you may already know," I said, hating myself for the uncertainty in my voice, "my name is Thom, and I—" I remembered it out of the blue, like a thunderclap. "I've never actually seen a dragon up close."

HAL

I was supposed to meet the Margrave for our daily walk. I don't know how it became a ritual but it did. And, after a few days, I couldn't imagine my life without the ambling path we took every noontime along the Locque Nevers, occasionally speaking, but most often not. It was awkward at times, and once I stumbled so that I almost took a dive into the water, but I think it did the chatelain's brother some good to be out and about. Fresh air was the cure for all ills, or so said Cooke, the chatelain's stableboy, with a laugh and a toss of his head much like a horse. And the Mme said it as well, though she never took fresh air for herself, claiming it made her dizzy.

The first time I'd thought it would be worse than it was, the two of us walking not quite side by side, and the Margrave's profile very sharp and lean against the sunlight.

"Well," I said.

I'd said "Well" three times now. It seemed only fair that I continue to fish for conversation like any other man would for—well, fish, I supposed—casting the line out into the dark, quiet waters and waiting each time hopefully, though I was granted no answering bite. The Margrave didn't enjoy talking, which was funny, since he seemed as if he might have been the sort of man who had enjoyed it. Once.

His unhappiness had begun to poison him, though I wasn't sure exactly how. I'd never seen someone so unhappy in my life. I wanted to reach out to him with something more than a *Well,* halting and inadequate.

This time, however—the fourth time—the Margrave stopped by the edge of the river.

"What fish," he said, "do you suppose frequent these waters?"

"I have no idea," I replied.

That was the extent of our first conversation. From the sigh of disappointment he heaved, I assumed I'd let him down somehow, but it wasn't my job to teach William or Alexander about the Locque Nevers, which meant I'd never been given cause to teach myself this unexpectedly necessary information.

I asked Cooke that evening, and he said there weren't any fish at all in Locque Nevers, though in some places there were tadpoles and newts and bullfrogs.

"Interesting," the Margrave said, when I relayed this knowledge.

That was the extent of our second conversation.

The third was longer, and seemed to make him almost happy before it made him much more *un*happy. He spoke to me about the city—his own inspiration, though I felt guilty nonetheless.

"What sort of man you are depends on the bar you frequent," he explained to me, quite patiently, while I listened wide-eyed as a child—and to him, I suppose, I was one. "And I don't mean bar as in your provincial equivalent—a roof and a few stools and a great sweating hulk of a man slamming out dreadful, diseased drink for fools who don't know the difference. No. Pantheon Bar, for example, is a great cobbled stretch right by the Amazement, which is the entertainment district, though I'm sure you've heard of that. Men from the Basquiat tend to prefer Pantheon over Reliquary, which I'd say is something of a more . . . old-school feel, for those who still claim loyalty, for whatever reason, to the spirit of the Ramanthe, while the students at the 'Versity are all for Chapel, which is cheaper, you see, and caters to the flashier sensibilities of the young."

I soaked it all in like a wet stone soaks in sunlight. "Oh," I said happily, but I couldn't imagine it.

Then, all at once, the Margrave's eyes shuttered and closed completely. I could see pain etch itself deeply around his eyes and mouth, so that it was hard for me to believe that he was a good many years younger than the chatelain himself.

"Are you all right?" I asked, worrying my lower lip but not daring to reach out to him. A cold wind was blowing in over the water.

"I'm going back," he said.

I didn't understand his moods, nor did I understand the private miseries he nursed. The Mme needed her smelling salts whenever his name was mentioned, and the rumors Cooke passed back and forth with Collins and Ramsey and Miller—who might not have known what they were talking about, but might also have known more than I did—were vicious.

I couldn't ask the chatelain. It wasn't my place, and he would have bellowed all the window glass out of their frames.

I wondered to myself, the night I heard Cooke and Collins and the rest talking about it, whether or not it mattered what he'd done—if it was what they said, or something like they said but different, or something truly bad, or something so stupid it didn't merit thinking about. I decided that it wasn't, rolled over in my little bed, and fell asleep soon after.

CHAPTER THREE

ROYSTON

It was raining, hard like walls of water whipped sideways by the howling wind, when my brother came to me, hair wet and plastered over his brow, face wet, lips blue. I'd been sleeping—or rather, lying in my bed with my face to the wall—and was about to muster some snide quip from the depths of my weariness when I saw his expression fully, not just obscured and backlit from the hall.

I sat up.

"William," my brother said, dripping all over the floor. It would warp the wood. "Damn child, always thinks he's playing when he isn't—never mind, never mind. He was out earlier, before the storm hit. Hal went out to find him, only the idiot boy didn't tell anyone, and we'd only just noticed them missing when Cooke came in to tell us he'd seen Hal set out—"

I was already pulling on my boots. What my brother thought he'd accomplish by running out into the rain was beyond me, but it stirred some trembling emotion in my chest to see how deeply he loved his children, despite how helpless he was to express any of it.

"What do you think?" I asked, not relishing the idea of going out into the rain. My left boot was giving me trouble, but unlike my brother's, my hands weren't shaking. "Where do you think they'd be?"

"William thinks it's *funny,*" my brother said, then his voice broke on something wet and cold, "to play by the marsh."

"And that's where you think they are?"

"Hal would have gone there to check for him," my brother

confirmed. He pushed his wet hair back off his forehead, then grabbed my arm with his wet hand. "Can you—?"

He meant: Was my magic something that could help in this matter. My brother had never bothered to learn the specifics of my Talent, which had hurt me once and now no longer mattered. It was too complicated to explain to a man so bent on remaining mired in country feudalism. In short, my Talent wasn't going to be especially helpful, no, but I had common sense and experience in similar matters; I'd saved an entire garrison of Reds on an afternoon as piss-poor as this one, and I was the only person in the entire household who had the head for doing what needed to be done to make sure no one was marsh-drowned by morning.

"No," I told my brother. "But I'll find them."

"Yes," said my brother. "Right. What do you need?"

"I'll need a coat," I said at length, for I realized that none of my clothes had been tailored specifically for a downpour in the countryside.

"A coat," my brother repeated.

"Yes," I confirmed, then stood up. There was a moment when it seemed I'd done it too quickly, and the blood rushed from my uppers too soon, but I held in place for a moment and the dizziness passed. I took my brother by his wet arm and steered him out of the room and down the stairs. I was not un-accustomed to telling men and women what to do in their own homes; mercifully my brother seemed to have gone into a kind of frozen waterlogged trance, where he was numb to tri-fles such as hurt dignity or misplaced rivalry.

Once on the landing, he went to the closet while I kicked the toe of my left boot against the floor, still dissatisfied with the fit and feel of it.

The rain hammered down against the roof with a force that sounded as though it had the entirety of the Locque Nevers behind it. This was foolish, I knew, as rivers could not be pulled from their beds without at least three days' advance planning and a geographical knowledge of the area.

"Here." My brother handed me an oilskin raincoat. His own, I presumed—too wide in the chest and too short in the arms—but it would have to do. I put it on. "If you can't find them," he began, and I silenced him with a hand.

No matter what had passed between us, between my brother and me, I did not wish to see him harmed by the loss of his child.

"I'll find them," I said, and went out into the rain.

The lay of the land surrounding Castle Nevers could only have been designed by a countryman. There were no straight paths to anywhere, only the vague and winding curve that would lead you to the river if you followed it long enough.

In some ways, that reminded me enough of the city for it to weigh heavily on my heart.

Today, however, I had no time for the turning paths, counterintuitive to any man with logic at hand. The wind whipped at branches, drove rain sharp and bitterly cold against my face and hands. I wished I'd thought to bring some gloves, for in the cold your fingers were the first to be endangered.

Hal had pointed out the marsh on one of our walks, pleasant and innocuous as always. I'd not been paying attention at the time, but was thankful now for his insistence that I leave the house despite my contempt for both sheep and trees. If it hadn't been for those walks, I'd be incurably lost now.

All things have a purpose. My mentor's words came unbidden as they ever did, and I recalled them with the same deep regret that now tinged and tainted every part of my life. I picked up speed.

To my surprise, much of the grounds were *not* unfamiliar, almost as though I truly hadn't spent all my term of exile in an impermeable fugue of self-pity. There wasn't a path to the marsh, not exactly, but it had a way all the same, past the ring of stumps where Emilie had her tea parties in the warmer months, and the burnt-out wreck of a caretaker's cabin that had been destroyed in an accident involving the boys upriver.

Much as I liked to believe myself separate from the goings-on in my brother's house, I knew with a sureness that flowed in me to the core that I could not—would not—go back to the house without my nephew and Hal. Those who knew me well might have called it stubbornness and they wouldn't have been very wrong, for I was a stubborn man in all things, and especially the ones I thought could not be amenable to change—weather and law and the movement of the stars themselves. This warm closeness in my chest was a kin of stubbornness, then, but it was like nothing I'd ever felt before.

There would be time enough to examine my discovery later, I told myself; now was not the time.

The trees were beginning to thin out when my boot made a squelch instead of a thump, which meant that I was getting close. It also meant that the wind, while being deprived of branches to snap at my face, was also uninhibited by such trifling cover. It tore at my brother's coat, freezing my wet skin and forcing my eyes to thin slits as I scanned the Nevers marsh for any signs of life. More than once I caught myself following the wind's howl with my gaze, thinking it a voice in peril. I rubbed my arms briskly to keep them from going numb as my hands had, then continued more gingerly. The ground here was soft, and nearly as wet as the air. I thought of William and his short legs and his appetite for mischief, and I felt sick at heart.

A shrill whistle went soaring past my ears, and suddenly the wind was calling my brother's name.

It was difficult to discern the direction from which the cry had come, but as I turned it came again, louder, stronger. Two voices instead of one, perhaps. I remembered various bits and pieces of lessons, training, how to narrow my focus, how to catch in my ears what I wanted to hear, and even as I put those theories to practice I forced my legs to move. There was water seeping into my boots, cold as the rest.

It made sense, in some strange way. Why should any part of me escape the frigid consequence of the rainy season?

I was thankful at least that the voices I was following were taking me back to the marsh's edge rather than farther in. No matter what confidence I had in my own abilities, I hadn't relished the idea of fishing two people from the watery depths of a piece of land that couldn't make up its mind whether to be solid or liquid and was treacherous enough to be both.

I saw a flash of something pale waving among a tangle of

branches and rain, and I realized with a shock that it was an arm. My sigh of relief was immediately snatched away by the wind. The boys were in a tree.

"Papa!" William's voice was reed-thin, screamed ragged. I hated to disappoint him, but that was what came of wearing my brother's coat. I struggled over to the tree, laid my hands against its gnarled trunk. Hal and the boy sat tangled together on a lower branch, hair and clothing glued to their skins. Neither was in danger of drowning in the marsh, but their chances of surviving the night outside would have been slim indeed. As it was, we could all be reasonably certain that in a matter of days, everyone in my brother's castle would be sniffling and sneezing and harboring some version of the same cold.

"M-Margrave Royston," said Hal, blue-lipped and shivering. He was holding tight to William, who looked ready to hurl himself out of the tree at the slightest provocation.

"Have the pair of you quite finished scaring my brother to death?" I asked.

William made a miserable sound that reminded me how young he was, so I checked my tongue and held out my arms for him, instead. My most-disagreeable nephew clung to me like a newborn kitten, tiny freezing hands crawling under my collar, thin arms looped about my neck. I felt something pierce the fog of indifference I'd held around me like the blanket in my bed, and I comforted him as I had when the children had been much younger and my brother visiting Miranda for the first and only time.

There was a rustling sound from above our heads, and I looked up to see Hal halfway out of the tree himself but moving slowly, careful of the limited response his frozen limbs must have been giving him.

"Here," I said, shifting William to one arm so that I could hold out a hand to Hal.

He took it without compunction, squeezed my fingers tight, and slipped from the tree with a wet thump. His lips were pressed tightly together, I assumed to keep his teeth from chattering. When he opened his mouth, the words came rushing out in a halting flow, as though he had a lot to say and not the words to say it.

"William—I had to come. Didn't think it would be so *cold,*" he managed, before falling against me much as William had done.

"Take my coat," I said, though it was too late for any coat to do much more than trap the cold that had already got into them.

Hal shook his head, wet hair brushing against the curve of my chin as he did so.

"Here," I said again, as reasonably as I could. I fumbled at the buttons of the coat with numb fingers until I could pull a side of it free. In a swift motion that let as little rain in as possible, I folded Hal in close, and brought the oilskin around him, so that it might serve a dual purpose.

"Oh," I heard him say quietly, an icy and immediate presence against my chest. "Thank you."

I swallowed, feeling the small movements of his mouth as he spoke against my shoulder. His hands were larger than William's, but they clutched in exactly the same way, holding tight to my shirt as though I were an anchor in the storm. With a slowly trickling certainty, like the water running down my neck, I felt that same hand as surely as if it had clutched at something deeper within my chest.

"Well," I said, gruff and businesslike. William was weeping against my shoulder. "We'd best get back to the house."

ROOK

I didn't have a mind to be sharing *or* caring again anytime soon. Only when I said as much to Adamo, he looked me square in the eye and said he'd string me up out the window even if I *was* the only soul who could fly Havemercy in a straight line. I wasn't in a mood for that kind of horseshit— especially not with all the horseshit I'd been forced to swallow lately—so I told him as how he knew he wouldn't; and then his jaw got hard, and we were just staring at each other for a while, breathing heavy like right before a fight. We'd've just about gutted each other on the spot, except then Ghislain stepped in with more news from th'Esar: that like as not we were going to have to show the little shit professor around our digs, let him observe us day to day, and not accidentally feed him to one of the girls. (That last being Ghislain's own phrasing.)

We'd known, barely and sort of, what to expect when we all piled into the atrium for our rehabilitation. Before the fact, Balfour kept talking about how it was just a punishment in theory and not in actual practice, and how it was better than all the things the Arlemagnes were demanding for punishment, and how it was a clever idea when you thought about it, pleasing both sides—a real compromise instead of one of those fake ones where both parties leave the table dissatisfied. But I knew better than that. I knew it was a demotion in status and I knew how it made us all look, like kids who'd stolen cookies from the jar, like no better than naughty puppies, with th'Esar rapping newsprint against our noses, and I was screaming pissed. No matter which way they tried to spin it, I wasn't going to do what the little shit said, and I wasn't going to cut him any breaks, either. Whatever he was here to accomplish it was all just more of the same: weak words 'Versity students and Margraves and members of the bastion tossed back and forth like birdies in some pussy's badminton. We were different from all that—*exempt,* to use their own rhetoric—'cause this was the Dragon Corps. We weren't supposed to abide by the usual rules, and whatever the fuck th'Esar thought he was going to accomplish, it sure wasn't inspiring no fighting spirit in me, leastways not the kind he was looking for out of any one of us.

"I'm flying out," I said.

"You aren't," Adamo told me.

But I was all energy and nerves and wanted to burn something, and we hadn't been flying in months. "Havemercy's pissed," I said, which was true, and didn't just mean *I'm pissed.* Havemercy liked flying better than anything, and these days when I visited her for a polish or a chat, she looked at me over one metal claw like I was a fucking disappointment. Yeah, sweetheart, I'd say, we're all fucking disappointed right about now. Then I'd say a few other choice phrases, and Have'd just snort like she didn't care one way or another, so long as I saw fit to get her up in the air again.

I needed to fly all that name-and-private-detail business off—and the idea that the little shit was coming to get the grand tour and we were all going to have to roll out the red carpet like he was some kind of king rather than all green and pissing his pants terrified of us.

Good, I thought. At least he had one thing straight, if nothing else.

"Don't be a fool," said Adamo. "You've already had your ride this month, same as the rest of the boys. It isn't my fault none of you takes the time to understand rationing a thing out once in a while."

Th'Esar had come to some sort of agreement with Adamo more than ten years back about how we each got one free ride a month during peacetimes. I guess he thought that any damage we could do up in the air was *miles* less than we could do on the ground, getting stir-crazy and all riled up at one another without nothing to let off the steam.

But mostly, we figured, he'd agreed for the dragons, partly 'cause keeping them locked up all the time made them cranky, and partly because he thought it made them rusty, too.

"I'm takin' her *out*," I repeated, and that was final-like. He wasn't going to string me up, and he could give me dog rations all he liked knowing I wouldn't give a rat's ass about it, and he sure as fuck couldn't dismiss me.

He was right in some sense, 'cause the thing is, the tech the magicians use for making dragons is all pretty hush-hush, and you can't risk some lucky Ke-Han getting his hands on you so he can figure it all out in his sweet time and start building up his own air force. When you're an airman, you've got to be careful and you've got to be precise—but all that doesn't mean anything unless you're *good,* and out of all of them I was the *best*. Everybody knew it—even Ace, though he wouldn't admit it, and especially Adamo, who was stubborn as a brick wall but smarter than he looked.

I wasn't going to take her far, I said, getting on my gloves. I was just going to take her *up,* wheel her around a bit, give Volstov a show, then return her so she could sleep easier, having had the exercise.

And so I didn't kill anyone from being so fucking mad.

"Thirty," Adamo said, which meant if I was up for more than half an hour, he *was* going to string me up.

Whatever. We both knew who'd won that round.

So I went on down through the bunks and the mess and the showers and through the leisure door—rather than the one you take when the raid siren's sounding, which shoots you straight from the bedroom to the docking bay—and then there I was, the wide, low-ceilinged room clean and dark and smelling of metal and burning things, and my palms itching to get Havemercy harnessed and get us *both* up in the air.

See, unlike most of the men here, I hadn't been trained properly or anything. I'd volunteered to be one of the muck boys who run around after the real airmen and keep the harnesses polished and the dragonhide gleaming and all that bullshit, like with mops and yessirs and nosirs every two seconds, scraping and bowing and otherwise making an ass of myself. Only, I volunteered at the right time, just when Havemercy was fresh off the table, and she was being real picky and real precise about not having anyone flying her no matter how they coaxed, until she took one look at me and it was love at first sight, only we both knew the other one didn't have any heart for loving to speak of. She was beautiful then, and she's still beautiful now, though there's a clip off her left wing from getting in too close to the real fighting one time, but we turned the tide of the skirmish and sent the Ke-Han packing back over the Cobalts where they'd come from all cocky and proud, so I guess we did all right by that.

"Hey, sweetheart," I said.

Havemercy saw the harness in my hand, that I had my gloves and my riding boots on. She yawned and flicked her tail. "Bell didn't ring," she said.

The thing you have to understand about the way dragons sound is this—they're not really talking. I mean, they're machines. They're made out of metal, and then there's a little hole in their chests where a magician pours some vital piece of his Talent and his love, and that's the dragonsoul. And if the magician's peculiar or eccentric or completely off his nut, the way they usually are, then that comes out in the dragon's personality. Only they don't have any blood, and their voices grate out from their hollow metal bellows, so it's more the echoing memory of words than actual words themselves. They aren't hes or shes, either, only I liked to think of riding her like I'd ride any woman, only it was better than all those times rolled up into one, my legs wrapped around her powerful neck and her wings beating the air, throwing it against my back and whipping my hair around my face.

"Just a spin," I said.

"Good," said Havemercy. "I'm getting rusty."

"Shit," I said, "you ain't."

"Aren't," Havemercy said. "You common little fucker."

There was a time when the powers that be were concerned I was going to be a bad influence on Havemercy, the pride of the entire dragonfleet, but she wasn't some prissy little politician's wife, just power and musculature and sleeking grace, and she didn't fuck around with being proper even from the start. I taught her all the good curses and she'd melt any man tried to separate us, leastways until I could get my knife in between his ribs and stick him like a pig.

Anyway, I harnessed her up and she lowered her neck for me to swing myself around. There were loops in her jaw like chain links for me to latch the harness on and I did, then she'd turned herself around and the door to her stall was lowering like a bridge-ramp, same as always, though slower since this was no more than a leisure jaunt, and also for reminding everyone as had a pair of eyes on them who *really* ran this city.

Us.

I snapped the goggles down over my eyes. They're made more for actual emergencies, when the flying's going to get sticky and there's ash and smoke and all sorts of shit you don't want getting into your eyes, not to mention clouding up your vision. I put them on, though, out of habit and because all I needed was to catch a bug under my lid to piss me off even more.

Havemercy stretched her wings—not all the way, since she wouldn't have the room 'til we really got out of this damn room and off this damn ground. If she'd been a horse, or some common animal made of meat and bone, I'd've dug my heels in a bit—so keen I was to get in the air—but Havemercy wasn't any kind of common anything, and even with my boots on it would've hurt my feet more than she could've felt it at all.

"So," said Havemercy, making a thoughtful sound like metal grinding. "Any direction in particular?"

"Anywhere," I said, then, "everywhere. Shit, Have, let's just make sure the city hasn't forgot about us."

She snorted and unfurled her wings with the sharp whistle of steel through air. They caught the sun, flashed bright and blinding down to the ground below. I laughed my approval, loud and indifferent to the people who turned away and those who pointed and stared alike. My girl knew how to get attention.

We rose into the air, and all them people with their cares and concerns fell away at once, the steady beat of Have's wings buffeting the currents all around me. On a clear day, a no-war-fucking-lull day, flying could be as smooth as a virgin's thighs, and as soft and easy, too. On a rough day, it was like riding the eye of a storm, snaking metal and magic under me.

"Let's go to the water, then," said Havemercy.

Volstov was a city built on a hill, with everything slowly sliding down to ruin in the water. That wasn't how the 'Versity types put it—"tiers" they said, the city was built on three tiers, Molly closest to the water and Miranda closest to the palace, with Charlotte in the middle, cold and unhappy as a child in the same position. It was all like some complicated cake for weddings, and right on top was the Basquiat. It rose from the center of Miranda, tall and arrogant as any one of the damned magicians and Margraves who occupied the place, with swirled onion-shaped domes set in too many colors. The only thing I liked about it was that it near rivaled the palace in size, and that pissed th'Esar off real nice every now and again when he caught sight of it out the windows. Or so I'd heard.

Nearest landmark to the Basquiat—stuck up on a nice little hill of its own, neat as you please—was the 'Versity Stretch. That was where good boys and girls went to drain their mamas and papas of their hard-earned cash in order to learn how to speak all proper and read things in dusty books that happened to no one left alive today. Not nothing or no one *useful* ever came out of the 'Versity Stretch, and our sensitive new piss-pot professor was only further proof of it.

"You're clenching the reins," said Havemercy.

I was. Just thinking about that little whoreson and his *plans* and his *research* made me want to spit, so I did, since there was no one to give me black looks in the air.

'Versity students didn't have much money, of course, after spending it all on books and whatever the fuck, so if you followed the Stretch it'd run you right into the Rue. The Rue d'St. Difference—where you could buy anything except slaves and sex—was where the merchants established themselves and vied for customers every sunup to sundown. Foreigners coming to the city from elsewhere had a real problem with the Rue, since it was the only place where the roads ran straight instead of all crabbing crooked in the same direction. Niall, who spent more time on the ground and in the city than any self-respecting airman should, said that this year the Rue was crowded with milliners, and women in fancy wide-brimmed hats with feathers and ribbons. I tried to get him to bring me one back so we could stick it on Balfour, but he went on whining about the price until I wanted to punch him in the face; and then he said he was never going to do me any favors, ever.

Whatever. Adamo would only have torn me a new one for it, anyway.

The roads went crooked again sure as rain as soon as they bent off into Charlotte. The middle sister was where most men found their sport. Grouped together were the unmistakable red roofs and pointed, storied buildings marking the Amazement, Volstov's entertainment district, filled with opera and theatre and a bit of whoring just to keep things interesting afterward.

'Course there were restaurants, if coffee after was more your bag, but you were like to be laughed straight back into Miranda with a priss attitude like that. Charlotte didn't coddle, and it made no bones about someone's ideas of segregation. If they wanted you out, they'd let you know. It was only a madman who'd want to live in Charlotte after Miranda, but you had to respect her attitude.

Through the center, just to one side of the Amazement, ran a road that was sharp and jagged as a lightning bolt. This was man-made. Wolf's Run, where the Provost's men made their digs, and they didn't have time for meandering around slow, sloping curves. The Run was located special in the center of things, so the wolves could duck into upper or lower as neat as they pleased whenever they had to keep the peace. I don't know why they didn't just stick the whole thing on the Mollyedge and keep the troubles out that way, but there's no accounting for what some people think is sensible.

I didn't have any desire to fly over Molly—Hapenny Lane, Tuesday Street, and an over-fucking-abundance of dirty, diseased urchins being its only commodities and sole export of the lowest maiden with her skirts soaking in ocean brine. No, I didn't want to get near it, and not *even* to get to the ocean.

I said so sudden and firm to Havemercy as she twisted and climbed, fickle in the wind.

"Fuck that," she said. "I wanted to see the boats."

"No time," I replied, though honestly I didn't know whether it had been twenty minutes or forty since we'd took off.

She made a wheezy sound, like a cranky bellows, and flicked her tail in a way that meant she knew I was lying.

Twenty-five, I decided impartially, and only for the harbor. We continued on.

The harbor was a deceptive place, clean and bustling as it was. Thremedon City wasn't a port town in that we needed the trade or nothing, but boats came and left just as often as they pleased since the Ke-Han had no use for the seas. They'd been fucked over more than once trying to cross them, which was why it'd been such a big surprise when they'd snuck up and took the Kiril Islands right out from under th'Esar's nose.

Took 'em a good few years to manage that one, and not from their fighting skills or nothing—because it took them that long to get across the water without capsizing in the storms.

Thremedon's harbor was filled with ships built by people who knew what they were doing, else I didn't think they'd have made it to us at all. Caelian barges with their dark orange sails like buildings on fire; little merchant vessels from Arlemagne; the fishing boats of the Molly-dwellers that were almost too small and insignificant to make out, like everything else that made up part and parcel of Molly.

I only felt sorry for the poor bastards who didn't realize where they'd landed, smack in the middle of the city's poorest and filthiest.

I was so fucking glad to be out of there.

Havemercy was humming a tune I'd taught her myself, picked up in one of the bars and memorized 'cause I knew she'd eat it up with a spoon. The bawdy songs were her favorite, and I could tell when she was in high spirits because of when she broke out with one. Anyone who says the dragons can't have emotions 'cause they're made of metal's never flown one, see, though that sort of talk never bothered me. Have and I understood each other.

"Feeling better?" I asked before she could get to the line about the earl with a girl on each knee.

"Are you?" Havemercy beat her wings extra-hard, like she was jumping in the air, and evened out again.

I thought about it. "Always better when we're off the ground," I answered, at length.

"Bastion's own truth," she said, and went back to her song.

THOM

"So," Marius asked that evening. "How was it?"

He was being kind about everything—treating me to dinner in Reliquary's finest—because he pitied me. And though I didn't relish being pitied for prolonged periods of time, I knew that the more I spoke to him, the more I could postpone heading back to be given the grand tour. Anything to avoid that, I thought; and, because Marius was paying and had assured me it was all right, I ordered the duck.

"You're asking after the grand offender himself, aren't you," I said, suddenly very interested in the design of my salad fork.

"Well, I was going to wait for a while to bring it up. But since you mention it . . . Indeed, I am."

"I think he might have been raised by wolves," I replied. "Or at least by the Ke-Han themselves."

"Ha," said Marius, though somewhat humorlessly. "Hilarious. That dreadful?"

"We already know he's an abuser of women," I said darkly. "The first exercise I had planned—"

"Introductions, yes; I thought that was very clever."

"Thank you." Marius always knew what to say—and, surrounded by the friendly candlelight of the Amory Rose, I felt comforted, less fatalistic. "When it was his turn, he spoke at great length about the joys of forcing his way between a lady's legs."

"It's said he comes from Molly," Marius pointed out. "So of course, he's bound to be vulgar, isn't he? It's common enough. He'll be a nuisance, but at the least you can always remind yourself how much smarter you are."

"I don't know," I said. "Whether or not he can write his own name seems to have very little impact on his ability to be an ass."

"So he's the heart of the trouble, do you think? The ringleader?"

As much as I wanted to ask Marius how he managed the most troublesome of students, I was nearly certain that much of it had to do with his age, his experience, and his own confidence. I had none of these three tools, and was rather certain of my imminent doom. "Yes." I sighed.

"I have no advice for you, Thomas," said Marius, though he did look rueful. Perhaps I wasn't so averse to pity as I'd thought. "You must weather it—and you mustn't let him win."

I thought of the stark gray lines of the Airman, where the pilots slept close by to their dragons. It was a new building, an ugly intrusion on the landscape of Miranda. And, like its inhabitants, it was made too many allowances.

"I know," I said, firmly. "I won't."

HAL

If I'd known getting myself almost drowned by the rain would help improve the Margrave's spirits so enormously, I would have done it sooner.

Well, that mightn't have been entirely true, and at least, if I'd been clever enough to plan it beforehand, I wouldn't have involved poor William.

After the chatelain recovered from his short-lived period of relief, the boy was confined to the indoors for the rest of the month, and by no more than the second day of his punishment he was nearly climbing the walls with boredom. I myself was suffering from something of a cold and was also cautioned to remain inside the castle, so I tried to entertain him with a few storybooks, but soon we ran out of stories he hadn't already heard. If we were left to our own devices much longer, I feared he might run away and *really* be lost to us for good.

Yet Margrave Royston was like unto a different man, and so we weren't left to our own devices at all.

I'd given up on the storybooks entirely and thought to try a bit of the lesson plan I was forever amending to please William's ever-changing interests. It began with an explanation of Volstov's war with Xi'an, its history and the reasons for it—though I'd never been able to find two textbooks that agreed on the latter—but to my dismay, there wasn't anything more recent than fifty years ago, and it had none of the detailed descriptions about famous battles that William was so enthusiastic about.

"I don't understand," he said, peering at the book over my shoulder as though he was angry with it.

"What don't you understand?" I asked, in a calm voice that I'd been perfecting for just this purpose. I thought that if I at least sounded like a proper tutor, it wouldn't matter so much that I didn't feel like one at all.

"You keep talking about the war," William said, "and about the mountains and those others, the Ramanthines. But I don't understand. Who are the villains?"

"I . . . well," I said, turning to the table of contents in the front of the book and stalling for time. "I'm not sure. It's not exactly that simple."

"Oh but there *must* be villains," William insisted. "It isn't a proper story without them. Papa always does the villains with a scary voice, but Mama says it hurts her throat, and she pretends like there aren't any in the stories she reads me. Does it hurt your throat too?"

"No," I said, reaching for another book that might have the answer I was looking for. "It's not that. I only think that there may really *not* be any villains in this story in particular. It all depends on what side you're coming from."

"Or whose side of the table you're sitting on," said the Margrave Royston from where he was standing in the doorway.

"Oh," I said, and stood, brushing dust off the backs of my trousers and fighting away the urge to rub my nose with the back of my sleeve. (Such behavior was countrified, vulgar, and unacceptable, said the Mme; only sometimes I forgot myself, and there was no kerchief handy.) "I'm afraid I don't quite follow."

I thought at first that the Margrave must have caught a fever from being out so long in the downpour the same way I'd caught a cold, but on that second day, as he showed no particularly feverish symptoms, I realized that what he'd actually caught was the memory of a purpose.

It changed him, chased the darkness from his eyes. He shook his head as though he'd only just remembered. "I'm sorry, I forgot. It happened before you were born. The last time we attempted diplomacy with Xi'an, William, our ambassador had some bad eel, which caused him to be ill all over the Ke-Han warlord's favored niece."

"He *threw up*?" William asked, with scandalized delight.

"Yes," the Margrave said, looking very serious. "She thought it was an attack, poor creature, and defended herself with a knife."

William was now looking at the Margrave Royston as if he were the last slice of chocolate cake at dinner.

He was not so absent a man that he did not notice the attention. "Have you run out of stories already, William?"

"Yes, well—" I couldn't help speaking up, since I was feeling somewhat responsible in the first place. "You see, we've read most of them before."

"Yes," William said sullenly, "we *have,*" as if it were the worst fate in all the world. Part of me very much agreed with him.

"What, even the one about Slipfinger the Penniless?" the Margrave asked.

"And his fifteen different adventures," I confirmed.

William scuffed his toe against the carpet, and added under his breath, "Which weren't so different, not *really.*"

"Well, after the tenth they do tend to get a bit similar," the Margrave agreed. He took a moment to look around the room, half of its shelves miserably empty and the dusky sunlight sinking low just outside the lone, squat window. For a moment I thought he would reject it and be lost to his fog just from the sight, but then, to my surprise, he stepped inside and clasped his hands before him. "If you'd like, William, I could always tell you about Cobalt Range."

That was the most famous battle in the past fifteen years, and William's eyes widened enormously. "Were you *there,* Uncle Roy?" he asked, all his sullenness forgotten.

"More or less," the Margrave said.

"Would you like a seat?" I asked, admittedly eager to hear the story myself.

"If it's no trouble," said the Margrave, who seemed to have only just realized there was but one comfortable chair in the entire room.

"Papa broke the other one," William said sagely. "He was very angry."

"He'd lost his favorite horse," I explained, then drew up the chair for the Margrave. I caught him looking at me with a curious expression—I couldn't understand it—but by the time I'd thought to look again for any clues to the puzzle, he wasn't looking at me at all, turning instead to helping William scramble up beside him on the chair. I sat at his feet, knees drawn up to my chest.

"Are you quite all right down there?" the Margrave inquired. "Surely—though this *is* the country—there are other chairs to be had somewhere about the place."

"Hal enjoys sitting in strange places," William confided.

I felt my ears grow hot, and knew without having to see them for myself that they were as pink as my cheeks.

The Margrave cleared his throat; not entirely in disapproval, I thought, but it hardly mattered, as I was still blushing. "Is that so?" he said. "To each his own, it would seem."

"Tell the *story,* Uncle Roy," William pleaded, and I was grateful for the distraction.

"Which story was that? Oh, yes, Cobalt Range." The Margrave closed his eyes for a moment, and sighed—not entirely happily, but with a certain pleasure in remembering. "Yes. Ten years ago, almost eleven. It was only my second campaign, and the first had hardly given me any experience at all. Now, a curiosity of the mountains is that no one wants to fight there for long. Though the higher ground is what counts, of course, in a battle, it's a lot of mean, close-in fighting. You can't get any space to fight, trapped like that, and space becomes very important when, well"—he paused, with a glance at William— "when there are a frightful amount of explosions going off all at once."

"*Brilliant,*" said William happily, and the Margrave looked relieved. If he'd been worrying over William's appetite for violence, he needn't have done. Mme was often chasing him away from Cooke when he told his stories of terrible riding injuries and horses with broken bones.

"On the other side of the Cobalts," he went on, "there is a valley. Imagine it like this: The Ke-Han city closest to our mountains is like a blue bowl, carved deep and smooth into the earth." He spoke of it like a beautiful thing, respect lighting his eyes and touching his voice, though I thought that where the Ke-Han were concerned every man was a barbarian and in no position to be concerning himself with beauty.

"Now, this city of theirs," the Margrave went on. "We thought that if we could push them back to it, get out of the mountains and into the open space, those of us with . . . particularly useful Talents—skills that were doing no one any good all pinned together as we were like sardines in a can—the fighting would end more quickly. And we did need it to end, because while much of our battle magic was rendered useless by proximity, theirs was doing just fine, and many men were dying.

"No one quite understands the Ke-Han magic. We do know that it's something unique, feral and uncultivated when compared to ours. Something to do with the elements, though, and they seem *particularly* fond of wind. I think they focus on that because they know our air force—the Dragon Corps—is so vital to our successes past and present.

"Seven days they hammered at us with everything they had. The Reds took it the hardest, being commanded to fight no matter what, and most of them with no knowledge of magic save what their grandmothers had told them about the Well." He shook his head, as though the memory was painful for him, but it was clearly an old hurt, long since healed over, and nothing that I recognized of that deeper hurt with which I was already familiar.

"They'd only spared twelve magicians on the Cobalts, and there were two and a half times more than that against us. Their leader was a man named Jiro, and he was clever, as much as I hated to admit it. He was going to keep us holed up in those mountains until we died of starvation, or ran out of soldiers, or both."

"What about the dragons, Uncle Roy?" William's mouth hung halfway open as though he were under some spellbinding enchantment.

"I'm getting to them, nephew of mine," the Margrave said, poking the end of William's nose with a heretofore unseen affection. Then he looked at me.

I swallowed, feeling peculiar—as though I were under some kind of enchantment myself. I tucked my knees in closer to my chest.

"We moved just after noon," he went on, and this time his eyes did not leave my face. "Waiting until night would have given us better cover, but those dragons you love so much, young William, aren't worth piss in the daytime. Pardon my vulgarity. By then the Ke-Han had done us so much damage that they'd grown complacent—assumed they'd already won the battle. There were the eight of my fellows left, along with the Fourteenth Company of Reds and a handful of the Ninth. The rocks were sharp and loose from over a week of near-constant assault, and pushing down through the mountain passes became like sliding on an ever-shifting sea of shale. One of our members had a Talent for concealment; this may very well have saved all our lives.

"Intelligence and more than an appropriate amount of guess-work told us that the Ke-Han were operating from an elaborate network of tunnels in the mountains. Of course, those tunnels were the only spot on the whole damned mountain—don't tell your mother I used that word, William—where wind hadn't hammered the rock to death. We slipped into the tunnels silent as shadows, the other magicians and I, while the Reds advanced farther into the city. We'd been promised air support if the dragons could untangle their wings from their asses in time. If they weren't there by nightfall, then it wouldn't much matter, either way."

He sighed, rubbing his long fingers over his forehead as though he were suddenly weary, though in a moment it passed and I was left wondering if I'd been seeing things. I still didn't understand Margrave Royston and his all-too-mercurial moods, but he smiled with far more teeth than strictly necessary, and it was better than the resignation from days before.

"It all went wrong in the tunnels. Jenkins knocked over some rock-rabble shrine, and released some damned wind spirit that started *howling* like fury. Of course the Ke-Han woke up, came pouring in from every direction; it was like being trapped in a rat warren. We ended up racing for our lives. By some miracle we ended up outside. I—I went last, collapsed the entire setup behind us.

"By then, of course, we'd caused such a ruckus that the city below was sending off alarm fireworks, bright red like fire in the darkening sky. Our colors.

"With the element of surprise lost, many of us no longer had anything to lose. The sun was dipping below the edge of the mountain range at our backs; in a few hours it would stain the sky as red as the soldiers' coats. We descended into the city, Ninth Company at our backs and the Fourteenth with me in front.

"I . . . operate better if there isn't anyone in the way, you see, as it wouldn't do any good to go blowing away our allies.

"I don't remember who it was who started singing the anthem, low and rolling. It moved through our battered little platoon like a wave until we were shouting it to the skies, song punctuated by blasts of rock and the shouts of our enemies. We made it nearly to the gates before they'd mustered almost enough of a force to greet us. We'd caught them off guard, remember, and most thought our campaign in the mountains quite over and done with.

"Jenkins died with a spear in his throat; it was a terrible way to go. And that's—Well, that was when I lost my temper and blew a hole in the cerulean wall surrounding the city. Nearly killed myself in the process, interestingly enough, as there's only so much a magician can do with his own Talent before it starts to tug at his blood, and the wall was built with a very old magic. Still, it seemed like we might almost be massacred then and there, after all, with the Ke-Han screaming bloody murder with their deep-throated war cries, and crashing their enormous war gongs, and pouring out from behind the city walls like an endless stream of ants.

"Then the dragons came.

"It started as a high whine, like the whistle of a kettle. Then the sound changed, became akin to that of the wind spirits that had rushed through the tunnels earlier that morning. It was, of course, the sound of wings, metal and magic, beating the air—and turning the tides of battle, I like to think. They covered the sky, streaking copper and silver, platinum and gold, flashing their bellies and glinting ferociously in the moonlight. I'd never seen anything so beautiful in all my life."

"Do they really breathe fire?" William asked.

I realized my mouth had been hanging open and closed it abruptly.

"In a way," the Margrave answered, and his eyes lost the distance they'd gathered with his story. "The city certainly burned, I know that much."

"It's a mechanism," I said. My throat was dry, my tongue no more useful to my needs than a rock. "I . . . I think," I added, very soon after that, for this was the Margrave's story, and surely he knew better than I.

"Indeed, it is that," the Margrave confirmed. "A complicated business—another story entirely—and perhaps one I'll tell you tomorrow. What do you say?"

"*Please,*" William said, though he never liked to use the word unless he was coerced or tricked into it. I couldn't help but smile. "Is that *really* your Talent, Uncle Royston? Blowing things up?"

"Ah," the Margrave replied. "That's . . . well . . . in a way. It's very hard to explain."

"Will you explain that tomorrow, too?" I was grateful for William's questions, since they were the ones I wanted to ask for myself but couldn't. I tried not to look too eager for a favorable reply.

"Indeed," the Margrave said. It wasn't the first time I found him watching me—as if he could see my wishes because I was very poor at hiding them. "I think, nephew, that I shall."

That night I dreamed of the war cry of the Ke-Han, and Margrave Royston in the tunnels at Cobalt, at that time scarcely more than my own age, much as I would have dreamed of any

favorite roman. When I woke, I was almost disappointed to recall it had no bearing on my life at all.

THOM

Chief Sergeant Adamo and Airman Balfour met me at the
door. From within, I could catch wisps of a melody—one
I didn't recognize—as picked out on the keys of a piano. I
could smell, too, the scent of the clove cigarettes certain professors and Margraves of the Basquiat smoked.

Above all that, though, was the smell of fire.

It wasn't simply something as commonplace as the sulfurous gasp of a match struck or a candle lit. It was *real* fire,
the killing kind, the sort that ripped through cities and trapped
children in their little rooms—fire hot enough to melt metal—
and the thick, dark smoke groaning at its heel, cruel and suffo-
cating. I didn't like fire of that unpredictable, violent nature. I
had my reasons for that, too.

My stomach turned over at the scent, but it was a grounding revulsion, one that reminded me who I was and the relative insignificance of what I'd been asked to accomplish. I
didn't know where the dragons themselves were—I assumed
I wasn't important enough to see them up close—and rather
than overstepping my bounds, I simply allowed a young,
rather grimy man to take my suitcase.

"Your quarters're this way," Adamo grunted.

Balfour fiddled with the thumb of his left glove. "It's only a
couch," he said. "And a sort of . . . standing curtain. It won't
be very quiet. Niall wakes up early and he likes to sing while
he makes breakfast, but in any case—I wanted to tell you—if
you wake up and your hand feels funny, wet sort of, whatever
you do don't bring it up to your face."

"Oh," I said, and I must have looked something awfully
unhappy, because Balfour's face fell.

Adamo stifled what might have been a laugh or might have
been a cough behind the palm of his broad hand. "If you're

stupid enough to fall for it," he said gruffly, "then you get what you deserve."

"No one deserves a blue face," Balfour said quietly.

I was inclined to agree with him.

As I already knew, the Airman was a hideous, blunt building, erected in the modern style and designed for efficiency over beauty. It was somewhat nicer on the inside, I was relieved to note, though not by very much. It was also a mess. There were boots strewn about the hallway, and coats in disarray, so that I almost tripped over one. There was even a shirt and what appeared to be a pair of ladies' undergarments. I realized all at once that these men had no idea how to clean up after themselves, and no awareness that they even should. I wondered what unpleasant smells the permeating scent of burning and the clove cigarettes masked, and found myself quite relieved I might never have cause to know.

I wasn't their nanny, and I wasn't their maid. I was their instructor in the skeleton of basic decency; I would teach them how to interact as humans rather than animals. What they did with their women's undergarments was up to them.

"And there's Niall's bunker, and Magoughin's," Balfour was in the process of telling me, "and there's the first row of showers. You sign up in advance, unless you've been out on a raid, and then you've got first priority whether you've signed up or not."

"Um," I said, though I didn't mean to sound stupid. "Why's that?"

"Oh," Balfour said, as if it were perfectly common sense, "to wash off all the ash, of course."

"Ah," I said, and promptly decided to keep my mouth shut.

"That's the common room, the one for music and smoking—and there's the private common room, for when you're engaged with a . . . ah . . . companion for the evening, or the afternoon, or whenever you've got off-hours."

A belch of perfume hit me from beyond the half-open door. It reminded me of my childhood, and I stepped quickly past it.

"That's command," Adamo said, jerking a hand toward a room across the way. "You don't go in there."

"Yes," Balfour agreed. "No one goes in there but Chief Sergeant."

"Duly noted," I assured them both.

I wondered where the rest of my welcoming committee was, or if they'd sent Balfour and Adamo ahead to lull me into a false sense of security while they waited just around the corner like jumping spiders, ready to strike.

"And there's my bunker, and there's Rook's, and there's Merritt's," Balfour continued, still giving me the grand tour. I didn't entirely see that it was necessary. I didn't think I would be spending much time inside any of these forbidding little rooms, their doors staunchly, disapprovingly, locked against me. It was, however, good to make note of which room *not* to stumble into in the dead of night, thinking it would be the right place to have a drink of water or to relieve myself.

"You may notice the rooms are all scattered-like," Adamo said. Indeed, I had, and I said as much. "The docking area's below," he explained. "Each man sleeps above his dragon."

"When we're needed, the air-raid bell sounds," Balfour added. "There's a trapdoor for each of us that lets us down into each of our private bays directly."

"The long way 'round isn't one you need to know, either," Adamo said. "The docks are off-limits." And that was most emphatically the end of that.

"Understood," I assured him.

"Now, Rook's out tonight," Adamo added, privately, and I was embarrassed to learn how easily everyone had seen through me, embarrassed to feel Balfour's eyes moving between the two of us. "We thought it'd be for the best. And, knowing him, he won't be back for a day at the least."

Before I could stop myself, I said, "But th'Esar—"

Adamo's look hardened. "We're not much used to having th'Esar in direct command of us," he said evenly. "Seeing as how he doesn't pilot a dragon, himself."

"Ah," I said. As they'd have noted in Molly, I'd stepped in it. "Of course."

I was quickly beginning to understand that conversation with any of the airmen outside of the requisite teachings would be akin to running the gauntlet. In a Ke-Han minefield.

"Here you are," Balfour piped up, gesturing to a plain standing screen that had been pulled haphazardly across an alcove. This was where the couch was.

I examined my new living space—it could hardly be called a room—with trepidation.

It was a largish couch, I'd give them that. Of course, it made sense that th'Esar would spare no luxury when it came to his precious Dragon Corps. I wondered if he even knew the extent of what went on down at the Airman when his influence wasn't physically present. I wondered if there would be certain things that I was to omit from my reports, and how I would know what was to be deemed information to which th'Esar didn't need to be privy. I felt the onset of a headache creeping from my temples to the bridge of my nose, knowing that if I got it wrong, the airmen would likely feed me to the dragons.

You are accountable only to the Chief Sergeant, I reminded myself. I would make my report, then Adamo himself could discern what information he wanted to share with the head of the nation. That would save me from trying to navigate the pitfalls of that particular arrangement, and also from trying to understand the strange circadian logic that governed these men. I did not at all cherish the deep anxiety fostering in my gut that came from not knowing what to expect.

"Ivory's on your left." Balfour tugged his right glove on tighter, gesturing farther down the hall to another room, which had been placed as all the rest: with no real rhyme or reason. The man who had designed the building must have been a genius or a madman or both. "He's very quiet, so you might not be . . . bothered."

He tacked on this last as if he hoped very much that it were true. On my other side, Adamo snorted; he didn't even bother trying to hide it.

I had never before felt so strongly the urge for a door of my very own that I could lock, not even when I'd been living in the very depths of Molly, where a lack of things to steal did not necessarily preclude break-ins.

Small blessings, I told myself again. Rook would be out for the evening, likely the entire night, and might not have the care to coat my hand in something strange and wet. I felt some helpless frustration once again at my predicament, that I'd allowed myself so easily to be caught at the tender mercies of the very type of system I'd made strict measures to avoid my entire life.

"Well," I said, and was promptly cut off by a bloodcurdling scream that echoed down the hallways.

"My books!"

"Ah," said Balfour. "That will be Raphael."

"My *books*," said Raphael again, louder this time and with a quivering timbre to his voice, as though he was a volcano on the edge of eruption. "What have you *done*, you piss-drinking sons of Ke-Han *whores*?"

"Shit," Adamo said, the curse torn rough as crushed cobblestone from his throat. "I'd better go. Docks're off-limits," he repeated to me, as though I were simple.

I could take no offense at his attitude, though, instead nodding to show that I really did understand. The Chief Sergeant was a man I did not want on any side but my own, and if that meant a little more bowing and scraping than usual, so be it.

He marched off down the hallway to the tune of a muffled crash, followed by a series of undignified hoots and hollers that sounded like nothing so much as an entire band of wild chimpanzees let loose from the zoo.

I thought about calm things: the surface of a lake on a windless day, the grant money I would receive for my studies upon completing this assignment. The knowledge that, even if they killed me, I was still much, much smarter.

There was another scream.

"*Madeline!*"

"I bet it's Niall and Compagnon," said Balfour confidentially. "They've had this big secret project going for weeks now. Papier- mâché. I guess they ran out of paper."

"Oh," I said, because I couldn't think of anything else to say.

Balfour nodded. "It was going to be a scale model of the city, only Compagnon gave it these, you know, enormous breasts, so now it's just a misshapen sort of woman. She's in the common room—not the private one, but the other one."

"And that's . . . Madeline?" I asked, with a sense of looming dread.

"Yes," said Balfour. "She's kind of like our mascot."

CHAPTER FOUR

ROYSTON

If asked, I couldn't have pinpointed the exact time or day when Hal's tradition of reading to me in the evenings became reversed, so that I was the one telling the stories, but it had happened. Some nights we would retire to the drawing room and—William having bragged to his siblings both younger and older—I would find myself seated hearthside, speaking to a rapt semicircle of bright, dark eyes as my brother's wife drifted in and out, mostly to "tch" noisily at the most violent parts. I prided myself on only ever having made Emilie cry once, and I thought perhaps that if William hadn't jeered at her so mercilessly, the whole mess might have been avoided entirely.

It was during these stories that I was most aware of Hal, the open wonderment on his face, the careful attention he paid to my words, as though I were one of the romans to which he was so devoted. A folly of mine perhaps, but it inspired me to find somewhere inside myself the parts that hadn't yet been ground down to rubble and compost by the country, and I was glad of it.

There was little news from the city, though I freely admitted to my friends in written word that the fault was mine for allowing the lines of communication to dry up. A colleague of mine from the Basquiat wrote that there was some great uproar in the Dragon Corps, that they were being made to take etiquette classes. I immediately wrote to the only touchstone I had ever cared to have among the Esar's colorful band of self-important animals: Chief Sergeant Adamo.

The letter I'd got back confirmed everything I'd been told,

and what was more—the man doing the teaching was a student barely out of the 'Versity.

He seems very clever, Adamo's letter read. *And I think he'll do all right so long as he survives the first few weeks, which he might not, and so long as he's quiet enough that Rook forgets him completely when the lessons aren't on. I don't really know what th'Esar's thinking having him stay here, of all places, but it'll work out or it won't.*

Everything's going swimmingly in the country, I hope. Don't go so long without writing again, or I'll have to break th'Esar's rules myself and fly upcountry way to pluck you out of there myself.

At the very idea of this I laughed so long and loud that Hal came to investigate. The letters from home, coupled with my newfound audience for what stories I'd collected, had made a world of difference in what I no longer viewed as the most terrible of exiles.

And then, of course, there was Hal.

He was, I liked to tell myself, the ubiquitous essence of that part of the countryside I still couldn't bring myself to hate. One of my mentors had told me that in order to be embraced by Thremedon, a man must cast aside all other lovers and take the city as his one and only—for then her secrets would be spread wide open, as in a card trick or a whorehouse. It seemed a very apt theory—though with my proclivities, I was required to modify the analogy somewhat.

Yet at the same time—though Thremedon was always my *other lover,* as it were—and as much as I hated to admit it, the country was my home. I'd been raised not in Nevers but in Tonnerre, on its border, and no matter how much time I'd spent learning the city as I would have learned a lover—and no matter how I yearned for that *other lover* during my exile— no man could ever completely expunge all trace of his first lover from his heart. I, too, was a victim of this pattern. In my own way, I suppose I still yearned to be accepted by this place I couldn't quite bring myself to accept in return.

If I'd been a philosopher and not a Margrave, I would have solved this problem for myself already. Or, at least, I'd have owned a better vocabulary for grappling with it privately. Perhaps that would have assuaged my bruised ego somewhat.

Unfortunately, the truth of the matter remained: I had conflated Hal with something taken from my own needs, and I found myself seeking out his company for reasons I should not have allowed myself to act upon or even to indulge in thought. His approval meant everything to me—the way he wrapped his arms around his knees and held them tight during the most frightening moments in my memoirs, or insisted on sitting on the floor at my feet, even when there were ample chairs for him to make use of. In his eyes I saw admiration and fascination both, as if he wished to read me like a book. And Hal, I knew, was a voracious reader.

It sparked something untoward in me, some answering desire to be read. He had a sharp mind and was cleverer than he thought he was, than the country had allowed him to be. Still, it was hardly in selflessness that I offered him all the knowledge I had that was fit for more innocent ears, hardly in selflessness that I endeavored to keep him near to me whenever I could.

To measure how impossible I had truly become, how stubborn and how self-involved, one need only take this for an example: I sought him out myself, though I always made it seem as if I hadn't. After his cold had ended I even mentioned our usual walks by the Nevers, more than once, though I tried with the coy neediness of a schoolboy to seem thoroughly disinterested in whether he could spare the time for me or not.

Hal wasn't the sort of creature suited to such games. I didn't think he had any idea I was playing them.

What did I want? I was certain that I wanted something— I knew it because I'd found once more the will to rise and bathe and knock the dust out of my own curtains, to demand some servant's punctuality to air the choking smell of dust out of the entire room—but it was there that my self-awareness ceased to be useful. I had no doubt I was protecting myself from the nature of my eagerness to please and to be favored above all other members of the household. This last wasn't very hard, for he was treated quite abominably, despite his tenuous kinship to my brother's wife. I don't mean that he was in any way overtly abused. It was simply that most pretended he wasn't there, and while he seemed not to mind overly much, it was nevertheless true that every time I made overtures or reached out to engage him in conversation his warm eyes, the pale blue color of a dreaming sky, lit up immediately. Now that I was no longer steeped in my own self-pity I could recognize the signs at once. This was an affectionate young man who was being starved for warmth.

He was also clever, and being starved of something to test his cleverness against. This, I supposed, was the reason for all the reading he did—for the way he tore into new books the way desert sands swallowed any and all water for which they were so burningly parched.

It was once again selfish of me, but I loved to watch him read. He had nimble, long fingers and he turned the pages of his romans with a trembling reverence—trembling, I realized quickly enough, because he was keeping a necessary hold on himself, that he wouldn't become so overeager as to tear a single page. He read as he walked; read in small, snug corners of every room; read outside in the branches of trees and tucked up against tree trunks. When he was at the table he wished he was reading. Only when he was at my feet and listening to my evening stories did that wistful expression fade from his face. Only then was the same hunger he usually reserved for the secrets between the pages fixed on someone alive and breathing in this world.

I admit freely that I lived to be sole proprietor of that expression. I dreamed of it at night and waited all day long to see it again.

Was this so selfish of me? Perhaps it was. Yet, in all honesty, I kept the children entertained and kept William from going mad during his confinement, which also kept the burden from resting solely upon Hal's shoulders. The Mme even fainted less. In my own way, I was useful in a house that still didn't entirely forgive my presence; and I was glad, also, to be wanted, by someone. It was a small thing, but it gave me a purpose, even if I'd never fancied myself the country bard before.

One evening, William asked me, "Are those stories *all* true, Uncle Royston?"

"As true as any story can be," I replied with a smile.

At that moment Hal caught my eyes, his own bright and wide. I understood, with a sudden and fierce thunderclap of epiphany, what it was I had cobbled together and pinned all my hopes to.

I excused myself from the room at once, worrying Emilie and troubling Hal and sending William into a fit of a tantrum in which he made Etienne's nose bleed all over the brand-new rug my brother's wife had just procured for the sitting room.

If we were to go about labeling things, then I will readily admit *that* was selfish.

Sometime later, I heard a tentative knock on my bedroom door. I knew whose knock it was; I'd memorized it. How I hadn't realized before the extent and the particular quality of my feelings, I didn't know. I was an idiot.

"Come in," I said. Even in the depths of condemning myself, I couldn't keep Hal out. I simply didn't want to.

He entered the room and closed the door very quietly behind him, perhaps to keep the light from the hallway from bothering me. There he stood, his back against the door and his hands behind him, still holding the doorknob, I presumed, and worrying his lower lip as he so often did. My heart made a strange revolution in my chest. I was sunk, as surely as I lay there.

"Are you feeling unwell?" Hal asked at last, when the silence was too long and too thick for either of us to bear a second more. "I thought perhaps, since you left so suddenly—"

"Something of a headache," I replied lightly. I hated myself not simply for worrying him, but for lying to him now— as if it made even an inch of difference.

"Oh," said Hal. Then he nodded, as though this were a perfectly appropriate reason for leaving as abruptly as I had, rather than merely excusing myself as any gentleman would have done in my place.

He would accept any answer I gave him, I felt certain. Except for the truth.

I had a fleeting, foreign wish for my old fog of indifference. Then I might have something at least to shield me from this awareness, new and raw. It *was* rather akin to having a headache, in that every movement seemed magnified, but my affliction was—for mercy or tragedy—centered only and irrevocably around Hal.

The doorknob clicked as he let go of it and came forward, hands clasped still behind his back.

"Would you like me to read to you?" His brow creased in a rare frown. "No, I suppose that wouldn't help, would it?"

It would help neither my fictional headache nor what truly ailed me. And, as selfish as I was, I could not stomach the idea of lying in bed while Hal read to me as though nothing had changed.

"No," I agreed, too quickly for manners, too quickly to stop the hurt from flashing across Hal's face, visible as print on the page. I felt like a brute, protecting myself at the expense of his ego, but trapped here as I was in the house, the country, I could think of no other way. I would not indulge in the same mistake twice.

"Would you like the drapes shut, then?" Hal's face had a curious look to it, wary and uncertain.

I realized then what it looked like, and that his concern revolved around the idea that I might have given up once more on life in the country at large and decided to shutter myself away. How could I explain that it was quite the opposite? The idea itself was laughable. Only I wasn't laughing.

"That's all right," I said at length, then sat up straighter so as to reassure him. "It's only a headache."

"Of course," he said, relief passing smooth as glass over his face. Hal, I understood, had quite simply never been given cause to hide his emotions from anyone. It was rather a dangerous skill to be without. "Well, you'll call if you need anything? There are always servants about—or me."

"I'm sure it will be gone come morning," I said, no longer in control of my own lie nor even clear on the good it could possibly be doing. After all, I would doubtless wake up in the morning exactly as I was now, lest I took as desperate measures as the men in the historically inaccurate books Hal had been reading in earlier months: which was to say, cut my own heart from my chest and seal it away for safekeeping.

"I hope so," he confided. "Otherwise, William will be inconsolable. And, well, you've seen him when he's inconsolable. It tends to lead to bloodshed."

I nodded and felt that this would be an appropriate place for an apology about the rug. "You may give him my deepest regrets," I told Hal instead. "And inform him that no one was eaten by ravenous sea creatures."

"That will disappoint him," said Hal.

"He'll get used to it," I said, too coldly again. It wasn't right or fair of me; I knew that Hal was made for no such pretenses, and that a good man, a better man, would have been perfectly clear with him.

There was a short silence, wherein I could see Hal struggle for a clear direction to take the conversation from there. I should have warned him that it was impossible. In the country, as I might well have known, there were many trees to become tangled in.

"Are you quite sure that there's nothing I can get for you, Margrave Royston?"

The mere fact that I'd grown less self-indulgent, dragged myself from a mire of self-pity, did not mean that my brother's request had changed, or that Hal came to see me out of anything resembling his own volition. Remembering this fact made things a little easier, like digging one's nails into the palm of one's hand to ward off distraction, or the advances of those with mind-reading Talents. A bit perverse, perhaps, but it was a small and necessary pain, there for me to call out of the ether whenever I so happened to need the reminder.

"Yes, Hal," I assured him. And then, buoyed by some fool capricious impulse, I looked at him directly. "You needn't address me that way, in case you haven't noticed. The rest of the family certainly doesn't bother."

"Oh," he said. The tips of his ears went a helpless, bright pink so that I had to look away. "I only thought—I'm not true family, see."

"Be that as it may," I said patiently.

I was not normally a patient man; it was the reason I'd turned down a position at the 'Versity Stretch when they'd offered it. Professors had to enjoy the gift of teaching and I was no teacher. I was too impatient, too scattered and self-interested. I wanted nothing to do with someone else's ideas and wanted to share none of my own. This curious new generosity was a change and—despite the contempt I held for the country and its own fear of progress—it affected me.

"All right," he replied after a spell, and I thought he sounded pleased, though I couldn't bring myself to look and see.

HAL

The night I learned for certain of Margrave Royston's reason for coming to stay with us started just the same as any other night, with no warning signs nor any indication that it was to be something out of the ordinary.

I'd prepared the children for dinner as best I could. Earlier that day, William celebrated his release from captivity by immediately finding the largest and squishiest mud puddle left by the rains; he'd used it to spark a war between himself and any of the others who came near, myself included. By the time we'd all got clean again, we'd run short on hot water, and that put Mme in a foul temper.

Mme was in a foul temper often enough these days, though she was fainting less. I came upon her arguing with the chatelain in the study about influences—specifically, the sort of influence the Margrave was having on the children and William in particular, who now proclaimed to anyone who asked that he was going to move to the city just as soon as he was able. He'd also picked up one or two words that had slipped into the stories in the heat of the moment, words that caused our cook to chase him about the house with a wooden spoon.

In general, though, I felt that things had been running more smoothly since Margrave Royston had taken it upon himself to occupy the children's fancy. I myself enjoyed the help as much as I did the stories, and would have been very sorry if anyone had convinced him to spend his time otherwise.

The children marched downstairs in a queue to the dining room, which I privately thought of as the finest room in the house. It was certainly one of the largest, paneled all in fine, dark wood with high-backed chairs and a long, rectangular table of exactly the same shade. The servants polished the table daily, whether we were using it or not, so that the wood always had an exacting gleam to it, as though it was not wood at all but marble or glass. I knew it couldn't compare to the likes of what they had in the city, but I thought it very fine, all the same.

"Any news from Thremedon?" The chatelain seemed relieved to have found that the city was no longer a subject taboo with his brother, and he asked after it often now; though whether he was truly curious or if it was only a peace offering, I couldn't tell.

"Well," said Royston, and his eyes crinkled at the corners the way they did whenever he was about to relay something particularly amusing. I leaned forward on my elbows—too eager as always, but then no one was looking at me. "It seems the Esar has come up with a particularly unique way of dealing with our airmen and the diplomat from Arlemagne all in one."

Mme took a very long drink from her wineglass. She didn't seem to like talking about the city very much.

"Out with it then," said the chatelain, who had no patience for the way his brother paused in order to build suspense.

Margrave Royston put down his fork and smiled so widely that it still looked rather foreign on his face. "They're calling it 'sensitivity training.'"

"*What?*" The chatelain's broad face went slack with shock.

The children broke out in a smattering of laughter, though whether they truly understood or whether they were laughing at their father's expression, I didn't know.

"It's a stroke of genius really," said the Margrave, fingers toying idly with the stem of his wineglass. "It humiliates the Dragon Corps without any blood drawn, which I think the diplomat was quite keen on initially; and perhaps they might even learn something from the whole ordeal though I sincerely doubt it."

"Oh, Arlemagne," Mme said, in a tone I thought rather strange. "They never *do* know what they want over there, do they?"

There was a short pause before the Margrave answered. "Well, I don't know about that."

"They've certainly had some problems in the past," said the chatelain, in support of Mme. He smiled jovially, and refilled his glass with wine. "Especially after their king took ill."

"This new one is completely useless," agreed Mme. She dabbed at her mouth neatly with a napkin and gestured for a servant to take her bowl of soup. "The prince, or whatever they insist on calling him."

"Now," said the Margrave—and he'd told me not to address him as such but remembering was hard, especially in my own head. His voice came out a little colder than it had a second ago, and I had the unexpected sensation of a sudden frost. "Now, that's not entirely fair. The heir apparent has many fine leadership qualities."

"Oh I'm *sure* he does," said Mme, her expression as sharp and brittle as glass. "But that wasn't exactly what we were talking about, now was it?"

"Marjorie." The chatelain said his wife's given name, quick and quiet like a rebuke. It was obvious that she'd said something rude, though for the life of me I didn't understand what.

"Yes, Royston," she went on. "Perhaps you should tell us of the enormous . . . *talents* the Arlemagnes possess."

Mme had partaken of rather a lot of wine. I could tell from the way she spoke, kneading the words in her mouth as if they were dough.

"Brother," said Royston, and in his voice I thought I could hear the rumbling of falling rock in the Ke-Han tunnels, "tell your wife to hold her tongue, else I may lose my temper."

She laughed, high and shrill, and I found myself wishing she would be quiet, or that the chatelain at least would quiet her. I stole a glance at the children to find William watching the Margrave with an eager sort of anticipation, while Etienne and Alexander stared at their uncle with a mixture of horror and awe. Emilie's hair hung in her eyes, the way it did when she was trying not to cry.

"What are you going to do? Blow me to smithereens, perhaps?" Mme asked pointedly. There were two spots of color rising high on her cheeks, and she was trembling. Despite the poor constitution she spoke so often of having, she seemed in no danger of fainting now.

"That would be against the law," the Margrave replied. His voice seemed to have two layers, the external worn thin to reveal the one beneath, which was sharp and unpleasant as a row of crocodile teeth. "I'm quite sure that I needn't go to such extreme measures to shut your mouth."

"*Brother,*" the chatelain warned.

"This is an outrage," Mme pressed; a moment later she'd slammed her wineglass down on the table so vehemently I was stunned when it didn't break. "We've given you our home, our *hospitality—*"

"And it has been *truly* hospitable," the Margrave replied, on the edge of a sneer.

"How dare you?" Mme said, her lips trembling. "How *dare* he!"

"I merely feel," the Margrave countered neatly, "that you should keep your mouth shut when you know so very little about the subject at hand."

"I know this much!" The Mme had never struck me as frightening before—inflexible, yes, and often selfish, but never so unforgiving or unkind—but now I found myself drawing away from her, wrapping my arms around Emilie and letting her hide her face against my shoulder. "You did a disservice to your country—betrayed your king by taking up with that fool in the first place—and because you did, why we . . . we might have gone to war over it! It's unnatural, and yet you—you had the audacity to be so indiscreet—"

"Marjorie," the chatelain almost shouted.

He never called Mme by her first name. In the course of five minutes, he'd used it twice.

I hardly dared, but suddenly I found myself looking at the

Margrave in the midst of all this. His face was white as a ghost's, his jaw clenched, his eyes fiercely dark. When I combined what I knew of the Margrave as he was now with his stories from the past, I wondered if he *wouldn't* set something on fire or use his Talent out of anger.

Surely he wouldn't, I told myself.

Emilie was on the verge of crying. I stroked her hair.

"Madam," the Margrave ground out in a voice like sharpening knives, "this may come as an immense surprise to you, considering how highly you esteem your intellect, yet I must confess there is a great deal in this world about which you know less than nothing. I say 'less than' because you are informed *incorrectly*—and being both tenacious and pompous, you cling to this misinformation as a pit bull to the bone, which makes you far more dangerous and contemptible than even the stupidest of men."

After that, no one said anything for a very long minute. I could hear the sounds Mme made as she searched for something to say, her breaths rasping; I could almost hear the moment when the entirety of the Margrave's insult had sunk in at last.

Then everything happened at once, the chatelain and Margrave Royston and Mme shouting at one another; the Mme's wineglass being knocked over; the chatelain pounding the table with his fist over and over until it threatened to split along the grain; and above all that, a crackling tension that made the hairs on the back of my neck stand on end and which came from where the Margrave was seated, perfectly still. I knew at once that it was his Talent, and whether he was searching to employ it or to check it, I wasn't sure.

"Only an *idiot*," Mme was screaming hoarsely, "would be so incompetent as to—"

"The Arlemagnes are damned shirkers, that's what they are," the chatelain was bellowing over all that. "Shirkers of responsibility, dogs in a fight, cowards and bastards all, and I can't say, Royston, I can't say as I approve of any of your damn choices, but this—"

"Is *too much!*" Mme barked. She clutched at her breast.

"To come here—to poison our children—to allow them to worship you, when you are no more than a common—"

"As I said, Madam, I have no further use for you or a single one of your ample prejudices," the Margrave interrupted smoothly. "I should like to think that you and your ilk are the reason most of Volstov has gone to piss in the past four years, and the reason why I fled the countryside in the first place. You epitomize everyone I've ever hated—every fluttering, close-minded maiden aunt with no beauty of feature or soul—"

"Now *see here,* damn it," the chatelain snarled. "Royston, you ass, if you hadn't noticed, she's my *wife*—"

"I'm very sorry, brother," the Margrave replied. "That was an unfortunate choice you made, and it's an unfortunate fate you suffer. I'd not even wish such a terrible thing on the Ke-Han—"

"All this from a man who bedded an Arlemagne prince!" The Mme spat on the floor; William, in what I assume was uncomfortable horror, barked out a dreadful laugh. Neither his parents nor his uncle seemed to notice. "I'd say, of everyone here, *you're* the disgrace to our country, *Margrave*," the Mme went on, inexorable. "As evidenced by the Esar's all-too-lenient punishment. If you ask me, it should have been far worse!"

It was then that the Margrave exploded the dining-room table.

I believe, even provoked as he was and shaking with rage, he was still in enough control of himself not to harm any of us with the outburst of raw magic; the explosion was oddly contained, as if some invisible protective dome existed between us and the blast. Splintering, burning wood skittered underneath our chairs and to the four walls of the dining room like some sort of fireworks display. As quickly as the fire began it was doused, and all we were left with was a singed rug and pieces of table everywhere.

Emilie was too shocked even to cry. Etienne was gripping Alexander by the arm, and William's eyes were wide with disbelief. I, too, felt myself staring.

Once again, the Margrave had rendered us speechless.

In the silence that followed, the Margrave said, very quietly, "I'll pay for that."

"Yes," the chatelain replied, clearing his throat. "Well. See that you do, brother."

The Mme fainted; Emilie immediately recovered from her shock and began to bawl. It was into the ensuing chaos that William asked, "Will you do the china cupboard next, Uncle Roy? Mama always says it's so ugly!"

"To your *room*, William!" the chatelain commanded.

While I attempted to round up the children and lead them out of the dining room—which appeared now to be more of a war zone than anything else—I saw the Margrave sink into his chair and put his head in his hands. I feared the fog would descend around him; I feared Mme's tongue had been too sharp. I feared a great many things, but Emilie was tugging on my sleeve, desperate to leave this battlefield. Instead of doing anything I would have liked to do, I ushered the children out into the hallway, where the servants had gathered to stare, openmouthed, through the door and at the scene before them.

"Would you?" I asked the cook.

"Of course," the cook said, gathering Emilie close. "Come now. Tut, what's she crying for, then?"

I turned back to the dining room. One of Mme's maids was kneeling on the floor beside her, waving smelling salts underneath her nose and trying, in vain, to rouse her. Now and then, Mme would let out a trembling groan; she'd stir, her eyes would flutter, and she'd fall back into deathly stillness. She'd done this before. It only meant she was scared and unhappy and faced with something she didn't understand and couldn't predict. By morning she'd be fine, if complaining of a headache.

The chatelain was unexpectedly quiet, staring at the tragedy his dining-room table had become.

"It was a very nice table," he said, at length. Mme took that moment to let out another groan, and I saw the Margrave wince.

"I'll buy you another," he repeated. "My apologies for the mess, brother."

"Well," the chatelain said. "Marjorie has that effect on even the best of us."

The Margrave returned his head to his hands, and I took that opportunity to step back over the threshold and into the madness. When I rested my hand on the Margrave's shoulder, he stirred and looked back at me, and did not smile.

What I'd learned was in some ways very much what Cook and the others had been gossiping about before—the rumors that had preceded the Margrave and made the servants so uncomfortable. There must have been more to it than that, however; I could tell as much by the unhappy slump of the Margrave's back.

"Would you," I said carefully, "like me to accompany you back to your room?"

"Oh," he said, and didn't seem able to answer my question.

"It's just that I think you might benefit from some company," I said, more quietly, so that only he could hear. I hoped that intimated what I thought—that no man should be left alone with such thoughts as were obviously haunting him—but I couldn't tell if he was pleased or displeased to hear my motives.

"I've made something of a mess," he said, still refusing to answer me.

"It would appear so," I replied. I looped both my arms under one of his and helped him to his feet. "The servants will look after it."

"Hal," he began.

"Come," I said. "You won't even have to talk to me. We can sit about in silence, if you'd like, or I can read to you. Anything you'd like."

The look he gave me then was one I'd remember for the rest of my life. "Well," said the Margrave. "All right."

I took him upstairs. I thought it strange that the Margrave, after such a display of power, could need to be led anywhere, but he didn't make any effort to lose me. I myself was glad of it, because I had the uncomfortable feeling that Margrave Royston had transformed into someone else again before my very eyes, and I wanted him in sight until I'd got it pinned down.

At some point during the tenure of his long and difficult stay at Castle Nevers, I'd somehow convinced myself that I knew the Margrave, knew what sort of a man he was by the way he interacted with the children and with me. The stories he told were fascinating, and I'd never heard the like, but until tonight they had remained only that—stories. Now, with the memory of the dining-room table fresh in my mind, it seemed as though the things I'd known about the Margrave were only a very small part of a much greater whole.

It was as though a character from one of my romans had leapt from the pages, full-blown and hale. I could scarcely look at him, I found, and not for lack of wanting to.

"I should apologize," he said, when we reached the landing. His voice was quiet, private, as though he were still half-lost in thought.

"You've done so," I reminded him, even if it was uncharitable of me. "And you promised to pay for the table."

"I lost my temper," he said. "I shouldn't have."

"Well, you heard the chatelain. Mme has that effect on everyone."

At that the Margrave laughed, startled and hoarse, so that I knew it had sounded quite as rude as I'd feared. I didn't care. At that moment, I felt as though I would say anything at all if it would keep him from retiring once more into depression.

"Indeed," he said, with a rumble in his throat that sounded pleased. I felt a strange sort of swelling in my chest—like pride—to know that I'd caused it, that I could effect such a change.

It was, after all, what I'd been aiming for.

The Margrave stepped away from me as we reached the door, turned the knob, and opened it halfway so that he might slip inside alone. He paused at the doorframe.

"I suppose," he said, turning slowly to meet my gaze, "that if you have any questions about the details aired so publicly this evening, I should offer to answer them now."

I blinked, felt a momentary scramble in my mind as I sought for the right question, or even any question at all. I wanted to ask a great many things. I wondered what the prince of

Arlemagne had been like, or whether he'd been anything like me, though that seemed a terribly inappropriate thing to ask, and not at all the sort of question I imagined Margrave Royston would feel up to answering.

"Would you," I said at last, "like to finish telling me how they built the Basquiat?"

He smiled again, and again I felt that peculiar flush of gladness.

"I would."

ROOK

Our Lady of a Thousand Fans was nice enough, but there was way too much fucking ceremony involved for my tastes, too much hoopla for the end result. I mean, everywhere *else* you have to sign your name and such, so if you kill somebody they've got your calling card if you're stupid enough to leave your real name, but in Our Lady they make you leave a surety—that is, a piece of yourself they keep until you're done, the kind of personal item they can track you down with if you were smart enough to sign with an alias. But Our Lady, if you counted it all up and weighed it out, was just about the same as anywhere else, so far as I could tell. Sure, they taught a few of the girls some real exotic stuff, just so they could charge us extra, but underneath all that they weren't nothin' special.

I had to go to Pantheon after Our Lady, get the sludgy taste of their sweet tea out of my mouth. That and some other things, 'cause Our Lady was all silk and softness, and I was too hacked off at everything to deal with any of that shit. Pantheon had gambling, and a man with one eye who was offering knife fights in the corner, even odds. Adamo'd told me off more than once for knife-fighting in the city, 'cause I was better'n most and more than once we'd had to have a little "talk" about what was fair and what was murdering a man in broad daylight. I still say that if you've got a knife and the other man's got a knife, then it's a fair fight no matter what angle you're coming from. It just shakes down that what *isn't* fair in this world is some people being better than others at killing.

But I liked being allowed in the bars more than I liked stabbing men in the gut, and soon enough we came to a sort of compromise.

Didn't stop me from laughing fit to burst when the one-eyed man nearly lost his other eye, though.

I ended up on the road back to the Airman much quicker than I'd've liked, the whole night having constituted nothing so much as one giant disappointment. At least, I reasoned, I'd be getting a good night's sleep and maybe tomorrow would be less of a complete fuck-up.

I lost sight of *that* notion the minute I walked in the door. Something in the air smelled different.

The people in the streets—laypeople as they're called, in technical terms—are always yammering on about the Dragon Corps and what we can or can't do. I've heard stories so wrong that I was sure they'd mixed us up with magicians or the Ke-Han or worse. Anyway, we can smell fear-sweat, but it's not like it's some mystical power; it just smells different than anything else. Train any animal early enough, and there isn't much you can't teach it. In the end, people are animals too, no matter how they dress themselves up or teach themselves to speak proper, and we're the same as anything else when it comes to training. The airmen got trained up real special to smell the things most people don't, but it didn't mean we were some bogeymen with Talents like magicians. Anyone with a nose could do it. Anyone with a *brain* and a nose could do it, which unfortunately cuts out a good portion of Thremedon since there are a whole lot more people with noses than with brains wandering around.

Merritt's boots were in the doorway, and I'd've tripped if I hadn't been expecting them. They were always in the doorway, no matter how many times I broke into his room to throw them at his head. I even tried jamming them down his throat once, but Magoughin and Ghislain had pulled me off. I kicked them out of the way, and cursed, loud as I pleased 'cause anyone awake wouldn't care and anyone asleep had thick steel doors between them and me, but it still hadn't made an impression.

But then: "Oh," said a voice, and worse it was a voice I recognized, 'cause there were only about fifteen voices I bothered to recognize in this world, Have's included. The rest fell by the wayside unless it was someone I really hated.

The professor and all his hugging-kissing philosophies definitely qualified.

"Bastion fucking cunt," I said, soft this time, like I knew I didn't need to be loud to intimidate this one. No, the 'Versity brat intimidated real nice and easy on his own. He had too much imagination for his own good.

From down the hall, something made a scraping noise against the ground. I thought it must have been that curtain thing Raphael'd dredged up from fuck knows where. Probably stole it from a whorehouse, seeing as how it had cranes and snowy mountaintops painted on it, and that sort of business had gone out of fashion about five years ago.

That didn't matter though. What mattered was: They'd *moved him in.* Brought him right into the fold like he wasn't some outsider, which anyone with eyes could see perfectly well he was. I picked my way down the hall, neat and quiet like some big Ke-Han panther. Little-known fact was that I could be as quiet as I pleased when it suited me. Just so happened that it didn't suit me often enough.

Zeroing in on the source of the noise came easy enough, as the halls weren't exactly dark and there was only one body moving in them. Everyone else—due to *another* rule they'd instated a couple years back—was doing their moving behind closed doors, shuttered and locked as was proper and decent. He'd moved the screen aside, to find the source of the noise, I guessed, and was in the midst of moving right into his little corner, making everything all home-and-cozy-like.

Just looking at him got me so twisted around that I wanted to hit something. No, what I wanted to do was get up into the air again, only there was a strict policy against flying by night unless we heard the raid siren. Strict enough that I stuck by it, same as everyone else. Don't take your girls out for pleasure unless they're tearing the place apart for a fly, *and* it's during the day.

"What do you want?" The professor didn't look up, just went on digging in his beat-up old trunk.

They'd got him set up on the couch they'd had put in when Niall started complaining that the walk from one end of the building to the other was too long. It was almost appalling what a man could obtain if he implied to th'Esar that he was unhappy. 'Course it all counted for horseshit if you couldn't convince Adamo first, but he picked his battles. Knew when giving in might be the better option.

It was, as he was often fond of saying, what made him so much smarter than me, though I couldn't see what he was going on about. I got on just fine.

"Chief Sergeant said you were out tonight," the professor added, which wasn't an answer to the question at all. He'd made himself a fortress—a stupid little wall with his two suitcases and the screen—like he thought it would actually stop anyone wanting to get in. The whole idea made me so mad I kicked one over, just to show him.

It landed on the floor with a satisfying smack. I showed all my teeth, but it wasn't a smile.

The professor made a noise in his throat that sounded like he'd thought the better of something, which ticked me off. I wanted him to say whatever it was *he* wanted to say. I'd been spoiling for a fight since the one-eyed man in Pantheon, and my nerves were humming with alcohol, thick and golden.

"He's not my fucking nursemaid," I said instead. "And nei-ther're *you.*"

"Yes, well, thank the bastion for that," he muttered, unfold-ing a pathetic homespun blanket and throwing it over the couch.

"What was that, Cindy?"

"My name—" he began, like he was doing me a favor by acting all patient.

"Let's get a few things straight," I cut him off, marching over the suitcases and sitting square in the middle of the couch.

He turned to face me, glasses catching the glare from the low red emergency lights they kept on and burning in the hallways. He looked angry, which was funny, and more than that it was stupid. Rule number one: I could sit anywhere I liked, and he'd have to learn to get over that if he was going to survive any longer than a day.

Which he still probably wasn't.

"You're not a guest. And you're sure as fuck not one of us, so you know what that means?" I leaned back easy on the couch and spread my arms across the back, in case there was any dispute as to whose couch it really was.

"I can't *imagine,*" he said, throwing on his professor look while he bit his words sharp, kept what he meant back there in his throat, all for himself.

The professor had a pinched look to his face, small and hard. Real stuck-up, like he belonged on the face of some coin instead of breathing and living around real people. Even in the red light, with nothing proper to 'lumin him, he looked younger than the boys running about with their nanny-nursemaids in the city. I wanted to spit in his face.

"Means you're a waste of space," I said instead. "Means you ain't never going to get done what you came here to do, and you might as well go back to the 'Versity while they'll still take you back, all in one pretty piece."

"Your concern," he said, dry as a Ke-Han desert, "is touching."

There was rage coming off him now, clear as a waving flag—it had a different smell than fear, anger—and it stopped him saying whatever it was he'd been about to say. He turned his back to me, went back to arranging his suitcases, and picked up the one I'd kicked over.

"Not very many men who'd turn their backs on me," I said as a point of interest.

He didn't say anything, but his shoulders twitched together like he was getting his hackles up about something. Then they evened out again and he answered flat and calm, "I'm not afraid of you."

That was just about the stupidest thing I'd ever heard anyone say. I laughed to prove it, quiet and sweet and taking my time, because the longer I took, the more scared he'd be. That's the way to get someone to provoke you—you just wait it out. It's the only kind of game I've got patience for.

"Yeah?" I asked. " 'Cause it sure smells like you are."

He stiffened, his hands stilling on what might've been a pair of socks. Real intimidating. Not scared of me at all; him and his socks were going to mess me up good and proper. "Perhaps you're imagining things," he said at length. "I certainly don't smell anything."

"Try again," I said. "Breathe in deep, get a good whiff of yourself." I didn't lean forward; I didn't have to. "You *stink* of it."

I saw him work his response around for just a moment; it was too split-second for him to do much thinking beforehand, and it was a big mistake he was about to make. I didn't even have proper time to relish the anticipation of it.

"*You,*" he said, "smell rather like a whore."

That was when I came off the couch, quick as a Ke-Han panther could be when he wasn't lounging back nice and easy and tracking every movement you made before the pounce, and grabbed him by the collar, threw him up against the wall. "Say it again," I snapped. It was easy this way, to let the anger out piece by pretty piece. The blood was pounding between my ears and I loved the sound, the feel of it.

"You smell rather like a whore," the professor said, but there wasn't nearly the same venom in it as the first time. Maybe he'd finally figured out what a stupid thing it was to say, just him and me, and no one around to vouch for me having killed him. No witnesses: That was the fancy way the Provost would've said it, or one of his wolves.

"That's 'cause I've been with whores," I said, drawing each word out sweet and mean, vowels like they'd pronounce them in Molly, all long and hard-edged. "I've been with whores all night long and, you know, sometimes it's so good I don't even have to pay them."

"I sincerely doubt that," said the professor. It seemed like he already knew he was going to die, like he felt it wouldn't make no difference if he went down swinging than if he went down meek and mild as a babe in arms. "I'm rather well acquainted with the system of prostitution and, if I recall, the frequenter is required to pay before the act. So unless one or two individual women who know you by name harbor a particularly soft spot for you— But even then, it's the madam who takes the money, and not the woman herself, so you see that's rather an empty and unnecessary boast. We both know better."

I tightened my fist in the front of his shirt and shoved him back against the wall so his head knocked against it and the fear rolled off him in waves.

"Yeah?" I asked. "You've been following me? You know how I get it done?"

"Well," said the professor, who by now was just babbling and waiting for death to come, and if he'd've been anybody else, I might've grown to admire him a little for it, "it's just that unless you climb in through the windows and rape the madams, what you've said is rather impossible. But, considering your style, it's not all that unlikely you *would* do things that way, in which case certainly you might not have to pay at all. Except of course there *are* bars on the windows, for keeping both deranged rapists out and kept women in. So once again we find ourselves at a fork in the road of logic— a logistical impasse, if you will—wherein you say one thing and I counter it very effectively with, ah, the truth."

I was gearing up to hit him. "Like you've spent all your school trips getting used to the way they do it in Hapenny," I snarled. Our faces were real close, and I could see his eyes get panicked, like he thought I was going to bite him.

Not likely. I don't put my mouth on just anybody.

"Actually," he said, in a squeezed voice, all reed-thin, "I have done much research on Tuesday Street, so you see I am rather well acquainted with the way things work in that *particular* business, Messire Rook."

If he thought he was so familiar with Tuesday Street just because of doing some research, I thought—all blind rage and preparing my fist to break his face—then he didn't know anything at all.

I raised my fist and let him take a good look at it. I was still wearing my flying gloves—it gets a man better service no matter where he goes—and I watched him square himself against it, when of course the real way to let yourself get hit is to go soft and relaxed to try and keep any bones from breaking.

It was kind of like hitting a puppy.

"No," I said finally, "I don't think I'm gonna."

He looked startled; even more so when I released my grip on him and let him slide down the wall, his knees shaking, his eyes not trusting my sudden relenting. That was smart of him, at least. "You're not going to— What?" he asked. Like he hadn't been pissing himself about what I was about to do this whole damn time.

"Later," I promised him. "Don't sleep too deeply or nothing, 'cause, well. You know." I flashed him more teeth than I needed to.

"Do I?" he asked, struggling to regain his composure.

"On the point of a pin, like," I replied. "And sometimes I get up in the night and look after unfinished business. That's all."

"Oh," he said.

And, quick as you please, I turned on my heel and headed back to my bunker, where I locked the door and lay down and slept nice and easy, while he was no doubt still shivering in his socks right there in the common room, by his couch and his fancy screen that wasn't going to help him none soon as I got the other boys behind me.

CHAPTER FIVE

✹✹

THOM

I was doomed.

I'd always been doomed, and to be honest I'd always known it, but it was really the words we exchanged my first night sleeping—or trying to sleep, rather—in the Airman compound that I realized just how doomed I was. Every time something creaked, every time a sound infiltrated my troubled sleep, I jerked awake with a start, my heart pounding. And that, of course, had been Rook's plan all along, which made me realize how clever he was and how I might have underestimated him, thinking he was no more than a common hooligan raised above his capabilities to control himself. No, it was quite the contrary; Airman Rook was a dangerously clever sort of person, without any formal education or moral upbringing, so that he was something like a live wire without any outlet, no backbone of kindness upon which all his intelligence could be structured and thence put to good use. He was exceptionally smart, which meant that his brain was naturally frustrated because he'd never known the right way to channel his own intelligence or expand his mental horizons. This frustration made him angry, made him lash out at people, made him punish them without enough self-awareness to understand why.

Also, he was going to kill me.

Whether he was going to do it on purpose or whether he was simply going to get a bit overzealous while torturing me, it didn't really matter. These were trifling details. The end result remained the same, no matter how I measured the contributing factors.

I wasn't ever going to sleep again—at least, not if I could absolutely help it.

Luckily, the first day I had slated for no more than observation, and so I sat upon my couch and watched as each man filtered out separately, went about his business separately, left separately, and returned separately, interacting now and then to tell a joke, or pick a fight about boots left by the front door, or shout about how that had been Ace's sandwich and not Ghislain's, and what sort of rat bastard ate a sandwich without making it for himself first in any case, whether he thought it had been abandoned or not?

Now and then I took notes, though what I thought they'd accomplish I wasn't sure. A few of the men were early risers, and a few of them hadn't appeared even now that lunch was long since over. Thankfully, Rook was in the latter category; I hoped, privately and cruelly, that he would sleep all day, or perhaps be smothered with his pillow. The way he treated his fellow men was reprehensible, the way he treated women even more so. He was exactly the sort of man I'd always loathed, both during my time in Molly *and* during my years at Primary, then at the 'Versity.

"This is often what it's like during the off-seasons," said Balfour, obviously taking pity on me. If I looked as tired as I felt, it was no wonder. "May I?"

I gestured to the empty space beside me. "By all means," I said. "Though I don't wish to get you in trouble with the other men."

"In trouble?" Balfour looked at me quizzically.

"For fraternizing with the enemy," I confided, leaning in close as Evariste and Compagnon passed through the room.

"Oh, no," Balfour said, a little too quickly I thought, then flushed. "Well, actually, yes. But it's not really important. Have you eaten? What are you writing down?"

"Nothing much," I admitted. "On both counts. Only I thought that I might first—observe you in your . . . natural habitat. Undisturbed by my presence."

"As if we're zoo animals?" Balfour asked, but I saw his smile at the corner of his mouth and knew he was only teasing me. "We are zoo animals, some of us," Balfour added, and I didn't miss his pointed look down the hall, in the direction of Rook's bunker.

"Well," I replied noncommittally, "it's not entirely for me to say."

"Ah," said Balfour. "Yes, I see. What have you found out thus far about our . . . natural habitat?"

"You never really talk to one another," I pointed out. "I mean, I've seen you. You all know one another very well, but during the morning like this, there aren't"—I struggled for a way to explain it properly—"aren't any lines of communication open among you," I finished lamely. "Does that make sense?"

"Some of us aren't the sort who feel friendly in the morning," Balfour tried to explain. "At night, it's very different."

"Yes," I said, though I didn't really see how such vastly incompatible men who refused to talk to one another beyond the occasional explosive argument or filthy joke could possibly work together in the air effectively enough to save all our lives from the Ke-Han hordes. Perhaps there was something I was missing, but I was rather dubious, from what I'd seen so far. "If you don't mind my asking, what was the outcome with Merritt's boots?"

"Oh, no one was hurt too badly," said Balfour cheerfully. "But I do think Merritt is going to need a new pair."

"Why's that?"

"Ghislain dropped them out the window," Balfour explained. "It was better than if Rook had done it, any case."

"Oh?"

"Well, because Rook would have thrown them, you see, with Merritt in them," Balfour finished. "No, all in all, I believe it was good Ghislain was the one who dealt with it first."

"Ah," I said, as though I understood, which I didn't at all. The general meaning I did take, though, was that not all the airmen were as unnecessarily cruel as Rook. They were products of the same system, perhaps—and therefore spent some time interacting with no more social grace than the zoo animals Balfour had suggested—but they were different, still.

Better somehow, as though in them there was still the basic human instinct of decency, long buried perhaps, but in existence nonetheless. Nothing I had seen from Airman Rook gave me any indication that he had a *soul,* let alone any sense of human decency.

Still, this indicated some sort of a system among the men, under which it was recognized that it was better to have some men deal with certain problems than others. It was a start, at least, and pointed toward what knowledge they might have as to each member's strengths and weaknesses.

I realized then that I'd been writing instead of speaking, and that Balfour was patiently waiting for me to finish.

"At the 'Versity, we learn to write things down as we're thinking them because you never know what you might forget or what might end up as important later," I explained.

Balfour nodded, then seemed to hesitate over something. "I'd find a safe place to put those notes," he said at last.

My dismay must have shown on my face, for he quickly smiled, reassuring and nervous at once.

"Not that I think— Not that there's any reason for you to be paranoid, certainly," he went on, in a tone telling me that paranoia would be a very wise choice at this juncture, trapped in the jaws of the dragon as I was. "It's only, if they're important to you, you should keep them safe."

That night, I began writing double copies of everything. This served a dual purpose in that it also kept me awake much more effectively than I'd expected. The gentle hum of the strip lighting even became somehow comforting, though I jumped much more easily than I'd have liked to admit when Luvander kicked down the door to the common room, announcing he was going to bed. He didn't look at me as he passed my couch, where I'd set my cases one on top of the other that I might use them as a makeshift desk.

The building was suddenly much noisier with the door open.

I hadn't realized quite how much sound was blocked by those particular doors, nor had I really even given it much thought, though of course any man who'd met the airmen would have certainly thought to provide them with as much insulation as possible. I didn't want to think of what they'd have done to one another in the 'Versity, where the walls were thin as paper and everyone observed a strict noise curfew so as not to curtail studying.

Balfour had said things were different at night, and indeed they seemed so. The sound of a piano floated down the hallway, scattered and abstract as though it were a tune someone was picking out of his very own head, which explained why I didn't recognize it. Over the music were layered voices: the airmen, in what seemed to be either fourteen different conversations, or one very large and tenuous argument. Every now and then, the voices would be punctuated by a bout of raucous laughter, and someone called something to do with points, which I understood to mean they were playing some sort of game.

More than anything—for the sake of completeness and my notes—I wished there were some way to observe them in this state, obviously much closer than the separate irritability of the morning. I wasn't foolish enough to think, however, that my presence would be welcomed, or even tolerated, and I had no more of a mind to invite a show of open hostility than I did to tear up my notes and sleep like a baby.

I stayed where I was, on the couch as if rooted there, though my progress in transcribing went much more slowly with the noise. Once or twice I thought I heard a feminine voice, high and tittering along with the rest, for of course there were no rules regarding a female presence in the Airman. I wondered if any of the ladies present that night was the owner of the undergarments I'd nearly tripped over my first day. I wondered how any woman could come here and not be disgusted by the utter male essence of the place, and how they didn't feel, upon entering, like foreigners on the brink of some strange and distant land of squalor.

Either they were exceedingly silly, or I was missing something—some small and hidden quality that made the airmen appealing.

At that moment, a voice unmistakable in its arrogance

crowed victoriously above the rest. "Winner takes the red-head!"

The common room erupted in noise, booted feet stamping the floor, hands slapping the walls or the tables, or any surface they could reach by the sound of things.

I finished my notes, final punctuation jabbed with slightly more emphasis than was needed. The first set I folded, placed them inside a notebook so that they wouldn't crease. The second set I slipped into an opening I'd sliced into the lining of my very first suitcase, which I'd come into possession of when I'd still been living in Molly. A safe hiding place could mean the difference between whether you ate or not the next day. I didn't know how effective the tricks would be, but the best experiment was a live one, I felt.

Then, despite my best efforts and the noise emanating from the common room, I eventually drifted into a restless sleep.

When I awoke, my first set of notes had been transformed into a rather generous pair of papier-mâché breasts affixed to my chest. The breasts themselves proved rather difficult to remove, the properties of flourplaster not being adapted for the curious particularities of human skin. The sound of giggling haunted me all morning.

"You've got to sign up in advance for a shower," Ghislain pointed out when I exited, feeling soggy and humiliated.

They'd told me and I'd completely forgotten, I realized with a pang of shame. There was no point in doing this at all if I wasn't going to do it right, or if I was going to lose what little regard they held for me by making them wait for showers.

"My apologies," I said, in what I hoped was a tone that conveyed my sincerity. Ghislain was very large and seemed quite clever enough that he could kill me and have it look an accident. "I hope you've not been waiting long."

He shrugged broad shoulders before he smiled with a flash of white teeth, bright and mocking. "I thought they looked rather nice on you," he said.

The next morning when I awoke, my hand felt strange, and a little wet. Following Balfour's advice however, did not lend me that much help, as further examination found a large pan of what might conceivably have started out as warm water at my bedside—well, couchside—and my hand submersed in it.

"Oh no," I said, quiet and desperate for this all to be a dream. *Surely* it was a dream, and grown men did not indulge in this circus-ring behavior. "No, no, no."

A crack of laughter, sharp like a whip, snapped past my head from above. If this were truly a nightmare, it was doing its job with marvelous attention to detail.

"He's *pissed* himself." Rook stood over the couch, eyes glinting with such a malicious amusement that I had to look away. "He's not *even* twelve; he's a *baby*."

Shortly thereafter I found myself in the unenviable position of having a long discussion with Chief Sergeant Adamo regarding the laundry services for the Airman, what constituted a true "emergency," and no, I could not have my own room with a door that locked.

"Fourteen rooms, fourteen men," Adamo said gruffly, in a tone that brooked no argument.

For the sake of my dignity, I had to try anyway. "Well, well what about the common room? That private one. It's got a locking door on it."

He leaned forward, raised one thick eyebrow. "If you want to be the one to tell the men what's the reason they can't bring their entertainment home with them. Of course, if it were me, I'd consider the fact that might make them mad enough to take the whole door down."

"Ah," I said weakly. I hadn't considered that.

"Door won't stop them," he continued. From his tone alone, I couldn't tell whether he was trying to be kind, merely informative, or whether he was trying to scare me. "Not if they've really got a mind for doing whatever they've got into their heads."

"I see. Yes." I was starting to get a clearer picture of what my stay in the Airman would be like, and the picture had very bleak colors.

"Nothing," Adamo said finally, "stops them. Not in the air, not on the ground. Best to remember it."

I nodded, eager to excuse myself from the conversation. It was a piece of information I would have to remember, write down, even as I wanted to protest that I was not a Ke-Han campaign, that such blind hammering force was not acceptable with civilians as it was with the Ke-Han warriors.

The problem with the airmen, I noted, seated in a welter of blankets on the floor while the couch was out being cleaned, seemed to be simply that they were men who had been trained in a specialized kind of behavior, for a specialized kind of environment, and no one had thought to mention that such behavior was unacceptable outside the bounds of that environment itself. It was a common enough phenomenon among soldiers returning from the war, or prisoners released from long captivity.

I began to realize the extent of what I'd been charged with—the rehabilitation of a group of men who had no idea they were in need of rehabilitation at all. As I couldn't very well quit, I had two options open to me. Either I'd soon be very successful, lauded throughout the city as a man who'd accomplished the unprecedented, or I'd soon be dead, from my own shame or something more immediately physical. And then it wouldn't matter.

When I woke up on the fifth day, they'd stolen my clothes and put them under the showers.

On the sixth day, there were beetles.

It was maddening to catch these glimpses—cruel and detrimental to me as they were—because in some ways they were picture-perfect examples of what I'd so desperately sought after: an indication that these men could work together as a seamless team to accomplish a common goal. Of course, the common goal of beetles in my hair was considerably less exemplary than, say, saving the city from the invading Ke-Han, but in some things it was just as important to examine the abstracts as it was to accustom oneself to the specifics.

I showered twice and shook out all my clothes and both suitcases, discovering another wealth of beetles in the second trunk. I sent them tumbling in a shiny black rain out the window, some of them too dazed even to take flight.

I was completely and utterly miserable, but when I thought about all I was learning, all I'd been privy to, and all the mystery that surrounded the Dragon Corps—when I thought of what a thunderclap my dissertation would be to the academic world, to say nothing of th'Esar's fiat—I concluded I had to stay. Often this conclusion was accompanied by the impulse to retch, whereupon I would casually make my way to the nearest bathroom in case of disaster. Often I ended up staying longer than was strictly necessary, knees drawn up to my chest and staring with dull fixation at the tiled walls, as though they could somehow offer a solution to my problems.

On the eighth day I made the mistake Balfour warned me against, bringing my wet hand to my face in confusion, and spent the rest of the day with a blue handprint stamped across my nose and cheek.

"I *am* sorry," Balfour told me privately. "I thought I warned you—"

"I think it's dashing," said Luvander, as he strode by.

"I *am* sorry," Balfour repeated.

I believed him, and I was sorry for him, but I was even sorrier for myself, and spent the rest of the evening hiding by one of the toilets trying to remember a time I'd been unhappier than this. Try though I might, I couldn't think of a single one.

ROYSTON

A week had passed since the incident of the dining-room table, and by that point I'd discovered two things about myself. The first was that—despite all evidence to the contrary—I was in fact the epitome of self-restraint and there should have been a portraiture of me in the encyclopedia entry on the subject.

The second, which was rather more troubling, was that I was only a man and not a god, that I was completely besotted, and that eventually I was going to crack and do something very, *very* unadvisable.

We'd been spending a great deal of time together in the past week, Hal and I, whether out of loneliness and a mutual need or some deeper connection, I couldn't tell. I taught him about the Basquiat, about the Esar's bastion, about the Well itself, and I learned soon enough what I'd been too blind to notice straightaway: that the way to Hal's heart was through my veritable archive of stories. Soon enough I found myself surreptitiously sending letters to my friends in Thremedon requesting the latest romans—those they would in their infinite wisdom recommend for a relatively young but voracious reader—and I anticipated their arrival with a keen and almost laughable excitement.

Beyond that, my daily walks with Hal grew longer and longer each time through my own careful machinations. I must have appeared to have discovered a new lease on my life, as well as a new hunger for exercise, when in reality I was keen and all too eager to increase our time together. He was companionable; our silences were comfortable. Now and then we were caught in a brief afternoon shower, on the tail of the heavier rains, and we took shelter beneath hanging willows, during which time I tried my best not to parade all my war successes in front of him the way William would display his favorite toys to impress one of his local friends.

In all, I felt something like a child again. Now and then I was struck by the sight of Hal, his kind mouth, his warm eyes, the uneven splash of freckles over his nose and the gentle, vulnerable line of his jaw and throat. His hair was still too long; it was always getting into his eyes. Walking beside him, I had more than one occasion to see him drift into some cloudless daydream, or chew the nail on his thumb, or gaze off at the tree-cluttered horizon as if it held the secrets to some unanswered question. I didn't dare break into such reveries and treated them with my own private reverence, until he noticed he'd fallen silent and flushed to the tips of his ears, cheeks pink and eyes shy.

I thought I could be content simply to walk beside him, to listen to his thoughts on what books he had read, to know he sought my opinion and my approval on the theories he'd formed. We agreed on poetry—which was an unexpected detail, considering my obstinate spirit and his dreamier one—and I spent much of my time before finally catching up with sleep lecturing myself on how little this meant.

He was young. He was good-natured. He was kind to spend such time with me, starved for the attention I gave him, more like my student and friend than anything else. It was circumstance alone that brought us together, and kept us side by side on the twisting paths alongside Locque Nevers. It was luck, not fate, and there was a resounding difference between the two.

I'd cause no more trouble in my brother's house.

However, I hadn't counted on the tenacity of the rainy season. And I hadn't counted on the storm that trapped us beneath a willow tree, soaking wet and shivering, but nevertheless laughing together happily, out of breath from running so fast for some kind of shelter.

"Do you get caught in the rain this often?" I asked him, over the pounding of the rain, the howling of the wind, and the occasional booming clap of thunder.

"Not really," he replied. "I think— I think it might be you, actually."

"Accept my most sincere of apologies," I told him, near giddy, feeling my teeth chatter. "Your lips are quite blue. How long do you think this will last?"

"It's difficult to say," Hal admitted. He wrapped his arms around his chest, chafed them with the palms of his hands, and stamped his feet to keep warm, though the weather was turning to winter, and we were both soaked through to the bone. "It could be ten minutes or it could be an hour."

"We'll have to get back to the house," I cautioned, "else you'll catch another cold."

"Oh," Hal said, worrying his lower lip—a habit he had, and a very distracting one. "Well, we're rather far from the castle."

"And you feel it would be rather impractical to take our chances and return now?"

"I do," he said, and the sound of his voice, blue-tinged as

his lips were with the wet and the cold, made me shiver, too, though for a different reason.

"Is there anything you'd suggest, then?" I asked.

He paused for a moment, still chewing at his lower lip; and then all at once his eyes lit up, and I found my breath catching on something rough and untoward in my throat. "Well," he said, some of that light fading, "it isn't used very much now, but it would be warmer than standing here under this tree and waiting for the rain to pass. That is, the boathouse. If I remember it right, it's not too far from here."

"Not so far that we could make a dash for it?" I asked.

Such a situation as this one—the two of us wet and wild from the rush and new heat that surged in our veins—had never swept me up before. I *was* like a child no older than William again; anyone who knew me from my old life would never have let me hear the end of it.

Luckily there was no one here but Hal and me.

He reached forward, across the space between us, and grasped my hand in one of his own. "Yes," he said. "Let's make a dash for it."

I caught his fingers and held them tight; and then we were running together, slipping in the mud, along the banks of the engorged river, laughing and shrieking into the howling wind and rain, half-blind in the downpour. No doubt we nearly lost our footing on more than one occasion, and were both perilously close to being swallowed whole by the gurgling river. It didn't matter. Nothing mattered. Hal's fingers were ice-cold in my own, and there was a form in the distance, just visible through the sheeting rain.

That, I understood, must be the boathouse.

We tumbled inside the door, gasping and choking and still laughing. The hinges were rusty and we nearly knocked the damn thing in, and the wind was blowing so hard that we almost couldn't close it again, but eventually we managed, collapsing back against it with our legs shaking and our whole bodies trembling with the cold.

At last, when I could speak again, I said, "It's very dark in here, isn't it?" then we both collapsed into laughter again, Hal sliding down the wall sudden and hard. Soon after, my knees gave way and I followed him.

This wasn't going to do either of us any good. We needed to light a fire, get out of our wet clothes, and glean as much warmth as we could from one another until the rains had passed and we could return to the house.

Realization hit me like a punch beneath the belt. We should have done this—but we couldn't.

Rather: *I* couldn't.

"Is everything all right?" Hal asked into the silence, as the wind slammed itself again and again against the thin wooden walls and the rain made the whole roof shake.

"Yes," I said. "Quite. I was simply trying to think of how we might best get warm."

"Oh," Hal said. "Yes, of course; you must be cold." His words were hard to understand, as his teeth were chattering, but I knew my own limits. I couldn't allow myself to reach over and warm him with my own body for a number of very real, very compelling reasons. Yet at the same time I couldn't let him fall ill due to my own shortcomings as a reserved and unselfish individual. "I'm sorry," Hal added, after a long moment. "This is my fault really."

"Is it?" I asked, my tone of voice not betraying my darker thoughts. "I wasn't aware you controlled the skies. How marvelous!"

"Oh," Hal said again, and I knew without having to see him that he was blushing.

"You might have said something earlier," I went on speaking, in order to give my thoughts as little entertainment as possible. "It's a useful Talent, that."

"No," said Hal, warm and familiar. For better or worse, he'd come to recognize when I was joking, and he knew what was serious and what wasn't. "I didn't mean that."

"I am aware," I assured him, and cast a glance around the long, low building for anything that we might see fit to burn. I did not wish to incur my brother's enmity by destroying any more of his possessions than I already had—though to be fair, I hadn't seen them use it much——so the squat little row-boat leaning up against one wall was out of the question. So too the oars, I assumed, though I knew myself that if it came to a choice between freezing to death and the family's recreational pursuits, I would take the blame wholeheartedly.

As if to add to my conviction, Hal lifted his hands to rub at his arms, one enormous quaking shiver at my side. He must have noticed me looking at him, for he offered a sheepish smile. "It's not as warm in here as I thought it might be."

"Do you know if there's anything that we might burn?" I asked.

The look in his eyes told me I'd phrased the question wrong, or perhaps the memory of the dining-room table was altogether too fresh in his mind. "I mean, for a fire. I am not *always* in the habit of exploding property. During times of peace, in any case, when I'm dining with my brother's family or taking shelter in my brother's boathouse."

"It might," Hal began, forcing the words out between his chattering teeth. "If you can, I mean, that might be the only way we've got of starting a fire. I didn't think to bring matches." He smiled at this, as though I'd been the one to teach him sarcasm.

"Ah," I said.

"Well, or, there's an oil lamp in the back corner," he said, using the wall to lever himself into a standing position once again. "Of course, that might burn the whole boathouse down, which would be warm, but . . ."

"Not entirely the solution to the problem I was hoping for," I agreed, following suit and standing as well. The wind drove itself into the boathouse walls with a force that set them trembling as surely as Hal was. Remaining in this state was most certainly not an option.

Further exploration of the boathouse yielded a small skiff with the bottom torn out. William, Hal explained, had thought it just the perfect size for a sled down the gravel mountain that was all that remained of an old quarry upriver, and the boat had been quite ruined by the time it reached the bottom. I thought that as a source of wood it would serve quite marvelously, and set about dragging it to the center of the boathouse, praising William all the while.

"Here," said Hal, pale and tinged with blue. "What can I do?" He was dripping all over the floor, and my own feelings on the matter made themselves known as surely as though I'd been kicked in the chest.

"Clear everything else out of the way," I said, for fires were only ever a good idea when they were controlled, and with my wits and hands half-frozen, I wanted to take no chances.

Hal nodded and picked up the oars, taking them to the very back of the boathouse. I circled the wooden skeleton of the boat my nephew had destroyed, trying to judge whether it would indeed be safer to use oil from the lamp. I knew that it wasn't, and that even entertaining the thought was simply a means for me to ignore the fact that I was reluctant to use my Talent again so soon, and in front of Hal. I was too old for such flights of fanciful self-consciousness, but there it was. If I were being perfectly honest, I assumed that it was only that I did not want him to look at me in a different way, which was patently ridiculous.

If I'd wanted that, I might have taken a care not to send the dining- room table out of the house in splinters.

"Are you going to light the fire?" Hal held his arms tightly, as if by doing so he could keep himself from shaking. A thin rivulet of water trailed from the ends of his hair, down his nose and mouth. Something shifted within me, sharp and bright.

My Talent for combustion—or exploding things, as seemed to be the layperson's preferred definition—had proved particularly useful during the war. The Esar had never bothered to learn the specifics, once he knew what it was I could do, nor did it seem to matter much after that. All I really needed was the oxygen readily available in the air. The scientists had explained it all very concisely, chemical reactions resulting in a great deal of heat. Theoretically, my explosions began as all fires did, and all that dictated their intensity was my own level of concentration. It was for that reason, among others, that I had had to learn very quickly to control my temper. Mishaps like my brother's dining-room table couldn't happen. They *shouldn't* happen.

"Stand back," I said quietly. Hal stepped back, though his eyes were on me, clear and pale as the rainwater.

I concentrated, drawing on my own store, the Well of my own power, from within, where it lay coiled like an enormous, fat serpent. It could strike as easily as allow itself to be charmed, and without the proper experience many magicians could quite easily end up destroyed by their own Talents, poisoned from within.

The boat lit with a soft whooshing noise, a pale echo of the wind and rain that howled outside. The fire was large, though, and rose crackling and cheery toward the ceiling, so that the room was flooded with a shaky orange light.

I could see Hal still over the curling edges of the flames, face framed by fire like the burning portrait of a lover. "That was . . ." he said at length. His voice was still shivering but it had grown quiet and restrained, as though he were trying to quell his shivering—which of course wouldn't help in the slightest. "That was very . . . Well."

"Come here," I said. I had to ignore the fluttering within my own damned chest that so mirrored the flames. I held out a hand and smiled without regard for anything else in the world, the rain or the wind, or my own considerable discomfort in clothes both clammy and frigid.

Hal crossed to sit next to me at the fire, taking off his sodden jacket with an unself-conscious shrug of his thin shoulders. "In . . . in the last roman I read, they went into a lot of detail about the best ways to . . . to get warm again when you're cold," he explained, and I knew by the quality of his voice and the uncertain way in which he would not quite meet my eyes that his thoughts had been the same as mine.

Well, likely not *exactly* the same as mine.

I nodded, acquiescing to at least this bit of wisdom. My own jacket was a soaked weight over my shoulders, clinging and useless. I peeled it off, and pushed it a careful distance closer to the fire to let it dry.

"This is a right sight better than the marsh," Hal said, almost cheerful now that his teeth had stopped chattering so violently.

I laughed, as I often did at the unexpected glimpses of glib good humor Hal possessed. Then the sound died in my throat, swift and abrupt, as he lifted the hem of his shirt and tugged the wet garment over his head.

"Here," I said, and my voice snagged on something low and dangerous, so that I had to clear the propriety back into my throat. "Here, let me." Thoughtless of my actions, I reached over to help him, freeing his arms and, in a moment, the rest of him.

"Oh," said Hal, his dark hair mussed in places and stuck to his scalp. The freckles on his face stood out like ink dots, sharp against his pale skin. His lips were still tinged blue, and he had freckles on his shoulders as well as on his shoulder blades. "Thank you."

If he smiled then, I knew quite well that I would be lost, and so I turned away quickly. "It's nothing," I answered, quiet and gracious. Careful.

There must still have been a touch of what I was wrestling around in my voice, however, because he put his hand on my arm.

"Is— Are you quite sure everything's all right? You sound as though you may be getting a cold."

I laughed again, but it was at my own expense, and not a kind laugh. How I had ended up in this situation was immaterial, as it was most certainly my own fault and therefore my responsibility to keep my private feelings at bay. "I'm quite sure, Hal. Thank you."

He brightened, as he always did when I used his name, and set about kicking off his boots with a thudding sound against the wooden floor of the boathouse. "You should start getting your clothes off, too—that is, if you don't mind me saying so, of course," he added quickly, as though I were staying clothed out of some insane obstinacy that wouldn't allow me to take the advice of a country ward.

"Well," I began. This was not a proper beginning at all, and so I elaborated. "I'm not all that cold, actually."

He tossed me a look full of a fondness that made my chest ache, and which also suggested that he thought me insanely obstinate. No doubt he was right. "Of course you are. You were caught in that rain same as me. There isn't any place for modesty; you could catch fever same as I, if you don't take better care of yourself." His voice was uncertain, unused to taking charge and yet armed with the simple conviction that he was right, and this gave him courage. "I'll close my eyes, if you like. And keep them closed until the rain stops, too."

"That really won't be necessary," I said, smiling in spite of the trap that had sprung up around me. With the air of a man headed to the noose, I began to undo the buttons of my shirt.

Hal looked away, and I had to assume it was out of a real sense of modesty rather than any promise he'd made me one way or the other.

I removed my shirt in precise, deliberate motions that meant nothing; I dropped it on the floor next to Hal's by the fire. The boathouse gave a particularly violent shudder, followed by an ominous creak.

Hal whistled low. "It could go on all night, by the sounds of that." When he did look at me, he kept his eyes cast down, so I knew that, for all his sensible talk, in some ways this was as difficult for him as it was for me.

Only in some ways, of course.

"Hal," I said, loud enough to be heard over the storm that raged outside—but only just.

"It's a good thing we've got this fire going," he went on as though he hadn't heard me, hands traveling to his belt. "Going by the size of the boat, it could last all night if we needed it to, without having to burn the one whose bottom hasn't been torn out."

"Hal," I repeated. The light from the fire stained our white skin to a deep, flushed tan, as though it was the height of summer and the cold season was not upon us. It was warmer without clothes, and I was no fool. I knew perfectly well how to survive a winter in the mountains, or a wet night in a boat-house. This was simply a road I could not take, and the knowing of it overwhelmed all the sense in my head.

His belt hit the floor with a dull clunk. I caught his arm above the elbow, so that he turned to look at me in surprise. "Margrave?"

Our mouths were too close. I could feel his breath against my lips, warm and hitching and uneven. I knew what I'd intended all this time. To think that I'd pretended to myself that I'd even considered resisting him! I was much more of a fool than I could ever have guessed.

I could have kissed him.

I almost did it, forthright and honest. And it was a very rare occasion on which I was perfectly honest about something, with someone.

I had been honest with Erik. I was honest with Hal.

I could have kissed him, and I almost did. He must have sensed it in me, for he made a small noise in the back of his throat and his lips parted as though he was expecting my mouth on his. It was an invitation, however clumsy and inexperienced, and with it his arm came up to lock thin and tight around my neck, pleading with me to wait—just a moment.

That was when I forced myself to draw away.

He was too much younger than I, too desperate for anyone's affection. Even though it was not my place to decide for him whether what he thought he wanted was what he actually *did* want, I couldn't have that uncertainty drawn between us. I didn't want to have to doubt him for any reason; likewise, I didn't want to give him cause to doubt me. Above all, I was the elder, and it was my duty to protect him from at least the same blunders I'd once made myself when I was his age. It wasn't so very long ago as all that, and because I cared for him, I refused to kiss him.

It took all my strength not to do so, to turn my face from his and toward the firelight. I was still holding tight to his arm, and we were close enough yet that I could feel as well as hear the sound he made, as if I'd doused him quite suddenly with ice-cold water.

There must have been something I could have done to reassure him, yet for the life of me I couldn't think of a single
thing.

We were silent for a long time. Hal didn't remove his hand
from the back of my neck, nor did I entirely release him. To
do so now would be to scorn him completely, and that would
have taken advantage of his position just as surely as kissing
him would have done.

He made that sound a second time, softer than the first. I
felt him stir against me; his hair tickled my neck, so that I
knew he'd bowed his head.

Above all else, I told myself with sudden remonstration, I
couldn't allow him to think this a defeat of any sort.

"Hal," I said.

There was an unfamiliar quality in my voice—it said too
clearly all that I was feeling, torn, ragged, on the edge of some
deeper need—and his fingers tightened against the back of my
neck. I didn't know who'd moved first to make it so, but quite
suddenly he was tucked in close against my chest, warm and
impossibly soft. Everything important about Hal was softness,
I decided, his hair and his mouth, the sweet curve of his jaw,
and the way it fit neatly into my palm. I ran my thumb along
the line of his cheek, marking its shape the way I'd only ever
had occasion to with my eyes.

And there we were. I held him against me, his skin clammy
and cold and still damp against mine, and his lips parted, his
half quirk of a sorry smile. I could feel his heart pounding
inside his chest, against my forearm, which was trapped
between us and would soon start cramping.

Now should have been the time when I used this leverage
and maneuvered us apart from each other. Now should have
been the time when I put my wealth of experience in these matters to good use, to the task of keeping him as far away from me
as was possible in the small boathouse.

But now wasn't the night for it. And at least I'd mustered
strength enough not to kiss him.

Then, his fingers clutched at the base of my neck, tangling
in my hair. He murmured something that sounded like my

name, and I allowed myself to harbor the foolish notion that it was exactly that. He was young, I thought wildly; he was separated from his parents and desperate for affection in my brother's cold, uncaring, selfish house. We'd grown very close. We were intimate friends, and Hal had obviously longed for such companionship. He didn't know what it was he asked for, the fingers of his free hand seeking purchase against my shoulder.

Yet, the treacherous shadow-half of me whispered, these lies would be to demean him. Hal was no idiot country boy, and inexperience was quite another thing from stupidity. I longed to rationalize his actions within the context of what I presumed him to be thinking—yet for all the time we'd spent together, I realized I had no way to judge or measure his thoughts at all.

"Hal," I said again.

At last we pulled away from each other, and Hal let his hand fall to his side, fingers curling against his palm. In my terror and self-aborted desire, I'd made certain my hand moved no farther than where it remained, still cupping his face against the palm.

I could see his eyes, blue flecked with gray, and they were shining for me.

"I didn't," he said, and licked his lips. "I—"

"It's warmer now," I said lightly, not betraying even so much as a shred of my feelings. "Isn't it?"

Hal began to blush, and quickly after that he looked away, ducking his head to hide it against my shoulder. I was sure that, considering how close we were, he was bound to hear the pulse at my throat beating wild and desperate for him.

The sound of the fire crackling, eating away at the poor ruined skiff, must have obscured the sound. I allowed myself to move my hand, to rest it against his pale back ghosted with freckles. His fingers tightened against my shoulder.

We should have spoken about it. We should have said something. We should have done anything other than curl against each other in silence, frozen in time, doing neither one thing nor the other.

I held my small triumph close about me like the mantle of a warrior, and said instead, "That was an adventure, wasn't it?"

"It was," Hal said. There was sadness in his voice, deep and dark.

I rested my nose against his temple and stared beyond him at the fire. We were holding each other because it was practical; I loosened my embrace though I didn't let go entirely.

Soon enough I could hear the even keel of Hal's breathing as it slowed. The storm had ended, and Hal was sleeping. When I tried to move he protested, mumbling in his sleep, and buried his face against my throat as if I were both his pillow and his bed.

I didn't fall prey, as I'd thought I would, to unhappy thoughts. Instead I followed Hal's example and slept comfortable and deep.

CHAPTER SIX

✂ ✂

ROOK

So the morning after the professor spent the whole day trying to school us in appreciating other people's feelings, with his whole face looking extra special on account of the big blue handprint, Adamo rounded us up and sat us down in a circle in the common room, where the professor—no longer blue, all the more the pity—was waiting for us.

"Right," he said, like he was facing down a whole horde of Ke-Han. "Today we're going to try something different."

For a long time no one spoke, and it got pretty uncomfortable, and I was grinning the whole time.

"Ah," Balfour said finally. The little snot. "What's that, then?"

"We're going to play roles," the professor replied, "in order to better understand those who are different from us."

Another silence. This time, though, it was Luvander who spoke up. "You mean like . . . role-*playing*?" he asked, all incredulous.

"Yes," the professor said. "Exactly."

"But isn't that like when the redhead's been a very naughty schoolgirl and the brunette's also been very naughty and they're spending all this time being punished by the blonde, who does it all with spanking—" Luvander began, but Adamo cleared his throat all of a sudden, and I supposed I'd have to ask Luvander for the rest of the story later, and who he'd been to see, and who I should ask for to make it happen.

The professor also cleared his throat. We were all looking at him now, and every man thinking the same thing: ba-

sically, that we weren't playing schoolgirls for him *or* with
him, no way and no matter if th'Esar himself commanded it
be done.

"No," he said patiently, though I could see him grinding
his teeth and on the edge of his patience. "No, that isn't the—
Those aren't the roles we're going to be playing."

"What other roles *are* there?" Compagnon asked, probably
'cause he didn't have the imagination our fine genius of a
professor had.

I was almost busting my seams, I was laughing so hard.

"You'll soon see," said the professor. And, just like that, he
was handing out these pieces of vanilla-colored paper to
each of us—the stiff, good sort, with something written on
each. When he stopped in front of me and handed me mine,
whatever the fuck it was, he gave me a kind of smile I didn't
like, no matter which way I turned it, and not just on account
of the more general dislike I had for his entire face.

"Now," the professor went on, returning to his place at the
center of the circle, "you'll find that on each of these cards
I've distributed is a name."

"It's not *my* name on this card," said Compagnon.

"No," the professor confirmed. "Indeed, none of your names
is on any of the cards."

"So they're all our roles," said Raphael.

"Exactly. Three points for you, Raphael, for that apt assessment," the professor said. Raphael looked way too pleased
with himself after that, and the rest of us a little sour that we
were playing a game with points, that none of us had known it
before now, and that Raphael was already winning. "The rules
and information are as follows. One: The names and the cards
have been distributed completely at random. Two: If you ask
to exchange your card for another, three of your points will
be deducted. The purpose of the game is to represent the character, the emotions, the viewpoints, and the sensitivities of
the name written on the card currently in your possession.
Each time you make an astute and insightful observation as to
the nature of your particular role, you will be awarded three

points. Whoever first achieves thirty points will win the game."

"Excuse me," said Niall, "but my card says on it 'That Whore Rook Insulted the Other Day for Having Ugly Breasts.' "

"Indeed," said the professor. "Indeed, it does."

"Mine says 'The Arlemagne Diplomat's Wife,' " Balfour said, looking at me, then at the professor, then just looking real distressed at no one in particular.

"Mine says 'The Arlemagne Diplomat,' " Adamo said. "So I guess you'd best sit here by me."

I didn't want to know what was written on my card, but I guess I had to look so I would know the right way to kill this whoreson standing here in front of us all, smug as you like. I flipped my card over. It read, "Margrave Royston," that fucking Cindy magician.

"I'm not doing it," I said. "Fuck you. Take these cards and fucking shove 'em. I'm not doing it."

"Ah," said the professor, "that puts you at negative three points and Raphael at positive three, and everyone else at zero."

"I feel," Ace said, sudden and sly, "that as the 'Prince of Arlemagne,' I'm kind of in a tight spot right about now, don't you think? What with everyone gossiping about me, even though I managed so cleverly to place all the blame on that *ever*-so-foolish Margrave of mine."

"Indeed," the professor said. "Very astute. Three points for you as well, Ace."

"And I," Balfour piped up, "I definitely didn't enjoy being called a whore in front of so many of my peers, or . . . or treated so abominably by that heartless airman of the Dragon Corps!"

"*Two* astute observations," the professor said. I was beginning to get the feeling he was all Cindy, one hundred percent, and was sort of especially hot for fucking Balfour. "That's six points, I think."

"Maybe, as 'The Arlemagne Diplomat's Wife,' " I said, with a real nasty sneer, "you shouldn't've *acted* like a whore to avoid getting *called* one."

"I don't know if the 'Margrave' would have said that, actually," said Adamo, and the professor looked as pleased as spiced wine.

"Well I wouldn't know," I said, feeling boxed in at all sides. "Seeing as I *ain't* no Mary Margrave."

"Oh, no one said you *were*," snapped Jeannot, short and sharp, like a current through the air. He was a quiet one, Jeannot, but he got serious real fast, and faster when he thought someone was wasting his time. "I, as 'Chief Sergeant of the Airmen,' wish to get through this with as little incident as possible."

Adamo made a sound in his throat like he was growling, amused and happy as an old dog.

"Excellent," said the professor. "Thank you, Jeannot. Three points."

"I guess, as one of the 'Handlers' down where the dragons are kept, I'd like it if no one tried to tell me how to do my job," piped up Merritt, with a pointed sort of look at Ivory, who'd been known on more than one occasion to pitch a fit at his muck-boys if Cassiopeia got touched wrong. But, if you asked me, Ivory was a little touched wrong in the head, so it all washed clean in the end.

The professor nodded, made a note real quick in that damned book of his that let us all know Merritt'd got his points, too. Something in the air shifted somehow, changed the way it did when you were on a raid and had to get primed for the fight to come. There were points adding up, fucking *Balfour* was in the lead, and all fourteen of us keen on winning now that there was something to win.

I knew the professor had planned it just that way on purpose, the way he'd planned my card on purpose, so I just kicked back in my chair. I wasn't going to play his game, not even with negative three points.

"As 'Provost,'" Compagnon said eagerly, "I really wish people would stop breaking the rules. It'd make my life a sight easier and I could kick back and enjoy the sweet little paycheck th'Esar tosses me every other week."

"A little obvious, but I'll grant it to you," said the professor, in a voice that sounded like he thought he was being really gracious. Staring at him reminded me of one other rumor I'd heard about the magician, when he wasn't biting the pillow with foreign Nellie princes.

"If *I* were the Margrave *Royston,*" I said grandly, grinning from ear to ear, "I'd blow up your 'Versity-stuffed head and dance in the gray matter."

Someone who sounded an awful lot like Ghislain made a disapproving sound. I didn't care, I still thought it was clever as foxes and no two ways about it.

"Well," said the professor after a moment. His mouth was drawn small and tight, so any words that came out looked forced. "I suppose I have to give you points for at least being accurate on his Talent."

"Suppose you do," I said cheerfully.

"That puts you at zero," he snapped, and crossed something neatly out in the ledger.

"I'm pretty sure Rook hurt my feelings, saying I had ugly breasts," Niall said, diving into the silence headlong, and his pronouncement was punctuated by Compagnon dissolving into a fit of giggles. "I mean, he'd paid me and everything, sure, but what about my *feelings*? Just because I'm a whore doesn't mean I don't have feelings," he concluded, enjoying himself far more than seemed natural.

"Ah, yes." The professor stopped looking angry pretty quick, turned to smile at Niall. He did that to everyone, looked straight at them when they were talking as if it made any kind of a difference. "That is almost two observations I think, Niall. You're at six."

Adamo cleared his throat. "As 'The Arlemagne Diplomat,' I'm still fuming mad that anyone would be not only stupid enough to sleep with my wife, but also to slap her ass and call her as good as a Hapenny whore in front of everyone."

"I'd imagine so," agreed the professor with that stupid little smile of his.

Did they teach him how to do that in the 'Versity? I wondered. Maybe that stupid face cut it with a passel of school brats, but here it was just out of place, same as the rest of him.

"Yeah, and it's all your fault we're here in the first place," I jeered, but I shut up real quick when Adamo shot me a glare.

"Suppose it's mine too, seeing as I'm th'Esar," Ghislain said. "I had a real difficult time of it, pleasing everyone sharpish in that meetin' room, and it didn't help having two incidents with Arlemagne happening around the same time, either. Guess it was the only thing I *could* do."

"*Very* good," said the professor, and he sounded so happy I thought he was going to piss his pants again. "Wonderful observations. That definitely makes six."

"I'm 'Head Mademoiselle at Our Lady of a Thousand Fans,' and I wish people would stop asking me 'how much,' because I'm quite happily married," said Luvander. There was a sort of quiet that settled over the room after this, with no one able to decide whether they wanted to laugh or not, and everyone turning to look at him. "What?" He sat up straight in his chair, looking ticked off. "It's *true.*"

"Well, that's news to me," admitted the professor. "But I'll take your word for it."

"Hey now," I said. "What's stopping the rest of us from just making stuff up and spoon-feeding it to you, huh?"

"The goodness of your hearts," he replied dryly, in a tone that I didn't like at all. It thought far too much of itself, that one.

"Are you calling me a liar?" Luvander spun around in his chair.

"As a 'New Recruit' to the Dragon Corps, I'm either really fucking lucky or doomed or both, and after my first week it's like enough to be the latter even if no one's pissed in my boots yet." Magoughin smiled, looking particularly proud of himself.

Balfour was looking a little pale, like that hadn't all been years ago anyway, and him with a new pair of boots whenever he wrote home for one.

"Ah," said the professor, looking a little under the weather himself all of a sudden, like getting his boots all fouled was something he hadn't thought of yet. It was almost sad, really, him with such an active imagination and all. "Well, very good, three points for you, Magoughin."

"Um," said Evariste. "My card says, 'That Kid Ghislain Hit on the Head When He Dropped Merritt's Boots out the Window.'"

"It was really an accident," said Ghislain mildly.

"Yes," said the professor.

"Well, I guess my head hurts," finished Evariste.

"Oh, well, I don't know if I'd exactly call that an astute—"

"If I'm th'Esarina, I probably wish my husband wouldn't make so many trips to the 'Fans," cut in Raphael, clearly eager to take his lead all over again. He paused. "Because it violates the sanctity of our *marriage*. You know, we took *vows*."

"Holy shit," I said. "'Violates the sanctity'? Why not just put on the damned dress and a tiara, Raphael?"

He sniffed. "It's not my fault that you're losing, Rook," he said.

"Actually, talking of marriage, I'm still very angry with my wife," said Adamo, and Balfour looked over at him for a moment, all hurt-like before he got ahold of himself, and that was nearly when I lost it. This game was going to drive us all mental.

"All right, I get it now," said Evariste again, quickly. "I wish whoever had been dropping heavy boots had been more considerate of . . . who might have been standing there. Below. I wish they'd looked."

"Yes, that's much better," said the professor, scribbling away like mad in that notebook of his. I wanted to snatch it right out of his hands. "Both of you, well done."

"As a Member of the Basquiat," said Ivory at last, in a bored sort of tone, "I am—depending on my political interests— watching this situation with the diplomat from Arlemagne unfold with interest. I want to see how th'Esar will handle it, certainly."

"As th'Esar I'm thanking the bastion one of yours got

mixed up in the mess with Arlemagne," Ghislain threw back at him. "Evens us out nice and square, don't you think?"

"Was Margrave Royston a member of the Basquiat?" Balfour slipped out of character, not that he was nearly nice-looking enough to play the diplomat's wife.

"Why don't you ask him?" Ace grinned at me with a mouth full of teeth that were just asking to be broken.

"I'm not fucking *playing*," I said.

"Well you've managed to raise your score to an even zero," said the professor, calm as you please. He seemed to have decided that if we weren't going to let him sleep proper through the nights, then he might as well not bother being all careful and polite with us. It even worked; some days he didn't even stink so obviously of fear and rage.

"I cry myself to sleep at night," Niall spoke up, touched by a sudden inspiration. "I ask countless clients whether *they* think my breasts look all right, and if they hesitate for even a moment, I know that terrible airman was right."

"Hang on," said Compagnon. "How do you know she cries at night?"

"Well I'm elaborating, aren't I? It's one of the skills of the theatre," replied Niall, in a voice like he thought it was obvious instead of totally insane.

"Has anyone won yet?" Merritt leaned forward in his chair. Maybe he expected the professor to show him his book when he held it that close to his chest, like it was his baby or something.

"No one's got to thirty yet, no," he answered, and studied the page for a moment. His eyebrows went up in surprise. "Niall's in the lead, though."

Almost like they'd planned it, everyone started shouting at once, Raphael even doing some ridiculous high sissy voice that he thought made him sound more like th'Esarina.

Right then, I knew I'd have to start making a list of my own, in order of noses that needed breaking so I didn't off and kill anyone 'cause of pent-up steam.

And I'd start with the professor—wipe that smug grin off

his face for once and for all. I flexed my fingers in anticipation. It was going to feel *real* nice after all of this.

HAL

Though I expected him to read what had nearly happened right off my face the moment I set foot inside the castle, all the chatelain actually said was that we'd best be more careful next time and not wander so far off—as if we were both his children, no less—and then he sent us on our way, my heart still pounding fit to break inside my chest. I'd almost kissed the chatelain's brother. I knew I still wanted to, but no one had guessed it.

Royston, meanwhile, didn't say anything at all.

This distressed me more than I could say, and above the unsteady rhythms of my heartbeat, nervousness began to creep into my blood instead of a fever. Perhaps it was a fever of another sort, a fever I'd been too busy with my books to experience until now, but it transformed me: I was at once too large for my skin and too small to find myself. I answered Royston's silence with a shamed silence of my own and longed for him to say anything at all. When I dared sneak glances at his face, I could find no clues in his expression that would illuminate his thoughts; rather, he was unreadable as a text in ancient Ramanthe, and I no scholar well versed enough to translate this unfamiliar language.

If only he would take my hand, I thought, or give me some sign. Then my thoughts contradicted themselves; I told myself that for certain he was only being cautious, as at any moment William or Etienne might have rounded the corner, or Mme herself, or any one of the servants. We were certain to talk about my foolishness; Royston was merely waiting for the appropriate time.

I bowed my head. I couldn't bear to look at Royston's face again only to find it so foreign to me. Yet, despite my fear, I followed him through the halls and back to his room, as per the chatelain's instructions, where Royston paused with one hand upon the door and pointedly didn't look over his shoulder at me.

"Hal," he said.

It was as if my own name had been turned into a spell to be used against me however Royston wished. I knew he wouldn't harm me, and yet I felt suddenly as if I *were* being harmed, all the same. After all, I'd made an enormous blunder; had assumed too much from his expression, had asked too much of his experience and his patience. He'd done such things before, perhaps more times than I could imagine, while I knew only what I'd read in books—and, until now, had been content to know only that. I seemed very foolish to myself, and very young.

I should have been more circumspect.

At last, I managed to speak. "Yes?" I said, barely hearing the sound of my own voice as it passed my lips.

"We must speak, at some point," Royston said. His voice and his words were all very careful; they seemed to me to be a precarious tower of cards, which the slightest breath of air would send tumbling all at once to the ground. "Whenever you are ready."

I was ready now, I thought stubbornly, but I reminded myself that we both needed warm baths and fresh clothes and some breakfast. "Shall I come to you tonight after dinner, then?" I asked.

My voice sounded as careful and as tentative as his. I didn't know what game we were playing. All I knew was that I didn't like it and missed the honest companionship we'd shared before.

"Yes," said Royston. "Tonight."

I spent the rest of the day in a jangle of nerves. No matter what I did, despite the hot bath I ran for myself and my fresh, warm clothes, I couldn't coax warmth into my fingertips. I tried to read: I could not. I spent time with William and Alexander: I was too distracted. Emilie remarked that I looked as if I'd been spirited away by a faerie circle—and was that where I'd been last night?

Royston was nowhere to be seen; I assumed he was inside

his room, though whether it was because he too was cold and tired, or because he didn't want to face me, I had no way of knowing.

I dined with the children and he with Mme and the chatelain. We didn't seek each other out in the halls as we were lately accustomed to doing, nor did I make an excuse to bump into him before our appointed hour for reading.

"Something's the matter with Hal," I heard Emilie say to Mme.

"Perhaps he's caught a cold from staying out all night in the rain," Mme replied. "Keep away from him the next few days. You don't want to catch it from him, do you?"

"No, Mama," said Emilie.

At long last it was half past nine, which was when we usually met in the evenings. We'd been in the middle of discussing an anthology of Ke-Han war verse that Royston had brought to the country with him when he left Thremedon, and though his thoughts on rhythm and assonance were thrilling, it was not the book I wanted to discuss this evening, however terrified I was of the new topic to hand. I had to promise myself to be calm, to be receptive, to be polite.

I rapped twice on the door, which was our signal, and from within I heard him say, "Come in."

It was too much for me.

All at once I was inside, breathless, helpless; I craved reassurance, and felt that without it I would break all to pieces. If only I could know that our friendship wasn't lost to us for good. "Please— Royston—" I began, but he lifted one hand to stop me, and I all but bit savagely into my lip to keep myself quiet.

Fool, *fool,* I scolded myself. Let him speak; don't trouble him so!

"Hal," Royston said. His voice was warm but guarded. I pushed away from the door and walked uncertainly to sit at his bedside in what I'd so presumptuously come to think of as *my chair.* Of course, it wasn't. It was Royston's, and should he no longer want me sitting in it night after night listening to the long, refined cadence of his Thremedon vowels, I would obey

his wishes not simply because he was so greatly my superior
but also because I cared so greatly for him.

"Shall I," I began, licking my lips. "Shall I begin where I
left off? With the war verses, that is; we'd just come to the
time of—"

"Hal," Royston said again, more gently. "There is— I
know it may be uncomfortable for you, and I'll not allow it to
continue this way." There was a strain behind his words,
which informed me at once that my presence here was troubling him, making the corners of his eyes crease. Some more
dramatic part of me wanted to fall to my knees and beg for
his forgiveness.

"I should not have acted the way I did," I said, picking my
words with excruciating care, "and if I've— If I've done
something that can't be fixed—"

"Is that what you think?" Royston swore under his breath,
a city curse, and beneath the anger in his eyes I saw familiar
sadness. "I've made you feel that way, haven't I? I didn't
think— No, Hal, this is very hardly *your* fault at all."

"Must there even be a fault?" I asked.

"You were very cold, and very close," Royston informed
me, as if I hadn't also been there. "I felt a certain . . . instinct,
a certain desire, and I found myself almost incapable of re-
straining myself, until I forced myself to consider the reper-
cussions of my actions. I led you to believe I wanted—even
required—something in particular from you. You acted upon
that cue I gave you. It was a most ignoble thing for me to do,
being so much older than you, and—I think it's safe to say—
better versed in the subtleties of these entanglements, though
obviously no wiser for my experiences, as my recent actions
have so deftly proven."

He was hiding behind the comfort of words, as he often
did when he was most unhappy with himself. I reached out—
impulsive, clumsy, but unable to stop myself—and quickly
took his closest hand in both my own. For a moment, I feared
he'd shy away or pull back as if burnt, but he did neither of
these things and merely allowed me to hold him, though all
the while I could see how wary he was of it.

"If you *can* find yourself capable of forgiving me," Royston went on, still picking his way across the landscape of his words as if they were eggshells, "then I hope we can continue as we were, forgetting my, ah, indiscretion."

I wanted to tell him that I most certainly would not forget it, feeling suddenly fierce and protective of what had very nearly passed between us. It had almost been *ours*. Was I to give it up so easily?

"If you wish," I said finally, my fingers tightening against his. "There is nothing to forgive."

Royston watched my face closely for a moment, and though I tried to conceal my feelings, I felt as though he could read them as easily on my face as if they were words on a page.

"I know it is very much to ask of you," Royston said. "Are you sure that you can forget it? You must know this: I'm not saying that I took advantage of you, not entirely." I could detect a note of panic in his voice, as if this wasn't progressing the way he'd rehearsed it. "You're twenty years old, fully capable of looking after yourself, a very clever young man, and I hold you in the highest regard possible. If it were within my power, I would take you from here to Thremedon, where you could learn as you so clearly crave to do. It is a . . . different matter here."

"You didn't take advantage of me," I said carefully, "because nothing happened."

"Ah," said Royston. "I— Ah. Yes. Well— Not *entirely,* as I said."

"And I'm not one of the children," I added, knowing full well how foolish *that* claim must have seemed, blushing as I was to the tips of my ears with the compliment he'd just paid me.

"No," said Royston. "But Hal, you *are* still quite inexperienced. I find myself in a curious position, keenly aware of your promise as a student, and—" He cut himself off then, shook his head, and said no more.

I sought to reassure him somehow. "It's all right," I said. "Nothing happened. We were cold, we would have both caught fever if you hadn't acted as you'd done. I'm grateful for it."

All these things were true—Mme had once told me I was

no better at lying than a child of three or four, and what was more, I didn't *want* to lie to Royston. I felt a strange kindling longing in my chest, but I was so enamored of his friendship that I knew then and there I'd do nothing to endanger it.

"Thank you," Royston said at length. "Thank you, Hal."

"Is it all right, then?" I asked uncertainly. "It isn't—I haven't ruined anything?"

Royston reached out to brush the troublesome fall of hair out of my eyes. "No," he said. "Though if you continue to ask that question, I shall become very angry. Not with you," he amended quickly. "With myself, for giving you cause to think such preposterous scenarios have any merit to them whatsoever."

There were his words again. He had an entire library of them for keeping the rest of the world at bay, and I wondered if this was the sort of tactic one was required to learn in the city. I'd never met anyone with the propensity for it in Nevers; men like the chatelain, who preferred to avoid uncomfortable matters, did so generally by clearing their throat and changing the topic with gruff, inexorable insistence. (I knew this much from the time I'd sought to get the chatelain's permission for securing Etienne further schooling with his art, a natural talent the chatelain seemed determined to ignore.)

The silence between Royston and me grew awkward without warning; it did so at approximately the same moment his fingers became stiff in mine and I wondered if I'd once again presumed too much.

I didn't know where the boundaries were between us. Nor did I know what we were to each other, too informal to be tutor and pupil, too close to be mere friends, and not yet close enough to be anything more.

That was the purpose of this conversation, I supposed: to establish what it was we actually were to each other.

Even as I watched him, I caught him stealing glances at my face. The sight filled me with inexplicable hunger, and the more I sought to suppress it, the louder it clamored to be acknowledged. I felt my cheeks grow hot, yet though I looked away, I refused to release Royston's hand.

"What *are* we to do, then?" I found myself asking uncertainly.

"Things have indeed been very . . . unusual between us," Royston conceded. After a moment, he even shifted his hand so that our fingers were twined together, and from that small movement I gleaned disproportionately large relief. "The plan—at least, *my* plan—for this evening was that we might attempt to explore the nature of our peculiar friendship. I would like it very much," he added gravely, "if you would trust me and allow us to continue to meet this way."

"And discuss your books?" I asked, feeling breathless at once. For a moment my eagerness eclipsed my disappointment.

Nothing had changed because, as I'd said already so many times, nothing had happened. This would have to be enough, I told myself firmly. I would be certain not to mistake Royston's intentions again.

"Yes," Royston replied. "And discuss such matters as I think you already quite capable of discussing." After a moment's pause, he added, "But we must be careful, you realize."

I couldn't entirely understand it, and I looked at him in perplexity before I grasped at a possible explanation. "I remember that I was once reading a collection of more . . . common verse," I said, "and Mme said that I mustn't read such garbage where her children might be able to see it."

Royston lifted a brow. "What did she do with the book?" he asked.

I'd never quite been able to forgive Mme for her reaction. "She tore the pages out," I whispered, shaking my head sadly. "Tore all the pages into little pieces and threw them into the fire."

"Ah," Royston said, and turned to look at me fully.

Royston's eyes were very dark, and I'd known it for a long time, but close to the center there was a light in them, warm and wondering. I felt a sort of wildness skip below the surface of my chest, as though I'd do anything to get him to look at me this way again.

No, that was a lie. I could do nothing at all and I knew it.

I was the one who broke the gaze first, and Royston cleared his throat a few seconds later.

"That is precisely my point," he went on smoothly, as though nothing at all untoward had passed between us in that moment. "If we are to learn—and learn properly—my brother and his wife must be completely unaware of our studies. There are many cases wherein they would assume, through whatever prejudices they are content to harbor, that the nature of our studies is unfit for their household, and certainly unnecessary for *your* education. In their minds, you are to be a children's tutor and nothing more. They have no sense of learning for its own sake, of learning for the beauty inherent in the struggle."

I wanted to kiss him again. I settled for gripping his hand tight within my own. "Yes," I said. "Would you—*Will* you teach me?"

"If you'll have me as your teacher," Royston replied. "But as I said, we must keep it private. My brother and his wife see only a single goal before them and, I admit, would suspect me of foul play."

"Foul play?"

"They might think I was training you to leave them," he replied slowly, as though he were struggling to explain it simply. "In the city, certain Margraves—certain magicians—have had much use for an assistant, a pupil, whose intellect and honesty they can trust as much as they trust their own."

More than anything, I wished to be that person for Margrave Royston; but at the same time, I knew that wasn't all. My desire had a baser connotation, something less pure and less loyal, and one that betrayed all our arrangements even as we made them. I fought it down again, until at last it curled around my heart and remained there, taunting me. I needed to find some way to silence it.

All I managed to say was, "Oh. Oh, yes, I see."

"I wouldn't wish to be so ungrateful for my brother's hospitality as to steal from him the tutor he's been training all this time to teach his children," Royston concluded. "I doubt also that you would be the sort of young man who'd wish to worry them so, having them think you'd taken advantage of their kindness, only to leave them at the last."

"Of course not," I said, almost too fiercely. "I made a promise to them—"

"And I can see plainly enough how much you love those children." Royston closed his eyes for a moment, and swallowed. "What I think is this. During the day, we must keep away from each other. We must stop this madness of meeting in the hallways every chance we have, or whispering between ourselves in the living room. You do understand what this would appear to them to be?"

"Yes," I said, though I regretted it. "Yes, of course. I can't neglect the children, after all."

"Exactly," Royston said. "We'll keep our hours of study to the evenings—perhaps earlier?"

I nodded, and then there was nothing left for us to discuss. We'd solved everything and nothing at once.

If my life worked as a roman—as it secretly unfolded page by page in my innermost thoughts—I would have pressed myself against him and told him to teach me all those things he knew that I did not, to cup my face in his hand the way he'd done before in the boathouse. I would open my mouth to his, and this time, he wouldn't pull away.

Instead, I opened the volume of Ke-Han verse and asked, "Ah, yes. Where were we?"

"Page twenty-eight," Royston said softly, leaning close to flip the pages for me, and without a moment's pause he leaned back once more against the pillows to listen to me read.

CHAPTER SEVEN

THOM

The first air raid I was privy to during my stay at the Airman came in the middle of the night. I saw no one and heard nothing above the blasting, howling cry of the siren, though I had made my way to the hallway to see what I could discover. There was a light flashing on and off in the hall, but by the time I'd collected my thoughts and realized over the stuttering of my heart what must have been happening, the siren had stopped ringing and the light was only flickering, unsteadily, over my head. In the siren's wake was an awful, swallowing silence—the kind of silence you imagine at the bottom of a country lake or well, deep and dark and unforgiving.

I was tired, uncertain; my heart was still hammering. I'd not been schooled in these procedures. They were of utmost state secrecy, and I'd already been given more information than any other person of my standing and position—and for all I knew everyone had gone, leaving me alone to fend for myself in this eerie silence. It would have been much easier, I thought, if I'd been given a contingency plan: some slip of paper that told me what I should do in case of an air raid.

It was just when I was about to give up and head back to my makeshift bedroom, where I would try—and no doubt fail—to rediscover sleep that a doorway at the end of the hall opened and from it spilled a golden shaft of light.

I recognized the location after a moment of searching for the knowledge. It was Adamo's room.

"There you are," Adamo said, stepping out mere moments later. "I take it the alarm woke you?"

"I take it the alarm was designed with waking people in mind," I replied. My ears were still ringing.

"Only Rook, Ace, and Ghislain have gone," Adamo explained brusquely. "It's the weekend, which means they're the ones on night duty."

"I see," I said, which was a blatant lie.

"Everyone else went back to sleep," Adamo said. I was going to ask how they managed it—I would never be able, no matter how many times I heard that bell in the middle of the night, simply to roll over in my bed and fall back asleep in a matter of seconds—but then I supposed this was why I wasn't a member of the corps, and held my tongue. "There might be another raid tonight, but probably not. It might even just be a false alarm. Raids are usually only called for one of three reasons, those being that the Ke-Han are at our doorstep—which is pretty unlikely—or that one of the watchtowers to the east's been attacked. Third reason's if we've been fighting awhile already and th'Esar gets it into his head that a preemptive hit's necessary. Since we *haven't* been fighting in a while, and since you don't hear the alarms that'd indicate a city-breaching, I'd guess it's the guard towers."

He fell silent, seemingly unaware that this was the most he'd ever spoken to me.

I realized at once what I'd been too dazed, too tired, to understand until now. Adamo was being kind to me. After all, he wasn't required to explain the situation or indeed any of the particulars to me. And yet, if I understood correctly, he'd stepped out of his chief sergeant's quarters to let me know. Perhaps it wasn't so very important to him, but considering the month I'd been having, I could have kissed him.

On second thought, I added dryly to myself, that was clearly not a system of rewards I should put into play at the Airman, of all places.

"Ah, yes. Thank you. I had wondered," I said.

"So you should try for some more sleep yourself," he concluded, then jerked one hand behind him. "That's where I'm headed. And tomorrow, you might want to lay off it. The boys'll be tired, on edge. It's been a long time since the bell sounded, if you catch my meaning."

"I do. I'll keep it in mind. Of course," I said, all very quickly. "Thank you again." I was on the verge of adding a tentative but nevertheless friendly *good night* when the door snicked shut, leaving the hall empty and dark and utterly silent once more.

Well, I thought. It might have been second nature to the members of the corps, but I'd only been there a month. Though I returned to my couch, I found myself wide-awake, nerves still jangling, heart still skipping its usual rhythm when I remembered the shock of the raid bell, or when I thought that at any moment it was likely to sound again. How any of these men managed to sleep, I had no idea.

For a long time I stared at the ceiling, calming my thoughts, but the comfortable ambling path of my mind just before sleep continued to elude me. I let my mind wander, but it was too much engaged. I was thinking about the dragons and, admittedly, their riders. What sort of men, I wondered, would volunteer for such a job? It shouldn't ever have come as a surprise to me that I was dealing with madmen, with lunatics, with perhaps the criminally insane. They were capable of waking instantly at the sound of the bell, suiting up, and shipping out before I'd even rubbed the sleep from my eyes. It was a miraculous talent, certainly, but who would ever knowingly choose such a way of living?

The dragons' choices had something or other to do with it, but they chose from a group of volunteers—from men willing to die at the drop of a hat or at the sound of a bell. Though for many of them, I began to realize, it's what they had been trained for since birth, perhaps creating a mentality an outsider would find difficult to understand.

My mind veered off after that to uninformed theories on the dragons and the mechanisms that ran them, half motor and half magic. Their greatest attributes were speed, stealth, the ability—despite their limited capacity for fuel, and what it did to their range—to raze an entire Ke-Han city to the ground. And, of course, there was the fact that the technology was ours and ours alone. The Ke-Han had no comparable army in the skies. The corps was th'Esar's greatest triumph and Volstov's ace in the hole. Admittedly, the Ke-Han had still found a way to make things particularly dangerous for them. In the earlier years it had been the catapults, firing great rocks into the sky before any of the first airmen had really got the hang of flying their dragons. We'd adapted around that, though, and the next dragons created had been sleeker, swifter, and the catapults had become relatively obsolete. Next, and perhaps most successfully, the Ke-Han had capitalized on their skills with wind magic, coupled with the mountains that so often landed dead center of the battlefield. They'd never brought a dragon down in large enough pieces for it to be of any use to them, but they'd brought one or more to ruin in the mountains, along with their airmen.

These days, the biggest vulnerability concerning the dragons was the amount of fuel their sleek bodies could hold. It wasn't enough to get into Lapis and back properly, and Lapis was where the Ke-Han kept their magicians. The more fuel they carried, the heavier they were and the slower they flew, and so on. The system hadn't yet been perfected, so that the farthest the dragons could reach were the Ke-Han watchtowers stationed along the mountains and their troops stationed around them.

If the war continued for another fifty years, perhaps the technicians would have time to solve the problem.

Still, there was a lot riding on the airmen, both on nights when the bell rang and on nights when it didn't.

I passed my hand over my eyes, rubbing blearily at them. What I couldn't get behind, I decided at last, wasn't the sound of the siren, nor even the flying, for I had no fear of heights. Rather, it was the fire. Most children who grow up in Molly or along the Mollyedge are trained to hate and fear fire; in Molly's cramped, winding streets and cluttered tenements, fire spreads too quickly to contain and kills without prejudice and without remorse the unlucky, the lame, the very young, and the very old. I lost my brother to one such fire, and naturally have been averse to them ever since.

After that, I was taken in by a few young women who tricked their trade at a House on Tuesday Street; a fire nearly claimed them two years later, when I was five. I can't say they moved up in the world after that, but rather cut their losses and dove deeper into Molly, bringing me along with them. I stayed for ten years, even once things became a bit dodgy. It was there that I forgot my brother's face—since, after all, I'd only known him for three years—and there that I taught myself three languages, the requirement for applying to 'Versity Prep, by studying in the prop room behind the hapenny-for-a-peek burlesque to the sound of Gin the Rattler's uncertain piano tunes. One year there was even a trumpeter, but he was a hopeless sot, and he was found halfway through his contract facedown in a gutter, and once that happened it was only old Gin hammering away at the half-remembered melodies.

All of this was long past. It was only the late hour and my unfortunate bout of insomnia that caused me to remember them. I wasn't often prone to such nostalgic indulgences.

I was just on the verge of drifting off again—in the midst of wondering what it was my brother really *did* look like— when I heard the sound of a door slamming, followed by raucous laughter and approaching footsteps. The voices I heard a few moments later I recognized immediately. Rook, Ace, and Ghislain were coming toward the common room, and my only recourse was to pretend I was sleeping.

Luckily, they stopped just beyond the door; I heard them talking, muted, through the wall. A few nervous laughs punctuated the distant conversation.

"Fuck"—and that was Rook—"if I wouldn't've taken a dive if it wasn't for that trick you pulled at the last fucking second!"

"You've been holding out on us, Ghislain," Ace—it must have been Ace—agreed.

"It was just a dive, only without the falling off," Ghislain pointed out. Only Ace laughed at that one, but it was the sound of Rook's voice that fascinated me most. It had changed. It was no longer a sullen child's, neither stubborn nor prideful, defensive nor prejudiced, but laced with fierce excitement.

"Fuck, but it *was* sweet," Rook said. He was entirely breathless.

If only I could have moved, sat up, or even reached for something to write on. I had the strange and sudden urge to document this moment for posterity, that I might remember it in the morning as real and not the deluded fabrication of my mind left to its own devices. Even with the airmen's distraction, I didn't trust my own movements to be stealthy enough to escape their attention, especially keyed up as they were from the raid.

No, with my luck, I would knock a table over, announcing my eavesdropping presence more assuredly than any air-raid siren.

"I only did what I had to," said Ghislain, and his voice sounded calmer than the rest.

"Saved my life or damn near to it." It was the first time I'd heard Ace sound wide-awake, focused. He cursed cheerfully. "I thought I'd never see anything outside of that tornado again! Lucky for me you've got lead weights in your ass the same as your dragon. Ke-Han; who'd have guessed? They've got balls on 'em, if nothing else."

"Thank the bastion for that. Another day on the ground and Havemercy'd've lost it."

"You mean *you'd* have lost it," said Ace, but it was a cheerful rejoinder, with none of the venom or snapping I'd grown accustomed to hearing from them whenever the airmen interacted in a group, or especially when Ace and Rook were alone.

Breathing shallowly, holding carefully still despite the fact that no one had attempted to enter the room, I remained possessed by a feeling I could not name or did not want to. In short: I was awestruck. I'd spent weeks trying to divine what it was that kept these men together and allowed them to function as a team when all I'd seen of them appeared to be grave dysfunction and an unwillingness to do whatever it was they were told. These were men contrary as cats and solitary as lone wolves, and all the information I'd gathered to this point added up to indicate that logically, they could not and would not function as a team.

Except logic appeared to have taken a leave—perhaps the sirens had scared it away—and outside my door the three men continued to converse as perfectly natural human beings. A little nervous and on edge, certainly, but it was the kind of jump that anyone got from a rush of adrenaline, and it held none of their usual sparking hatred.

"Think the war's on for good again?" Rook's voice practically trembled on this last, with enough eagerness to inspire in me a peculiar mix of revulsion and intrigue. Only a man so cold as Airman Rook would crave the resumption of something as destructive as Volstov's hundred-years war with the Ke-Han.

"Don't think anyone'll really miss that guard tower. Anyway, that isn't the important part. They hit us. You know what that means." With my eyes closed, I thought I could almost picture the smooth, rolling indifference of Ghislain's broad shoulders.

"We hit back," Rook answered, with violent exhilaration. "Shit, I don't think any of them's going to be forgetting tonight real soon."

"I don't think I'll be forgetting tonight real soon," Ace complained.

"Better be on your guard," said Rook, "or else Ghislain'll be taking your spot on that board pretty quick."

"Maybe he'll take yours," said Ace, but quietly, and it was only then I grasped that I could hear him because he was standing just outside the door.

I threw the blankets over my head. The room lit up with a spark and a hum, and the sound of laughter and booted feet flooded the common room.

I cursed silently in the three languages I'd learned to speak, which had indirectly led me along the path to being *here*, sleeping on a couch—a grown man, hiding from other grown men.

"Well, if it isn't the littlest fucking professor." Even with me, Rook's voice did not regain that glass-sharp cruelty to which I'd become accustomed. "Up and out. This is a private party and I know you ain't asleep. Ain't nobody who sleeps after the raid siren on their first night."

"I *was* asleep," I said stubbornly, which defeated my purpose in concealment, but I thought perhaps in the long run it might save me from the indignity of being sat on, or coated in tar, and then dipped in feathers, or whatever other horrible plans they had percolating behind their laughing eyes and smug, secure grins.

When I opened my eyes I saw immediately why anyone back from a raid procured inarguable rights to the showers, as all three men were covered in thick, uneven layers of ash that had been smeared into their clothes and faces like a second skin. Their gloves were stained greasy and black, and there were bright, pale rings around their eyes that I supposed meant they had been wearing goggles. When Rook smiled, his teeth flashed white and uncomfortably pointed against the black of his skin.

They looked less like men and more than a little like the portraits of the Ke-Han warrior gods I'd seen inked in the textbooks at the 'Versity.

"I know I've left it here somewhere," said Ace out loud, though to no one in particular. He was rummaging through the cupboards set into the far wall.

"Leave him be," said Ghislain, meaning me. "I'm too worn-out to be fighting with anyone as isn't dressed in blue and screaming curses on my family to all eternity."

"Sometimes *he* wears blue," said Rook, nodding toward me with a maddening obstinacy.

To my great surprise, however, he didn't press the matter. He only leaned against the wall and folded his arms, as though he were too tired to stand and too wired to sit.

"Ha!" Ace produced a bottle from one of the cupboards, which bore a seal resembling that of the private store of the Arlemagne noblesse. I recognized it because their diplomat had spent a very long time wetting his throat with it in between detailing how exactly he wanted Airman Rook torn to pieces by wild dogs.

Ghislain—who'd procured a chair and was studying the floor as though he were now trying to decide whether it would be an adequate place to fall asleep or not—smiled, his mouth knowing and expectant, then asked anyway. "What's that?"

"I thought we might celebrate, it being our first raid of the season and all."

"Make it quick," said Rook, leaving a long black smudge against the wall where he'd been leaning against it. "I'm gonna sleep like the dead tonight and I *ain't* getting up for any lessons." He threw this last with a look at me, which was jarring after having been so ignored.

"There aren't any lessons tomorrow," I said, uncomfortably clearing the sleep from my voice as the other two turned to look at me as well. "I thought— Well, the Chief Sergeant suggested, I mean— I don't have anything planned," I concluded lamely, ashamed of myself for being so surprised by the change in the airmen that I no longer knew how to interact with them.

It was as though they'd undergone a metamorphosis, and where I'd once made myself comfortable in a cocoon of sarcasm and heavy-handed wit, I now had to reevaluate everything I'd learned. I got the feeling they'd brought the shadows of their dragons back with them, hidden but transformative, and were both less and more like real human men for it.

If I hadn't known better, I'd have thought they did it on purpose.

"There, see," said Ace, pouring the bubbling liquor into large cups obviously not meant for the expensive vintage they now held. "No lessons. That means you can all celebrate and stop pretending like you're sleepy as babes in arms."

"I am sleepy," said Ghislain, but he held his hand out for the glass all the same.

I could no more attempt to go back to sleep now than I could after the air-raid sirens had gone off. Even ignored as I was, even aware that I was an outsider, I could not help but observe with fascination the difference in process. My fear, that as the novelty and the adrenaline wore off them it would be replaced by the sullenness and anger I'd come to think of as characteristic, turned out to be unfounded. Instead, a kind of calm had settled over them. It was partly exhaustion, perhaps, but when Ace thrust his cup out in front of him, even Rook begrudgingly joined the toast.

What I realized then—with the clarity that could only come from having been powerfully, painfully wrong—was that much of the behavior of the airmen came not from a fount of cruelty and stupidity, but rather a gratuitous squandering of ability. These were men who'd been fed from birth, as Marius had so aptly put it, on their own importance to the realm. Each member of the Dragon Corps knew this about himself, only to be met with the stubborn reality that, when the war was no longer being waged, th'Esar had no need for them. It must have been a bitter tonic to swallow. It was as though the siren and the resulting raid had bled off some reserve of poison and drained them of their shaky, pent-up rage.

They no longer seemed a separate species, like proud, ill-behaved animals, but appeared to be men at last.

That was not to say I excused their behavior, for in truth I still found their society as oppressive, cruel, and elitist as I ever had, but I felt for the first time as though I understood, infinitesimally, the smallest piece of the puzzle that caused them to operate the way they did.

ROYSTON

We had to be careful. That much was of paramount importance.

A knock on my door—my brother, briefly inquiring after my health that evening—jolted me from a thoroughly incautious examination of the shadow of Hal's eyelashes against his cheek while he read.

My own private feelings on the matter would have to be kept just that: private. It was all there was to it, and with no room for argument I thought that I could readily convince myself of the new way of things.

All too soon—or seemingly not soon enough—Hal had finished with his reading. At least, I applauded myself, I'd kept from descending so much into my thoughts that I no longer had the wherewithal to converse with him properly.

"Hal," I spoke to remind him, quiet and low, though it was as much for my own benefit as it was for his. "You mustn't forget what we discussed. We cannot meet with such frequency, and you must try your hardest not to seek me out so."

"I will," Hal said. Then, flushing, he added, "But it will be difficult."

"You *must* do it," I insisted, more forcefully than was perhaps necessary. I had to make him listen and, beyond that, I had to know he understood me. I thought of my brother's wife, her intolerance fueled by a sharp but nevertheless closed mind. I thought of what she might do if she suspected Hal of having any manner of feelings for me which she might deem unseemly, and it was enough to make me ill.

"I know," Hal said, the light in his eyes dimming. "The Mme—"

"Hang her," I muttered. "She doesn't know anything. Yet— and we must both remember this—it is as much her house as it is my brother's, and though he is a good man in many respects, he is content in the simplicity of his countrified existence. He isn't searching to expand his mind or open his heart any further than his wife is willing. It's enough that he tolerates my presence here, and that his wife does. Despite their differing levels of graciousness."

Hal reached out as if he meant to touch me again, then thought the better of it. "I know," he repeated sadly.

"And you should take your leave," I continued. I knew full well I was exhibiting more self-restraint than I ever had in my entire life, but if my brother was making his rounds that evening and found Hal missing from his tiny corner of a bedroom—and yes, I'd seen it, and yes, it was bordering on the inhumane, his bed cramped in a slope-ceilinged corner, barely more than ample closet space—then doubtless his suspicions would be aroused. My dignity and my status in the household would not withstand any more blows than they already had. It was Hal and Hal's place in my brother's castle that worried me, and, I felt, out of Hal's best interests that I acted so decisively now. Such a thing could not be rescinded nor could it, in the country, be defended. Hal was going to be a tutor, and I saw very keenly that he was eager for the post; he loved my niece and nephews very tenderly, and was better with them than one could imagine possible. He was goodness through and through, and therefore his heart was more vulnerable than most.

I could protect him, even if I'd never been able to protect myself.

"All right," Hal said, and he stood from the chair very slowly, as if it pained him to do so. After that he slipped away—his silhouette outlined for a moment in the doorway—and closed the door carefully as he left.

And so began our little charade.

Hal didn't have the requisite nature for it. It was well enough when I wasn't there, when Hal was playing with the children or discussing a book with Alexander, engaged in the task of testing the young boy's comprehension and depth of critical thinking. Yet when we were in the same room together—and when we weren't alone—I saw him struggle with the task I'd set him. Whether or not it was in his own best interests had nothing to do with the way his face fell each time I was curt with him, or turned down his entreaties to come and join him and William for another story. It pained me to be cruel to him even in appearance alone, but I was certain he was clever enough to realize I was only acting my part of the shadow play we'd decided on.

Yet it seemed that I was much too convincing in my role. He came to me that first night, hesitant and unsure.

"I thought . . . you might have changed your mind," he said.

At once, remorse engulfed me. I could never apologize enough, I thought, and stepped firmly on a blooming impulse to cross the room and hold him as closely as I had in the boathouse.

"Hal," I said carefully. "I was acting. We'd both decided—"

"I knew that," he said, shutting the door and ducking to hide his expression. "I knew that, and yet— You were so convincing, I *did* think it might have been possible you'd thought things over again, and—"

"I would have told you," I promised, over a rising sense of uneasiness that it was not my tutoring he spoke of. "Barring a sudden onset of madness, I don't believe I'll be thinking anything over anytime soon."

We looked at each other for a long moment after that. I took it upon myself to choose the text for that night, a small and meaningless gesture of apology for the things I could not change. If I thought about it in this way—that Hal was my pupil, and I his mentor—then like any good teacher I must allow each new discovery to take its natural time. When we were alone, it grew more difficult to ignore the temptation to encourage and reward any way I pleased, mix poetics with the physical, guide his study of the complicated structure of old Ramanthe and kiss him for the pleasure of seeing his neck bowed to the task, or the pleasure of seeing his eyes alight when he'd solved some new, more complicated problem.

I did so want to kiss him yet knew that I could not.

There were times during the day when I was unnecessarily sharp with him. There were also times when I was no more than brusque—and that, I thought, was what hurt him most of all. After a few days of this behavior, of his eyes the color of bruises at every hurt, however scripted, I decided against my better judgment that to prolong our studies together in the nighttime hours after the rest of the house lay abed would not be too much to ask. There was a certain privacy to working late into the night, as though the silence of the house enveloped us, left us cut off and safe from the country and its prejudices.

The only problem in this plan was that Hal had exhausting days taking care of the children, and the more hours he spent conscious and studying, the more meals he required to relieve his fatigue, so that a mere week after my proposed extension of our time together, we began sneaking down to the kitchen like children to concoct something suitably filling with which we might fuel our studies.

My only concern was the cook, and what she would say to

my brother's wife if she found the two of us quite alone together in the dark pocketing bread and cheese and whatever else we might find left over from that evening's meal. I found myself quite keen on never learning what *would* happen if we were caught, and so it was that I discovered the pantry, with its simple array of plain spices and herbs. It was not particularly large, and there were certainly cobwebs about the ceiling, but it would do, I decided, if ever we were in a pinch.

Additionally, there were few things that didn't go down better with a sprinkle of rosemary.

After that, our routine carried on in very much the same fashion, with our breaks at midnight to rifle through the kitchen like common burglars. I mastered the urge to suggest that Hal stay, when we finished our studies and his head drooped low to nearly sleeping in his chair.

I wasn't made for the role of a teacher for the same reasons I'd never been a good student: I was too selfish, too impulsive. What I needed I took, and there were a few times when I nearly gave in to my less noble desires, without any thought for what would come of my capriciousness.

Hal didn't seem to mind. Indeed, he didn't seem to notice a single one of my flaws. And, as I'd suspected, he was as eager and quick to learn as he was to please. He was as open as the country gentry were *not*.

I would ruin it, I was certain. It was only a matter of time. It was not in my nature to deny anything I wanted so wholeheartedly, and to my dismay I was gradually beginning to discover that Hal fell into that category. On some days when I was feeling particularly maudlin, it seemed Hal *was* the category.

We stole rolls from the kitchen at night—by light of a candle-lamp we read together and tangled in the handsome words, but not in body. In this setting, I did my best to tutor Hal on the correct pronunciations—but there was no more than that. There were times when I thought Hal disappointed with this reserve on my side—what must have seemed part-infuriating coyness—but he said nothing and was content to let me brush the hair back from his brow and out of his eyes, and watch him as he read with the unsteady flickering of the candlelight illuminating his face and causing the freckles to stand out sharply against his pale skin.

Then, things changed.

The first change came a few weeks after we began our system of reading late into the night and descending upon the kitchen to raid the leftovers, experimenting with the heady aroma of the cook's spices and trying not to disorder her most prized possessions.

It was a weekend, I believe, and Hal had completed a very difficult text in the old Ramanthe. Though by then it wasn't much of a reward, I still took it upon myself to congratulate him and suggest we take pains to discover what had happened with the unfinished dessert from that night's dinner.

We'd been in the kitchen, speaking softly, and Hal had found us spoons and everything had been going very much as it always did until I heard the footsteps from outside the door. Without a second thought, I whisked Hal with me into the pantry.

All around us was the smell of the simpler herbs and spices—cinnamon, rosemary, sage, and thyme—and I stood close to him so that the little spice bottles rattled when he trembled and stumbled back against them.

"Careful," I whispered.

He said nothing at all, only inhaled soft and sharp as though he'd seen a spider.

When I looked down I met his gaze, touched with nervous apology, and I scarcely had the time to wonder why before he put his hands on either side of my face and kissed me.

For a moment I could do nothing at all, frozen in place and the blood pounding at my temples as if anticipating a fight. There was silence in the kitchen.

His mouth was very warm.

As if jerking awake from a deep sleep, I forced myself to straighten, in a slow but firm refusal to give in to the dizzying wave that threatened to break over me. I saw Hal's eyes, wide and frightened of what he had just done.

We both recovered ourselves at the same time.

"Please," he said, just as I was stepping away. I didn't hear what else he said after that. I'd already made my swift escape, smoothing out the front of my shirt and all but fleeing back to my room.

It wasn't the right thing to do. I knew this even as I did it. Whatever promises we'd made to each other, whatever stage we'd agreed to play upon, I knew full well that our rules didn't extend to this matter. My leaving was no act for our audience, for there had *been* no audience to witness Hal's declaration; it had been only me and the cook's spices, mute in their bottles. It was not for their benefit that I'd flown, and certainly not for Hal's.

No, it was only for me, selfish as I'd ever been. I'd always known, of course, that I would do something to ruin our cautious happiness. I just hadn't suspected it would be so soon.

I closed the door behind me, the dead bolt sliding into place with a sure thump that echoed the lead weight in my stomach. My only reprieve, so small as to be almost laughable, was that the cook hadn't caught us at our game. Luck was on our side, but I knew how simply and how swiftly luck could turn. We'd been far too careless.

Hal didn't follow me back to my room.

It was a reprieve, then. It gave me the time to think over what exactly it was I thought I was doing and what I'd already done to Hal.

I felt charged with an overabundance of nervous energy. I picked up the book we'd been reading for two nights now, but the text assumed a certain mutability. It danced and skittered across the page so that I quite lost my temper with it, and hurled the book to the floor.

Frustration roiled in my veins as I thought of Hal and what his reaction would have been if he saw me now, throwing one of the books; and then I thought again of Hal, and what would doubtless prove the irrevocable destruction of something I'd not allowed myself to name or label.

I sat on my bed, facing the empty chair. As it almost always was when I'd been too self-centered to see the truth of the matter, I felt impossibly foolish. I couldn't even blame Hal's feelings on something I'd done, not entirely, as—he was fond of reminding me—he was quite old enough to be capable of understanding his own emotions. Though inexperienced in many ways, Hal was not a child and hardly needed me to tell him what it was he felt or thought. He was clever enough that to think otherwise would be to do him a dishonor, and I had no great wish to lump myself among the other residents of my brother's house who no more recognized his intellect than they would have recognized a dragon come to roost in the trees.

Finally, to pretend that Hal did not understand the gravity of what he'd done would be an insult to both of us.

He *had* meant it, then. I knew it was childish—and acknowledging that I could still be the child in a relationship with a boy a full fifteen summers younger than myself was humbling fare—but more so than that, it had been a coward's province to flee from someone brave enough to declare his feelings by acting without thought. I was not a complete coward, that at least I knew, but the idea of having to scramble for a reply in the faint cobwebbed light of the pantry had ignited in me a desperate, throttling urgency to be somewhere, anywhere, other than where I was.

It wasn't my finest of moments. And it wasn't fair to Hal—especially to give him no reply at all—to protect myself and garner ample time to sort out my own emotions, leaving him with nothing but silence and doubt.

What, then, did I have to sort out? Staring at the empty chair didn't help me any, as all around it hovered the specter of Hal, smiling and freckled about the nose and shoulders. I stood up again, paced the length of my small room, as though an excess of bloodflow would help me to think better.

Instead, I could think only of Hal.

He was a creature entirely lovable, and I feared that in allowing myself to love him, I would somehow extinguish the intrinsic optimism he held in his heart.

For the fact of the matter was that Hal was someone made entirely to be honest, in an environment that would not allow him to be so. I couldn't ask him to become entangled ever further into this mess I'd—we'd—created. He was to be a tutor come the summer, and the children's attentions would become far more important than my own. I had no wish to upset Hal's standing in the house any more than I already had, and by allowing things to continue along their progressive course, I knew that I would.

My time in my brother's country house was an exile of indeterminate length, and pretending otherwise was what would sink us.

In this I was quite resolved until I heard the knock at my door, twice, as was our signal. It was *very* late. I felt my determination struggle to be set free like a stubborn bird and I held it in place even as I held still in the center of my room.

"Please," said Hal, quiet, but not quiet enough should anyone have been passing through the hall, which I sincerely hoped they were not.

The door was locked, which I realized too late was a clear sign that I was indeed within. Too late, and always too slow. I cursed myself but crossed the room to unlock the door and pull it open.

Hal had a wild look about his eyes, anxious and desperate in one, and I knew that I'd been right to leave the pantry.

"Hal," I said unsteadily, drawing him in after a perfunctory check up and down the hallway for curious young eyes. Then I closed the door.

He stared up at me, misery radiating from every small motion, worrying his lower lip in a way that I was often quite fond of, but not now. Not when I knew I'd been the cause.

I sought for the proper words, some fitting apology that I could make, and found that there were none. "I'm sorry," I said instead. It was no more than a fraction of the true apology I wanted to make. "I should not have left," I added, and hesitantly touched his face.

This seemed to be the signal he'd been waiting for, as he all but threw himself into my arms. I held him tight; it was all I could think of doing.

"Please," he said, close against my neck. "I didn't mean—" He stopped then, as though he couldn't even pretend to take it back.

The rules of the game hadn't been so clear when I'd set them, and once again the fault was all my own.

With Hal caught close in my arms, I found that my words had deserted me. It was an unsettling realization, as I depended on words more often than I would have liked to admit. They were my citadel and stronghold; they kept me afloat when everything else was a swirling, cooking stew of what I knew and what I felt.

There were no words that would set this right save those that couldn't be unsaid.

"Can we just— Can we pretend that never happened?"

"*I* can't," I said, honest as I only ever could be when it was completely inconvenient to be so. Hal's fingers tightened so fiercely in my shirt that I was sure for a moment it would rip. "And, even if I could, Hal, I wouldn't."

"Oh," he said, and slumped a little as he exhaled. I put an arm around his waist, as much to hold him up as to keep him close. "I was afraid of that."

"It isn't— It's not something I would ever want to pretend hadn't . . . happened," I said clumsily. "If I teach you at least one thing during my time here, then let it be this: There is no kiss we can undo, nor any word we can unsay."

I felt him nod. Then he lifted his head to look at me, visibly struggling with something he wanted to say. "Is that why you left, then?"

"Likewise, I can make no excuse for *my* actions," I said, helplessly aware that an apology wasn't what he wanted. "They were inexcusable. I am sorry, Hal."

I found I had no way of explaining it to him. But I had faith that his intrinsic intelligence and empathy would guide him to discern my true emotions and to understand why they could not be expressed.

I was afraid, but I was also certain of what we needed. I would endeavor to avoid such situations again.

"We should perhaps," I said haltingly, then tried again. "We should perhaps . . . meet with less frequency."

I could at least teach him, however, though I knew what a poor compensation it was. But I could hope that he might soon be able to see that my rejection was not born out of a lack of affection. There were things I could say without speaking, and I hoped only that Hal would understand them.

"Would you care to finish that passage on the laws of the bastion?" I asked lightly, still holding him foolishly close. Despite all my fine words and upright sentiments, I could not release him until I heard his reply. If he refused, I knew I would be bound to do something even more foolish, and my beseeching must have been evident in my expression, for he hesitated only a moment.

"I'd like that," he said, seemingly relieved, though there was a shadow of disappointment that hung far off in the back of his gaze.

I held him for a while longer, and in the bright moonlight that streamed through my unshuttered windows, it was almost easy to believe we were not so trapped.

ROOK

Pretty soon our period of lazing about was all over, and, quick as that, it seemed like every night the siren was howling and we were grabbing our boots and getting out just as our palms were itching to do for too fucking long.

The way to ride depended, to begin with, on what kind of airman you were and what kind of dragon you were flying. Balfour's Anastasia was small and sleek and kind of the same as riding a horse, I'd wager, though I'd never been astride her myself. If you were a big motherfucker like Ghislain, then you could get away with straddling Compassus and steering her through the air without cramping up your legs something crazy, not to mention breaking both your arms just to jerk the harness and bring her around. But you've got to be a real serious son-of-a to ride a girl as fast as my Havemercy—or Thoushalt, Ace's girl, who was the only dragon of the lot to match my darling for speed.

Basically, our girls were all designed by different men who

I guess were thinking completely different thoughts at the time they designed them, so things are real different depending on whether you find yourself saddling up a swift like Anastasia or a fire-belcher like Ivory's Cassiopeia, or a Jacqueline-of-all-trades like Havemercy, who's the greatest beauty of the lot and who kills like none other, not even Thoushalt. Havemercy was the best, though, since she was almost as fast as Anastasia herself and easier to rein in, besides. And where fire was concerned, she was the most precise and so could hit them hardest and fastest.

The Ke-Han call Have the fire god, and that's about as good a name for her as any, not to mention one I'm particularly proud of for my personal hand in.

The problem with the Ke-Han was that they were smart, and they knew the lay of the land better than any of us, seeing as how the Cobalts were theirs to begin with, so of course they had these tricks, like hiding in the mountains or using the winds against us. That was how Balfour's brother—who rode Anastasia before him—died, the first time the Ke-Han got their magicians together and turned the skies against us. After that we figured pretty quick how to fly even when the wind was shrieking us down with all it had; leastways, it's easier for the bigger girls to resist a sudden gust from an unnatural direction, the kind that always means the Ke-Han've spotted us and the race is on. If you're on a swift, you've gotta let yourself be pummeled along until you can duck down below the gust, double back around, and hit the sons of whores when they least expect it. Of course flying against the winds used a hell of a lot more Well's-piss fuel than normal, so whenever we got hit by the magicians we had to move double quick to make sure we got back to the Airman in time and didn't cause a national crisis by crashing into the mountains or getting caught by the Ke-Han.

The fuel thing was what got under my skin like nothing else, since there were nights when we could as good as *see* the magician's dome, blue like an overturned bowl and nestled in the heart of the city. Any trip out that far'd be a suicide mission, without enough fuel to get back, but I couldn't help thinking some nights—if I was angry enough—that it'd be worth it to put the Ke-Han in their place once and for all.

The way rounds worked was that you signed up for at least two shifts a week, and it was best if you were working in threes with a swift for recon, a fire-belcher for razing, and a crusher like Compassus, or a Jacqueline-of-all-trades like Havemercy. Once things started getting hot and heavy I was working with Ghislain and Balfour pretty regular, but also with Ace 'cause there was no beating us when we worked together, hitting the Ke-Han from both sides no matter which way they went scurrying, toward the mountain or their cities.

They hadn't even rebuilt their fucking lapis wall. They had no clue what they were doing, and the way everyone was figuring it now was that because of the corps and our dragons, it was going to be over pretty soon. We just kept hitting them and hitting them with all we had, magicians and dragons both, which meant we were being called for every fucking night for a period of about two, two and a half weeks.

It was pretty fucking great.

I mean, I wasn't supporting war or anything—just my role in it. I wasn't some kind of half-wit and I knew that this was my place, up in the air whooping like crazy and steering Havemercy until we were right overhead—Compassus or even Adamo on Proudmouth watching my tail, and one of the swifts scouting out the next target. Sometimes we even got in two, three hits a night. Soon enough we were going to absolutely crush them—I mean, absolutely have them *crushed*. They knew it. They weren't even being smart about their moves anymore, just scattering every which way, so's knocking them off was like picking out ants beneath a magnifying glass, until there wasn't any point in it anymore and we were too close to sunrise and were recalled.

Because that's the thing about riding a dragon into battle: You just can't do it in the daytime. Well, you *could,* but you'd have to be pretty fucking stupid or pretty fucking desperate or a really uncomfortable combination of the two to do it. It's too easy to see a girl in the sunlight, and too easy to bring her down. The Ke-Han don't depend all that much on catapults anymore, but that'd change real soon if they could see us even halfway clearly. Everything's done by moonlight, and you've got to hope to whoever's actually listening that you can just get out there on a night when there's clouds and shit mucking up the starlight. Dragons can see pretty well in the dark, so basically you've just got to trust your girl and she's got to trust you—and the two of you have to work together to live through the night.

Havemercy and I had it down to a science, to an art. I signed up for all the extra shifts no one wanted, and we were up in the air near on to every other night, the wind making my hair even more of a knot than usual, and on our off-days we slept like the fucking dead. In the skies, we didn't have to answer to anyone and we didn't have the time to think about what our actions meant, what poor bastards they affected. You do unto others or they do unto you—that's the first rule of the skies and the one you stick to like the words are your brothers.

The best thing about all this was that the professor didn't have any time or any orders to keep torturing us with our feelings, and whenever I did see him—mercifully more rare now than ever—he was just wandering the halls looking lost and alone.

And that's when I got my idea.

Adamo was going to tear me a brand-new one, since there's laws against taking a civ up into the skies without filling out all kinds of miserable paperwork. But the idea was too good and, anyway, there was no real punishment for an airman when the war was on. I mean, Adamo could give me rations that tasted like dogshit and make sure I never slept on a comfortable bed again, but the truth was I wasn't sleeping much anyway and I didn't care what I ate so long as it kept up my strength for flying.

So I sat on my brilliant idea for the whole day I was off duty, and made sure to eat all my favorites in the mess since I might not be able to for a long while after.

The logistics were kind of hard to figure. Like: How the fuck was I supposed to get the snotnose into the hangar decks?

And where the fuck was I going to get an extra pair of goggles so that the smoke didn't make him go blind?

Anyway, I got the whole thing prepared; I just had to make sure I was awake and dressed when the siren started its wailing. That'd give me, I figured, about a half minute extra to find him, grab him, get him down below, and strap the goggles on him without nobody seeing it. And, since nobody was going to be out and about with the raid bell ringing, it wasn't all that hard to maneuver. I just had to be quick enough, and smart about it. And I was.

I didn't even figure for sleep that night, and when the bell started to clang I was out of my room like a shot and inside that common room in, possibly, *negative* time, grabbing the professor by the collar and hauling him to his feet. Before he was even awake enough to protest I had a hand clamped over his mouth.

"Angh!" he said, very angry, and tried to bite my palm.

Too bad for him I was wearing my riding gloves.

"Shut up," I said, "and pay close attention. I'm going to show you a little something about the Dragon Corps—for *mutual understandin'*, that kind of thing."

His eyes were wide and I didn't wait to hear him complain any further. We only had fifteen seconds, and in just that time I'd dragged him back to my room and shoved him through the chute, coming down fast behind him.

Then, we were inside Havemercy's private quarters. I flung the harness on her and strapped up, shoving my feet into the stirrups and holding my hand out to his highness the sensitivity trainer.

To my surprise, he didn't hesitate—just reached out and took it, just like that.

"Goggles behind you," I said, grabbing my own and putting them on. I heard him struggle for a moment, then the familiar snap that meant he'd got 'em on, but the wrong way. That'd leave a bruise for him in the morning.

"Havemercy's a go!" Perkins, the prep for that evening, shouted at us from the main deck. I dug my heels in.

"Hold on tight," I said.

The professor barely had time to follow my instructions before the doors opened and we were thrown out into the night—Havemercy held tight beneath my thighs and my boots strapped to the stirrups, with the professor hanging on around my waist. That first push once you're off deck was a necessary propulsion to get us flying in the first place, but most fresh blood doesn't expect it, and I heard the professor grunt somewhere next to my ear as all the breath got knocked out of him like a sucker punch to the gut.

This was probably a piss-poor plan from the professor's point of view, since there was no one to say he wasn't going to get thrown at any minute the rest of that long, bloody night. There wasn't a single thing standing beneath him and the distance to the ground—dropping away beneath us every second of rushing wind and cloudy moonlight—except for his arms wrapped around me. He was still in his fucking pajamas. If he did survive the night, he was going to be covered from head to toe with ash and he wouldn't be able to wash it out of his hair for at least a week, but if that was all he suffered, then he could consider himself one lucky bastard, and thank the skies for treating him proper.

"What the *fuck* do you think you're doing?" he shouted, while meanwhile Havemercy was leaving all of Volstov behind, and the wind she was creating pummeled his words so as I could barely make out what he was saying.

It was easier for me, since I was in front, to keep my words from getting swallowed up somewhere just a ways behind us. "Introducing you to my particular lifestyle," I snapped back. Adrenaline was working its magic on me even as we spoke.

It was always like this, when I got close enough to the mountains to see the little Ke-Han lights dotting the desert in the nighttime—like a miniature sky flipped onto its belly.

"You're crazy," I heard him mutter, though it must have been louder than that or I wouldn't have heard a thing.

"That isn't *any* kind of a thing to be saying to a man in my position, professor," I said, real easy, like it didn't bother me in the slightest—which it didn't, not really. There wasn't much that could bother me once Have and I were in the air, which was how come I would be able to stand being close to the professor for any length of time.

He fell silent, and as far as I could tell that meant he was thinking it over. With that big brain of his, I was sure he'd come to the right conclusion, which was not to insult me on my own fucking dragon when no one even knew he was here except me and Havemercy, and her with no loyalty to anyone but herself and me.

Ghislain's Compassus rose huge and terrifying at my right. The professor's reaction was real sweet; I could hear him swear the way I was sure they didn't ever teach in the 'Versity, and after that he nearly pushed the air from *my* lungs with his skinny arms.

I remembered what he'd said about never having seen a dragon up close before. Now he was face-to-face with two in one night. Let no one say I never did the kid any favors.

"It's three for a raid," I said, loud over the wind as we were climbing now, and the higher up we got the more it whipped around us sudden and fierce. "Unless the fighting's hot, then we got no need for recon because the Ke-Han are barreling out from the hills every which way and we just got to plug them up no matter what."

"Ah." I felt him nod, sharp, into my shoulder. He was paying attention, I realized, and let loose a snort of amusement. The little freak was paying attention like this was some *class,* where he'd be *tested* later, and then graded on his memory of everything he'd learned.

If he'd known to bring a notebook, he'd probably be taking notes in that, too.

Whatever. If the kid wanted to treat me like one of the Nellies who taught at the 'Versity and didn't ever once figure on going out to learn things for themselves, that was fine.

"Who's the kid?" Have'd been pretty quiet for her usual quick self up until now, but that was only because she was smart, trying to get the lay of the situation before she said anything. She was deadly, my girl, and wicked sharp in a tight situation just the same as I was.

I hadn't told her about the professor, least not in as many words.

"Did— Did you say something?" He was yelling practically into my ear, which I didn't appreciate, and I let him know by shrugging my shoulder so that it bounced his jaw. *"Bastion,"* he swore again, as if he'd bit his tongue something painful.

"I'm not deaf," I told him. To Have, real close to her neck, I said, "This is the man who's been teaching me all manner of speaking pretty and not treadin' on the feelings of others."

Havemercy made the sound I'd come to think of as her laugh, all machinery and metallic amusement. "The one you said you were going to slit open like an envelope from end to end?"

"I— What?" The professor was speaking quiet again, I'd give him that. "Did you . . . I could have sworn you said something."

"That was just Have," I said, not because I took pity on him or nothing but because I could see his questions getting really old really fast, and for a clever sort of brat he didn't seem any closer to figuring it out.

"Have?" he asked, proving me right. "Have what? Do you mean . . . oh, I— I didn't realize . . ."

It was almost painful, keeping my laugh in, but then I knew Ghislain would want to know what I was laughing at, and chances were that up until this point he hadn't even seen the professor hitching a ride with Havemercy and me. The dark's pretty good for keeping secrets.

I knew Balfour would see him, though, because Balfour saw everything. It was what he'd been trained to do. But he also wouldn't be likely to go running to Adamo on me, mainly 'cause he didn't want piss in his boots anytime soon, whereas that kind of retribution wouldn't be weighing too much on Ghislain's mind—stony bastard that he was.

"She talks?" The way the professor said it, I could tell exactly what kind of a look he'd have on his face: the exact same dumb, incredulous expression he wore when he woke up with beetles in his hair or missing all his clothes.

"You bet your sweet ass she talks," said my girl. "Now be quiet, would you? We've got important matters to look after. And stop all your fucking cursing. Haven't you seen a proper dragon before?"

"I can't say that I have," the professor said, and maybe more that the wind swallowed.

Balfour had come up on our left from the rear, Anastasia sleek and hidden behind the clouds. Even if he had girl parts, Balfour was still good for recon, had a mind for understanding that, when it was important to stay in one place, he should damn well *stay* there. That's harder'n most think, especially when you've got a fight happening around you on all sides. But, as Adamo was fond of reminding us at full pitch, someone has to keep their heads when the battle's going on.

I knew sure as dragonfire it wasn't ever going to be me.

We picked up speed with the cresting slope of the Cobalts— they're real smooth and easy for a while, tricking you into thinking they're all pretty and welcoming, until they get jagged as alligator teeth and you know the truth. Once we crossed over those mountains I'd go in fast and hard, hammer the bastards first and give 'em a bit of a show, something to chase. Ghislain'd be right behind me, crushing the sons-of so thoroughly they'd never get up again.

The idea was that Balfour would use this distraction to get close, fly in deep over the Ke-Han city territory, and see if there was anything th'Esar needed to be worrying about; then we'd all go scurrying back to the rendezvous point and make it back to base before the sun came up over the range's edge.

We'd tried it the other way round, recon first and us guns coming in later if the swift got into trouble, but I was too damn impatient to be put into the sky for any kind of a waiting game, and after several instances of Adamo trying to explain the way of things to me yet again, we all just figured it'd be for the best that we changed the plan around so as it suited us rather than trying to fit *us* to the plan.

'Course what had helped my case was Balfour's brother getting into the trouble he did, and us not knowing anything about it until it was too late. We almost lost Anastasia in that one, and *then* we'd have all been nobly fucked harder than the chambermaids in th'Esar's palace. We only had two swifts. Recon was dangerous flying: the point of being small was to get close, and if you got too close, there was always a chance you wouldn't get out again.

It was funny—not so funny that I was laughing—but I could hear the professor breathing in my ear, piss-terrified no matter what he said and holding tight to me like a kid hiding under his bed from monsters.

"You want to ease off so I can say this," I said. I heard the quiet *oh* before I felt the vise around my waist loosen marginally. "It's going to get loud real soon. Real fast, too, and real messy. Nothing'll get in your eyes with those goggles on, but don't look directly at nothing that seems too bright, and don't fucking scream or I'll throw you to the Ke-Han and let them sort out the pieces. You got that?"

He nodded mutely, fingers worrying dedicatedly at a button on my coat.

Well. It was better than screaming, I supposed.

"What about you, sweetheart?" I twitched Have's harness fondly, knew what the answer'd be before I even asked it, but it was a politeness I knew she liked. It was probably the only one.

Most of the guys talked to their dragons like they were real ladies, so it wasn't out of the ordinary. If the professor knew what was good for him, he'd forget he ever heard it.

"Just don't spin around so hard this time," she said. "You'll break my neck."

I laughed, feeling the air all around us as she began to plummet. "I won't."

I didn't warn the professor or tell him to hold on, so as we made our descent I felt his hands scrabbling for a safer purchase, like he wasn't so sure just holding on to me would be safe enough. I really hoped he wasn't going to tear the buttons off my coat or nothing, 'cause then I'd have to make him sew them back on.

I bet he knew how to do it, too.

Finally, his arms locked tight around my ribs again, like he figured we weren't going to be doing much more talking anyway, and I wouldn't speak up to complain. He was at least right about that.

The wind hit us like a bucket of cold water, sharp and freezing and all at once, which meant that it wasn't real wind at all but the work of those fucking magicians. I held our course, steering Have right through because I knew that if there were anything stronger they could have hit us with, they'd have done so right up front. We'd caught them unawares, the lazy cunts, and in the time it'd take to cook up anything really threatening, Ghislain and Compassus would have them flattened to the ground.

I let out a war whoop, wild as any of the Ke-Han's breathless, ululating screams, and took out a guard tower on the far wall. The trick to getting Have to breathe fire was a different kind of jerking the harness, pulling against the mechanism just behind her tongue; and then the gasoline caught the fuse and she was *screaming* fire. The guard tower burst into flames—orange and the faint soul of green that was the dragonmagic. These were fires that couldn't be easily quenched with sand or water.

The tower lit up our section like a beacon, and below us the tiny scrambling silhouettes of Ke-Han warriors came pouring out from behind the wall, as though there were anything they could possibly do against three fucking dragons.

"That seems a—a rather showy way of announcing our presence, doesn't it?"

It took me a full minute to figure out one, why someone was talking to me, and two, why that someone wasn't Havemercy. The thing with flying is, you've got to get your head into an almost completely separate mind-set, deep focus, and you can't be taking breaks to ask yourself: *Gee, I wonder if there are families down there,* or: *Hey, I haven't seen Ghislain and Balfour in a while,* because that's the kind of thinking that can get you killed. The first thing you learn is how not to get all distracted like that.

"Not trying to hide," I gritted out, twisting with Have to

one side as a sudden push of wind beckoned us closer to die on the rocks.

"Those look like catapults," he said, in a voice that meant he'd been shocked calm, or was a little bit of a sociopath, our professor.

"So they are," I said. Then, just for revenge, I added, "*Trebuchets,* actually."

We took off like a streak of lightning, wind howling in my ears as Havemercy let out a screech to make sure everyone on the ground knew just who was the god of fire around here. Something molten crashed against the mountains behind, where we'd just been.

"I don't understand," the professor said, loud as he could over the boom of the catapult. "They don't even seem to be trying!"

I wanted to tell him no, professor, that we were just that good, but the trouble was that I didn't quite understand it, either.

Catapults were inelegant, a clunking technology the Ke-Han had given up on years ago when it became evident that they weren't quick enough to hit us even flying half-blind and on one wing. They hid behind their magicians when it came to matching us, and if I'd been in any kind of a charitable mood while dealing with the Ke-Han, I'd have said they did all right. Not well, because when you were pitting anything against the Dragon Corps it was just a sad inevitability that we'd send 'em screaming, but all right.

Now things almost seemed too easy. I was suspicious of easiness from anything, excepting women, and thought I might make a point of saying as much to Adamo when we made it back to the Airman after we were finished.

It was like the Ke-Han emperor had gone on a holiday and left his fourteen-year-old nephew in charge.

They were lining the catapult up to us again when a long, earth-shattering groan pierced the skies, and Ghislain came roaring down on Compassus like he didn't have a care in the world for the little breezes the Ke-Han magicians threw at him.

Ghislain said the Ke-Han called Compassus the sky-shaker. Fuckers were apt, if nothing else.

The catapult creaked and swung loose, and we soared wide of the mark, Havemercy's long, gorgeous framework glinting silver in the arc light.

The sound of screaming was louder now that the sky-shaker had arrived and was mowing down everything they sent forward. In moments, the catapults were no longer a threat, and neither was the second guard tower, resolutely pealing its alarm to all that could hear—as if they couldn't already hear from the screaming and our dragons, gnashing and roaring their pleasure to the skies.

"*Oh,*" said the professor. I felt his hands go slack as interest got the better of him and he tried to sit up, presumably to get a better look while still holding on.

A twister of a spell hit Havemercy square in the jaw left of nowhere, so that I had to turn us hard like she'd told me not to, and for one sick moment I felt the professor's hands slip against my stomach.

"Sit the *fuck down,*" I snarled, harsher than I'd meant to. I couldn't grab both his hands in one of mine, they weren't at all tiny like I'd've thought, but I held tight to Have's harness with one hand, tighter to his wrist with the other. If the air had been perfectly still, I'd have been able to hear his bones grinding. Or maybe that was my teeth. "Let go again and I swear, by Havemercy, I'll let you fall."

I released my hold on his wrist in disgust, gloved hands put to better use trying to steer us clear of the litter of tornadoes that had popped up around the city walls. I was as mad at myself as anything—I'd been watching and thinking when I should have been moving, and that was what came of bringing the professor up where he didn't belong for a second.

It was my own damn fault, though, trying to teach the professor some kind of reverse lesson.

Below us, Ghislain was still wreaking havoc with Compassus; she was big enough that the twisters merely nudged them with a suggestion of a twirl this way and that.

Holding close as he was, I could feel the professor shaking like he was out-of-his-mind-terrified, which—for once—I couldn't blame him for.

The sky was losing its pitch-darkness fairly quickly by this point, so I hoped Balfour was planning on heading back our way real soon. Anastasia could move when she had to, but I knew Compassus would need a fair time's warning to make it back by first light.

Something shifted in the clouds.

You never heard Anastasia before you saw her. That was one of her talents. And even then you didn't see her unless you knew what to look for, silver and blue like skymetal, and in the clouds she was fucking invisible. Still, when I saw the flicker of movement wide of the city, I knew what it meant. Time to go.

I didn't warn the professor this time when we dove either, and I could hear him cursing all the way down, soft in my ear as the wind whipped around us and Havemercy started to sing.

"I didn't know they taught *that* sort of pretty speak at the 'Versity, professor," I called without looking back at him. When we got closer, I let Have take out a barracks Ghislain had been heading for with Compassus, because I knew it would get his attention.

"No, *that* I learned from you," the professor answered. He sounded almost sullen.

I laughed, wild and exhilarated with the wind in my blood. Have laughed, too, all creaking and sweet, rattling beneath us and making the professor curse again—so that I had to wonder if he wasn't really a Mollyrat, same as I was.

Have and I circled once around Compassus, in case Ghislain hadn't got the message and thought I was trying to start some kind of a game on my own with the barracks, which I'd also been known to do.

He got the message though, and I let them go tearing out ahead of us, smoke spewing in all directions and streaming into my nose and mouth.

The smoke you got used to, but for the first few nights it

was pretty terrible, and when the professor started coughing behind me I knew it'd be at least a week before I heard the end of it.

I thought I could hear cheering when we went back over the mountains, like we hadn't just razed their city forces to the ground, and over half the towers they used for their magicians with it.

It was like they weren't even trying to win anymore—which of course I'd heard could happen when you just wore a man down for so long he didn't even care what the outcome was, so long as he could get out. But this didn't feel the same as that.

I didn't like it, and I didn't like having to *think* about it neither, but with the professor breathing quick and uneven in my ear, Ghislain up ahead, and Balfour out in front, it was all I could do.

Well, almost all, I thought, and joined Havemercy just in time for the verse about ladies' undergarments. There was a moment where I wondered if a third voice hadn't joined in with ours, but that wasn't too fucking likely, and in the end I blamed it on the wind.

We got back to the Airman a little more than an hour later, with the sun just peeking her head up above the horizon at our backs. Ghislain and Balfour were flying on ahead and not looking back, so I figured I might've made it out of this without it being noticed I'd taken the professor out for a spin with me—though of course if the boys noticed the soot under his fingernails and the grease in his hair, they'd pretty much realize straightaway what we'd been up to, what I'd done, and have a list of all the rules I'd broken. Whether or not they actually set that list down on Adamo's desk was another matter. It depended on what kind of a mood they were in and whether or not they saw me sharpening my knives beforehand. Anyway, Adamo had more important things to be worrying about than something that hadn't made any difference in my performance in the first place.

I'd make sure they saw me sharpening my knives.

When we got back into the hangar and I got myself unstrapped, easing my aching feet out of them stiff boots and tossing them aside for the mess-men to deal with and have polished and ready for me by sundown that same day, the professor came down off of Have's back like his legs didn't have bones in them any longer and his knees were made out of nothing more useful to him than water. The airmen called that kind of wobbling Civ Legs, short for civilian legs, and those who'd got over all that shaking soon forgot their own misery about how it felt, all your body gone numb from the force of riding a dragon all night long.

The professor was lucky. He'd made it out alive, and he hadn't had to fucking *steer* her or *anything,* just hold on and make sure he didn't slide off, and he could barely even manage to do that. He hardly deserved a fucking medal just for staying alive.

I took off my gloves next, pretending like I didn't see him wobbling all around and fumbling with the straps of his goggles, trying to get them off so he could actually see. My fingers were stiff from gripping the harness reins all night long and didn't move quick as they might've done. There's some things a body can't get used to, no matter how many calluses it builds up, no matter how much the muscles shift to accommodate whatever crazy flying you've been doing of late.

At last, when I was sorted out and all the things that needed washing were in a corner of Have's dock—my jacket and my gloves thrown over to join my boots—and I made sure Have was settled in nice and comfortable for the night, I turned finally to look at the professor. He was watching me with his big green eyes sort of eerie—but not accusing—with the rest of his face soot black in streaks, and only the shape of the goggles marked pale as a backward raccoon.

"Why?" he asked at last.

I scratched the back of my neck, just to get my fingers working again. "Don't know," I answered lazily. "Thought, in the interest of sharin' and carin'—"

"What did you think I'd learn?" he pressed—not quite snapping, and his voice trembling beneath its calm. "Or did you think perhaps you'd kill me while we were up there?"

"I coulda done," I pointed out. "But I didn't. Even caught you once."

The professor barely moved his blackened lips as he spoke. "And as I said, I want to know why."

"Would've landed me in fuck-all trouble," I said. "Would've been some nasty explaining."

"No one knew I was up there with you. There'd be no body. It wouldn't be any trouble at all."

The professor was smarter than he looked. Must've been, any case, in order to get so far as to be given this position of wrangling us. I could've hit him right there, but my hands would've cramped up if I tried to clench 'em into fists. Instead, I said, "So what *do* you think, then? Bein' the genius among us."

"I don't know," he replied, almost helplessly. "That's why I asked."

"You want to know that bad?"

"That badly," he said, then winced. "Yes. I do."

"Inspiration, I guess," I said. "Thought maybe I could scare you off, make you piss yourself. I don't fucking know."

"I just—" the professor began. He cut his own self short, though, and had to swallow around something that seemed a little too thick for him for a moment, like he was choking on his own thoughts. Not many men could have held on the way he did—not many men would still be standing now. Any second I expected him to collapse to the floor, but he didn't. "I wish you'd tell me," he finished, finally.

"You want to know why?" I stepped closer to him, too tired to be *real* intimidating, but drawing myself up to full height and managing a grin—covered in soot and ash and grease as I was, I must've looked like some kind of monster out of a storybook. He met my eyes, and there was this weird electric kind of charge between us, like when two dragons fly close enough that their tails or wings scrape against each other and sparks rain down onto the world below. I'd never got that feeling anywhere other than in the air before. I hated it; I wanted to be sick. When my words came, they were even angrier than I thought they'd be. I wasn't so tired I couldn't get charged up by some idiot 'Versity civ thinking he had me figured. "I'll tell you why," I went on, ignoring how strange it was. "It's 'cause all those pretty things you say—all that horseshit you try to feed us about weighing both sides and learning every man's story and getting to know your fellows—all of that doesn't mean *fuck* when you're up there. I can't stop to ask myself questions when I've got Have to think about. I can't even balance out what my own fucking feelings are when I'm in the air—and I sure as shit don't have time for anyone else's. All I gotta know—all I've been trained to know—is how to not get my ass killed. And maybe tonight I figured that was something you needed to know, so as you could get a clearer vision of your *big picture*."

I was breathing pretty heavily by the time I was finished, since I wasn't usually a man who talked so much in one go. The professor—who usually *was* the sort of man who talked so much in one go—didn't seem to have anything in particular to say to that. No two ways about it: It felt good to get it off my chest. Now it was all out there on the table, how much of a stupid civ he was and how he didn't know the first fucking thing about any of us. All he was doing was coming in uninformed, disrupting our flow and looking down his snub nose at us—like we weren't saving his ass and every other ass in the whole of Volstov, leastways when the war was on.

My blood was up and I could barely see straight, I was so tired, my skin heavy with dragonsmoke. He deserved what I threw at him, whether he'd been man enough to keep his feet after first flight or not.

He did, but only barely. When he wobbled out, if I'd been less firing mad, I would have chased him out of the room just laughing at him, the way he had to hang on to the doorframe and the wall just to keep himself upright.

"You weren't any better your first time up," Have said, snorting through her flared nostrils. Dim light from the hangar glinted off them, and I turned back to see her trying to wipe grease and soot off the corner of her mouth. She didn't like the way it tasted, and it was a bitch to clean if it hardened overnight. I didn't trust snot-nosed Perkins, or anybody else for that matter, with her.

No one knew how to take care of my girl but me.

"Was fucking too," I said, rubbing down her neck next. "You told me I was the sweetest ride you'd ever had."

"I was young then," Have said. She sounded wry and echoed like inside she was grinning. "Impressionable. I didn't know any better."

"Save it," I told her. "I'm too tired."

"I'm just a Jacqueline," Have replied. "I can't do anything but tell the truth. He wasn't half-bad. Didn't even piss himself on me. I appreciate that in a man. He reminds me of you. Not so dirty, but no one is."

"Are you on his fucking side or something? Is that it?"

Have looked at me the same way Have always looked at me, ever since we first met and my fingernails were dirty and she didn't waste any fucking time in letting me know what she thought about *that*—and all the other things, for that matter. It wasn't a way I enjoyed being looked at, not even when Have's dark eyes were doing the looking.

"I'm just saying, I get a sense of people. I've got good taste, and there isn't anyone out there who's ever smacked of *you* before. Though one of you's quite enough, to be honest."

"Did I keep you on the ground too long, is that it?" Of course, dragons couldn't go crazy the same as people did, but any machine stopped working if you kept it from doing what it was meant to long enough. Some of the prototype dragons had just—stopped—during the first really big lull they'd hit between battles. Since Have was the newest, not to mention the best, I hadn't thought we'd be having that problem, but she was talking some dreadful nonsense now. "I ain't *nothing* like that professor."

"Not a drop? Not a hint?" Have asked, sounding more like some sly, calculating mistress than my sweet girl. "Anyway, I didn't say you had any of his good qualities, the brains and the fancy manners or anything like that. What I mean is, he's got your bad qualities, the poor bastard. The stubbornness, and the language, too. Doesn't smell as bad as you do, though."

"Never took you for a traitor," I said. "You're sure nothing hit you in the head when I was saving that idiot's life?"

I was getting real angry, and there wasn't any point in getting angry with someone who couldn't get angry back, so I just breathed real deep and clenched my fists in tight.

"I'm not taking anyone's side," she said at last, which wasn't a proper answer at all. "Go take a bath."

"Didn't know you were my mother," I snapped.

"Am not," Have replied smoothly, eyelids slipping shut. "I'd've raised you better."

I didn't do as nice a job cleaning her off as I should have— I didn't have any time for spending on turncoat traitors when I could've been catching some much-needed shut-eye—but the whole thing set me off so bad I didn't have the time to talk to Adamo about how crazy the Ke-Han were acting, and by morning it didn't seem half so important as I'd made it out to be in the dark.

HAL

The way I felt for Margrave Royston was at once a strange and terrifying sensation. I had no other experiences against which I could measure it. In my ignorance I kept it safe, treasured it, held it private and unanswered and often lonely inside my chest. But for all the misery I felt in not being allowed to express it, I knew also that I'd never exchange the way I felt for a safer, less painful course. It was my own wound, my own loss. Royston was kind and he was brilliant and he told me of the city and suffered my endless questions; he even gave me a gift without any occasion, a parcel of books he'd ordered specially from a friend. Their bindings were strong, their pages thick. They were so expensive that I did all I could not to accept them, but he insisted and insisted until I could no longer protest without seeming rude. I lined them up one next to the other on the little shelf next to my bed, and gazed at them with almost the same reverence I reserved for Royston himself.

There were times when I cried. But it wasn't for any purpose or reason in particular, and they were few and simple tears, and I kept such moments secret. I was being quite silly about everything, since in truth I was luckier than I could believe.

I *was* happy. I knew I was. I felt alive and hungry for the first time in my life—and it was only now that I realized how little I'd known before Royston arrived, what darkness it was in which I'd have been content to live out my entire life had he not shown me there could be more to *real* learning than the handful of foolish tools I'd been given.

The days were bright. He answered every question I posed to him. He'd forgiven me the kiss I stole from him—though it was still between us, a shadow like a blow whenever I forgot myself and remembered it. When I was alone, I traced the shape of his mouth over mine and wondered always if it were possible—if I gave him enough time—that Royston would ever return my feelings. But these were silly wonderings—foolish, juvenile, the mark of an innocent country boy. He must have thought me very careless to have fallen so quickly and with so little reservation.

I'd promised myself and him not to make the same mistake a second time. If I did, I'd prove an unworthy student. I was determined not to lose that which I still had, and so I was doubly careful, and tried very hard not to take advantage of what concessions he afforded me.

Yet, on the whole, things were well enough. I cherished the moments I had with him, the books he'd given me, our conversations that ran late into the night.

Then everything changed at once.

The post to Nevers arrived twice a week, once just after the weekend and once just before it. When the man on horseback arrived that afternoon, I thought I must be mistaken as to the day—or that it might have had something to do with the war, since last night's raid had woken up half the countryside; the guard tower they'd hit had been nearer to us than Thremedon proper—but William sat bolt upright from where he was sprawled, creating a fortress out of pots that he'd stolen from the kitchens.

"It's the wrong day for mail!" he announced delightedly.

As excited as William was, I felt a cold sort of dread settle over me. It was a premonition, perhaps, no more than a feeling—but in all the time I'd spent at the chatelain's castle in Nevers, the post had only ever come at its appointed time and on its appointed day. The only variable that had changed was Royston's presence here, and because I could think of no one else, I was certain this sudden development had to do with him.

I was right.

William tried to eavesdrop on the conversation in the lower hall, where Royston and the chatelain and Mme were talking with the man on horseback. And, although I wished to hear their words for more immediate reasons than William's general curiosity, duty required me to guide him away from the banister and do my best to distract him from matters that weren't any of his business. Nor were they, I supposed, any of mine.

Though I tried my best to keep William entertained, I could no more keep his attention from wandering to the business with the untimely post than I could keep mine from doing the same. We were both wretched to each other, and I admit a pot handle was broken that afternoon when William had a fit over how strict I was being with him.

Perhaps I was. I apologized to him, and we endeavored to fix the pot handle, but all the while I could think of nothing but Royston, standing there at the bottom of the stairs, his back to me.

For all I knew, he was going to leave.

It was later—too much later—that I spoke to Royston and learned what the trouble was. In fact, it was he who came to me, knocking twice upon my little door. He'd never done so before, and I knew at once that there was *real* trouble.

I let him in, and we stood before each other awkwardly.

"I've been called back," he said at last.

"Oh," I replied stupidly. "To the city."

"Yes," he confirmed. "It means they need my Talent."

"For the war?"

"For the war."

The tales Royston told of battle were distant; I'd always assumed, however naively and stubbornly, that they were in the past, and he'd never be put in the path of such danger again. Yet he was still a young enough magician with a vitally useful Talent. I'd never had any cause to believe what I believed beyond my own private hopes. The idea of being separated from him was not so terrible as the knowledge that he would be leaving me to go to war.

I felt as if I were going to be sick. A moment later my knees gave way and I was sitting down heavily upon the edge of my bed, gripping the sheets until my knuckles were white.

"Hal," he said. I barely heard him.

"When?" I asked.

"Tomorrow," he replied, his voice very distant, coming to me over the thrumming of blood in my ears. "As soon as possible, but I've been given tonight to set my things in order and settle up matters in the country. My carriage should arrive sometime tomorrow morning."

I shook my head against it, closing my eyes. If pressed to categorize how I'd come to feel about Royston, I didn't believe it in my capacity to phrase a response. I cared for him—more than anyone else, I cared for him. I knew what life here would become without him. This change was unimaginable. "I don't want you to go," I said. The selfishness inherent in the words made them sound poisonous to my own ears, but I couldn't stop myself from speaking them.

"I cannot very well shirk my duty," he said, and I thought I saw the ghost of a smile in the corner of his mouth. No matter how bitter it seemed, I couldn't bear to look at even the imitation of a smile on his face in that moment. "Not when the Esar has so . . . graciously agreed to end my term of exile in the country much sooner than expected."

I let the words roll off me, even as I recognized what he was doing.

"But you live here," I said, soft and insistent. I couldn't make myself stop.

"Hal," he said again, and he knelt on the floor so that I would look at him. Under normal circumstances this might have stirred some small wonderment in me, for Royston was not given to such sweeping gestures. Yet all I could feel was the dull throbbing in my skull, the sound of my pulse proclaiming that Royston was leaving both the countryside and me. "Hal, I would like you to listen to me since I'm going to be gone in the morning and I—"

"Stop *saying* that," I said, meeting his eyes at last. "I heard you the first time, I'm not *stupid*."

He moved to take my hands, and found that he could not, as I was still holding tightly to my bed. Instead, he laid his palms somewhat awkwardly over my clenched fists. Something worked in his jaw.

"I know you aren't stupid," he said. "It is one of your particularly unique qualities, Hal, and I don't have a mind toward forgetting it anytime soon. No. Nevertheless, I've decided— at least, I thought—to have an eye toward asking you something."

He was thinking out loud, babbling in the way I'd only heard very rarely, which meant that he must have been quite nervous.

I was in no mood to console him, terrible and selfish as my misery had become, but my hands unclenched a little from their iron hold on the bedspread to wrap around his own. "Say it, then," I whispered.

"Come with me," he said, all at once, as if he were afraid it might lodge in his throat halfway before he had the chance to get it out.

It startled both of us, and me so much that I found myself unable to speak.

"I—I would be most honored if you would come with me," Royston quickly revised, looking down at the floor with what appeared to be considerable interest. "I've thought about it. Or rather, since I received the news I *have* been thinking about it, and, well, I think it's the best solution. In any case, there it stands. My invitation may come as quite a shock, but I am nevertheless very serious about it."

I was too shocked to laugh at the way he was speaking, overly serious, as though it was a business proposal, and so I did the only thing I could do: I just flinched. My surprise was tempered with pleasure and dismay at once; I wanted to pull my hands away to cover my face and found that I could not— of course, because Royston was still holding them.

In all the strangest fantasies I'd entertained since I began studying with him—and there had been many, in this very room, extravagant and off center as my thoughts ever were— I had always imagined that I'd give anything to hear him ask this very question of me. *I would be most honored if you would come with me*.

In as many words, that was all I'd wanted. Yet it was one thing to imagine it in the dusky moments between waking and sleeping, and quite another to be faced with the possibility, real and whole in the waking world.

I knew at once the complications; they were why I'd always assumed it would be no more than a daydream.

"I know that I would be depriving the children of a most excellent tutor," he went on, seeking to draw me from my silence. "I merely find that I have grown . . . accustomed to your conversation, as well as your company, and while there are a rare few people in this world whom I consider my friends, I find quite suddenly that you are one of the dearest. As I said, the request is selfish. Yet it isn't entirely ludicrous, either. We could— There are some things, Hal, that would be greatly facilitated by a move to the city."

I didn't dare to imagine what he meant by that. In the moment, with all that I stood to lose, I couldn't afford to presume myself into even further disappointment.

"If you wish to stay with me, then you shouldn't leave," I said, horrified at my own selfishness but still unable to stop myself. I freed my hands to hold his face, tilting it up to get a real, full look at it. "Don't leave."

He looked at me with dark, miserable eyes, and I felt guilt settle heavy in my chest like a burden.

I hadn't meant to be a burden.

"Hal," he said at last.

"I can't go," I whispered, pulling my hands away and drawing my knees up to my chest. I wished quite suddenly that he wouldn't kneel so before me: Our positions were abruptly reversed, and I found myself unexpectedly averse to the change. It was one of many changes. I couldn't bear to look at it straight on. "Since I was a child, my father promised me. And the chatelain has done so much for me, funded my entire education, brought me here to live in his house and fed me, clothed me. My bed is his, the clothes on my back, all the books on my shelves, save for the ones you gave me. I couldn't be so ungrateful. I can't go."

"Please," Royston said carefully, as though he had no idea what an effect such words had on me. He moved now, unfolding from where he knelt, and paused but a moment before he sat beside me on my bed. He almost knocked the back of his head against the sloped ceiling—something I'd done countless times before.

"Be careful there," I murmured. "The ceiling is very low."

"Ah," Royston said. "Yes. I see."

We sat for a time in uncomfortable silence while I fought off the urge to cry, or indeed to think of anything at all. My thoughts were treacherous, and my fingers felt impossibly cold.

At last, I heard Royston draw in a measured breath. "I would pay them very generously in thanks for their understanding," he told me, with a straightforwardness that stunned me. "They would understand, I think—and it is not as if you are the only tutor in all of Nevers. You wouldn't be leaving them in such dire straits as all that."

"That would be asking too much of you," I replied, as soon as I'd found my voice.

"I think it a negligible detail," Royston replied, "when *I* have just asked so very much of *you*."

"It's quite different," I told him. On the whole I felt as if my mind had been oddly separated from all my emotions; I was speaking, certainly, but at the same time not entirely sure I was in control of the words I spoke. I might have been a mechanical dragon more than I was myself, for all I had control of my actions, or understood the recklessness of my own heart.

"It isn't so very different as all that," Royston said. He turned his face as though he sought to capture my gaze and, after a moment of unnecessary perversity, I allowed our eyes to meet. There was something in his gaze that made me wonder if he was trying to say more than I'd heard. I felt something clench tight within me, unruly and curious despite myself. "If," Royston continued, gently, "by this offer, I presume too much—"

This was hard for him. I saw it in the tight lines around the corners of his eyes, the matching lines, just as tight, around the corners of his mouth. I knew enough of Royston to know he wasn't the sort of man given to such persistence; when he was denied so firmly something he wanted for himself, he withdrew to prevent any further infliction of the same hurt.

Yet here he was, importuning me further. I was repaying him for all his kindnesses by being stubborn as a mule and heedless as a child.

"I'm sorry," I told him, all at once and in a breathless rush. "Royston, please, you mustn't think me ungrateful—"

"I don't."

"—and you mustn't think I wouldn't *want* to go with you," I went on, "because when I think about what it will be like once you've left, it's *too* insufferable."

Royston's eyes lit up for a moment with warmth and good humor, and something that looked a little like relief. "I'm glad to find us in agreement on that point, at least," he said.

I flushed, and pressed on, determined to make myself heard. "Only," I stammered, "only I *can't* do it. To leave without any warning—to abandon Alexander and William and Etienne, even Emilie—"

"It is quite sudden, yes," Royston agreed.

"And what's more," I added, blush growing deeper, "I don't know the first thing about the city." I realized all at once that the majority of my altruism stemmed not from my desire to repay my distant aunt and her husband's kindness, nor was it to save the children from the sadness of parting. Rather, it was my own intractable fear of the city herself, all three maidens, whatever specter of it I'd concocted. I was raised in the country, and I thought of it without reservations as my home. While I wished to follow Royston, and I did—it was almost feverish how completely I wished it—I was also terrified.

I faltered then, and Royston saw through my protestations at once.

"Hal," he said, taking one of my hands in both of his own, "you are far more clever and far better-read than most students at the 'Versity. What separates you from them is their monstrous sense of self-entitlement, but no more than that, I assure you. The city, too, is no more than the countryside with a great many more houses and a great many more opportunities." He paused for a moment, then allowed himself a slight, self-deprecating smile. "Perhaps that is somewhat oversimplified," he continued, "but there is *some* truth to it. I asked you to come with me when I leave tomorrow with some considerable measure of selfishness, but at the same time I would never have made the offer if I didn't think you would benefit from the arrangement just as much—if not more so—than I. There are some people who aren't made for the limitations of the countryside. You are one of those people, Hal. If you say that you will be happier here reading what little my brother can procure for you, teaching the basic patterns of grammar to my nephews, then I will not press the matter further, and though I will be quite distraught to take my leave of you, I *will* do it. But can you truly look me in the eye and tell me with all honesty—and do not let fear temper your answer, Hal—that the city does not hold for you something you crave, something you have always craved, something you have longed for ever since you first imagined it might be out there, just beyond your reach, waiting for you to have the chance to attain it? Tell me—it is the same longing you foster when you read, is it not?"

When he was finished speaking, I found I could scarcely breathe. Royston was a peerless speaker, and had he asked me at that moment to leap out a window, I suspect I would have done it for him without hesitation. His eyes were very bright and his face alive with the meaning behind his words. I felt my heart stutter in my chest as my breath stuttered in my throat.

This was one of many reasons why I so often dreamed of kissing him. He spoke more beautifully than the most exquisite passages I'd ever read.

The expression on his face was too overwhelming, the force of his words too pure. I looked away from him and knotted my fingers in the bedsheets.

"It is," I whispered. "I do wish for that."

"When I was somewhat younger than you," Royston told me, "I left my home in the countryside. I had no such offer as you have before you now, and—I've never told this to anyone—I was completely terrified of all that lay ahead of me."

"But you did it yourself," I replied. "You have no reason to feel beholden to anyone now, for the . . . the price they paid for you when you were that age, to rescue you, to show you all the things you speak so eloquently about." I was near to shredding the sheet, and I forced myself to let go of it before I really did tear it. "It is almost . . . *too* kind of you. Your offer."

"I won't hold you to it," Royston promised. "I don't expect to be repaid."

I shook my head. "Then you undervalue me," I said. "It would seem that I owed you too much."

"Then think of it in terms of my selfishness," Royston said candidly. "In the terms I have tried my hardest *not* to think of it. As I said, you are more than worthy of the city, but if you would do me the favor of considering it from my perspective— Hal, I am quite close now to begging for your company."

It was much the same as the way I'd begged for him to stay.

We were unexpectedly equals, at least in terms of how greatly opposed we were to being parted from one another. After a moment, I found myself laughing, then Royston was laughing with me; we ran the gamut from nervous to relieved in no more than a second, and I fell against him, hiding my face against his shoulder, muffling the sound of my laughter in shades of gratitude and delight.

"Would you really?" I asked him, when I'd quite composed myself once more. "Would you really take me away from here, take me with you to the city?"

"This is no jest, Hal," he said. "I would never have offered it if I didn't have every intention of seeing it through. A good assistant is a rare thing to come by; a good student even rarer."

"Mme will be so angry," I added. "She'll be likely to faint all week."

"Let her be angry," Royston said. "She deserves you less than anyone else here."

I sobered for a moment when I thought of the others. "I *will* miss them," I said softly. "I'm very fond of the children."

"They shall come to hate me, no doubt, for whisking you away from them," Royston replied. "I will be their evil uncle, who stole the light out of their lives without any warning."

"Don't," I murmured, and nudged his shoulder lightly with my own, but there was no vehemence in my rebuke.

"Hal," he said, and I wondered what it was about his voice that could make my own name sound like a title both foreign and beautiful. Despite what good sense had taught me about the extent of Royston's personal feelings, I turned slightly, and tilted my head up.

He touched my cheek, and looked at me with an expression that I'd only ever seen him wear when he spoke of Thremedon, his beloved city. Then he winced, and took his hand away to press it against his forehead, a faint glimmer of unhappiness crossing his face.

"I'm sorry," I said quickly. I didn't know why I had thought . . . but it didn't matter. If Royston was going to take me to the city with him, I would have to be more circumspect.

"No," he said, though his argument sounded halfhearted at best. "It isn't that. I've only . . . I've got something of a headache, that's all."

"Oh," I said, accepting the lie, because it was clear that was what Royston wanted me to do. "That's all right. We can—we don't have to talk."

We were silent for a while after that, but this time it was without the prior awkwardness. I toyed with one of the rings on Royston's left hand, and he allowed me to do it. It was a ring for poison, with a complicated, stiff catch, and the silence that stretched between us was punctuated by the sound the ring made when I managed to open it.

At last, Royston said, "Will you come with me, then?"

"Yes," I told him, without hesitation. "Yes, I'll come."

"Ah," he replied. The pleasure and relief flooded his voice, deepening it. "Well," Royston went on, and I was sad to hear that quality disappearing from his voice, "it's rather late to talk to my brother about the matter."

I hid a yawn against the inside of my elbow. "I don't know what I should pack," I admitted.

"Don't worry," Royston said. "I shall see to that. Would you . . . ah, would you like me to stay with you awhile? If you have any questions about the city—about what will be expected of you there—I wouldn't mind answering them."

I had a few, and we stayed up a while longer, talking in hushed voices. Only once more did Royston show signs of the headache that had bothered him earlier, but he insisted it was nothing. He spoke instead of what Thremedon would be like this time of year, what plays would be having their runs in the theatres, and how he was friends with one of the airmen in the Dragon Corps—none other than the Chief Sergeant himself. It all seemed rather like a dream, and indeed I must have drifted off without noticing it, for all at once I was opening my eyes to the sound of birds chirping outside.

The first thing I understood was that I was alone; there was no other warmth curled against me in my small bed.

I jerked awake all at once. Something was wrong, but for the first few reeling seconds of consciousness, I couldn't remember *what*.

Then, I remembered everything all at once. Today I was leaving for the city—Royston had been with me before I'd fallen asleep; he'd asked me to go—but he was beside me no longer, and all at once I couldn't tell if what had passed the night before had indeed been no more than a dream. I could remember, only in bits and pieces, what it had been like in the night with Royston beside me, the anxieties that plagued me waking me and his warmth at my back. At one point—if I could be certain that I hadn't dreamed it all—I'd even turned to press up against him, one arm around his shoulders. He'd let me.

My cheeks were too hot and I was frozen in place—not just because of the cold—staring with unthinking misery at the rumpled sheets drawn clumsily but unmistakably around me.

So Royston *had* been with me last night, and before he'd left, he'd seen fit to cover me.

We'd spent the night together. I'd slept with Royston by my side, a thrilling and awful realization at once. What if I'd kicked him in my sleep, or elbowed him in the stomach? What if I'd snored, or mumbled while dreaming? And where had he gone, leaving me here alone?

There was no clock in my little room. I didn't know what time it was, if I had overslept or imagined everything. For all I knew, Royston was gone already.

I was beginning to doubt myself for a complete raving madman when there were two short knocks against the door.

That was our signal.

My hands froze, and I couldn't help but wonder if perhaps I hadn't imagined the whole thing after all.

A moment later my suspicions were dispelled. "Are you decent?" Royston's voice called through the doorway, and I could have laughed or cried for gladness, however much the question made me blush.

"I am always decent," I replied, feeling somewhat impish in my relief. Though that wasn't entirely true—a few of the buttons on my shirt had come undone—and I was in the middle of fixing them when the door swung open and Royston stepped inside.

Royston stood there, expression inscrutable but his eyes impossibly warm. In his left hand he held my best pair of boots, the leather ones that the chatelain had bought for me when it was first decided I'd be staying at Nevers to teach Alexander and William their basic grammar and histories.

"Those are my boots," I said lamely, pausing mid-button.

"Yes," Royston said, not looking away from me. "They are indeed. You're going to need them, I should think, if you're to leave with me in ten minutes. I've settled it all with my brother; I have miraculously managed to convince him that you deserve a finer education than is available to you here." Without betraying a single emotion, Royston set the boots down just inside the door. "I believe you might also want to change into your weekend finest, though of course once we come to Thremedon I'll have an entirely new wardrobe made for you, should you like it. They're terribly obsessed with fashion there, and I think you'd look very fine in high-collared blue, unless that's gone out while I've been away." He must have seen my bafflement, for after a moment's pause he continued, "Don't worry. It won't be any trouble at all. I shall have to have my tailor make up new clothes for me as well if I want to look presentable. I simply thought that I might bring you along and make a day of it."

"Royston," I began, then snapped to attention at once. "When must I be ready?"

"Ten minutes, if you can," Royston said. "I'll leave you to it." He gave me a private smile before ducking out.

I was ready in six.

CHAPTER EIGHT

THOM

I began to have dreams of flying.

This wasn't so surprising. I'd never been up in the air before Rook manhandled me onto Havemercy, and it was such an incredible thing I didn't wonder at the impression it left upon me. Yet at the same time, in the course of just one night, Rook had managed to throw off my entire balance, ruin all my equilibrium, and send all my assumptions into the sort of tailspin he'd maneuvered at one point over the Cobalt Range. I didn't know what to make of it—or of him.

The most I knew was that I couldn't stop dreaming about it.

I couldn't get the grease out of my hair or the soot out from under my fingernails, and sometimes in the night I startled myself awake by catching the lingering smell of sulfur still clinging to my skin. Naturally, this meant I spent most of my time weary and also useless—for now that the airmen were back in the air, it seemed that the purpose for my presence was obsolete. At any moment I expected to kiss all dreams of a grant from th'Esar good-bye. My one reprieve was, now that all the airmen were doing nightly raids, everything smelled of smoke and ash and grease, so at least Chief Sergeant Adamo wouldn't notice one more man in the Airman who reeked of it.

It was then that the invitation arrived. Or rather, all fifteen of them.

There was one for each of the airmen, and one for me. We were all guests of honor at th'Esar's ball tomorrow evening as a part of the citywide festivities to celebrate our impending victory, which was apparently much closer at hand than anyone had known until now. The few times I'd left the Airman to clear my head, the city had been full of uncertainty, men and women not liking what it meant that the raids had started back up again without warning. Thremedon was too far from the border to see the effects of the war in the city itself, but the people weren't deaf, and those in Miranda especially must have heard the raid siren going off every night. The last thing I'd expected now was a festival. Then again, it would probably do everyone some good, and if the end of the war was truly as close as th'Esar said, then we were all due a little celebration.

It was only that, to my eyes, th'Esar's ball was going to be much more like a performance evaluation than a party. I was reminded that the Dragon Corps was especially required at the ball, in order to show off their newly acquired etiquette and manners.

I thought I was going to be sick when I read this final, personal addendum on my invitation. We hadn't done our exercises in weeks, and there wasn't a man in the lot who had any reason to make anything other than a fool out of me for all the torture I'd put them through. Showing them up in front of one another with those role cards had seemed a brilliant idea at the time, but it certainly hadn't done anything to dispel the animosity between me and Rook. I knew that without Rook's support, I would be completely disgraced in front of everyone. It was quite possible there'd be another international incident.

In short, I was going to be ruined.

Since there was no way around it, I resigned myself to it. When th'Esar himself sent his personal tailor to fit me with suitable attire for the coming festivities, I held out my arms and let my measurements be taken with a sort of mechanical numbness.

And I was still dreaming of being up in the air, the electric friction and the sheer exhilaration of almost dying, the world falling away beneath me, the wild madman's cries Rook let out as he dove toward the ground. It was quite obvious I'd lost my mind.

I didn't see much of Rook himself after that night, for it seemed that he was called out most often despite the arrangement of signing up that Adamo had explained to me one day when we'd found ourselves both in the common room at the same time with no polite way of excusing ourselves. As for Adamo, he continued to display the same peculiar kindness toward me that he had since the war had started back up, and whether it was simply pity rather than an appreciation of my position or skills, I didn't know.

I had a feeling it was the former, but I would still take what I could get.

Curiosity continued to overwhelm me—or perhaps it was simply that I could still smell on my skin the evidence of a city being burnt weeks after the fact. In any case, when next I found myself accompanied in the common room by a noisy game of darts that appeared to have no rules to it whatsoever, I let my interest get the better of me.

"Why is it that Rook goes out so often?" I was combing over my notes in an attempt to gather at least a concise report of what I'd learned in my time here, that I might have *something* to present to th'Esar when he demanded it.

"Well, he's the best, isn't he?" Niall threw his dart, whereupon it stuck deep into the wall. He punched the air, and gave his companions a condescending look. Whatever their target was, I could only assume he'd hit it dead center.

"Well," said Raphael, "and he signs up for all the extra shifts."

"Is he kind of like a madman?" I said without thinking.

Niall only laughed while Compagnon went to the wall, examining the shapes made by the darts with what I thought looked like a compass.

"It doesn't count," he said at last, and Raphael held out his hand as though expecting to be paid.

Niall ignored him. "There're the fourteen of us, yeah? Three a night, if we go out every night, then it depends on what you fly because you've got to balance out your attributes."

Compagnon set to giggling over "attributes." I listened like a student.

"Anything more than that is extra, see? So if the fighting's really bad, and we want a leg up, we'll take the girls in twice

a night," Niall went on. "The extra shifts used to be real necessary when the war was wilder years back and th'Esar didn't
want to give them any kind of a chance to rebuild. And it's a
volunteer system, see, only no one really wants to sign up for
any of *those* shifts unless they're assigned to 'em proper,
since it means that much less sleep, so Adamo used to just put
our names up there; didn't even bother disguising his handwriting, just wrote 'em up there neat as you please."

I nodded, swallowing the urge to polish his speech. With
the ball looming in my mind's eye, I had to be particularly
gracious if I had any hope of earning their sympathy and co-
operation.

"Don't get me wrong," Niall concluded, "because we're all
keen on the flying, else we wouldn't be here, you know? But
Rook's—Rook's built like a dragon himself—more comfortable in the air than he is on the ground, plus he'll blast right
through anyone as tries to get in his way."

"Also," said Compagnon slyly, "he's made of metal, so that
he can go all night long."

Raphael groaned and threatened to stick him with the
compass in what sounded like a not only painful but quite
physically impossible feat.

I wanted to ask how many of them had ever flown with
passengers, but something bid me hold my tongue.

There hadn't—so far as I could see—been any consequences for Rook having taken me up on his dragon. It seemed
odd to think that no one might have noticed, when it had
changed something so surely within me. I felt as though the
information must have been branded across my forehead in a
way entirely different from the ash under my fingernails and
the greasy smell of firesmoke still clinging to my hands and
hair.

More than once after that night I'd dreamed of the fires in
Molly, and woke with my heart pounding to find myself
alone, a shaft of moonlight spilling across the floor of the
Airman's common room.

If Rook had known how I felt about fire, then surely he
would have done it on purpose, but I couldn't see fit to ac-

cuse him of the things that weren't his fault, *especially* as those occurred so few and far between.

I went for a walk that evening to collect my thoughts.

Certainly, when I'd been put to the challenge of rehabilitating th'Esar's Dragon Corps, I hadn't agreed to anything like exile. The city stretched from the door of the Airman, same as it had from the 'Versity, and there was no reason for me to stay locked away like a heroine of fairy tales—though as luck would have it, the airmen would have paid more attention if I'd been possessed of breasts and a skirt—and my obstinacy in this regard was faintly maddening. The more time passed, the less inclined I was to leave the building; now, when I went for a walk, it was simply up and down the halls, being turned about by my surroundings like a rat in a maze.

Some small irrational part of me knew that if I allowed myself to leave now, even for an hour, some sea change— some disastrous rolling of the collective mind—would destroy any work I'd managed to accomplish with these men, and they would go back to being exactly the way they'd always been, as opposed to exactly the way they'd always been with an ever-so-slight variation: the occasional kindnesses they afforded me, by habit or by forgetfulness. My only hope was that slight variations were all the fashion this season, and that th'Esar, while not providing me with a grant, would at least allow me to leave in one piece.

Everything depended on Rook. That was the plain hard truth, and mine was not a comfortable position to be in. While the other airmen seemed to have taken to me with a reasonable tolerance—similar to what one might project toward a neglected family pet—Rook had experienced no such change of mind. In the end he held sway over the others—with perhaps the notable exception of Chief Sergeant Adamo—and I knew that they would follow his lead, both here and at the ball.

In Molly there was a saying that you shouldn't think too hard on the things you *didn't* want to come to pass. It was superstitious nonsense, of course, woven by mothers who didn't wish their children to dwell on negative thoughts, as though by merely contemplating something or someone you could draw it from the ether like a ghost from the darkness.

My luck, however, was a matter entirely different when it came to suspicion, and when Rook stumbled from his room, reeking of acrid smoke and covered in ash, as if he hadn't bothered to shower before he'd rolled off Havemercy and gone right back to sleep, I knew that it had nothing to do with whether I'd been thinking of him or not.

He barely spared me a glance, pale-rimmed eyes bright and awake despite his rumpled appearance.

"I—" I began before I could stop myself, and he halted.

I realized with a fleeting panic that I didn't know what I'd meant to say, that I'd only called out to keep him from ignoring me entirely the way he'd begun to do of late. Normally this would have been a blessing, to be overlooked after months of malevolent attention, but instead I only felt cut off, alone. I thought it must have been the flying, that in him somewhere there was the evidence that had stripped my theories from me as surely as old bark, and I couldn't let it just pass by.

I was certainly losing my mind, then.

"I'm waitin'," Rook said roughly.

"I, ah, I wanted to thank you," I said, taken aback at the words coming out of my own mouth.

Judging by Rook's expression, so was he.

"Don't know what for, unless it's not killing you in your sleep." He smiled then, and I waited for the familiar fear to grip me. It did not. Instead when he looked at me I felt his expression was not unlike my dreams of flying—the faint echo of something elusive and strange.

"For, well, the additional perspective," I answered honestly, recovering myself as best I could. "And for . . . not letting me fall."

"Yeah, well. I didn't do it for you." He shrugged, though whether he was talking about catching my wrist or taking me up into the air in the first place I couldn't guess. His hair looked filthy, almost tan instead of golden, and I wondered how it would be possible for him to be clean by tomorrow night when it had taken me over a week to get to anything near resembling my state before I'd clambered onto that dragon in the first place.

"No," I agreed quickly, for no matter how I'd lost my mind, I was quite aware that nothing Rook did was for my own benefit. "I know that. I only—I didn't know. I mean I suppose I *knew*, but not in the same way as, as when we were flying."

"You mean when *I* was flying," Rook cut in. "*You* were hanging on and screaming like a whore either done *real* wrong or *real* nice."

I drew a deep breath, determined not to allow him to get the better of me so close to this trial set by th'Esar. "I was not," I said, "screaming."

"And you don't know everything about everything, even with that fancy 'Versity education of yours," he went on as though he hadn't heard me at all. "We act different 'cause we *are* different, not because we never had the right nannies come around to teach us all how to play nice and all that shit."

"You're still human," I said quietly. "So I suppose you can act like one."

"Then you'd be supposing dead wrong, professor," he replied, looking down his long nose at me. "Can't be human and fly the dragons. That's just the way it works."

It was the most terrible thing I'd ever heard, and truly maddening if that was what all of them believed. Yet somehow I got the sense that this was a notion particular to Rook, though it didn't make me feel any better. "You *must* be," I insisted, with no real idea of what it was that I was so insistent against. "You're just hiding behind the dragons, using them as . . . as an excuse for whatever reasons you have for wanting to act as though you're completely emotionless. No man is made of metal."

He shook his head, and stepped so close that I could smell the night's raid on him—dragonmetal and the burning strongholds of the Ke-Han. I wondered dizzily if it were possible that this man *was* made of metal. "You don't listen, and I ain't patient, but I'll say it again: It's not an act. In the air I can't be thinking about how I *feel*, much less how my *actions* affect everything going on around me. You go up, you do the job, you come back. Isn't anything other than that, and if you get it confused, you'll die because some other son-of-a was smart enough not to."

"But you can't spend your life on the ground as if you're still in the air," I said, clinging to my faint and crumbling resolve. For one wild moment I thought I could smell something below the fire, anger or something sharper. But scenting such human emotions was a particular skill of the airmen and not one I could have learned through propinquity.

Rook swallowed something back, frowning like it nearly choked him to do it, then turned on his heel. "Shit, professor. And you think *we're* the stubborn ones."

This time I was powerless to stop him as he walked away, my boots planted as though glued to the floor.

"Anyway," he called back over his shoulder, "I got some cleaning up to do. Have you heard? Seems we've been invited to a party—and from the looks of it, we're the Ke-Han-fucking guests of honor!"

He had impeccable aim. Perhaps it came from so long a time spent up in the air, or from his skill at the airmen's complicated and seemingly incomprehensible game of darts, but he managed to hit home each time with his sly words. It was obvious that the airman Rook had my number, that for all my 'Versity schooling we were on uneven ground, and we both knew it instinctively, in the same way cats know to chase mice or hawks to drop down from the sky upon rabbits with deadly accuracy.

I had the distinct sense that the ball was going to be a disaster. I knew my etiquette better than a single one of the airmen—except, perhaps, for Balfour, who'd been raised in high society—yet I wasn't so vital to Volstov's success in the war. And any slip I made, no matter how slight, would be on par with the most egregious of Rook's errors.

Th'Esar had no reason to be so lenient when punishing me as he did when punishing his elite Dragon Corps, scourge of the skies, heroes of the bastion.

I hardly slept at all that night, and spent the day before the evening of the ball trying once again, however futile the endeavor was, to cohere my notes into some semblance of an order. Surely I must have learned something vital in all my time spent sleeping on a couch in the Airman and enduring the cruelest of the corps' insults. Surely I must have in turn imparted some learning of my own. Yet the more I read over my notes, the more I noticed how uninformed I was. If the riders of the Dragon Corps were incapable of understanding the rules of the rest of society, then it was equally true that the rest of society was incapable of understanding the rules of the Dragon Corps. Each was governed by vastly different principles; the motivating factors for behaving politically were like the structure of outlandish foreign grammar to the airmen, and I was at last beginning to understand *why*. Still, it was no excuse for them to behave as pigs to their fellow-men, or for them to treat women as objects to be bartered and discussed like horses, or to look down upon all of Arlemagne for doing their best to stay out of our war. The airmen didn't have to agree with other opinions, and they certainly didn't have to follow other men's rules all that often, but they *did* have to acknowledge that these things existed.

I couldn't imagine what they would do once their services were no longer required.

This was always the trouble with learning, I remembered from my first few courses at the 'Versity. The more you were informed, the less you realized you knew, and the point between grasping new knowledge and abandoning the old was as precarious as straddling a great divide, being torn in both directions and terrified of falling between with neither side to support your theories.

I wished Marius were close by to tell me I was overthinking the issue and should take a deep breath and confront, as simply as possible, all the things I knew. If I were to do him proud, I would gather my results without any preconceptions and allow them to shape their own conclusion. This was the mark of a true scholar, if not a great one.

Yet there was no real time for such intellectual pursuits. Sometime after midday the tailor brought my clothes for their final fitting, and meanwhile all of the Airman was gradually being filled with the sound of new boots being broken in before that evening's dancing. While the tailor adjusted the inseam of my trousers, I managed to catch bits and pieces of a lively story Magoughin was telling about the daughters of the new Arlemagne diplomat—the other one, presumably, had been asked to cool his heels for a while, and was perhaps mending his now-tenuous relationship with his wife. I even caught, tacked on to the end of the story almost as an afterthought, Magoughin's realization that: "Now we've been trained to act like proper gentlemen, though, I don't suppose we can take them back with us afterward and show them a thing or two about Volstov?"

Compagnon's giggling nearly obscured Jeannot's wry reply, which was, as far as I could make it out, "A thing or three, knowing your tastes."

"I'd rather be at Benoite's party if all's said and done," Ghislain admitted, "but I guess a man can't turn down th'Esar when he's invited somewhere, and he's th'Esar anyway, so chances are he'll have the best wine, if not the friendliest ladies."

After that, all was drowned out by a chorus of laughter, whereupon the tailor said I was twisting around too much, and in order to make his job less impossible—and to avoid being stuck in the thigh by any needles—I stopped trying to eavesdrop on their conversation and consigned myself to my thoughts once more.

By the time my suit was finished, the Airman clock had tolled six hours past noon, and the members of the corps were beginning to gather in the common room, each one of them dressed in Volstov's most recognizable uniform.

I myself was wearing the sort of fabric I never had the cause or the money to purchase for myself while I was a student. It was soft and heavy at once, and fit slim where it needed to, rather than bulking up as a less expensive grade would. The collar and lapels of the jacket were wide after the latest fashion, the sleeves long. The tailor had decided that the best color for my eyes and my complexion was a sort of bottle green, and the outfit had even come with handsome, tall leather boots, heavy buckles at the ankles, and stiff white gloves.

It was safe to say, as the airmen came in to wait and laugh and joke with one another, and lounge easily in their finery, that I'd never felt so out of place in my entire life.

I was a plain-looking sort of person—neither ugly nor handsome—and though, as the tailor said, the color of the suit did hint at the green in my eyes, whenever I caught sight of myself in the mirror I felt startled by how different my usual perception of myself was from the present reality. When compared to the airmen, each man striking in his own way, I felt even more ridiculously common, like a little boy from the Mollyedge dressed up but nevertheless revealed for what he really was.

I wasn't one of these men, part of their brotherhood. Never before had I felt so much of an intruder on their comfort, their rituals, their way of life.

I sat on the arm of my couch-bed with my gloves held in my hands, waiting with the rest for our carriages to come, and yet not with the rest at all. When Jeannot came in, he was called over to talk with Ghislain, Ace, and Balfour; likewise, when Niall made his entrance, he was beckoned to the smaller group of Raphael and Compagnon. All the men were dressed in their Dragon Corps uniforms: dark blue jackets and silver buttons, gold epaulettes, slim white trousers, and high black boots. Grouped together, the airmen reminded me of a collection of gems, each one cut differently, but all of them polished so brightly they shone.

The last man to make his arrival was, of course, Rook; it wasn't because I was looking for him that I noticed this detail, but rather the ubiquity of his presence in any room. In that way he was *exactly* like a dragon: mythical, enormous, surreal.

He entered in grand style, kicking the door open and immediately engaging Ivory in some heated discussion about what had been done with Rook's favorite earrings, and how they fucking weren't lying around just so some son-of-a could give them to his lady friend. They were apparently the finest Ke-Han gold, fashioned into Ke-Han loops, and I wondered, not for the first time, at Rook's decision to wear his hair in Ke-Han braids and pierce his ears with demarcations of Ke-Han warrior status, when he was known throughout Ke-Han as a murdering god, capricious, merciless, and cruel.

In the spirit of the evening—and perhaps to match the royal blue of the Dragon Corps jacket—he'd redyed the blue streaks in his golden hair, and his eyes were bright in the candlelight.

There was a moment when I felt as if he were watching me, but all at once there was a commotion from without, then everyone was rushing toward the door.

"That'll be the carriages," Balfour told me, adjusting his white gloves one last time before he, too, followed the crowd.

I soon saw why they were all so quick to scramble for their carriages, for those left behind had no choice in where they sat, and everyone was shoving in every which way like children who didn't want to be left behind. Since I brought up the rear, I was stuck in with Rook and Magoughin—three men to a carriage—with them telling lewd jokes the entire way and occasionally looking over to me with quite pointed expressions, leaving me no need to wonder if they were doing it on purpose.

And then, we arrived at the palace.

It was lit up with countless glittering lights—the spires aglow, no doubt with magic—onion domes the color of the crown, golden and pearl white and midnight blue. It was a scene I'd viewed only distantly over the years from my various rooms along the 'Versity stretch, which was, I realized now, too far away from the palace to do justice to the sight.

I felt all my breath leave me at once. Yet, though I waited for Rook to mock me about my wide-eyed "civ" wonderment, he said nothing at all, although he did shove past me with no more than a grunt as he made his way out of the carriage and onto Palace Walk.

It, too, was alight with the shimmering of countless paper lanterns. They lined the pathway and the narrow flight of stairs up to the palace's main doorway. The whole palace itself, while dark and spindly in the daytime, had taken on new life.

To say I was overwhelmed would be something of an understatement.

The airmen had no reason to wait for me and so they didn't, filtering off ahead in chattering groups of threes and fours. I stood frozen, admiring the colored lights like a common child as the sharp sounds of their new boots against the ground faded off into the distance.

Then it occurred to me that it would be much worse to enter alone than in the wake of the airmen, where I might be able to escape attention entirely, and I moved quickly to catch up.

"Palace Walk ain't for running," Adamo said to me as I came up to him. There was something strange about his face, I thought, and I couldn't place it until I realized that he'd shaved.

"Isn't," I corrected him automatically, and slowed to the leisurely pace the other men were walking at.

He raised his eyebrows at me.

"Ah," I said, beginning to worry at my gloves the way Balfour did. "I'm sorry about that."

He shrugged. "Can't help being the way you are."

I nodded, offering him a shaky smile of truce. It felt uncomfortably as though he were trying to make a point, and I was too nervous to be taught any more lessons by the very men I'd been charged to teach.

Up ahead tinkled a distinctly feminine peal of laughter, and I saw that Rook had been enveloped by a group of fashionably dressed women, their hair curled and pinned, gowns voluminous in gold and cream, as if they'd planned them to match the palace—which in a way I supposed they could have. I didn't pretend to understand the minds of women, or at least *these* women. I knew that if I'd been female, the story of the Arlemagne diplomat's wife would have kept me as far away from hanging off Rook's arm as possible, and I would never have smiled so brightly at him, with teeth like rows of pearls.

Then Rook and his entourage of attractive young ladies disappeared, swallowed up by the light spilling out from the palace, and I was left frowning at the open doors with little reason or understanding.

"He's doing very well," said Adamo. I waited for a moment, to see if anyone else responded. Then, since I was still the only person next to him, I had to assume he was speaking to me.

"I—who?" I asked. "Rook?"

He nodded, finding it perhaps harder than he'd anticipated to hide his amusement without a full beard. "None of those women are even anyone else's wives."

HAL

The city was alive.

That wasn't to say that there were more living things in it than in the country, for all during the carriage ride away from Castle Nevers, Royston waxed enthusiastic about the lack of small winged insects, and sheep, and ducks, and trees, until I was forced to ask—with impossible fondness, and not at all the exasperation I'd aimed for—what it was they *did* have in the city, if not these things.

I should have known better.

My curiosity was rewarded with a sermon that approached the zeal of a man deeply religious or deeply in love; it spanned the length of our ride into Thremedon, transporting me out of our bumping carriage where my elbows jostled against Royston's. (The proper way to ride in a carriage I knew was to sit opposite your companion, but I found after the first mile or so, I was opposed even to this small distance between us, and had wedged myself quite firmly between him and the little window. I shouldn't have demanded so much, but he at least seemed untroubled by it, and was too caught up in speaking about the city to notice how I clung to his every word, or peered out the window like a child each time we turned a new corner.)

He spoke of the Crescents—a district filled entirely with magicians—and the structurally unsound homes they built for beauty and kept aloft with magic. From his descriptions, I constructed in my head some approximation of their long, crooked towers and crabbed iron spires, with staircases that spiraled within as well as without and balconies on the rooftops. Most magicians, he explained, liked to be high up; it made them feel important. He laughed, and I imagined the buildings, crowding in on one another like children huddled together to keep out of the rain. Royston said that the enchantment set in place to hold the houses in the air was older than his grandfather, though the technology was in some ways a precursor to the dragons themselves. It had been the first Esar who'd gathered all the magicians with related Talents to place a lasting magic on the district, so that he would always know exactly where his most powerful magicians were living.

"He likes to have all his chickens in one coop, so to speak," Royston explained, a fleeting stoniness in his eyes and around his mouth. "In case he is ever feeling less than favorably disposed toward them."

I nodded, wishing I hadn't asked in the first place.

Just off from the Crescents was Moon Street, he said, which was a bit of a step down as far as magic went. The people on Moon Street dealt in charms mostly, smaller Talents that could be bought or borrowed for a fee. They weren't true magicians—though their ancestors had been once—but the Well's influence in their blood was long diluted over the years. When Royston first spoke of Moon Street it was clear that he didn't think much of it, but after a time he paused, traced the outline of his mouth with long fingers and beseeched me not to be influenced by his snobbish prejudices.

"Don't worry," I told him. "I've not had that problem yet."

He laughed, and for what I felt was the first time turned away from the window to look at me and not the city. I felt the same as I always did when confronted with his complete attention, frightened and selfish all at once, as though I didn't want it, yet couldn't bear to lose it.

"Hal," he said, "now that we are speeding toward the city with all alacrity, there are some things that may become . . . much simpler, given Thremedon's relative tolerance, and what may or may not be done without igniting the fury of one's own brother and his shrewish wife."

Despite all the rules I'd set down for my own best interests, I felt something excited twist within my stomach. "Oh?" I managed.

All I could see of him then was his stark profile, framed in shadows and by the carriage window, and completely unreadable.

The trouble with Royston was that, for all the words he knew, he so rarely managed to employ them properly. They got in the way of what he wanted to say rather than aiding him. I was left next to him in the carriage, jostled with every bump beneath us, watching his face eagerly for some hint as to his deeper meaning—or rather, for some hint as to what he wanted.

It was as though he didn't know I would gladly offer it. It was as though he didn't know I already had.

"What I mean to say," Royston said, picking his words very carefully, "is that my invitation is not necessarily a shrewd business proposal, in need though I am of an assistant, nor is it solely academic, delighted though I am at the prospect of a student. That is . . ."

I hesitated, then reached out to cover his hand with one of my own. It was difficult to swallow, as though my collar were buttoned too tightly, but now that I had taken Royston's hand with my own I could hardly move, much less do anything so mundane as check the clasps at my throat.

"What you mean to say is that the city is nothing at all like the country," I supplied, nerves making me cheeky, "and more than nomenclature alone separates them so distinctly."

Royston turned to me at that, at last, some measure of amusement and surprise in his eyes.

"Something to that effect," he agreed. "Thremedon requires a certain amount of charades, it is true, but nothing so complicated as the tragicomic scenes we enacted in my brother's house."

I thought of his discomfort in the boathouse, his excuses in the pantry, how well he'd played his part. I thought of how educated he was and how much he had seen in comparison to my limited scope. Royston was a Margrave of the Esar; I had been a tutor to the reluctant, boisterous children of a country estate. There was a great deal for me to feel awkward about and a great deal to separate us, but right then all I could think was that we were heading away from the country, and there was only half a carriage seat's width between us.

A rush of giddiness at what lay before me—before us—flooded me. Royston was just about to say something further, some clarification that would no doubt have been even more convoluted, when I put my hands against the sides of his face and kissed him.

I would have liked for it to be less awkward than the first, when my elbows almost knocked over the cinnamon and I nearly thrust him backward into an open bag of flour. It wasn't. At that very moment the carriage hit a bump and our teeth scraped; our noses banged. I was ready enough to pull away, humiliated and blushing fiercely, just like the first time.

Only then Royston's fingers were in my hair, his palm against my throat.

He was better at this than I was.

I should have felt ashamed, or even more nervous; I should have frozen where I was, for all I'd been thinking about this since I'd tried and failed the first time. Instead, I scrambled forward, clutching at Royston's shoulders against the jostling of the carriage. His left knee knocked against my right.

If this was what Thremedon promised, then I was glad to have left the country, for all my littler fears. How had I failed to know all this time what I'd been stifling, and, in turn, how I'd been stifled?

It took me too long to notice Royston's hand moving from my throat to my shoulder, until I realized all at once with a sudden punch of disappointment that he was encouraging me to stop, or, at least, to pause.

"Hal," he said gently. I let my cheek remain pressed next to his for a few seconds longer before I allowed myself to move away. And still we were much closer than we might have been, so that I was distracted even by the smell of him.

I let out a long, unsteady breath. "Yes?"

"Thremedon's allowances aside," Royston said carefully, "I

would like it very much if we might refrain from . . . rushing into anything. Recently, I have had a great many rushed and ultimately disastrous liaisons, and you . . ." He paused for a moment, to turn his face against my hair; I thought, from the deep breath he drew in, he might have been doing the same as I was—savoring the moment. His words disappointed me but, I found, they did not surprise me. When I thought of the rumors surrounding the Arlemagne prince and Royston's reason for leaving the city in the first place, it wasn't only jealousy I felt, but a deep protectiveness, as though Royston were in some ways my ward. It was little wonder he was so reticent now.

"I see," I said, just as carefully.

"More than that," Royston continued. "Hal, you have never been beyond Nevers, and I am only a small piece of a very large city. There is a great deal more for you to see before you— Before you make any decisions."

It would do no good to protest, or to argue with Royston's meticulous, if somewhat faulty, logic. At present, he was pinching the bridge of his nose as though the headache that had been plaguing him for some time now had returned. This time, however, when I felt the urge to run my fingers against the few gray hairs at his temple, I did.

As my father used to say, you can't ask the summer flowers to bloom in the spring. This would be a different sort of hesitation, and I was willing to wait—long enough, at least, to prove to him that my exodus from the countryside was more about following him than anything else.

"All right," I said.

Royston leaned into the light touch of my fingers at his temple. "Thank you," he replied.

After what seemed like an age—though it was surely my own impatience that made it so—the city rose into view, nestled back against the land as if she were reclining, crowned with proud towers in the Esar's own colors.

There was another building farther off, built in the same style as the palace but with many more towers, and the swirling domes that topped them seemed to come alive, shimmering in the sunlight.

Royston rested a hand against my shoulder, leaning over to look out the window as well.

"That's the Basquiat," he said, and his voice held a low note of wonder that I'd scarcely heard before.

I'd never considered myself a jealous person before, but the look I saw on Royston's face when he spoke of Thremedon was enough to stir something decidedly wistful and selfish inside me.

"Oh," I said only. "Well, it's very nice."

He moved his hand down my shoulder to lace his fingers through mine. I felt reassured, even if I was still nervous.

"It is even nicer," he said, "from up close."

I didn't have the privilege of seeing the Basquiat that day, and on the next the invitation arrived.

There was only one, as the Esar had no reason to know or even care about a country boy barely into manhood, but Royston insisted I accompany him to the tailor's anyway, disappearing during my fitting and returning with triumph flashing in his eyes and a real, embossed invitation on stiff white paper. Even as he handed it to me, he refused to say where or how he'd come into possession of it, but it was the first intimation I had that Royston was a man with considerable power in the city. It wasn't any wonder he'd hated the country *and* his place in it.

High collars, it appeared, hadn't gone out of style during Royston's absence from the city, and mine was clasped against my throat with some strange silver-laced thread.

The moment my clothes were sewn into place, we were hurrying into yet another carriage before I could get a satisfactory answer out of Royston as to what, exactly, I was expected to do at a ball, and what did he mean *dance*?

It was all I could do not to stroke the plush fabric of my jacket when we stepped out together onto the main walk. It led narrowly to the palace, lit on both sides with countless flickering paper lanterns on high black stands. Before us was the palace itself, brighter than the sun; I had to resist the urge to shield my eyes against the sight of it.

I'd thought before that Royston had been going somewhat overboard by spoiling me with such finery, but as we mixed in with the other guests, I saw that I'd been quite mistaken. The truth of the matter was, Royston had actually been rather restrained in recommending solid blues for me.

Royston himself was dressed all in black, with gold detailing over his jacket and in a single stripe down the length of his trousers.

I hesitated when we came to the door, but he took my hand, entwining my gloved fingers with his own.

The main doors of the palace opened directly onto a balcony above the ballroom, which was so enormous that I felt certain it would have fit the entirety of Castle Nevers with room to spare. High tables had been arranged to overlook the floor on a more complicated set of balconies below the entranceway, where the noblesse sat drinking and eating all manner of very tiny foods.

The very best wine, Royston said to me in an undertone as we crossed the room, was made by the Ke-Han, and it was dark and red as blood.

I wondered if it been taken as the spoils of battle, for all I'd heard since I'd arrived in the city was how the war was almost certainly over, and how the Dragon Corps had assured us a swift and total victory. I didn't understand why Royston had been called back at all, if that was the case, but I didn't want to expose my ignorance to the people of the city so immediately. Surely, if they said the war was close to an end—and if the opinion was shared by a man as great as the Esar—then that was the truth of the matter. I couldn't bring myself to ask Royston what his opinion was, but I privately cherished the idea that he might not have to go away to war at all, however foolish that was.

Above the floor, at the very center of the ceiling, hung an enormous, three-tiered chandelier—not unlike an upside-down approximation of Thremedon, made all in crystal and spun gold. Its light illuminated the dancers with perfect clarity, and yet left many shadowy places in the corners where a person might hide.

I lost count of how many times I was introduced to complete strangers as we descended the steps halfway to the second-tier balconies, where the noblesse stood together talking, both men and women hiding their laughter elegantly behind lace fans. There were people staring at us, I realized. Or to be more accurate, they were staring at Royston.

"I didn't think he'd ever come back," a lady to my right whispered to her keen-eyed companion.

"I didn't think he'd ever be *asked* back," said a man dressed all in blue. He wore a mask over one side of his face.

"Never mind the Margrave," murmured the lady next to him. "Have you seen who came in after them? It's Caius Greylace! I'd have sworn up and down that the Esar would have *abdicated his throne* before he asked *him* back to court. And without any grand incident, either!"

"Perhaps it's for our grand victory," the masked man replied, in a tone that revealed he was delighted to show off his knowledge of the proceedings. "The Esar wants this victory to be decisive. That, and he wants it to be as flamboyant as possible."

The lady struck him on the shoulder with her fan, and I felt Royston's hand underneath my elbow, drawing me away from the whispering clutches to make further introductions. I didn't ask if he'd heard the people gossiping. Surely, if he had, then he had his own reasons for ignoring it. If he hadn't, then there was no need to upset him by drawing attention to it.

After that, I had little time to think about it, as I became lost among the sea of faces that Royston propelled me through. He introduced me to everyone, as though I belonged there just the same as they did. Amidst the complicated names of the Margraves and the *velikaia,* my own name seemed to retreat to one of the many small, dark shadows.

I wished very much to be able to follow it.

I knew—despite my valiant efforts to sit still in the elegant, wing-backed chair next to Royston and listen as his friends discussed political matters, the state of the Basquiat, and a

great many other subjects I had no way of understanding—
that I no more belonged here than did a sheep from the country.

Royston pointed out certain people of note as they entered
and were announced, warning me away from some and gossiping about others.

"And those," he said at last, sitting forward somewhat in
his chair, "are the airmen of the Esar's Dragon Corps."

I sat up with interest, curious to see the men who had fea-
tured so often in the romans I'd read that they were almost
like legends themselves.

They were very striking indeed, dressed all in uniform save
for a man in green who stood with them at the rear. He had a
look of forced calm that I knew meant he was in fact fright-
fully uncomfortable, and I felt an immediate kinship with him.
We were in the same dire straits, and I wished there was some
way I could inform him there was at least *some* company for
his suffering.

The airmen filtered through the crowd like royal-blue water, dispersing like rain through the cracks of pavement,
though they weren't any the less noticeable while separated
than when they were together. Every now and then I would
catch sight of a gold epaulette or a dark blue jacket moving
through the crowd—the chandelier light glinting off a silver
button—and I knew who it must be before I even turned my
head to get a closer look at him.

There was one who was especially striking. He wore his
blue-streaked golden hair braided and loose around his face.
When the corps split up, the crowd surrounding that particular airman seemed largely female, and the man in green was
left standing alone.

"The man in green," a pale woman murmured to her escort. "Who do you suppose *he* is?"

"Not one of their escorts, I'm sure," the man replied, with
an expression that made me rather uncomfortable.

"I assume it's the poor soul the Esar assigned to nanny
them," Royston replied, stifling a yawn with one hand. "Don't
you think? He looks very much like a 'Versity student."

"I can't imagine why he's been invited," said another woman at our table. She fanned herself wearily, though I saw her crane her neck to follow the movements of the poor man in green. "He seems rather . . . young, don't you agree?"

"Well," said the first woman, "it wasn't a *real* punishment, was it?"

Everyone dissolved into laughter, even Royston, who chuckled politely for a moment, then returned to watching the man in green with a keener interest than the rest.

I took my leave to visit the bathroom sometime later on, when various members of the Basquiat and Royston started in on a discussion about the war. No one else seemed to think it strange, their having won so abruptly when as far as I knew the raids had only just begun again. Once or twice Royston frowned, as though he didn't entirely like the direction the conversation was taking, but since he was quite capable of turning the tides of an entire discussion on his own, I didn't think he would miss me. I could be brave in the kind of way that got me through a fancy city ball, I thought, and I could be brave in a way that allowed me to accept the eventuality of Royston going away to war—if indeed it lasted that long—but I could *not* be the two kinds of brave at once.

As soon as I'd resigned myself to this, my newest problem was trying to avoid becoming hopelessly lost once I'd left the ballroom. It was not as difficult as I'd feared, as there seemed to be many servants scattered throughout the halls for specifically this purpose. That they didn't seem all that keen on speaking to me was only a small detail, but I was nevertheless very grateful when I finally opened the correct door.

"Oh," said someone, who was quite unexpectedly seated on the marble counter into which the porcelain washing-sink was inlaid.

It was the man in green.

"I'm sorry," I said as he slid to the floor, smoothing the creases in his trousers. "I didn't realize there was anyone, ah, using the room."

"Oh," he said again, straightening up at once. "Well, you see,

I'm— I'm not so much using the room as I am hiding. In the room."

This seemed to me a perfectly reasonable thing to do, as it had been my plan exactly. He was braver than I, however, for being able to reveal his motives freely.

"I think that may also be why I'm here," I admitted. "I'm glad to see I've come to the right place."

His smile indicated he'd been starved for basic kindness for a very long time, and my heart went out to him immediately. From what little I'd heard about the Dragon Corps—and if he was indeed the 'Versity student who'd been set to the task of rehabilitating them for proper society—then his life couldn't have been very easy of late. And now he found himself here, in this terrifying place, as foreign as if it weren't the center of our own Volstov capital. I didn't envy him his position.

"I haven't been here long," he said cautiously, as if he expected to be caught out and ridiculed at any moment. "In fact, I was just leaving—"

"You needn't, not on my account," I assured him. "I think it may be much more preferable to hide in the bathroom *with* someone than by myself. On my own it has a . . . more desperate air. Don't you agree?"

He laughed hesitantly, but when he'd finished laughing the smile remained in his eyes, lighting up his entire face. "Yes," he agreed at length. "I suppose it does. Do you mind my asking—it may be presumptuous of me—but your accent seems to indicate—"

"I'm from county Nevers," I told him. In truth, I was glad to have the secret out. It was so obvious from the moment I opened my mouth that I might as well have been wearing a sign pronouncing my country origins to the entire room.

"I thought so," the man in green admitted. "There's a certain— That is, one of my professors was a specialist in the dialects."

"Was he?" I asked. "What did you study with him?"

"The provinces, mostly, and the regional influences of the old Ramanthe," the man in green replied, a dreamy expression on his face. "We barely touched upon Nevers—it's unorthodox teaching to go so far as the river—but in any case, this is probably all overwhelmingly dull for you, isn't it?"

It wasn't, and I let him know it in no uncertain terms. "I've always wanted to study at the 'Versity," I added, almost shyly. It wasn't a dream I shared with many, but the man in green, I felt, would understand this desire. "I'm too old now, of course, but— Was there *really* a class like that?"

"Countless classes," the man in green replied. "Marius— Marius is my thesis advisor—often had to chastise me about spreading myself too thin by signing up for too many of them."

"Of course you did," I replied. "Attending the 'Versity is the only chance you'll get to learn such things."

"Exactly," the man in green said. There was a momentary silence between us—not entirely uncomfortable—and then a sudden flush of embarrassment came over him. "I'm sorry," he said, "I haven't introduced myself. I'm Thom. I'm here with the, ah, corps. Their reputation precedes them."

"I'm Hal," I replied. "It's rather a relief to meet you."

"You're here with Mar— The Margrave," Thom said quickly. There was a new blush on his cheeks, but I had to confess I was at a loss as to *why*. "Margrave . . . Royston. Yes, Margrave Royston. I saw you at his table."

It was my turn to blush. "Yes," I said. "He— You know, I'm sure, the—"

"The circumstances for his sojourn in the countryside?" Thom supplied for me kindly.

"Yes," I confirmed. "Well. I *was* to be the tutor at Castle Nevers."

"And now you're not."

"Yes," I said. "Exactly that."

Thom leaned back against the marble wall, toying idly with his collar. It made me feel much better about the stiffness at my own throat, and I took this as my chance to loosen the clasp there somewhat and breathe deeply and properly for the first time in what felt like years. "It's been a dramatic year," Thom said at last. "Hasn't it?"

"It seems it has," I replied. "I'm not entirely . . . up on my Thremedon gossip, however."

"My friend," Thom informed me, "I believe you are in the midst of that about which everyone is gossiping."

"I'm not sure that's preferable," I confided.

"No," he agreed. "Nor am I."

"Are you the instructor to the Dragon Corps?" I began.

Thom nodded. "I have some manner or other of a title, at this point," he said. "But all it means is that I'm supposed to teach the Dragon Corps to be respectful of others and to refrain from harassing every woman they meet, whether she's a common Nellie or a diplomat's wife. I admit that it's a thankless job."

I couldn't help myself, and asked impulsively, "But have you seen them? The dragons?"

Something strange and unrecognizable passed over Thom's face; it made him look rather more mysterious, darkening his eyes to the color of twin bruises. Rather than intimating some divine secret about the Dragon Corps, however, he simply said, "Yes. Once. Not *very* close, though."

"Ah," I said. "That was . . . rude of me, wasn't it? I'm sorry. I'm from Nevers, and—"

"Bastion," Thom swore wearily. "Goodness, *please* don't apologize. You're the first person who's actually talked to me—I mean really talked to me, rather than cursed at me or told me I had a giant blue handprint on my face or beetles still in my hair—in months. It seems more like years, to be honest with you. I'm grateful for it."

I paused for a moment to consider this, and found I had to loosen my high, tight collar a second time. "Is it really that awful?" I asked companionably. "I'm sorry. I'd no idea it could be that bad. After all, I've only ever read about the Dragon Corps. Naturally," I added, blushing again, "since I've been in Thremedon no more than two days."

"It's an experience," Thom said dryly. "One I'm sure I'll be grateful to have had one day in the very, *very* distant future, once I have fully recovered from all this experiencing."

We laughed together for a moment, a more friendly sound than the sparkling, tittering noises the noblesse made behind their lacy fans.

"Surely it isn't all bad," I said presumptuously. "I even thought perhaps— But, no, that's rather stupid of me. And silly."

"What?" Thom inquired, suddenly curious.

"Never mind," I insisted. "It really is unfounded. I don't know what I could possibly have been thinking to bring it up."

"Come," Thom encouraged, "let's try to be honest with each other, shall we? I'm in need of some honesty. What was it you were going to say?"

I struggled for a moment with the right way to phrase what I had in mind. At last, I formed my tentative words with the utmost care, certain that this *was* presuming too much familiarity. "I only thought—from the way he was looking at you—the man in blue, with the braids—I only *thought* you might have been particular friends—"

Thom's expression closed itself off to me at once, and I knew I'd committed a fatal blunder in our tentative acquaintanceship. "Why," he said, voice a little too hard; I thought for a moment he might even have been on the verge of laughter, but it was a dreadful laugh that stifled itself in his throat, and one which made my stomach feel ice-cold. "Why would you even think that?"

I felt awful. I didn't know what it was that I'd said that had so offended him. If I'd known which way to turn once I made my escape, I would have fled the bathroom then and there, but it was necessary I right my own wrong and patch up the damage as best as I could. "I'm so sorry," I assured him. "Perhaps I was mistaken? I only *thought* I saw . . . but of course I didn't. Do you have . . . particular trouble with him? Was that why he was watching you?"

There was a long and awkward silence, bristling unpleasantly between us. "Has he put you up to this?" Thom asked at last. "I wouldn't blame you; he's quite intimidating, and if he caught you while you were on your way here . . ."

I realized at once that whatever Thom had been put through during his time with the Dragon Corps, it was beyond my ability to imagine. The man with the gold-and-blue braids certainly made a striking impression; the intensity I'd mistakenly thought of as collegiality might have been something much more sinister. I wondered if there was something—anything—I could do for Thom, but we were no more than strangers exchanging our personal social ineptitudes in the bathroom of the Esar's palace. We didn't know each other at all beyond the barest of details and a kinship born of mutual anxiety.

I was a complete idiot.

"I haven't spoken to him at all," I said, hoping he'd believe me. "I'm not any good at lying—you can ask Royston, if you'd like. He'll tell you just how awful at it I really am."

"That won't be necessary," Thom said, his expression softening only somewhat. "You really— You really thought you saw him, as you say, looking at me?"

Perhaps it would have been better to lie about it, to assuage his worries, but as I'd already told him, I was dreadful at lying and he would have seen through my attempts immediately. "I must have been mistaken. I've never—"

"Please," Thom said, voice polite but clipped, "don't feel the need to excuse yourself. Whatever you saw or didn't see, it doesn't really matter, does it? Doubtless he has something planned, and was keeping an eye on me to ensure his—*Bastion!* If you'll excuse me, I really must be—Good-bye."

Before I could apologize for my mistake, he'd left the room, the bathroom door closing loudly behind him. I winced at the sound it made, the echoes through the marble room, and sank back against one of the countless, floor-length mirrors. I began to realize just how naive I was, and to understand that I was no longer in the country, where a look meant nothing more than the obvious.

My first palace offense, I thought wretchedly, and I wished it had been someone who better deserved it.

ROOK

All night long I was surrounded by ladies and their perfumes and their polished nails and their powdered breasts, some of them looking good enough to eat, decked out in their finest and all of them tripping over one another to dance with me. But I was too busy thinking about something else, against all better instincts and *real* stupid, and the more I thought about it the angrier I got—especially seeing as how about fifteen minutes after we all arrived the crazy professor disappeared, and nobody seemed to notice he was missing. My guess was that he'd been called to report on us, or maybe he'd gone to drown himself in the bathroom before he had to admit to th'Esar that he had no idea in the world what in bastion's name he was doing. Either way, there was no reason to torture him by being rude on purpose to the women surrounding me like sharks scenting blood in the water if he wasn't there to see it and sweat about it, even if they were the reason I lost sight of him in the first place. After that business with Have, I was bursting with an excuse to give him trouble. Without him around to witness everyone seeing how he'd failed, I wasn't even in the mood to find some poor bastard's brand-new wife and get her dancing in front of all the noblesse in all their gossiping finery.

When the dancing finally started up for real about an hour later, I saw him again. He was one of the only people wearing green—blue being in fashion these days and all because of our uniforms, despite th'Esar's colors being red—and so it was easy to spot him through the crowd, even though he stuck to the shadows.

And there I was with my ideas of revenge banging around, and the women pressing close to me asking me to sign their cards for more dances than I'd signed away to the lady before. Even though I liked dancing—and I *did* like it, not in the same way court dandies liked it for its stiff formality, but because when the music got wild, the women got breathless—I wasn't in the mood.

It was because of what Have'd said about me and the professor being like two peas in a pod. I wasn't forgetting *that* anytime soon.

It was this nagging sensation that'd chased me around ever since we'd gone up in the air together, like the tail end of a dream I could only half remember and needed the whole of for my own peace of mind. I guess it had something to do with how I really shouldn't've taken the professor along with me for a raid, how what me and Have did was private between the two of us, and how I couldn't fly a night afterward without thinking of him cursing like a gutter whore right in my ear, and me whooping up a storm and burning the Ke-Han as they scattered across the desert in the night. But most of all, I couldn't forget Have's reaction to him. She didn't have any loyalty to anyone but me. But then I'd never gone riding with anyone else alongside neither. Whatever it was I'd done— whatever my role in this horseshit was—I didn't like it. And I knew who was going to pay for it, too, soon as I knew right where he was and I knew that he could see *me*.

My whole evening was just spent waiting for a chance to embarrass him.

But you couldn't explain something like that to a lady, especially not the ravenous sort who frequented these balls. I figured it was because they'd married noble husbands and had to wait for just such an event to dance—or better—with a real man that they got so desperate. In any case, with the music going and my dance card full, I lost sight of the professor, skulking about in the shadows the way he was, like he knew he didn't belong *here*, neither.

In that way, I guess Have was right. I guess we *were* some kind of the same. The difference was in how we acted about it, and *that* was where I came out on top.

When I looked back he'd disappeared again, and just when I'd got it into my head what I was going to do with the redhead waving her lace handkerchief at me like a welcoming flag, too.

That was it, what sent my blood fizzing nice and warm and got my limbs all loose and hot like they were ready to hit someone or worse. I didn't much care about what the professor did one way or the other, but he'd spent all his time at our bunker loitering around like he thought he was too good to mix in proper with people, and now he was doing it here, too.

Some people didn't have any fucking idea about good manners.

I spun sharp with a pretty brunette who'd been batting her

eyelashes at me since I arrived. She was small enough so I could see right over the top of her head, and right on the dip, there was the thin green silhouette of the professor disappearing behind the fancy curtains. I knew personal-like how th'Esar had rigged those curtains up special to hang over the entrances to the balconies for when his honored guests got a little too hot and bothered for being in the public eye. I also knew, just as personal-like, that this particular brunette was the daughter of one of th'Esar's favorites, some stuffed pigeon from the bastion who kept her trimmed like a cake in a bakery window but wouldn't let anyone inside the shop.

The professor had a kind of talent for hiding, if nothing else. When the music ended I took the brunette round the waist a little tighter even than when we were dancing, and she followed me just like that. We cut easy through the crowd with none of that sidling off to one side that most people did. If you were slow enough to trip up dancing couples, then you didn't deserve to be on the floor at all was my way of thinking, and I weaved in and out a bit, bobbing like it was a real good fight that demanded all my attention. Sometimes navigating the dance floor was pretty close to how it was flying Have.

Then, we were out. Back inside, the musicians kicked into a popular tune that usually made me want to smash someone's head in, so it was just as well.

It was too late at night for the sky to be anything but perfect black, mottled with streaks of starlight here and there, and the filmy gray clouds that meant it'd have been a perfect night for flying.

I could see the professor out of the corner of my eye like a shadow nobody wanted, hiding behind one of the long red curtains. He must've snuck back there when he realized we were heading straight for him, and if he was gonna be no better than a coward, then my revenge was clear as day. It was easier than picking out the Ke-Han towers, and almost as satisfying.

"So," I said. "Magritte."

"Isobel," the brunette corrected me.

"Right," I said. "Isobel."

"It's all right," she whispered, toying with her glove and pressing back against the railing. "They're very similar."

They weren't, and I figured, if anything, that kind of thing would piss the professor off more than anything else. I took one of Isobel-Magritte's tight brown ringlets in one hand, curling it around a finger, but she didn't look up at me, just kept toying with her glove like it was the most fascinating thing she'd ever seen. I hated it when women did that, but liked it a little, too. They did it on purpose, but only the right kind of lady could pull it off.

I could feel the professor watching me, green eyes burning disapproval into the back of my neck, but my hide was thicker than Have's metal scales, and, since he was a 'Versity student and all, he should have known that kind of thing wouldn't make one speck of difference with *me*.

Isobel was breathing a little quickly—guess it had to do with her tight bodice and how fast I'd been spinning her out on the floor—and I dropped my hand without any warning, letting it hover above one of the fancy laces holding her bodice up that were in fashion this year, which made taking someone out on one of the balconies at th'Esar's celebrations pretty fucking complicated. By the time you got to anything, people were already gossiping about you behind their fans.

It'd've been even better if I could give the professor some kind of signal—like I knew he was there, like I was doing it all for him, just 'cause I could—but I didn't fancy getting slapped for all my troubles. This would have to do for now, and anyway, I could always let him know later I'd seen him there all along, make the look on his face even sweeter when I finally got to see it.

Isobel-Magritte had already turned her face up toward mine when I started kissing her good and deep and fierce, and I was just getting into it when the curtains shifted and the sound cut us off pretty quick. Stupid Nellie, I thought, and nearly swore, except Isobel-Magritte was scrabbling at me to get away because of her honor being compromised and all, and then the professor must have realized his game was up and decided to cut his losses before I knifed him for a spy.

Once all the smoke had cleared, and Isobel had cleared off for good, I was even angrier than before. My plan had all but backfired, except for the wary look in the professor's eyes and the flush on his cheeks, and I wasn't in the mood for taking any prisoners. I'd get even with him now or throw him over the fucking railing, no two ways about it.

"Couldn't take the show?" I asked, undoing the top button on my collar.

The professor took a step away from me, disgust and something else mingling in his expression, and I guessed I could count that, at least, as a triumph that night. There was something in his eyes that I recognized—I guess it was kind of a look you got to be familiar with, growing up in Molly where you had to be stubborn and fierce just so no one took the idea that they could fleece you. It didn't look at all strange on his face, either, and suddenly what Have had been talking about hit me but hard. The little snot was a Mollyrat, same as me, defensive as he was about doing things right and knowing all them curse words besides. I had him figured out. He looked so prim and proper, I wanted to smack the 'Versity out of him, only he was too stubborn for *that*, too. Just as quick as I'd figured him out, my plans for revenge changed.

"You're disgusting," he said. "Do you realize who she is? *And* she's barely of age!"

I shrugged, dangling my arms over the edge of the railing, all the while keeping a close watch. I was ready for him. He wasn't so smart as all that, and I was going to be the one to show him just how stupid he was.

"Figured you'd be hiding away and pissing yourself in the bathroom or something," I said.

"I tried that," he admitted bitterly, stiffening. "But I was . . . interrupted."

I knew there was some kind of an insult in there somewhere, and I knew it was for me, but I was already too caught up and angry over everything that had already happened to go getting mad over something else altogether. Instead, I laughed, because the way he said it was just so offended. *Interrupted*: like it was another one of his fiddly rules of etiquette. Maybe he should've hung up a sign that read, "Please refrain from using the bathrooms in which the fucking crazies are hiding."

I was surprised he hadn't tried to tack on a whole extra course in fancy court learning before we'd all gone rushing out the door, but then I remembered what I'd figured out—that he was an urchin from the Mollyedge, probably no better than a Mollyrat and no better than *me*, and didn't know any better than us even if he'd wanted to.

All the balconies overlooked th'Esar's gardens, probably because it got the ladies all wet to stand outside in the moonlight with the smell of climbing jasmine in the air. Bastion, it'd almost worked for me until the professor interrupted things with that way he had of twisting everything around no matter where he was or what he was doing.

I leaned closer to him, mainly because I liked the twitchy look he got at the corner of his eye that meant he was trying to watch me and trying not to *look* like he was watching me all at the same time. It only made him look jittery as a rabbit, or worse, like he couldn't make up his fucking mind. I just stretched my arms, letting him know I was comfortable as anything and perfectly happy to stay there all night until he had some kind of a fit right then and there and in front of me, even though deep down, I was bristling with fire.

Predictably, it was him who cracked first.

"I'd have thought," he said, voice clipped and cool, like he obviously thought he could fool me into thinking he was the same, "that *my* presence here wouldn't have stopped you from pursuing your *acquaintance*. Magritte, I believe it was? Or was that Isobel?"

"Magritte or Isobel," I said, "I didn't think you pillow-biters noticed that sort of thing."

He looked at me then, eyes green even in the dark and spitting-mad, like he wanted to hit me but was too smart to go through with it. Whatever I'd got into my head just now concerning the professor hit me real sweet and real deep, the way a particular drop did a number on my belly when I was riding Havemercy, but I wasn't averse to hitting him back—and harder.

Being a Mollyrat, he was too smart to hit someone bigger than he was, and better at fighting to boot. Dirty fucking sneak—just like the rest of them.

"Wrong, huh?" I guessed. "You must have had your eye on one of them, then." I wasn't getting right in his face, just reminding him that I could. "Which was it then? The blonde? 'Cause she screams like you wouldn't believe, only it's the dark one's got this trick she does with her tongue, like—"

"Don't," he said, eyes bright, jaw as hard as he could make it. "Spare me the sordid details. No one cares as much as you think."

"As much as I think? *Here's* what I think." I changed tack swift as if he'd flicked a switch, pushing forward like you had to in a raid 'cause once you'd touched off from the ground there wasn't no going back. "I think you don't have any idea who I'm talking about, that I could name them all and you *still* wouldn't know, because you weren't looking at a one of *them* no matter how much tit they were showing."

"I'd be surprised if *you* could name one of them, either," he said, "considering your embarrassing display earlier."

"She didn't seem to mind," I pointed out. The whole thing reminded me a little of that first night when I'd put him to the wall. The professor got like a wildcat when he was cornered, and it wasn't like I'd forgot the fact but more like I had to remember it a bit every time it happened. "Why, do *you*?"

"Actually," the professor faltered, "I think that this whole little performance was for my benefit, that you didn't care one way or another about being with that girl. You only cared about my seeing it and what my reaction would be."

Something sparked in his eyes like metal scraping metal.

"Do you?" I asked, soft and dangerous.

I leaned in close and his face changed, disgust and confusion and fear in his eyes. His lips parted halfway like he was going to protest or scream or something, and I felt a hot spike of victory hit me low in the belly.

It was better than a dive.

Swift as changing direction to find the right current, I knew exactly how I was going to play this one out. He was no different from anybody else I knew, and, given enough time, *everyone* saw reason.

"What kind of a brainless fucking idiot would say something like that?" I snapped. "You think you're so smart, better than every man-fucking-jack of us, but I can see right through you. A Mollyrat's always a Mollyrat, no matter *how* far he runs."

His eyes flew open again, as though whatever he'd been expecting, it definitely hadn't been *that*. I smiled, 'cause I had him now exactly where I wanted him, and for all his cleverness I didn't think he'd figured it out yet.

"Yeah," I said, like I'd been planning on it all along. Let him wonder how long I'd known his little secret, 'cause the look on his face told me I was right, no matter what he said after. "That's right. You're *that* fucking easy for me to read. Don't think all of them in there wouldn't know it if I let it slip, that it would be so hard to fucking believe with the way you walk, all nervous and small. You stink of it."

"I don't care if they know," he began.

I grinned, too certain now to stop. "Liar," I said, rolling the word fat and sweet off my tongue.

It caught him by surprise, and for a moment his mouth was as weak and soft as a woman's. Then, he must have remembered who I was—where he was—and his jaw hardened, chin tilting up in useless, stupid defiance.

"So what if I am," he snapped right back, that suicide streak in him showing itself, and not for the first time. It was a miracle he survived Molly, acting so proud as all that. "You're a 'rat yourself."

"And I'm an *airman*," I said, feeling dangerous. "What medals do you have? What lives have *you* saved? Speaking fifteen useless languages and being able to argue your way out of a paper bag—real fucking special."

His cheeks were bright red now and his eyes sparking bright, like I'd lit up a fire inside him. "Well, we can't all be upstanding citizens and heroes like *you*. Some of us weren't so lucky."

"Lucky?" I laughed at that, sharp and barking, and he

drew back again; maybe he thought I was going to hit him, or maybe the sound was just so fucking awful he thought I already had. Didn't matter to me either way, so long as he was knocked down a peg or fifteen by someone who could make sure he *stayed* down. No one else had volunteered for the job, and I was only too glad to take it on.

"You get to do whatever you want," the professor returned, shaking, but holding his ground. "You think you're above the common laws of courtesy—*decency*—basic humanity. You take what you want and don't think about anyone else—and it isn't that you're stupid, either. You're like every other Mollyrat who never bothered to learn beyond the gutters. You think that because your mother raised you in the streets, you can live by their rules—"

That was when I grabbed him by the collar and threw him up against the railing. His lower back hit against it and his breath whistled sharp between his teeth, and then we stared at each other for a long time, that same metallic scraping and flashing passed between us.

"We're not so different as you think," he said finally, just like Have. It was like he had some kind of death wish.

"If you believe that," I said, showing all my teeth, "then you're stupider than you look. If you thought I was watching you and putting on a show for you—maybe you were right. But you'd better keep just as close an eye on me," I added, tightening my grip at his throat, "if you know what's good for you."

"You're no more than a common bully," he whispered, voice trembling. I'd shaken him for good now, and it was deeper than just the physical side, my knuckles bruising his throat and his back aching for all his so-called defiance.

"I don't care what I am, so long as you're afraid of me," I said, and dropped him neat as that.

He really *was* that easy, that touchy about where he came from. Seeing as how he was no more than a stuck-up fucking 'Versity boy, I should've picked up on it sooner; maybe I could've spared us all the trouble of having him teach us how to channel our emotions good and proper.

The one thing I *could* say for him was how long he lasted—but then again, being from Molly, it wasn't any wonder he was a tenacious little bastard. People from Molly tended to hold on good and long and hard to whatever it was they had, seeing as how quick it tended to get snatched away from them once they were down past the Mollyedge, where everything was free game to them as could take it fast enough.

I took a handful of his hair right at the back of his neck and tugged his head back. Tilted up toward mine, his face was hard, like maybe I'd pushed him too far, but I could see something still struggling in his mouth, bitter and desperate like surrender.

"Yeah," I said finally, when I could be sure he was listening. "I thought so."

Then I turned on my heel and left him there without any warning, sagged against the balcony and limp as a forgotten pair of gloves. I needed some time to think about what had just happened, and what in bastion's name I was going to even *do* about it.

CHAPTER NINE

ROYSTON

According to Adamo, we really *were* winning the war, and while I was grateful for my reprieve from country life, the facts didn't exactly add up. There was a bad taste in my mouth about the entire business, and it wasn't just the bloodless, bodiless white wine that seemed to have come back into fashion during my absence from the court.

"Disgusting, isn't it," Adamo said. "Like drinking some horse's piss."

"I can't be sure if your comparison is *entirely* apt," I replied as we clinked our long-stemmed flute glasses together in a toast to our similar tastes, "but I'll take your word for it."

"Whoreson," Adamo said fondly. "It was a turn of phrase."

"Oh, yes, of *course* it was," I said.

Together we downed our horse piss in one great go, but I still had no better bearings on what the Esar thought he was doing. If we were winning the war, then there was no reason for him to have called me back to court because I was needed on the front. It was possible that he wanted all his forces for the last great victory, but then why was the entire city engulfed in celebration over a war we hadn't yet *exactly* won? His behavior was even more baffling than usual, and I sensed some smoke screen to the entire display. The Esar himself was conspicuous by his absence for most of the night, but that in and of itself wasn't entirely unusual, as he usually left it to the Esarina, who was very fond of fine parties, to devote her full attention toward them.

There were other faces, too—ones that I was expecting to see, a few I was expecting to have to suffer stultifying conversation with—that, though I was grateful not to be afflicted with their presence, made me more uncomfortable in their absence than the awful wine we were being served.

Something was happening this night, something very private, and as far as I could tell it pointed very much against our guaranteed victory.

For example: Both Margraves of th'Incalnion were missing. And as they were of the oldest magician blood in all of Volstov, venerated scholars in their own right and never the sort to miss a party, I was immediately suspicious. As I began to catalog the list of those missing—Barebone of Barrowright Abbey, Wildgrave Marshall from the Valence, and *velikaia* Antoinette were the most noticeable; I don't believe I'd ever been to a party of the Esar's at which any one of them was not in attendance, much less all of them absent the same night—I felt more and more uncomfortable. There was always the likelihood that Antoinette, at least, had left early as she always did. It was a possibility, however slight, that some of them had found other parties more agreeable, but it didn't seem likely. Not all of them at once. There was something being kept from all of us, and the Esar seemed to feel that, if he put on a grand enough show, we'd be too busy drinking, dancing, gossiping, and listening to the music—not to mention watching in rapt fascination our friends and enemies disappear in odd couplings onto the balconies—that we'd none of us realize what was really happening.

"Don't you think there's something a little strange about all this?" I asked Adamo, turning down the truffles as they passed me by.

"What, like how we're here and all but setting off fireworks, and nobody's *actually* handed the head of the Ke-Han warlord over to th'Esar yet?" Adamo asked.

I was grateful for his straightforward manner. "Exactly."

"Or maybe your being recalled like we're all in desperate need of you," Adamo added. "And—no offense, your Talent's been real useful, so don't take this any way toward being personal—but you're not the only one's been recalled, either."

"Yes, I saw Caius," I said. "I never thought he'd be . . .

invited back. Or come back, even if the Esar *paid* him, for that matter."

"And there's Berhane, too," Adamo added.

"Is there *really*?" I asked. "Bastion. Something *is* going on."

"Not necessarily. Th'Esar's the kind of man who likes things finished once and for all, and if the war's heading in that direction, then he could just be calling back all his best and brightest for the final push," Adamo finished. "Stop sending those truffles away."

"My apologies." I paused for a moment, both to think over the information as well as to summon the young man bearing the platter of truffles back to our side. Adamo plucked one off the careful arrangement of powdered sugar and lace and chewed slowly on it. I didn't altogether agree with his logic, though what he said about the Esar made sense. He was that sort of man. "What's your count on who's missing?" I asked at length.

"Fifteen," Adamo said.

"Does that number include Antoinette?"

"Sixteen," Adamo revised. "And I'll tell you another thing, only this is about the Ke-Han. They're not even fighting like they used to."

The musicians started up a cheery waltz and there was a commotion of partners being changed and fans being snapped open to flutter widely in front of flushed bosoms from which most of the powder had been worn off by perspiration. I cast an unhappy look out over the crowd, then turned my full attention back to Adamo. "I don't see how that entirely fits in with our present collection of evidence," I began.

"Most men about to get their tails beat in a game they've been fighting for over a hundred years—a game so important that losing it's going to cost them their lives—don't just give up fighting like all the wind's been knocked out of them," Adamo explained. "No, they fight like dogs. They go for the throat, the belly. They don't just lie down in the sand and call for their mothers."

"I take your point," I replied. "My mistake."

One of the members of the bastion passed too close to us

then for me to be entirely comfortable with his purposes—it would have been my own fault if our conversation were overheard by all and sundry, with us discussing it in the middle of the Esar's own ballroom—and Adamo cleared his throat, showing me he'd been thinking the same thing. This conversation was best left to another time and another place, and when we'd not been drinking so much horse piss, either.

"It's good to see you again," Adamo said. "And looking so healthy. For a while your letters had me thinking I needed to fly in there and pull you out myself."

"As dashing as that would have been," I replied dryly, "I did manage to take care of myself."

"'Course you did," Adamo said, as if he didn't believe me for a single second. "And the new, ah, apprentice you brought with you tonight had nothing to do with it?"

"Bastion," I swore, a little too loud for propriety. "Hal."

"I think he was in the bathroom, last I checked, having a fascinating conversation with Raphael—he's one of mine, flies Natalia—about third-edition gold prints," Adamo told me. "Weirdest damn conversation I've ever been privy to, if you don't mind me saying it."

"Bathroom," I said, then, "thank you," then made my hurried excuses and my equally hurried way to the bathroom, where I found Hal alone—no longer, it would seem, engaged in conversation with the young airman Adamo had mentioned.

"Royston," he said, turning at once. There were mirrors everywhere, allowing me to see him from all angles, and just where the blush began—at the back of his neck—before it suffused most of his face and eclipsed his freckles. "This must look—I mean, I intended to come back, but the whole sink is made of porcelain and marble, then I had a conversation with a member of the Dragon Corps. Did you know that Raphael collects third-edition gold prints?"

"Hal," I said, stepping close to him at once, and taking his hands. "Can you ever forgive me?"

"Why," Hal said. "What are you talking about?"

"It seems that I abandoned you most cruelly to a night spent making idle conversation with frequenters of the bathroom," I explained. "As curious a choice as that may have been for you to make, it was no doubt influenced by my utter selfishness this evening."

"Not at all," Hal said frankly. "You were glad to be back. I didn't wish to intrude, nor did I wish to embarrass you."

"Embarrass me?" I asked, baffled at this unexpected fear of his. "How in bastion's name do you propose you might have done that?"

"There were," Hal admitted, with the faintest ghost of a wry smile, "many times this evening where I have to admit I had no idea what you or your friends were talking about."

"Ah," I said. "Yes. That."

"It's very different here," he said softly. "I know that you love it. I want to love it, too—"

"The things most worth loving take their time in giving you reason," I told him. "I did abandon you tonight. There were matters weighing heavily on my mind, but this is no excuse."

"I didn't mind," said Hal, squeezing my hands with such intractable good nature that I felt it in my chest. "I met more than one or two interesting people."

"Did you," I said. "Interesting people at a ball? You've been much more fortunate than most."

"You're very strange." Hal did smile then, and it was a true smile, as true as all the ones I'd seen in the country. "You talk of your friends as if you don't care, but I know that you missed them."

"I am a cold and distant man," I answered, full of contrition.

Still, I couldn't help but be pleased that he'd noticed. Oftentimes I found that only the men I'd known longest, the ones who remained in my life throughout the years, were the ones who saw immediately to the heart of my strange deception.

Perhaps it was only my own foolish stubbornness, obligating me to conceal what it was I felt when I felt it. Hal had been the exception and not the rule in this regard.

"You aren't," he said, and he truly did seem happy, for all

I'd left him to the tender mercies of total strangers while I satisfied both my curiosity and my insistent craving for the city life. Then he leaned up and pressed his mouth to my cheek, chaste and warm.

He was abiding by the rules I'd set down for us much better than I had wanted him to, I thought treasonously. I held him close for a moment, until a stir of voices passed the bathroom door and I was forced to weigh my desires against the potential consequences of putting Hal at the center of the storming gossip of which I knew the noblesse were so very capable. Reluctantly we separated, though I wasn't quite quick enough to thwart my own urge to smooth the fringe from his eyes.

"Are you quite ready to leave the bathroom now?" I asked. "Or have you developed a rapport with your own reflection?"

"Strange," he said again fondly, then turned away to examine his hair in the many mirrors. I felt a small pang of guilt, as it was a concern I'd never seen him exhibit before.

"You look fine," I reassured him. "Better than fine, even. Luminous. Radiant."

He laughed, exiting the room ahead of me, but I saw the flush of color at the back of his neck, and I knew that, for all my foolishness, at least the words hadn't been in vain.

There were more people in the halls, and seemingly fewer in the grand ballroom than there had been at the height of the night's festivities. Of course, not everyone was for dancing, and once the requisite grace period had been observed—to show respect for the Esar and his particular brand of pomp and circumstance—it was generally considered acceptable to take your leave.

So perhaps it was only my suspicious nature, or perhaps I'd only been too long removed from the city to remember the subtle particulars of concealment and subterfuge, but everywhere I looked it seemed as though there was some great mystery happening just beneath the glass. The guests stood sequestered in groups of twos and threes, speaking at volumes no louder than a whisper. Every now and then someone would laugh, high and uncomfortable, or the loose, throaty guffaw of the very drunk. I pitied whoever that might have been, for they were sure to have the most thankless of headaches in the morning. Indeed, my own head was starting to feel too large, my skull too tight in a way that I'd unhappily come to recognize. I attributed it to the stress of my return and my tenuous situation with Hal, but it didn't make the aching any easier to bear.

What allowed me to nurture my suspicions instead of quashing them outright were the many faces I recognized and even respected. Marius of the Basquiat was there, and speaking to Berhane, whose presence alone would have surprised me if Adamo hadn't told me himself she'd been recalled. That she would have anything to say to Marius could bode nothing but ill.

"Hal," I said, feeling guilty even as I said it, "would you excuse me for one more moment?"

"They might be at Arnaud's party," Berhane was saying, in cold and brittle tones. "Or they might be elsewhere entirely. All in all I think it's dreadfully rude of you to ask me when you *know* I've only just got back. And when you didn't even bother to write!"

Marius had the bewildered and miserable look of a man caught without an umbrella in an unexpected downpour. "I *did* write," he said, then, noticing my approach he added, "Anyway, now is hardly an appropriate time, Berhane."

"Hello, Marius," I said cheerfully. "I'm not interrupting anything, am I?"

"Not at all!" Berhane answered. "I was just leaving."

"That's a dreadful shame," I said, "since I haven't yet had the honor of welcoming you back to our fair city."

She paused in thought at that, smoothing her immaculate hairstyle with one idle hand. "Well," she said, her tone softening. "I've heard I wasn't the only one recalled."

"Indeed not." I took her hand to kiss it, thinking about how best to fish for knowledge of what my colleagues thought of the Esar's ball and whether any of them found it as strange as I did. "I've heard that the Esar wants all his very *finest* for the battle to come, so it stands only to reason."

Berhane fluttered a fan in front of her smile and Marius made a noise of disgust.

"Oh come now, Royston, don't tell me this doesn't all seem a little . . . off to you," he said.

I shook my head, still holding Berhane's hand. I'd discovered that the secret to getting any information out of Marius was to go through Berhane first. I'd have felt a little guiltier over it if it hadn't been so apparent that she enjoyed the charade as much as I did. "I saw the young man you've been mentoring, Marius," I said. "He looked rather green around the gills if you don't mind my saying."

"He's had it somewhat rougher than you have," Marius replied dryly. "All things considered."

"Oh, come now, arguing when the gossip is so good? Royston, *Caius* was here just a moment ago!" Berhane confessed, leaning close that I might hear her whisper. "But he was called away by one of the Esar's dreadful, smirking servants. He can't have done anything so soon. I wonder if he's to be given an official pardon."

I felt my suspicions worsen, and for all Berhane's tone was light, her eyes were sharp and unhappy. She had her suspicions the same as I did.

Marius shook his head. He looked as though he wanted to hang the pair of us, but I didn't know for which offense. "Has your sojourn from the city caused the both of you to forget how easily one can be overheard here? Never mind it now. If there *is* something to discover, we can trust we'll discover it soon enough."

"Ever the teacher." I sighed. "It was good to see you, Berhane."

"Royston." Marius's voice caught me just as I'd begun to turn away. Berhane had dropped the act just as I had, and together we were three very grim magicians with nothing but our suspicions to hold us together. "The Wildgrave was here for about five minutes at the beginning of the ball. He excused himself from our table very quickly. Said he had some blasted fever."

"When I arrived, I saw him arguing with Caius," added Berhane. "And the pair of them disappeared down one of those awful corridors the Esar had built."

I nodded, not entirely certain what to do with the information now that I'd been given it. Wildgrave Marshall was the eldest son of one of the most distinguished magician's houses. As far as I knew, he had never been involved in any suspicious activities before. And it seemed as though Caius Greylace was appearing and disappearing as convenienced him throughout the ball, although that in and of itself wasn't exactly unusual.

"If we discover anything," Marius said, shaking my hand, "we'll let you know."

I rejoined Hal with much apology, and immediately explained my charade with Berhane to the half-baffled, half-hurt expression on his face. I even took his hand as we made our exit from the palace, too tired to pretend I didn't want what I did and in want of comfort at that particular moment.

"Are you all right?" Hal pulled me from my reverie and I returned with a jolt as if from underwater.

"Yes," I said, pulling my gaze away from Caius and a pale girl with blue hair by the door. "Yes, I'm fine."

"You only looked very far off," Hal said. "Like the way the chatelain used to say I did when I was thinking of a story I'd read earlier and where might be the best place for finishing it."

"I was merely trying to remember the names of some of the more important people at our table," I confessed, and felt all the better about the small deception when his face lit up as surely as one of the glowing lanterns lining the Palace Walk.

I felt an irrational wish for more time to speak with Adamo, and in private, where the long fingers of the bastion mightn't still reach us. My old friend was refreshingly straightforward, and such secretive matters fairly overwhelmed my appetite for delicacy. For court intrigue and rumors of the war, I would take nothing but honesty from both barrels, and be all the gladder for it. Adamo understood what few men did, and he managed it somehow while never quite turning into one of the near monstrosities some of his airmen had.

"I met the man charged with rehabilitating the Dragon Corps," Hal said, and I got the uncomfortable sense he'd said something just before it, that I'd missed a piece of his conversation while lost in my own private thoughts. "The one they were talking about. Is it true he's just a student from the 'Versity?"

"I believe so," I said, adding Marius to the list of people I would have to speak to shortly. Knowing Marius, I would have to bribe him to get him to admit whether he knew anything. Perhaps I would go through Berhane. "What was he like? Interesting?"

"He was," said Hal. "Only, I think I said something wrong, and he got quite strange and left in a rush."

"Oh, I wouldn't worry about that," I said, trying not to seem as distracted as I felt. "After what I've heard from the Chief Sergeant, I should think he 'got quite strange' all on his own."

The music seemed too loud, and the chandelier too bright when we reentered the ballroom. Now that I'd begun to dwell on it, the party seemed little more than a façade. I didn't know what it was the Esar was so keen on keeping under wraps, but I *did* know that he was underestimating the vast majority of my peers if he thought they wouldn't notice.

The problem was that I'd always been a little too interested in things that weren't any of my concern. And, punishment or no, that was a habit I found hard to overcome.

THOM

I'd taken leave of my senses. That was the only possible explanation. The Dragon Corps had damaged my mind so thoroughly that I hadn't even noticed they'd done it until Rook had cornered me at th'Esar's ball.

And I'd let him.

I'd more than let him. I'd encouraged it. I'd descended to his level.

I would no longer remember this night as the night I wore the finest clothes I'd ever owned, or the night I'd been invited to a ball—a real ball—at the palace, but rather as the night I'd thrown away all my careful restraint and let Rook get under my skin exactly the way I'd promised myself he wouldn't.

I was meant to be better than this; I knew better, I'd been taught better. I could either think myself better educated than Rook and follow up that assumption with my actions, or I could resort to brawling with him at every turn like a common Mollyrat. Which, as he'd so astutely discovered, I was.

I held no illusions as to the truth of what Rook had told me about the piercing obviousness of my roots and where I'd come from. Much as I hated him, I couldn't deny the simple fact that he was cleverer than most and could probably be quite sharp about keeping a secret when he thought it would benefit him. I couldn't say the same for many of the other airmen, and I knew that if my birthright really was common knowledge, I'd have heard it in more than a few taunts already. It was simply too good to pass up—a jumped-up urchin from Molly trying to teach anyone about anything. The worst of it was that there were no notes I could refer to for this, no piece of wisdom from Marius that would help me to clear my head so that I might get back on track.

The problem was simply that I didn't even know what track I was trying to find my way back to.

After Rook had left, I'd had to take a long moment to collect myself, breathing in the cold night air and waiting for the chill to pull me back to reality. I waited there until I could stand without the help of the rail, until the throbbing in my back had receded to something manageable, no longer a constant, heated reminder of how foolish I'd been. I'd thought I might run into Hal in the bathrooms when I ended up there again, but they'd been empty when I returned, which was probably for the best as I'd have only owed him an apology and I wasn't feeling much for words.

It was then that th'Esar himself summoned me.

I was waylaid in the bathrooms—that my whereabouts was so easily discovered unsettled and unnerved me almost as much as what had passed a few moments before on the balcony overlooking the gardens—by one of his servants.

"His Majesty wishes to confer with you," the messenger said, bowing low and all but tugging his forelock. He was obviously at a loss for what title, if any, he should employ when addressing me. I had as little idea as he for, of the two of us, it was quite clear to me *he'd* had the better breeding. Then again, as Rook had made perfectly clear, it wasn't hard to be a better-bred man than I was.

"Ah," I said, trying to gather my wits about me. "Yes. I shall . . . follow?"

"There is a more private way," the servant said, still bowing. "If you will mark my lead."

I followed him out into the hall as he walked calmly and unhurriedly past a group of three women talking to one another behind their fans. It hardly helped my composure that they were talking about Rook. I caught the barest threads of their conversation and felt my cheeks grow warm with anger.

It seemed I couldn't escape him, not in dreams of flying or on a balcony at the ball—which was in some part supposed to have been my own small triumph, the perfect way to showcase what I'd accomplished with the airmen. I hadn't heard any gossiping about any major and embarrassing incidents thus far, which would have seemed like its own small miracle were it not for the fact that I knew Rook had been far more occupied with tearing me down on the balcony than starting any trouble.

"Has he gone early?" one asked her closest friend. "Or do you suppose he's found someone?"

"He can't have done," her friend replied, looking as miserable as I felt. "He never decides so quickly!"

"Yes," said a third, who stifled a yawn with her dainty, silk-gloved hand. "I *did* think we had more time."

Only my purpose anchored me as the servant cleared his throat, waiting for me to quicken my step to follow him, when we turned a sudden corner into an unlit hallway which, if pressed, I would have sworn hadn't been there before.

"Come quickly," the servant said, most politely.

I doubled my pace.

Here, the palace was almost deathly silent; it seemed that even the air possessed the same stultifying reverence as one found in a mausoleum or tomb. It was quite the contrast to the ceaseless noises of the ballroom, where the rustle of silks and taffetas, lowered voices and whispered gossip built to almost the same crescendo as the music. Even the countless flickering magic-lights had their own certain noise—a relentless, ceaseless thrumming, a music all their own—but here in the shadowy darkness of the hidden hallway, the only sounds that disturbed the absolute silence were my footsteps.

The servant's footsteps made no sound at all.

I began to feel as if I'd entered into some secret world, one gravely different from my own. The change may even have occurred before Rook cornered me on the balcony, and I was too distracted by my own reckless temper and his taunting words to notice it.

The servant led me through the twisting halls, taking sharp turn after sharp turn, until I realized that the majority of our path was a complicated ruse designed to confuse me so completely I'd never be able to find my way in this direction again, even on pain of death.

The walls loomed narrow and tight at either side, and at times I had the slight impression that I was being led in a downward direction—countered only at times by having the slight impression of being led upward again. Occasionally I could discern certain shapes around me: the frames of paintings or heavy tapestries, a doorway, or what might have been a very old mirror. Yet as soon as I could make out what they were meant to be I'd already moved on.

At last, when I was disoriented and weary, the footman halted, turned neatly on his eerily silent heel, and bowed with a flourish to his left.

Where no doorway had been before—and this time I was all but certain—a delicate door swung inward.

"We are on time, I believe," the servant said.

Not wanting to know what sort of punishment lay in store for making th'Esar wait, I stepped into the hidden room.

It was larger inside than I'd expected, the walls surrounding a long meeting table. At the end of the table I recognized th'Esar, who was seated and drinking dark wine from an exquisitely delicate goblet. Next to him stood a woman I vaguely recognized—all I could know for certain was that she wasn't th'Esarina—and she, too, was drinking from a similar goblet, or at least holding it in one hand, while with the other she traced the rim round and round in deep thought. She was naturally very dark, with a sharp nose, and the makeup around her eyes and on her mouth was darker still, looking almost as black as her hair in the strange light of the room. If called upon to do so, I would have guessed she was a member of the old Ramanthe nobility; the structure of her face was nearly unmistakable. It reminded me of a portrait I had seen in my textbooks, of the *velikaia* Antoinette, who had been the previous Esar's choice of bride for his son before it had been discovered that she hid a quiet Talent. The text went on to say that a marriage between the Volstovic nobility and that of the lingering Ramanthines would have been enormously prosperous, but unfortunately the plans had fallen through.

She bent down to say something private to th'Esar, and a black curl of hair slipped free of its complicated twist, resting softly against her sharp, bare shoulder.

Then they both turned and looked directly at me.

"Ah," th'Esar said, beckoning me closer. "We have the Dragon Corps to discuss."

I'd seen th'Esar before, but in the company of so many of his entourage that he was barely recognizable on his own. It was a foolish remnant of my childhood in Molly, but I was surprised all the same to discover that he was no more than a man—and a weary one at that, if those were more than simple shadows marring his face. He had a strong chin, and salt streaks in his red hair, and his face was powerful, if not entirely handsome.

I bowed at once.

"No need for that," he said, waving his hand. "It's been a long night. Full of dancing, mm? Dismissed," he added to the woman beside him, who set her goblet down on the table, curtsied once—more for my sake, I thought, than for formality—and disappeared through one of many little doors set all along the walls.

It was without a doubt the strangest room in which I'd ever found myself.

"We called you here to discuss your progress with the corps," he said, and motioned for me to sit. By his leave, I did so; I was grateful for the permission, since my legs were shaking. "We find you've done an acceptable job, since there have been no diplomatic complaints yet this night, and we have had to placate no other men on the loss of their wives."

This was because Rook had been too preoccupied with exacting whatever punishment he thought necessary on me to go after any married woman. Should I have been grateful for *that,* as well? I didn't think so and, what's more, I wasn't about to point out that fact to th'Esar.

"Thank you, Your Majesty," I deferred instead. "I am most pleased to have served you adequately."

"Your services may be further needed in rehabilitating them," th'Esar continued, "once the war is over, and they find themselves . . . at loose ends."

I bowed my head lower and said nothing at all.

"You will of course be thanked amply and suitably for your work and service to the crown," th'Esar concluded. "We will have a man gather your notes. Perhaps we will forward your theories for publication, just as we were inspired to fund your participation in the matter." He paused to let the full weight of this praise sink in; I murmured my commoner's thanks without quite listening to a word I was saying, feeling riven by how little able I was to appreciate the promotion. I'd succeeded. I was to be funded in writing my own book. Whether it was the book I wished to write or something else entirely didn't matter. After I was finished writing it, I would be a scholar of fame and repute, and could pursue my own studies in whatever direction caught my fancy. It wouldn't matter then where I'd come from. I would have everything I'd ever striven toward. And that was surely more important.

And yet I was utterly incapable of feeling any kind of pride at this achievement. I knew why—I could chase the numbness right back to its source—and I kept my head very low indeed, so that th'Esar would not sense from me even a moment of ingratitude.

Rook was a poison.

I could not stop thinking of him and my defeat, even now, at the precise moment of my triumph. Additionally, I had the nagging notion at the back of my mind that if I were to follow proper channels, those notes should be going to Adamo, that the Chief Sergeant was the one who would then be reporting to th'Esar. Yet I could do no more than wonder why th'Esar would have asked me to breach this protocol.

"Yet let me ask you one more thing," th'Esar added unexpectedly, and I found myself looking up before I could help myself. "Since you have, no doubt, grown very close to our Dragon Corps these past weeks."

I nodded, swallowing dryly. "Indeed," I murmured, though it was a dreadful lie. "Indeed, I have."

"Have you noticed anything . . . odd, of late? About their behavior?"

I shook my head. "I'm afraid I don't quite understand the question," I began.

Th'Esar waved his hand again, the simplest of motions striking me mute. "No," he said. "Think carefully. This is a matter of utmost importance, and my query is one I must ask you to repeat to no one—on pain of execution, mind." He let *that* sink in for a few moments. "Tell me, and consider thoroughly: Have the airmen said anything to intimate that there is something—no matter how small—amiss about the way that our war is being won?"

Even if there had been, I wouldn't be the man to ask. I searched desperately for something to tell th'Esar, my supreme ruler and a man who balanced my life in his hand easily as he balanced his goblet, but all I could come up with was what it had been like to feel Have between my legs, or the way my stomach flew into my throat as we dove. I thought about the fierce, scuffling fights that had started up in the common room at all hours, some of them silent and over just as quickly as they'd begun, and some of them with Ghislain taking even odds and Magoughin jeering each party with equal delight. I had no idea if there was something amiss now that hadn't been before. Their behavior was idiosyncratic at best, and even if they did have more serious concerns, I knew that they wouldn't speak to me of all people about them.

"I see that you are uncertain," th'Esar said, relieving me of any need to respond. "That is all right, of course. You are no airman yourself. But perhaps you might do us another service."

I could do nothing but accept. "Your Majesty," I said, and bowed yet another time in my chair. "I will do anything you ask of me. I am your servant in this as in all matters."

At least I hadn't forgotten my most basic etiquette.

Th'Esar smiled thinly. "If you would be our eyes and ears in the Airman," he said, each word separate and distinct to give them full weight and bearing, "then I would find some way to reward you further."

I understood his meaning all at once. I had no loyalty to the Dragon Corps; I was no member, no airman, no brother in arms. I'd suffered certain indescribable injustices at their hands, and surely each time I'd craved just such a revenge as this to be mine. Hadn't I?

Above all, I was in no position to deny th'Esar what he wished. No one was—not even th'Esarina.

Yet neither was I in the position to be his spy among a group of men who barely even trusted me as it was, a group of men whose ringleader had pinned me into place like a collector might pin a butterfly. It was obvious which of us was fully in charge in this matter. I could no more spy on Rook than I could ignore him.

"You will do this task for us," th'Esar said. "I will expect your reports among those on the progress of the corps' new manners. Your service is invaluable; you are dismissed."

I made my way out of the room in a daze, bowing obsequiously and disgusting even myself. The servant was waiting for me at the door, and I was led backward through the tangled maze of hallways and darkness until we arrived once again in the real world, where the party was still in full flush. When I turned to thank the servant for his guidance, I found he'd already disappeared behind me and I was left once more alone.

I saw Rook in the center of the dance floor, twirling a flushed young blonde, but though I watched him, I couldn't get th'Esar or his impossible task out of my mind.

I set back for the Airman before the party was over and spent the remainder of the night on my couch, waiting for the sound of an air-raid siren—but, of course, everyone was at the palace, and the silence remained unbroken even until the first dawnlight.

CHAPTER TEN

❦

HAL

Things were different in Royston's home from the way they were at the palace—for which I thought I might be eternally grateful. When I was in his collection of magician's rooms, overlooking the entire city and swaying with the tower on its precarious foundations, I felt as at home as I ever had in Nevers, if not more so. From time to time I was gripped by sudden fear that the city would swallow us up, tower and all, but this was only my lack of experience, and I felt certain I'd soon enough grow past it. Royston had apologized for the unpleasantness at the ball—and indeed, he seemed rather less distracted—and the "day of recovery," as he called it, was a quiet one. We spent it alone, in private. I enjoyed it very much.

There were times when I still felt raw and thwarted over the rules that Royston had set into place for us, his infuriating stubbornness in doing what he thought was fitting, but he still allowed me to take his hand, and to rub at his temples whenever he got one of his now-frequent headaches. It wasn't so bad as all that. I knew I could be patient enough to prove to him what I needed to prove—and then the waiting would not seem so interminable as all that.

"I thought perhaps," Royston said that evening, "that we might see about enrolling you in a few classes at the 'Versity."

He was reading some letter that had come for him earlier, the importance of which he'd protested was completely negligible, but I saw the way he read it and couldn't help my curiosity.

As far as distractions went, however, Royston was quite the master.

"But I've no primary education at all," I protested, almost forgetting the letter completely. Royston seemed to have done the same; it lay folded by his cup of after-dinner coffee as if it were no more than a napkin.

"Nonsense," Royston said. "You're quite intelligent. I wouldn't have brought you here if I meant to keep you locked away inside this tower like some sort of maiden of old."

"Well," I said carefully. "But it seems— The expense—"

"No matter," Royston said. "I'm a wealthy man, unless I failed to impress that upon you earlier with my displays of foolish extravagance. And their purpose *was* to impress you, by the by. I thought I'd succeeded with the carriage."

"Four white horses," I said, toying unhappily with my spoon. "Yes, I was aware—"

"But something disturbs you." Royston's tone immediately grew serious, and I saw the creases along his brow deepen. "What is it?"

I struggled to find the proper words to express my concerns without seeming ungrateful. "I *would* like to attend the 'Versity," I said. "Very much, in fact. I never thought it would even be a possibility. But the cost *is* something. I wouldn't wish to take your money, any more than I already have—which has been too much, despite what you may think. I would feel . . . uncomfortable, knowing that you'd spent so much on me, without my having any way to repay you—"

"Your education would be an investment," Royston began reasonably. "It would be payment in itself to see your mind put to the tasks for which it was meant."

"If I attend the 'Versity," I said firmly, and with no room for argument, "then I will do so on my own chevronet."

Royston was silent for a moment. I saw him soften, and at last he said, "We use tournois primarily. In the city."

I flushed to the tips of my ears. I'd known that, of course, but old country habits died hard. "I thought perhaps I might offer myself as a tutor," I said. I'd been thinking it over since I scrambled into the carriage with him, and I thought it the most viable of my options. "Not children so old as Alexander or even William. Surely there are preparatory schools? Before the primary education? I might even act as an assistant. It wouldn't entirely pay handsomely, but at least I wouldn't be a burden."

"Whatever you do or do not choose to do," Royston told me sharply, "do not ever call yourself a burden, Hal."

I was blushing again. I hadn't meant to imply that, either. "No," I promised. "I won't. I'm very sorry. But I *would* feel it, Royston, if I simply did nothing."

Royston was silent again, mulling this over, stirring the coffee in his cup. I nearly dropped my spoon at one point, and so gave up my fidgeting. It was a disagreement between us—as close to any sort of argument as we'd ever come— and I felt miserable for it. But above all I couldn't allow him to spend money so heedlessly on me when I had nothing to offer him in return except myself if I ever managed to overcome his stubbornness, and I didn't wish for that to feel like any sort of common *exchange* between us.

"No," Royston said at length. "You are right. Of course you are. I've been distracted; I haven't been thinking clearly."

I stood then, and went over to sit on the floor at his side as I'd done countless times before when he was spinning his stories. "You haven't," I said. "Tell me what's been troubling you."

"In truth, I should not," Royston said. He paused, though, and I could see him waver on the edge of sharing it with me.

I pressed on, however recklessly. "I know the chances of my being able to help you with it are very slim," I said, "for I know little about the intrigues of the city. But perhaps I might be able to help even by listening. I'd be glad to," I added, letting my palm rest against his knee for a moment before I thought the better of it and let it fall. He dropped his hand to my hair and sighed.

"I don't believe the war is about to end," he replied carefully. "In fact, I think that we are all—very efficiently, mind you that—being lied to, but for what purpose I cannot divine. And the thought that something important is being kept from even those with reason to know it . . . I admit that it's driving me to distraction just thinking about it."

I let this information sink in. Despite Royston's assurances to the contrary, I couldn't help but feel my own ignorance when it came to discussing matters of the city, or its oddly structured politics—much like a tower in the Crescents, as far as I could see, in that there was no way of telling how it stayed up from the outside. "You don't have any idea as to what it might be about?" I said at last. Royston was the cleverest person I knew, and I found I couldn't quite wrap my head around the concept that there was anything he didn't understand.

He hesitated, then I felt his fingers begin to stroke my hair a little, as though he were in deep thought. I tried not to let the motion distract me too much, though I liked the small reassurance that these moments gave me. Some days, it was very hard to remember what Royston had told me in the carriage, and even harder when he hadn't *told* me outright. When he touched my hair, or placed a hand against my back to guide me up the stairs, it became easier to believe that I hadn't imagined all sorts of implications which hadn't really been there. Royston *did* care for me.

"I don't have any idea," he said at last, sounding as frustrated as I'd ever heard him. "There have only been . . . anomalies, of a sort."

"Oh yes?" I asked, and looked at him encouragingly. For all his brilliance, Royston was often a man who needed to be led like a horse by a carrot if you wanted him to finish his thoughts out loud rather than retreat back into his own mind.

He cast a glance at me and smiled just slightly in the very left corner of his mouth, as though he knew exactly what I was doing. "Only the paranoia of the rich and powerful, I'm afraid," he said, and I knew he was joking, could see it dancing in the depths of his eyes, warm and brown. "Spend enough time at the palace and everything starts to seem like a conspiracy."

If he really thought that, then there would have been no reason at all for him to behave the way he was, with considerably more distraction than had ever occupied him in the country, no matter his disinterest in sheep and trees alike.

As seemed to be my curse, I couldn't help but wear my thoughts plain as the nose on my face.

"I'm sorry, Hal," he said, fingers still making restless,

nesting motions at the back of my head. "If you are keen on the specifics, it is only that there were fewer faces at the ball than I'd expected to recognize."

"Oh," I said, trying to divine his meaning as he obviously expected me to. "Do you think they're at war, then? Off with the fighting?"

He closed his eyes to think it over, then sighed. "Hal," he said, "forgive me for burdening you with this; it is most unfair of me. But I must confess that the state of the war itself is what troubles me."

I felt a sudden plummeting in my chest. "Why?" I asked, and put an entreating hand once more on his knee. "Have they told you— Do you have to go away already? Was that what was written in the letter?"

"What?" His eyes went to the object in question though he didn't turn his face from mine. "No! Oh, certainly not, Hal. Of course I would have mentioned anything such as that much earlier. I only wonder how close to the end we can truly be if the Esar is so keen on calling back so many of my fellows in relative states of disgrace with the crown. That is what I was discussing with my fellows when I so rudely excused myself from your company in the hall."

"With the blond woman?" I realized my hand was still on his knee, and felt a flush rising in my cheeks when I remembered how jealous I'd been.

"Yes," he said. "And what I can't make out for the life of me is why the Esar would bother if we were just meant to attend fancy parties. Not that I'm not a devotee of fancy parties, by all means; they are infinitely preferable to leaving for war, yet not entirely as pressing a matter, if you catch my meaning."

Still bearing the emotional bruises I'd obtained from my first fancy party, I declined to offer my opinion on the subject.

"Most people do seem to think the war's quite over," I said, after a moment. It was the first time I'd said aloud what Royston must also have noticed. I didn't have any particular reason for keeping it to myself, only the unfounded fear that exposing it to the light and air would send it crumbling away as surely as ash.

As far as I could tell, it was the talk all over town: in colorful Bottle Alley, where Royston had taken me so that he could buy "something to reassure him that all of Thremedon hadn't gone mad for horse's piss in his absence," then all along the wide rows of the Shoals, where we'd gone to buy fish for dinner. Little old women with black teeth had even proclaimed it cheerfully, announcing the catch of the day as a special in celebration of Volstov's imminent victory.

So it was silly of me, perhaps, to have held my tongue on the subject as long as I had, as though it were a wish I'd made on a shooting star or something equally childish.

When I saw Royston's face, however, fondness mixed with a kind of deep sadness, I knew why I'd done it; I hadn't wanted to see that look.

"I know it's silly of me to say," I said, quickly, before he could speak again. "Why else would they have called you back if they didn't need you? Of course the war can't be over. I only thought that perhaps, with what everyone's been saying, there might be something else. Something you're missing?"

"Hal," he said, frowning as though he were unhappy with something, though I knew it wasn't me. "I can't say many things for certain at the moment, but one thing I feel as though I must *prepare* you for is that I will still very likely be called away."

I swallowed around something that rose in my throat. "I know that," I told him.

In truth I felt a little at odds with myself, not wanting to require the special treatment Royston often afforded me, and yet still craving the kind of reassurance—unreasonable to ask for, unreasonable to promise—that everything was going to be all right.

I was going to say something more when there was a knock at the downstairs door.

When first I'd come to live in Royston's rooms at the tower, the layout had confused me terribly. There seemed to be staircases with no visible destination, doors without any handles that couldn't possibly lead into new rooms. There was even a bright green trapdoor set into the ceiling, but when I'd asked after it he only mentioned something about the best houses having alternative points of exit and left the matter at that.

My consternation—weighted with the fact that this was in every way still Royston's house—kept me seated and waiting while he stood to answer the knock. I did clamber into his chair, though, watching the firm lines of his back fondly, as I tended to whenever I thought I could steal a look.

"There are people I might speak to," he said in passing. "If you are anxious to find a place as a tutor."

"Yes." I nodded. "I would be very grateful."

He smiled over his shoulder at me—seemingly in no hurry to answer the door—and then all at once a change came over his face, sudden and still as though he'd missed a step in the staircase. I watched his hand around the banister go white at the knuckles, as though he was forced suddenly to hold on very tightly, and I was out of the chair before I could help myself.

"Are you all right?" I was so close that I could hear his breathing, even and deep, the way it only ever was in sleep, or when he was steadying himself before trying to control some more basic human impulse.

It was a long time before he answered, so long that I'd begun to think he hadn't heard me at all. I asked again, near to feeling ill. "Royston? What is it?"

His head snapped up all at once, clearly startled, and he shook it quickly as if to clear it. "I'm sorry," he said, and there was a rough note in his voice that hadn't been there a moment ago. "It's nothing."

I thought it was self-evident that it had indeed been *something,* and I took his hand before I could think better of it. "I'll see who was at the door," I offered, and once I was sure Royston could stand on his own I hurried down the steps.

Whoever had knocked was at the door no longer, but when I closed it again I felt something slippery under my foot, and moved aside to examine it. At the bottom of the landing someone had pushed a square white envelope under the door. It felt expensive, heavy, when I picked it up, with sharp corners and stiff stationery. The handwriting on the front was impeccable and addressed itself to the Margrave Royston.

When I carried the envelope back up the stairs, Royston was sitting at the top. He still didn't look entirely right, and I had the useless, fluttering urge to offer him a cup of tea even though he preferred dark coffee or coax him into the comfortable chair by the fire.

What I did was neither of these things, but instead gave over the letter that had been delivered, then sat too close beside him on the top step.

He looked at me sidelong and I realized what it looked like: that I was trying to read his mail. Then he smiled, and it was something like watching the shadow over his face pass away with the advent of day.

"Thank you," he said, and opened his letter with ruthless precision.

The letter must have been short, as he glanced at it only briefly before crumpling it in his hand. All I could think, against the sudden hammering of my heart, was that it was not paper made for crumpling. It was of very fine quality, much too thick to be of no importance.

We sat in uncomfortable silence there on the stairs, Royston not willing to tell me whatever had been in the letter, and me too cowardly to ask outright, and both of us knowing it was inevitable. In the dull, dark stretch at the back of my mind that perhaps had known what was coming all along, I thought that surely the Esar would be the only man to use such fine stationery. After that realization, it was only a small jump to come to a reasonable conclusion about what exactly had been written there.

There was, after all, only one reason I could think of for the Esar to contact Royston.

As the minutes ticked by, measured by the large grandfather clock in the drawing room, I wrapped a hand around Royston's arm below the elbow. I was still nervous about touching him first, since there was always the chance that he would remember his rules and become stern with me. It had never happened yet, but my anxiety remained all the same.

"Hal," he began, careful and slow, as though I were a nervous horse that needed gentling to avoid being spooked.

"When?" I interrupted, startled by the hardness in my voice.

It must have startled Royston, too, because he refrained from answering, only put his arms close around me and held me tight the way he'd only ever had occasion to do a handful of times before.

I put my head against his shoulder and hated the war.

ROOK

I half expected the professor to have stormed his way back to the 'Versity by the time the ball ended, but to my surprise, when I got back to the Airman, I found him right where he'd always been: sleeping or not sleeping or whatever it was he did on his pathetic little couch.

Jeannot'd told me right before the carriage ride back that the little snot'd met with th'Esar private-like sometime during the night—which Jeannot knew because he was friends with all the oldest servants in the palace. You can't buy the respect old blood can get you some places. From the reports Jeannot and Ghislain had got out of 'em, it was pretty clear that th'Esar wasn't just trying to keep us acting proper, but was also using the professor to get all the information on us he could without us knowing about it. It was pretty fucking clever of both of them, and I only saw it as a shame we hadn't acted up enough to get the professor sacked, though maybe I'd wasted too much of my time with that stunt on the balcony and I doubted he'd be telling anyone about *that* anytime soon, even threatened by th'Esar, seeing as how I had him pinned. The last thing a snot like him wanted was everyone to know he didn't have a pedigree—and besides which, if Isobel-Magritte's father was to find out I'd cornered her so nice and easy on the balcony at th'Esar's own ball, there was no accounting for the shit the professor'd be armpit deep in.

Truth was that, after learning we had a real son-of-a spy in our midst, I hadn't had much mood for sport. I was too angry, and while there are some girls who like that kind of thing just fine, the overwhelming majority tend to call you a pig or worse, and I already had one professor to deal with. I wasn't completely fucking crazy. There are some things you just don't bring down upon yourself twice, and the professor was one of them.

Not because he was anything in particular, mind. Just because he was so fucking annoying.

The carriage ride back everyone was in a mood 'cause we were all wondering what that meeting meant for us, and whether we were going to have to hang the professor out the window the same way we did to new recruits who couldn't keep their stupid mouths shut.

Finally, I said, "I'll take care of it. Don't tell anyone."

"Oh?" Jeannot lifted a brow, sliding back in his seat. "And how are you planning on doing that?"

"I'm thinking," I snapped. "Just keep quiet about it."

It was just me, Jeannot, and Ghislain in the carriage. Jeannot and Ghislain could be out of their minds sometimes and they'd pulled some crazy stunts, but the one good thing about them was that you could always trust them to keep their mouths locked up tighter'n th'Esarina's cunt when it suited their best interests.

We were safe with the information being ours. For now, anyway.

But we had to *do* something, on top of that.

After a while I realized Ghislain was looking at me, which meant he had something to say about it and was waiting to be asked with proper grammar and everything to grace us with his brilliance. Ghislain was more or less that smug, but he was big enough no one could complain about it, and I didn't have the time or patience to be all coy like some Margrave's daughter.

"Spit it out," I said, "or quit looking at me like that."

Ghislain took his time, cracking the knuckles of his left hand and inspecting his nails. "It's you," he said at length, all cryptic and as smug as ever, like he wasn't spouting total horseshit. "You're the one who has to do it."

"Kill him?" I asked. I was only half-joking.

Jeannot snorted and rolled his eyes. "Don't you know anything?" he asked, like he didn't know how dangerous it was to say something that stupid to me. "Why do you think he sticks around?"

"Because he's got shit for brains," I said, but by now I was more than half-interested in what the boys were saying.

"Because he's as stubborn as you are," Jeannot said, and Ghislain nodded in agreement.

"And because he's got shit for brains," I added.

"Look," Jeannot said, leaning across the space between us as the carriage jostled us down the road. "If he was given reason to believe he's got through to you—if he was to think you'd had a change of heart, or perhaps had seen the error of your ways—"

"You can catch more flies with honey than with vinegar," Ghislain said, like some sort of Brother of Regina preaching to his followers. I wanted to punch him in his square jaw, but even I wasn't so stupid. Only thing *that* would've given me was five broken fingers.

"So you're saying I've gotta pretend like all this talk of— seeing the other side of things and opening myself up to my feelings has made a difference in my poor, deluded life," I concluded for them. "And this way, we can control whatever information he thinks he's found to feed th'Esar." An idea was sort of half-forming, and I liked the way it looked from where I sat. I was sick and tired of having some green-as-grass professor, barely out of the 'Versity, lording himself over me. I wasn't letting him spy on us, either, and the thought of seeing him trip all over himself just thinking I'd seen the light suited me just fine.

"You *are* the toughest pupil," Jeannot finished, leaning back again, for all the world as if he wasn't going back to a building infiltrated by an outsider, one of th'Esar's lackeys, a whoreson spy.

I wasn't just going to sit back and eat whatever th'Esar fed us. We were winning his war for him. I could take the professor. I'd taken worse.

"Seems like a plan," I said.

Then we were quiet, and I had the rest of the ride to think about how I was going to handle this.

The way I figured it—and it was sort of like a plan of attack, which occasionally I had the inspiration for—I'd have to keep him guessing, keep him on his toes. Had he changed me or hadn't he? He didn't have to know. If I seemed to be reformed too sudden-like, all the red flags in his head would start waving. I would still keep him scared as a rabbit who's just seen a fox, but I would also start to give some, to play to his sense of duty, his twisted-up morals he'd read out of a book somewhere and fancied himself the keeper of. I'd be some kind of an idiot not to use what Jeannot and Ghislain saw to our advantage, and I wasn't *any* kind of an idiot—no matter how mad I was I hadn't seen it in the first place for myself.

So anyway, when we got back to the compound and saw the professor sleeping, or pretending to sleep, Ghislain gave me one of his unreadable looks, like he was some god on high and whatever it was he was thinking couldn't be figured out by mere mortal men. Then he looked over at the professor and a kind of understanding passed between us, like how he knew what I had in mind and if it kept the professor's mouth shut, then he wasn't going to say a single thing against it.

Good man, Ghislain. Bat-shit bell-cracked, I sometimes thought, or just a hundred times smarter than any of us. But whatever way you cut it, he was still on my side—in a manner of speaking—and that was all that counted.

I closed the door behind me and came up on the professor real slow. This was *my* world now, not the professor's, and I could do whatever I wanted.

That was about the time I figured out he wasn't asleep: when his back stiffened as I came close, and I could all but see his face, eyes wide open and ready for the attack.

"I've been thinking," I said.

That sure as bastion wasn't what the professor was expecting me to say, and I had to clamp down hard as the vise of a dragon's mouth not to grin. I had the professor right in the palm of my hand, like Havemercy's reins.

The professor didn't say anything—not that I figured he would—but I sat down on the edge of the couch right up close to him, slipping off my gloves and easing out of my boots and pretending like I was struggling with what I had to say, when in reality the only thing I was struggling with was not laughing then and there. It was almost the same as acting at one of th'Esar's balls, pretending like I was listening to what my dancing partner was saying while she let me twirl her a little too close in the midst of the crowd, and maybe let me keep one of her handkerchiefs, a prize of a different kind of war.

The professor must've been too on edge to speak or move, and when I cleared my throat he might've jumped straight up into the air if he hadn't been lying down. "Like I said, I've been thinking," I repeated. "About what you said at the ball."

"Oh," the professor said. "What I said. At the ball. I said a lot of things. Most men do when they're feeling, feeling cornered, attacked. We say a lot of things we don't mean—"

"Don't fuck around," I said. "You said it, you meant it. I don't want to play any games. It's too fucking late for that."

"Oh," the professor said again. "I see. Yes. Too late, indeed."

"It's just, the way I see it," I said, swallowing back another laugh, "some of us aren't lucky enough to get to the 'Versity and make fine, *respectable* civs out of themselves. What I've got is flying. Maybe you can't teach me anything. Maybe you're too fucking late."

The professor turned real quick, like he just couldn't stop himself, like he just couldn't help it, and I knew I'd hit him deep and hard and in the place that wondered—same as I did, but only when I wasn't in my right mind—just how different we were. I knew the truth, because I was the one calling all the shots, and if I fed him the right combination of lines, gave him what he wanted, his standards would keep him here, trying to help me. As if I needed to be fucking helped. He was the one who needed help, and maybe after all this was over he could take a good, long look at himself and change *his* mind on a few things.

None of that mattered now, though. What mattered now were his big green eyes staring up at me like I'd just admitted my mother didn't love me enough when I was little, or my drunken Molly father beat me. Or no matter what, deep down, I was scared and alone and just lashing out so no one would see it. I wasn't any of those things, didn't have any memory of my parents and didn't much care, but the one thing that was important here was to keep the professor guessing.

"What are you saying?" he asked, eyes bright in the darkness.

I chewed my lower lip for a little while. I used to be the best grifter on all of Hapenny, before I met Have and put an end to that business, but there are some things you never forget how to do, and conning a man is one of those things.

"Sometimes," I said, "I *do* think about it. What I might've been."

"Oh," the professor said.

He wasn't so brilliant, just saying "oh" all the time and nodding, staring at me like *that* could fix anything.

I let the silence hang all heavy and important between us for a good, long while, then, without any warning, I stood up, leaving my boots behind.

"Doesn't fucking matter now," I said, and left him where he was. I could feel him watching me all the way out.

And that was how it started.

I mean, if you want to get precise, you could really say it started on the balcony; but that was just the beginning, a kind of prelude to the main event. This was when I knew the way to keep the professor guessing and keep his loyalties all mixed up like signals in the dark. It would be by dangling what he wanted so bad in front of his nose, and that was exactly what I did. Most would say that being an airman must've dulled any kindness I ever had in me, but the truth was that by the time I came to sign up for the corps I didn't have any of that kindness left, not even so much as a scrap, and it wasn't as if that sort of horseshit mattered to me, anyway.

I hit him with moments of my "vulnerability" like we hit the Ke-Han with the air raids, though it was more unpredictable than that; the Ke-Han pretty much knew to look to the skies soon as the clouds covered the moon. But with the professor, I had to be a whole lot less easy to anticipate and prepare for.

What really throws people off is if you don't give them any pattern to plan around. People are real routine-based creatures; they like it best when their days have some semblance of familiarity. So when you throw them off the scent like that, mixing it up every time, you get them below the belt no matter what they think they're expecting.

First and foremost, there were a couple of rules, and I made sure he knew them. One: I was gonna come to him, if I came to him at all. He couldn't seek me out or he'd ruin it, get my defenses up and my blood hot, and there'd be no talking to me at all, just silence or the sound of me sharpening my knives. I don't think the professor much liked those knives, since they were a reminder of where we both came from, and soon enough the professor picked up on the fact that if he was going to "get" to me, he'd have to be cagey. That made it pretty hard to go anywhere or meet any of th'Esar's men in case he had something to report, so I had to be sure the professor didn't want to miss a fucking minute of time just being nearby—just in case I *did* have something to say to him, some kind of admission to make, some kind of breakthrough thanks to his guidance.

The professor could sense I was on the verge of something. Then again, the professor was *real* smart.

Two: There was no talking about it. When everyone else was around and the sun was up and we were having a grand old time of it, he had to learn how to keep his eyes to the floor, as that was the only way he wouldn't look straight at me like he was starving for knowledge, for any little bit of information that could explain who I was, and give the game away. This was private business. I was a private man. I wanted him to think I didn't want the other boys to *know* I was questioning who I was.

Three: We weren't friends. We weren't going to be friends. We didn't talk about how our days were and we certainly didn't say good morning or good night to each other. It didn't change anything, just his allegiance to me.

All I was doing was getting his hopes up, but hopes are a dangerous thing in a man, and the professor was too proud for his own good. He wanted to see he'd made a difference, and I was feeding him exactly what he wanted to hear—if only sometimes.

A few days after I'd started, and was just beginning to "open up," I let him think he'd almost lost me again—called him a pillow-biter and a Nellie and worse than the Mary Margrave and everything, until I could see the despair in his eyes like a gray shadow, like ash.

"You're insane," he said.

"Yeah?" I said. "But you keep trying to change me, so what does that fucking say about *you*?"

Mostly this was my neat and simple way of keeping an eye on him, even when I wasn't trapping him in a box of his own making, giving him the idea that maybe this time I'd actually give him a little piece of me that would solve the puzzle and let him in, then snatching it back. I could feel him watching me all the time, careful and measured like he was trying to size me up and measure my actions against what I should be telling him, but he didn't want me to catch him at it. One day he was doing it in front of a couple of the boys, Ivory and Magoughin and Merritt and Luvander, and I lost it with him afterward, just lost it.

"What the fuck do you think you're doing," I snarled, close to his ear, my breath gusting hot back up against my own face. "I don't want you fucking *looking* at me."

He didn't stop, but at least he was smart enough to be more careful about it.

So I guess that took care of the professor for the time being. I saw Balfour worrying after him a couple of times when he caught the professor sneaking out of my room late one night— since after all, *that* was the kind of thing I liked to do, just to keep him on edge all the time, keep him tired and careless, not paying attention to anything else but converting me or whatever it was he thought he was going to do. I guess it upset Balfour something special, seeing as how they were two bleeding hearts and he thought he was losing the one person who actually cared what he had to say. But for all his worrying, Balfour didn't know what I knew, that the professor might've been a rat.

I wasn't too concerned about it.

Other than that, there was the war to think about. Even though we'd been led to believe it would be over in a week, things played out just like I'd figured they might, and pretty much right after the ball, all the magicians that th'Esar'd called back from disreputable exile were deployed quick as that, and the air-raid siren was still ringing out every night so not a man jack of us was getting enough sleep. Most of the time we caught winks during the day, long catnaps I liked to think of them, while at night we kept the Ke-Han busy even as the magicians made their way to the Cobalts, then through 'em, then right up to the front.

Something didn't smell right about it; it smelled like lying. A couple of the boys were thinking the same thing, but our job was to go where we were told when we'd signed our names for the week earlier, so whether we thought something of it or not it didn't seem to make much difference. I signed up for a couple of extra shifts, and it was the funniest thing I'd ever seen, coming back one night to find the professor waiting up for me, holding his own elbows, his knuckles real white.

I wiped some of the soot off my forehead and cocked my head to the side, giving him a look like he was the crazy one, not me.

"Do you know," he said faintly, "you can sometimes *hear* the sound of the explosions, even here? The ground shakes."

It didn't. Or, at least, it never had before, since Thremedon was nestled real cozy against the hillside and the water, miles away from the Cobalts. Most of the fighting since the creation of the dragons took place on the Ke-Han's side of the mountains.

"You're making things up," I said. "It's pretty fucking far away."

He didn't say anything, just sort of rocking in his place for a moment or two, then he surged off the couch all at once, like the tide.

"You're bleeding," he said.

Have'd got me a swish-flick with her wing. Nothing crazy like that'd ever happened before—we knew where the other one was down to the barest hairbreadth of a centimeter—and it'd spooked us both pretty bad. It pissed me off that the professor'd zeroed right in on it, like he knew, or was just a damn good guesser.

Then, because he was out of his right mind and straight into his wrong one, he started dabbing at the cut on my temple with the edge of his sleeve.

I was tired and I was still a little biting mad, but for some reason instead of breaking his jaw I let him do it. It was stupid of him to get so close to me after a fight and I could see he knew it, breathing unsteadily, waiting for me to lash out at him or *bite* him or something.

I figured not doing any of those things would freak him more than actually doing what he expected me to. When he led me over to his couch and went to get me a glass of water I stayed put like a little kid. Fuck, I even drank some of it.

"Was it . . . very rough tonight?" he asked, like he thought I was in the mood for discussing it with him.

"Not particularly," I said, rolling out the tension in my shoulders. I needed a shower pretty bad, but now all of a sudden here we were, sitting and talking like it was afternoon tea. "Ivory almost took it chin-fucking-on, but Have and I got him out. What the fuck do you care about it?"

"You can almost *hear* the explosions from here," he repeated, like it meant something I just wasn't picking up on. He colored, just a little, high on his cheeks. For a moment he even looked kind of familiar, but I couldn't place it. "The couch is going to smell like grease," he said. "There will be no getting it out, no matter how many times it's cleaned."

"You're the one who wanted me to sit down so bad," I pointed out. "I gotta clean up."

"If there's anything I could—" he began, then cut off short, like he thought now was the time to start being coy with me. That was what came of letting him come close even for a second, really. I had him in a bad place, cornered nice and good. "If you want to talk," he finished finally, and winced, because even he must've known how pathetic it sounded.

"Think I've been handling this for a long time on my own, professor," I said. "Don't fucking worry about it."

"I do," the professor replied, almost fiercely.

It was a pretty stupid thing to say, and I wasn't predisposed toward excusing him for any slip-ups anyway, but he had a strange kind of courage, and it made me hesitate, which gave him some kind of idea, I'm sure, about how close we'd grown.

Once that happened, the professor stopped trying to pretend he wasn't over-the-moon distracted after something or other. He didn't break the rules, though, no matter how many times the boys caught him at his notes, muttering to himself or looking after me the morning after a raid, asking me if I wanted breakfast, that sort of thing. The only thing that gave me some kind of amusement was Balfour, whose look of bitter disappointment that the professor had no time for him at all kept me laughing for hours after I saw it.

Then things with Have started to get messy, and I wasn't laughing at anything for a good long while.

It wasn't anything big at first, just the little things, like the first time when her wing had grazed my head. Only it didn't stop there, like it should've. Have and I were the best because we flew like one being, metal and magic, flesh and blood, without a heart between us. Some days, when it all went right, I could barely tell who it was that did the flying, her or me. It wasn't that the line was blurred; there was no fucking line at all. But that was before.

Like I said, it wasn't anything big. Leastways it wasn't so big that I could mention it to any of the others. I'd tried sneaking it into a question about something else to Ace, Thoushalt being the closest thing to Have in all the world, but he'd only given me a strange look with those sleepy eyes of his, like he didn't have a clue what I was on about and could he shower now?

So it was only me, then, or whatever was off wasn't so much that the others'd noticed yet. I wasn't any kind of egomaniac, despite what certain people and professors chose to believe. And even if I was the best, I knew that if there was something wrong—really wrong—with our girls, then there wouldn't have been a man of us not up in arms about it. I might've told myself it was all in my imagination even, only it wasn't, 'cause Have was real enough and things on her weren't working like they used to. We were flying like separate creatures, Havemercy and me, with no regard for where anyone put their hand or their tail. The scrape with her wing was the first, but it sure as shit wasn't the last, and when I gave her trouble for it, she seemed real surprised and 'bout as concerned as something that can't feel concern could be. She wasn't even talking like she had before, only the muck-headed Handlers didn't notice it, said I was making shit up or gone mad with signing up for too many raids.

One of them even tried to say it was my *fault* for signing up for so many raids, and that Have was probably just out of sorts on account of being overworked.

I broke his jaw.

I thought for sure that'd get me in some kind of trouble with Adamo, but even our grand Chief Sergeant seemed distracted like he'd never been before, spending all his time locked up in command like some real war general and us too distracting or not good enough to strategize with him. 'Course I knew it wasn't that, and that Adamo had been real good to me when he did hear about the fight, didn't put me on tight rations or nothing.

Instead of making it better, though, it just pissed me off even more. Nothing was acting like it was damn well supposed to.

With all that anger in my head it might have been a good idea to stay away from the professor for a spell, but I got the uncomfortable feeling that he'd start following me around like some kind of dog that didn't have another home if I stayed away too long.

Then he started hanging around me anyway, not anything like the rest of the guys did on downtime, but more like a real persistent shadow in the back of my head, reading in the back of the room or writing his notes down or even just eating his lunch while I was eating my breakfast.

With things going on with Have the way they were, and me coming back scratched or cut up or something most nights, it was like he'd forgot the rules. He was cleverer about it than he could've been, but not near as clever as he thought he was, like he thought he could look at me just because I had a bandage on my fucking face.

I didn't much care whether he was doing it on purpose or not, only it seemed worse if he wasn't, 'cause just what kind of a weak-willed son-of-a didn't even do the things he wanted to on purpose?

If he wanted someone to follow around, I told him one night when it'd especially worn on me seeing him there, calm as you please, then he could go and get himself some kind of a Cindy boyfriend. He got quiet after that—only the professor was always quiet lately—just clamped right down on his tongue and didn't let anything past that didn't force itself free.

I could almost see him questioning himself after that, and I swallowed my pride for a moment.

"Tired," I ground out.

"Oh, of course," he said, like that made all the difference. "They're riding you very hard these days, aren't they?"

It was like he thought he was getting everything he wanted just by sitting next to me and agreeing with me, making exceptions until the moment I saw the light, had my epiphany, and changed my ways. What he didn't know was that I made the rules and I was holding all the cards. Neither of these things was liable to change soon, and he'd just have to get used to it.

That night when I left, after dragging him along like a puppy on a string, I signed up for the next night's crush shift that Niall had been complaining no one wanted, knowing it was probably his turn. Have and I just needed to get back into the groove of things, I thought, and it wouldn't do no good ignoring the problem.

Paying attention to the problem didn't seem to be working any better, though.

Things came to a head the night I was out with Compagnon and Raphael, though it didn't happen for more than a flash and neither one of them noticed it, but I fucking lost control of Havemercy for all the time it took a man to sneeze.

Someone once told me that when you sneeze your heart just stops, not long enough to kill you, not so long that you're even aware of it, but it stops.

Feeling Have streaking underneath me in the sky while knowing I wasn't having a thing to do with it was a *lot* like a sneeze in that respect.

Anyway, losing control like that, for even a split second, was long enough for the magicians to hit me with whatever flying fucking debris on fire they'd caught up in the wind; trust the Ke-Han to fight with their own buildings. I got hit bad in the left side, knocking all the feeling out of my shoulder and burning me like I'd just been blindsided by a damn enormous coal, which I guess I had.

Through some kind or another of luck, Compagnon *did* notice and had the gall to act like we should retreat or something just 'cause my whole left side was on fire and I was riding a dragon who wasn't my girl except when she was.

"I think you should go with the retreat," she said, sounding enough like her old self that I could almost forget what'd happened. Excepting the searing pain, of course. "You stubborn jackass."

She was right enough about that, I thought, because by the time we landed in the hangar I felt all sharp and miserable the way I did when something was either going to make me pass out or sick up.

When we were really in the thick of it, the Airman had its own meds, but either th'Esar had cut their funding or he'd decided things weren't hot enough yet, 'cause we hadn't seen hide nor hair of anyone looking remotely doctory or useful or nothing, and the rooms they normally filled for this sort of thing were cold, clean steel and white walls.

Completely fucking empty.

I sat on the examination table before my legs got too shaky and I didn't have any choice in the matter. I closed my eyes and leaned back against the wall, grinding my teeth against the insistent throbbing in my shoulder and smack over my ribs.

The Rittenhouse was nearest, was what Compagnon said, and with Raphael still running point on recon, I'd just have to wait there by myself while he got the meds out of their nice restful sleeps. Compagnon had a terrible sense of humor, though, and when the door opened a minute later, him saying he'd run into someone in the hall who could keep watch over me, I didn't need to open my eyes to know who he was talking about.

I couldn't even smell the professor over the stench on my own flesh—cooked meat and charred coat and silver buttons sizzling where they'd hit my skin—but I knew.

The door swung shut with a quiet snick, and the professor breathed in deep.

"Might not want to use your nose there," I said idly, voice dull with the effort of controlling the pain. "Burnt flesh ain't so pretty."

He made a soft, useless sort of sound in the back of his throat, and I cracked open an eye.

"You just going to stand there?" I asked.

Even laid up as I was, functioning on only the most basic levels, it really amused me how the professor could go on looking so shocked after so long.

That galvanized him into moving forward, at least. There was something strange in his eyes—not pity, else I would have hit him and pain be damned—but *something* for certain. It stayed there, green and strange and bothering me when he sat down on my good side, even when he reached out to touch me, maybe to pat my hand, then seemed to think better of it. Some people just like to feel useful, especially the most useless of them all.

There wasn't anything the professor could do here and, for once, even he knew it.

"What happened?" he asked at last. His voice wasn't rough or dream-slurred or nothing, so I knew he hadn't been sleeping again. He didn't sleep much lately. The raid sirens and I saw to that pretty well.

I shrugged, only I couldn't shrug and I'd forgotten. Instead I swore until I ran out of things to curse, and body parts to curse them with, then leaned back against the wall again, breathing none too easily. I thought I'd give th'Esar a piece of my mind on moving out our resident meds, but then I remembered the professor and that, if he really was a rat and I played my cards right, he might be able to do it for me.

Except when I tried to focus on what might be the best way to go about it, my thoughts shifted, refused to come together like the mismatched pieces of the jigsaw puzzles that Evariste did in the common room when no one else was around to entertain him.

I gave up in exasperation, as apparently I'd got the ability to be clever knocked out of me along with the air when I'd been hit by bits of burning Ke-Han building.

I sighed loud and frustrated, then felt a cool hand against mine.

I opened both eyes.

"All right," I said. "Here's the thing. I could tear down the bastion all on my lonesome, amount of pain I'm in right now, so I don't want you asking any dumb-ass questions about how I'm *feeling* or what *happened* or anything like that, okay?"

He nodded, pale concern and a willingness in his face like he didn't know what he'd done wrong or what he could do to make it right. "All right."

"If you're going to be here, then you talk to me, distract me from pulling your head off, 'cause you're closer than the bastion by a long shot."

"Oh," he said, and I could practically *hear* him thinking, even when I closed my eyes again and I couldn't see it. "Well, Luvander won the game of darts in the common room today."

"Luvander cheats," I answered. "Everyone knows it."

"Well, then, they must have let him win," the professor amended. "And there was some commotion over who had used the gas burners in Raphael's room to make grilled cheese."

If this was the kind of information he was feeding th'Esar, I thought, then we wouldn't have any kind of a problem on our hands anytime soon.

"I think it was Magoughin and Merritt," he finished, going

all quiet at the end like he'd finally realized he was babbling on about nonsense no one in their right mind would have anything to do with caring about.

I let the silence fester, shifting infinitesimally against the wall 'cause I couldn't just sit still with all this fire and metal in me. I smelled like the burnt-out hull of a building, everything scorched beyond recognition. I smelled like death.

"Shit," I said into the quiet, and the professor's hand went tight where I'd forgotten it was on mine. He had big hands, but I knew that from before, when I took him up with me on Have. He was hurting me. I wanted to go to sleep, and I wanted the medics from the Rittenhouse to get themselves into gear. "I hate fire."

"I— Oh," he said, pretty damn stupidly. "So do I."

I wondered why he'd ever let me take him up into the air without putting up more of a fight if he hated it that much, but he'd won something out of me for not asking the fucking stupid question I'd been expecting: *What sort of airman hates fire*, that kind of shit, and I just wasn't in the mood.

"It spreads very quickly from house to house, on the Mollyedge and in Molly especially," he continued.

"Yeah," I said, and I don't know what I'd got into my head, whether it was the burn, or my coat melting into my shoulder, or the fact that I hadn't got more than catnaps for longer'n I could remember, but I didn't stop talking there like I should've. "My brother died in a fire like that. Guess it was about—well, a long fucking time ago, that's for sure. I mean, I must've lost track of how long it was." That was a pretty lie, and no mistake. "His name was Hilary. He was goin' on four and he used to eat fireflies. I don't know. I think *he* thought they'd make him glow."

I felt him go very still, like even though he didn't have any special skills toward reading *me,* he could still sense he was on real thin ice here. Maybe he knew me better than I thought, or maybe he just understood that men like me didn't talk about this kind of thing to just anyone.

He was right, any which way he was thinking. I hadn't said a word about Hilary since Hilary'd died.

I opened my eyes again, and slid down the wall a little so our faces were nice and close. "You tell anyone what I just said, I don't care if they wear a crown, I'll kill you first."

"Oh," he said, looking real white and a little sick, like I'd figured out his biggest secret. "Oh, no, of course not, I wouldn't *dream*— I'll forget you ever mentioned it." He swallowed hard.

The professor looked a little shaky, the way he had when he'd clambered on down off Havemercy's back, only there was that same electricity in his eyes that had given me the idea in the first place.

"Good," I said. "Just so long as we're clear."

By the time the meds got there, I was half-out, the professor breathing slow and steady by my side. My eyes were closed and, what with burnt flesh and the rest of my skin too hot for thinking, I don't know if he stayed with me the whole rest of the night. Knowing him, he probably did.

CHAPTER ELEVEN

✖✖

ROYSTON

We traveled only the first day on horseback. The rest of the trip was made on foot, and it took a little more than a week and a half—nearly two by the time we'd met with our commanding officers and our garrison of Reds—to arrive at our side of the Cobalts. The path we took was a necessary one, looping back through the foothills and twisting around, until we were well shot of Thremedon herself. If we hadn't been forced to take such a meandering route, we might have made it in five days, but it wasn't speed that was of the essence. It was our own victory.

I had some recollections from a few years back, when I'd been on the front just the same as now, but it was always such a shock to be reminded that the Cobalts were so aptly named. They were high and jagged and faded off into the clouds, and they were indeed very blue, at least until the ice caps made them very white. If I hadn't been about to be killing the men who lurked just on the other side of the range, I would have taken the time to drink in the sight of them. The first time I'd come here I'd been too young and too nervous to make proper note of them at all.

The way we were deployed was quite clever. It was a strategy developed after too many years spent fighting—well over a hundred by now—and one that had been only slightly modified by the advent of the Dragon Corps, whose service was invaluable but also limited to the night, because of what enormously obvious targets they'd have been in the daylight. Because they were so deadly and so precise and caused such destruction on so massive a scale, we avoided skirmishes in the nighttime. And so it was that we were able to engage the Ke-Han on two fronts: the more common form of warfare, between garrisons of Reds and Blues augmented by the particular specialties of magicians during battle days, then the more recent form, which took place only at night and was signaled by the howling, shrieking wind that had once worked against Volstov's air force, and the subsequent explosions that meant it no longer did.

The captain in charge of my Reds was a man who'd been no more than a common foot soldier when last I'd been to the Cobalts. I was always pleased to be able to recognize a face. It meant that a man I'd once known, however brief our period of acquaintance, had managed to keep himself alive and well for as long as I had, and it fostered a certain heartening camaraderie. The captain's surname was Achille, and as he explained it, he'd risen very suddenly in the ranks after a disastrous rout in which half of our generals had been killed and he'd proved himself quite the master at rallying half-starved men with no magician at all behind them.

"You'd be surprised what starving men and starving dogs are capable of," he said, over our first dinner.

"Hardly," I said, remembering the disasters in which I myself had been involved. "Shall we do our best not to arrive at such dire straits?"

"Indeed," Achille said, "I've been doing my best these days to accomplish just that."

We reminisced together for only a short period before it grew dark and Achille quiet.

"The dragons come sometime past midnight," he said, with a faraway look. I wondered what sort of man he might have been if the war hadn't claimed his quick mind and ample imagination and, I acknowledged privately, ample stubbornness. "If you listen, you can hear them from miles away."

Our garrison was marked in midrange territory and housed by one of the old mountain forts. As far as any of us knew, the entire trouble with the Ke-Han, which by now spanned the course of several lifetimes, hadn't arisen out of thin air but rather from an age-old border dispute. Since before most could remember, there had been mountain forts on our side and the Ke-Han—originally a nomadic people before they built their city of lapis stone—patrolled the Cobalt border during the summertime. Each country was eager to stake its claim to certain lands just beyond the mountains, but since the range proved such an excellent natural barrier, it was generally considered that east of the Cobalts began Ke-Han land and west of it was Volstov's.

Stories varied as to whether it was the Ke-Han who broke the entente by building their tunnels. One popular legend in Thremedon ran that a captain of a midrange mountain fort heard with his unbelievably keen ears the echoing sound of stone being blasted away by the ancient Ke-Han nature workers and immediately began drill work of his own to meet them in the middle. Another story had it that a group of overexuberant Volstovic patrolmen accidentally killed two Ke-Han warriors in a moment of zealotry or, perhaps, confusion. What Ramanthine history books I'd managed to gather over the years stated that the Ke-Han were always seeking to expand their empire, and the Ramanthines had been their next great conquest. Volstov had inherited their war with the Ke-Han: an unexpected parting gift from our conquered Ramanthines. Then, if a man truly wanted to drive himself mad, there was the matter of the Kiril Islands, which the Ke-Han had taken from Volstovic control while the Esar had been occupying himself with the conquest of the Ramanthines.

I had no opinion as to which of these stories approached the truth more closely than the other. Likely it was none and things had escalated more gradually, until some misunderstanding or even accident brought things to a head and brought us all to such an interminable length of fighting.

It was madness, and neither side would step down until the other had been annihilated.

I wrapped my coat closer around me—the sort of coat all magicians wore when they were sent to Cobalt deployment: a burnished wine red with ermine lining and an abundance of white fur around the throat and wrists. It was comfortable, at least, and very warm, for mountainside temperatures had the unreliable habit of dropping quite suddenly once the sun set.

As I understood it, and as Achille had confirmed for me as we went over our approved plans for battle, the emperor in his lapis city was all but crushed. Achille himself had been leading a garrison of Reds when the wall was torn down, half by magician work and half by the tail of two crushing dragons— Compassus and another whose name I could not remember. It was the farthest that any dragon had ever made it into the city before, and the men seemed to take this as a sign. In fact, it was commonly held among the soldiers, who were farther removed from the troublesome goings-on at court than even I had been during my stay at Nevers, that our next battle might even be the one in which we claimed final victory as our own. Whether or not I could join them in this anticipation, I wasn't yet convinced.

All I knew for certain was that, after the dragons hit the lapis city this night, all the Esar's forces were to come down on the city at once.

Our plan—the Esar's plan—was that we should take this city for our own. If all went according to plan, we would be able to take the Ke-Han emperor as our prisoner of war, toppling his throne and bringing an entire people to their knees.

Admittedly, there was a certain excitement buzzing with the cold in the air. I couldn't help but allow it access to my own blood, for we all wanted this war to be over. And I knew that, if nothing else, we *were* doubtless on the verge of something colossal—though I couldn't be sure if it was our own victory or something as yet unforeseen.

Be prepared for all eventualities.

I repeated this phrase to myself every time I threatened to get ahead of myself, and wished that those around me would attempt to be as circumspect as I was struggling to be.

I sat with Achille in his captain's quarters—the highest room in the mountainside fort, reserved for captains and magicians alone—waiting to hear the sound of the dragons sleeking through the distant air. I thought for a brief moment of Hal, for I was always stealing such private moments to think of him, and wondered how I might have told this story to him if we were together in the warm room at Castle Nevers, with William on my knee and Hal's eyes bright with firelight as he sat at my feet. I longed to have him at my side for a brief and impossibly selfish moment, until I remembered just how Hal would have suffered here. No; this was the sort of tale I'd bring back to him, and *then* I could allow myself to tangle my fingers with his and glean all my comfort from being so close.

Yet I would never have been able to do the moment justice with mere words. There was no describing the Dragon Corps.

It was true that we heard them before we saw them, and Achille and I went quickly together to the window, throwing it open. The evening was cloudy and dark, perfect conditions for flying, and almost half an hour passed, the wind changing constantly, before we saw anything.

We heard them more than saw them when they were at last overhead, the forceful boom of their bodies pounding too quickly through the air for us to see anything more than a momentary flash of silver dark in the filmy moonlight. They always rode in threes.

The wind they left in their wake shook the very building to its core. I almost imagined the Cobalts themselves being sent crumbling because of the disturbance in the air. Our side gave a great whoop of national pride to hear them pass overhead, and I could feel that pride replace the excitement, the air now stirred to a fever by the beating of the dragons' mammoth metal wings.

"Fuck," said Achille reverently. "Fuck me if they aren't the most beautiful things in all of Volstov."

"I agree with you," I said, with the faint offerings of a smile, "and thus I'm afraid I must decline your suggestion as to the rest of it."

He laughed and clapped me on the back and called me, somewhat affectionately, the greatest Cindy this side of the ocean.

I managed little sleep for myself that night, and what rest I did manage was laced through with nervous anticipation, the sound of the dragons in the air, and the explosions that shortly followed their arrival. I'd forgotten how reverberant such things sounded through the long, complicated system of tunnels the Ke-Han had twice used to overpower us; I'd forgotten how loud it could get, how bright, how nightmarish. I was losing my touch, I told myself wryly, and had best reacquaint myself with the peculiar sensation of having the ground shake like an earthquake beneath my feet by the time I was thrust into the thick of things long before this hour on the morrow.

There was also the troublesome matter of my headaches.

They had come and gone all throughout the trip, and while I told myself they were no more than my way of adapting to the shift in temperatures and altitude, I knew this for the flimsy lie that it was. Quite simply, they'd begun before I ever left for the Cobalts at all. The first, unprecedented and dizzying, had occurred during my exile, and it had taken all my skills at play-acting to hide from Hal how greatly it distressed me.

Now, the only man I had to hide it from was myself—and the entire rest of my garrison of Reds, their captain, and the Ke-Han Blues. It was only a headache. I'd been getting them since the night before my return to the city, and I'd managed to find ways to function despite the discomfort. Undue stress could have brought it on, or my own entrenched fear of returning to battle.

Yet it was accompanied by a certain mind-numbing lack of equilibrium, as if someone had quite suddenly jerked the world out from underneath my feet and I was left to suffer through a maddening spin of blindness. I'd never suffered such headaches before, and there was absolutely no warning for them—merely a sudden onset of pain, pinching sharp at my temples, followed by that whirlwind of confusion.

If I were to suffer from such a headache during the battle to come as I was suffering with more and more frequency these days, I did not want to think of the possible ramifications—not only for myself, but for my entire garrison as well.

A combination of my headaches and thinking about my headaches kept me up most of the night. So it was that I rose early and joined Achille for breakfast, both of us talking with

sparse, low words that anticipated too many possible out-
comes.

"We'll take their tunnels," Achille said. "Use their strongholds against them. We've been working out the system the
past year now and we've finally got it figured. We send a distraction up one side of the mountain to keep them busy, and
meanwhile the rest of us from all the other positions take our
mark through the tunnels and advance on them. Before they
know it, we'll all be out. And, the way they're depleted, there
won't be any stopping us."

He was repeating the plan to comfort himself.

I, too, was doing much the same, mouthing this speech of
his that I had memorized.

It was a simple plan, a *good* plan. There was no foresee-
able reason why it shouldn't have worked.

But the unforeseeable was what undid us in the end. The
Ke-Han had been waiting all this time, waiting for us to grow
cocky, and we'd done exactly that. We couldn't have suited
their plans better than if we'd been working with them toward their own victory.

In some ways, it was my own fault. That is not to say that
I was egotistic enough about my vital position among our
Reds and the other magicians along with us, but one must always accept responsibility for his own actions, and in that
way a great deal of the fault was my own. The troublesome
headaches—I realized it too late—hadn't been my own private suffering, but rather the indication of something much
larger involving many more than myself.

There was no such thing as a singularity. It was what we'd
learned first as magicians. It was the most important truth of
who we were and what we did, and I'd forgotten it as swiftly
as a dragon's pass through the air.

My headaches were no more *mine* than they were harm-
less, and once we'd passed through the tunnels to the other
side, that much became painfully evident.

The first sign was that the distraction wasn't working as it
should have been. Achille had sent several magicians with a

detachment of Reds to aid it in hanging together, but the magicians were the purpose, all with Talents made for flash and destruction.

When we exited the tunnels, we should have been able to hear the results of our ruse, or see them at least, great colorful fireworks and rumbling earth, or even the warrior cries of the Ke-Han that indicated battle was at hand. There was none of this reassuring evidence, however, and I felt an uneasiness heavy in my chest as I caught myself scanning the jutting blue rock face of the Cobalts, which were stony and impassive and gave nothing away.

The uneasiness spread throughout my arms and legs, too swift to be the onset of anything that I could tie back to a simple worry about our progress. No, this was entirely physical, and I occupied my mind with trying to gauge exactly how bad it was and how I might be able to go on standing so long as we kept moving. None of the others seemed to be exhibiting any discomfort, and I thought that even if we couldn't hear the various noises indicating that our distraction was under way, that didn't necessarily mean it wasn't. It was quite possible that the men and magicians on the other side were at that very moment experiencing the full flush of victory.

Then Alcibiades collapsed.

He'd been a soldier before he was a magician, and the latter was only due to the Esar's deciding some fifteen years prior that any man with a Talent fighting in the war would damn well learn to use it whether he wanted to or not. Still, he had some skill with water—once he'd got past his initial prejudice—and though we'd never interacted for any particular length of time, he was a singularly competent man.

Achille called us all to a halt with a silent gesture, signaling for someone to check on our fallen comrade. Marcelline, standing closest to me, adjusted the warm collar of her coat with fingers that shook almost imperceptibly.

"Do you feel it?" she asked, but I had no idea to what she was referring.

I shook my head. She looked a little green against the white and red of her clothing.

"That's what I mean," she said softly, more because it seemed as though she couldn't bring herself to speak any louder, rather than any caution toward being overheard. "There's nothing *there*."

I thought that perhaps she meant the wind, and certainly it was odd the Ke-Han hadn't begun to attack us with it yet. Then her eyes rolled up toward the back of her head, white and startling. I caught her before she hit the ground.

Someone shouted the warning, and even as I felt the headache begin like a battering ram at both of my temples, I turned to see the Ke-Han forces coming in from all sides, closing the net of the trap we had walked right into.

Out front, I saw a great gushing blast of water come exploding from the rock. There were veins of sulfurous hot springs running below the Cobalts, and I guessed that they were what now spewed forth from the land beneath us, scalding the men from the second midrange fort and giving our men some time to rally around a common point. I wondered if perhaps Alcibiades had regained consciousness, after all; this seemed something I should feel pleased over, if only I could bring myself to feel anything at all beyond the pounding in my temples.

I couldn't. Rather, it was more like what Marcelline had been describing, an absence of that familiar, constant presence—*my Talent*—which left me feeling vulnerable and hollowed out as a man made from straw husks. It was akin to the strange, flooding loss of strength I experienced when I had a fever.

I should have moved, or tried to do my duty as both a soldier of the realm and a magician of the Basquiat, which made the code all the more important: I must necessarily do whatever was in my power to stop the Ke-Han's advance. As a magician, whatever I had in my power was considerably more than the average man, and as such I knew that the soldiers had come to depend on our help, our protection.

As far as I could tell, however, after that first show of defiance from Alcibiades, everyone seemed to have been taken with the same affliction as I, for I saw no telltale rumbles of destruction, nor streaking jets of fire. Instead, the Ke-Han rallied around their injured, then surged forward once more, blue coats the very color of the mountain rock.

I placed Marcelline on the ground behind me, for I would need both my hands free, and even as I wavered on my feet, I drew a deep breath to draw on the place where my Talent rested, hidden deep within. My stomach gave a lurch in revolt against what I found there, and at last I understood what Marcelline had tried to warn me of.

There was nothing there.

It was as though someone had gone into my chest and scooped out something infinitely more vital than my heart or stomach, and the sensation brought me to my knees.

I heard around me all at once the clang and crash of metal as used in battle, the hoarse cries of men I'd known and eaten with as they fought on, despite the sudden onset of our debilitating handicap.

Achille wasn't in plain view, for even my vision had blurred distressingly for me, as though, with the absence of what anchored me, everything else was falling apart. Maybe I *was* falling apart. Nothing like this had ever happened before. I had no way of knowing.

The world went white in from the edges, erasing the scene before me as surely as if I'd lost consciousness—not a blackout, but a whiteout—with the sharp, blinding force of a lightning bolt.

Everything that followed was a blank, clean slate.

When I awoke, I was in a tent that, from the lack of light streaming in through the fabric, must have been in the garrison at the foothills.

I ached all over, and the headache pounded still in my head, as though it wished to force my eyes from their sockets. Something smelled very strongly of blood. I sat up at once—a grievous error, as nausea rolled through me so that I had to lean over one side of the cot I'd been placed on to divest myself of the meager contents of my stomach. In a streak of wild luck, someone appeared to have placed a pan there for exactly that purpose.

To my right someone chuckled weakly, more of a pathetic

coughing than anything else, and I lifted my head—slowly this time—to examine my surroundings. Alcibiades lay prone on the cot next to mine, nose like the prow of a dying ship and bandaged quite heavily about the head.

"Where are we?" I said, and swallowed to work the saliva into my mouth, which felt as dry as sandpaper. My throat hurt as though I'd been shouting.

Had I been shouting?

It took him a very long time to reply—so long that I thought he'd fallen asleep. When he did speak, the sound startled me and set all my nerves jangling as though I were a high-strung horse. "Base camp, med tent. 'Til we get moved, anyway."

"Ah," I said, and surrendered my head to the cool softness of the pillow below it. There were troublesome thoughts floating across my skull, but not a one of them seemed strong enough to break through the red haze of throbbing in my brain. "We're to be moved?"

"Soon as possible," said Alcibiades, in the same scratchy voice as mine. "Head doctor, she nearly had a fit when she saw us."

I didn't feel as though there was anything *visibly* wrong with me, and that surely the head doctor of a medical unit during wartime would have seen a great many terrible things. "Am I missing a leg?" I said at last, as it was the only thing I could think of, and might have gone a long way toward explaining why I couldn't feel either one of them.

"No," he said, without a trace of humor in his voice. "It's because we're *magicians*."

I overlooked the contempt in his voice as he said this last, because it had set something else turning in my mind, like a great, if slow-moving, waterwheel.

The Reds had gone on fighting when we'd been stricken, that much I did remember. It was just that they went on fighting without us. The others who'd been . . . taken, I supposed I could call it, by this infernal numbness, were Alcibiades and Marcelline, both of them magicians. When I tried to think on it now, I found that I could not remember having seen *any* of the ordinary soldiers fall prey to whatever strange illness had taken hold of *us*. If it had struck magicians and magicians only, I thought against the pain in my head, then . . .

Then I had to be sick again, and I very nearly didn't make it to the pan this time around.

I'd never heard of anything that could debilitate so selectively. There were illnesses that were intrinsically magic, of course, but they ravaged those with Talent and those without equally. That whatever had hit us in the mountains had hit *only* magicians was a curiosity I might have found fascinating if it had happened hundreds of years ago instead of just a handful of hours before.

An unsettling thought occurred to me, and I looked once more to Alcibiades. "The others. The captain?"

He shook his head, very slowly from left to right, and I felt a wave of sadness overtake my heart. "They thought we were *all* dead, I think—you were certainly *lying* there like you were—and I got pinned under Emeric while I was still out of it." Alcibiades paused to clear his throat, as though he'd got something caught in it all of a sudden. "When I woke up, it was all quiet—they'd moved on—and I'd have gone right past you too if you hadn't made a noise like you weren't dead but dying, maybe."

"Then I owe you my thanks," I said, speaking more to distract myself from the memories I had of those who were now gone: of the easy companionability I had with Achille, and the idea of his kind eyes open and lifeless in the far reaches of the mountain range. "It's fortunate that you were able to overcome whatever's attempted to bleed us of our senses."

"I was a soldier before ever I was a magician, Margrave," he said, breathing shallow through his clenched teeth. "We learn how to go on through a little discomfort."

I resented the implication that all magicians were soft, untested warriors, but I thought that it might be ungrateful to pick a fight with a man who'd in all likelihood saved my life. And besides, my headache was making it hurt to speak.

I grunted, instead.

Alcibiades went quiet after that, and I drifted into sleep,

more passed out from the pain in my head than any kind of a real rest.

When I awoke a second time, it was to the sight of a silhouette in the open tent flap, and I'd no concept of the amount of time that had been lost to me while I was unconscious.

"Margrave Royston," said the newcomer, in the curt, official voice of a bureaucrat or one of the Provost's wolves. "And Alcibiades of the Glendarrow, by order of the Esar you are to accompany me to the Basquiat with all due haste."

"Charming," I said, just as soon as I could work up the energy to speak. "I cannot speak for my colleague at present, but rest assured we will follow you as soon as we are able to get up."

The man didn't laugh, but I was thinking more about what it meant that the Esar had become involved and what it meant that there was already a system set in place to cart us off to the Basquiat, of all places.

The Basquiat *wasn't* the Esar's province.

I thought of who had been missing at the ball, and came up with the same answer every time, that each of them—whatever other qualities they possessed—had been some manner or other of magician. Were they in the Basquiat, as well? If only I could have made myself think, *think,* beyond the dull arrhythmic pounding between my ears.

"You are not to speak with anyone," the man went on, rolling his proclamation up as larger, burlier men with stretchers came in. "You will have no contact with the outside world. Any discussion of what occurred in the Cobalt Mountains will be viewed as inciting undue panic among the people and thus an act of treason."

The thought of Hal came to me then, smiling and sudden and so vivid that it almost stopped the ache that plagued me.

"My . . . apprentice," I said, too weak and out of sorts even to demand information from the medics. "I should get a message to him."

"Your family members and associates will be informed of your situation," said the man as rote, weary, and bored as if this were an everyday occurrence. I had to wonder how many times he'd recently said the same thing, rolled off the same reassurances. It was by no means a comforting thought.

"How long before we can *leave*?" From a ways off I heard the familiar voice, laced with irritability. Alcibiades had either just regained consciousness or chosen this particular moment to speak up.

Our only answer was the click-slam of twin carriage doors.

"Fucked as not," Alcibiades said wearily.

I was slid off my cot and onto the stretcher, and another period of emptiness claimed me.

THOM

I left the medic room with ash on my hands and grease on my mouth and my heart clamped round with iron wire, the sort they used to keep urchins out of the shops in Molly.

I knew no other way to say it and there was no hiding from it, either. Rook was my brother; I had no doubt in my mind. It made a sick kind of sense, really, and the more I turned it over in my head, the more I found that I could get around it. *This* was the reason I could never just walk away from him, or couldn't ever just let the matter lie, not even in my own head. I'd thought at first that it must have been some wild, proud streak in me that Marius had neglected to stamp out: a professor's instinct to impart wisdom, or my own stubbornness in having wanted desperately to be right about him, right about my own theory that within everyone was some capacity for change.

What Rook had given me instead was the knowledge that, at the very least, I had better reason than the Isobel-Magrittes of the world to follow him around like a stray. After all, I'd begun doing it since birth, despite what obstacles and separations in the road between us had fallen since.

His name had once been John, almost too ridiculously simple for what he'd become since I was told he'd died in the fire. Mine had been Hilary; the whores who raised me called me

Thom, and because it was a name my dead brother never called me, I allowed them to use it. Subsequently, it had stuck. I assumed a part of myself had died in that fire—the part of myself named by my parents—and I left it at that. Sometimes I dreamed of him, my dead brother, but he was always faceless, the features blurred. Understandable, since I'd been no more than three years old when the tragedy struck us.

He'd told me to stay where I was—he'd gone out for some reason—I'd later followed a bird, I think, or a dog. Perhaps a kitten. I never did as he told, could never remember, and he was often angry with me. I found my way back only just as it was beginning to get dark, and the house was in flames, and there was a lady crying; these were all the bare pieces I remembered, and no more than that.

Someone told me my brother was dead. I believed him, since my brother had always made it a point to get home before nightfall. I didn't remember our parents, though when I was older I realized that they must have been among the countless other young couples who realized just how expensive it was to raise children. They'd cut their losses early and left me in John's care. He hadn't been old enough to take care of me, and yet he had.

I hadn't cried when our parents left. When I lost my brother, I'd cried for days and days without end.

I was three then, and twenty-four now. Twenty-one years had passed in the interim—twenty-one years during which the one constant in my life was the specter of my dead brother—dead, I often thought, because he'd come back, thought me within the burning house, and run inside to save me. I only came to this conclusion when I was much older and sought to explain the occurrences that had stamped themselves, so unforgiving, on my memory in red-hot flashes.

What must have actually happened—for my own peace of mind, I needed more than anything to fit the missing parts of the puzzle together—was that John must have returned sometime after the fire had been put out, after I'd been led away from the conflagration by the neighboring women of ill repute, who'd taken pity on me. He must have thought the same thing

I had, or perhaps he'd been told by the same man that his brother was dead.

He'd told me to stay where I was. He had no reason to believe I hadn't done just as he said.

I believed I suddenly understood Rook better—but even as the thought crossed my mind I was struck with guilt, fierce and swift. I was pacing the halls of the Airman, and each time my path led me again and again to Rook's private door. I had a brother again.

I leaned against the door for a moment, pressing my cheek against the frame and, on the most foolish of whims, tested the knob, barely thinking about what I was doing.

It turned, and the door swung open. Before I could stop myself from intruding, I stumbled inside.

Here I was: in the belly of the beast. It smelled faintly of ash, of sulfur and fire, and most pressingly of metal. The bed was unmade, three pairs of boots by the closet; there was a trapdoor that I knew led to Havemercy's bay. There was a print of the famous portrait of Lady Greylace, the most renowned whore in all of Volstov, but no books at all. I nearly laughed; I nearly cried.

It smelled of him—on everything, every shadow in every corner—a glass half-full of water on the desk and a jewel box full of his earrings. Earlier this night, or on any other night for that matter, my brother might have died a second time without my ever learning that he'd *lived*.

I sat down on the edge of his bed and knotted my fingers in the sheets. When he returned to his room I would tell him— for he'd opened himself to me, whether it was from loss of blood or a sudden shift in altitude or any other stupid incomprehensible reason. He'd spoken my true name, and I would use his, and perhaps we might mend what had broken between us twenty-one years ago.

It was possible. I *knew* it was.

I waited there for hours, long past sunrise, rehearsing what I'd say and how I'd say it. *Rook,* I might begin, or perhaps *John,* though I thought the latter might be too sudden. You couldn't spring this sort of realization on a man the way it had been sprung on me, though that had been an accident. I wished to spare him some of that pain—for despite all his cruelties, I remembered a time when he was gentle and kind, bandaging the knees I always scraped, or catching the fireflies I clamored for. Besides all that, he was my brother. It wasn't every day that a man could be resurrected from the dead, and I knew that I must treat this as gently as he'd once treated me. It was more delicate, more precious, than any other secret I'd ever held.

Yet it was also the first time I'd ever had something on Rook, and it gave me a disturbing flush of some feeling I didn't want to identify, as similar as it was to victory. True, I was for the first time in a position of possessing some knowledge that Rook did not, and an *important* piece of information, to boot, but this was entirely different. This was family, and I was no airman who kept secrets just to be hurtful or to lord over them who didn't know.

At long last he returned, flinging the door open and half-kicking off one of his boots. They must have given him something to numb the burns—for there were great strides being made of late in medicines that eased almost any kind of pain—but his eyes were tired, and his shirt was open to reveal the bandage swathed across his chest.

He saw me then and stilled, wary as a tomcat on the prowl in an alleyway. This was his territory, and I a threat, engaged in trespass.

"You fucking waited up for me?" he said finally, his eyes still narrowed and all of him tensed and ready for a fight. He was too tired for it—despite his protestations, he *was* human before anything else—and I stood quickly. "Or were you snooping around?"

"What?" All my rehearsal seemed for naught; I'd forgotten every line as if I'd never thought of them at all. "Snooping?"

"I know about that pact you've got with th'Esar," he snarled, ranging past me and shrugging out of his shirt with some delicacy. The burns clearly must have still troubled him. Of course they did. I'd seen what they looked like a few hours before.

"About the— What?"

"Jeannot's got a friend in the palace," he said, "and if you tell *this* to th'Esar, I'll gut you from the belly up. But we know you met with him that night at the ball. We know he's got you in his pocket like a fucking puppet."

I shook my head, trying to clear it. "No," I said, "you don't understand—"

"You want to enlighten me, then, as to why it was you and His Majesty needed to meet so private-like?" He came close to me without any warning, nearly backing me up against the wall, and I could smell the burnt flesh, the medicinal stench of the balm on his chest, the metallic residue on his palms and, beneath that, blood lacing everything—always blood beneath. I should have told him then, should have let the knowledge come out of me all at once before I let my fear of it undo me, as it was already doing.

Yet if I told him now, there was no telling what he'd do. He was unpredictable, he was purposefully cruel, he was probably insane: All these things added up suddenly and startlingly to make an inarguable case, a perfect equation for why I should keep my mouth shut. It wasn't simply that I was afraid of Rook, for now that fear was laced with a kind of hurt running through it, a marbled vein of regret for what I'd lost from my brother because I did remember a time when he'd been kind. Looking at him now made all sorts of emotions rise that I didn't want to deal with at present, and certainly not where anyone so cunning as Rook could see.

So I held my tongue, and lifted my chin with instinctive defiance, and tried my best not to think about how he'd trusted me with his memories and the companionable silence that had followed.

I'd been so desperate for such a sign from him—any sign at all that all my work had not been in vain, that I wasn't simply pouring my efforts into an empty yawning mouth of contempt and trickery. Rook *had* seemed changed over our time since the ball, but faced with my own lack of perception now—my own brother in front of me, mad and bleeding and more than a little tired—I was forced to wonder. Perhaps I'd never even made a dent in that armor of his, thicker than dragonscale and twice as resilient. Perhaps all this waiting I was doing, looking for the barest shadow of kindness, something I could misconstrue as affection, was because I knew that I would accept it from him, and gratefully. Perhaps this was because I'd sensed in him all along my long-lost brother, who *had* been kind once, before time and whatever strange fate had befallen him ruined that instinct forever.

"Well?" he asked.

"I'm not spying on you," I whispered.

That much was at least the truth, but there were other truths I should have spoken—other truths I might have spoken—but when I opened my mouth to speak, the words abandoned me. He looked at me as though I were mad, gaping like a fish, and I had no means to protest this assumption. I *was* mad.

He made a sound, rather more like a grunt than anything that could be misconstrued as human speech. He either believed me or didn't, and the fact that I couldn't tell the difference upset me just as it always had, so not *everything* had changed.

"Better not be," he said, and brought his face so close to mine that I felt momentarily off-kilter, as though the earth had tipped sharply beneath my feet.

Then, just as suddenly, Rook turned away from me and the ground righted itself once more. I thought that I could say it then, unfair a thing as it was to sneak in on a man when he wasn't looking. I swallowed, and cleared the dryness from my throat. It was a poor charade; I could no more speak than I could move.

This wasn't to be the first time I kept the truth from him.

That night he didn't even kick me from his room, just flung himself down onto his bed and was asleep almost before he hit the mattress; he must have known he had me pinned beneath his thumb like a bug, incapable of crossing him. This was the power Rook had over me.

I watched him for a few guilty moments to see if his face eased at all, if the harsh lines of it grew peaceful with sleep. I wanted to recognize him, but I didn't. Then I forced myself from the room and curled against this secret as if it were slitting me open the way Rook had promised.

I think I understood now, if only a little, the reason for his sudden interest, his "change of heart": It was to keep me close, keep me where he could watch me and make sure I wasn't going to betray the corps. So long as there was a steady stream of reticent confidences and hesitant looks that *suggested* he would open up if only I stayed around, there would be no reporting to th'Esar. It was so clever that I would have experienced a grudging admiration were it not for the already-consuming wealth of guilt and confusion swamping me. Moreover, I was humiliated, for there had been some small part of me that had dared to hope at making a difference with Rook. And now, for all I'd thought it through so carefully, it was all dashed to pieces as surely as if thrown from his dragon as he sped her too quickly through the night.

Everything had changed, and nothing. I had failed on more counts than I could possibly name because I had come no closer to understanding Rook than I'd ever been, and I myself was now possessed of a secret almost too large to keep. I could no longer fault him for his questionable morals. He was my own brother, and I could not even summon up the wherewithal to tell him so. I told myself that I only needed more time to sort out *my* feelings before I took them to Rook, but I knew that a larger part of it than I wished to admit was rather the gratification of wielding some new power over him, and the lie became harder and harder as time passed. If pressed to choose, I'd say that I was worse than he'd ever been even when he was at his most vindictive.

I was too preoccupied with my own thoughts to notice the change that came over the city. Truth be told, I wasn't paying attention. My focus had so turned inward that I'd completely forgotten there was a city living and breathing all around me. And, because Rook was off duty for the following week, I was allowed to forget there was a war.

Yet I wasn't living inside a complete vacuum. Now and then I'd catch moments of the other airmen's conversation in the halls, hushed and grave. One afternoon I even heard Adamo shouting inside his private quarters, though to whom he was shouting I couldn't be sure and had no right to ask.

That night, when Rook cornered me in the hall, he grabbed my wrist hard, and said, "We have some talking to do."

Fear rose sharp and quick as the guilt, and I let him lead me, all numbness, into his room and shut the door behind us.

He looked uncomfortable for a minute, then gritted his teeth as though what he was trying to say was about to kill him, or worse. Finally, he managed a curt, "Have ain't right."

For a moment I didn't understand him. I was expecting him to tell me he'd known—that he'd read my thoughts—that he knew me for what I was and he never wanted to see me again so long as we both lived. Breathing ceased to be an autonomic function, and I concentrated on drawing air, along with as little attention as possible. I'd been prepared for the worst, not some garbled sentence I couldn't parse. "What?" I asked.

"Have," he snarled. "Havemercy. She ain't—she *isn't*—right. That mess I got myself into? Not for any reason I can figure. It's like sometimes she's okay and sometimes . . . she isn't."

I stared at him, relieved and terrified all at once. This, more than anything, cemented my place among the morally bereft and bankrupt. He was confiding in me a second time, this time of his own volition and not due either to pain or to blood loss, with no alternative motive, while I was keeping from him so massive a secret that I hadn't slept in days. "You . . . Havemercy," I managed at last. "She's— What do you mean she isn't right?"

Rook growled, clearly finding our means for communication ineffective. "She ain't *flying* right. It's like we're not speaking the same language. It's like we're fucking *strangers,* is what it's like, or worse. I tell her to do something and she just doesn't do it—like she doesn't hear what I'm saying or even recognize it for words."

"I don't know anything about dragons," I said carefully, moving to sit beside him. "I don't understand why you're coming to me—"

"Because you can fucking tell th'Esar about it," he said, nearly biting my head off with the words. "He's expecting a report back from you—so, tell him. Tell him that Havemercy's fucking *off*. It's quicker than going through the proper channels."

"Well," I said, understanding why he was confiding in me yet again. I didn't bother to argue my case—I wasn't spying on my brother, but he was close enough to the truth of what th'Esar had asked me to do that it didn't really matter.

He was looking at me, short-tempered and hot, and I realized that I hadn't yet given him a proper answer. "Of course I will," I said, quiet and low. He was my brother. I owed him that much.

I knew that the longer I stayed silent, the more likely it was that one day the odds would become irrevocably stacked against me, that I would break something that could not be fixed and that this lie would be the end of us.

"I'll write to him," I said.

"When?" Rook asked.

"Tonight," I said. "Now."

Because I'd promised him—because I was still under the strange impression I was a man of my word, if little else—I did exactly as I said, and wrote th'Esar a brief, formal note that I'd discovered something in the Airman that might be of interest to him.

I was almost grateful for th'Esar's summons when it came the following morning, for the need to prepare a report was a welcome distraction from my own thoughts, confused and tangled as they'd become. I spent the morning attacking my new task with all the zeal of a hunted man.

The summons had said that a carriage would be sent to meet me nearby—a special treatment that surprised me, but th'Esar was apparently very good to his spies. Just as I was observing the turn of the hour on the small round watch Marius had gifted me with to congratulate me upon some previous academic success, the carriage appeared, white and gold like something out of a roman, or some ludicrous rich man's fantasy. The Mollyrat in me couldn't quite get past being awed long enough to be contemptuous, but having spent so long as a penny-pinching student, I couldn't help but wonder at how many hot meals that carriage would buy. Somehow I thought it would be better if I didn't know the answer.

I clambered inside, clutching tightly to the sheet of notes Rook had dictated to me—and which I'd subsequently translated into the kind of talk I could use with a man like th'Esar—and attempted to calm myself. Thinking with a clear head was the only way I was going to get through this particular meeting with any kind of dignity, or more importantly, with my head still fixed firmly to my shoulders. During my time in the Airman, I'd adapted to thinking one way and speaking another. This need for duplicity was still no excuse for the way I'd behaved, the way I was still behaving, toward Rook, but it had been cultivated as a survival tactic the moment I'd stepped into that room on the dais facing those fourteen wing-backed chairs, and the undoing of it was proving more difficult than I ever would have anticipated.

Now, it seemed, I would have to learn and fast, for th'Esar was a man who did not like to be lied to. And if he sensed a disparity between my mind and my lips, he would surely not hesitate to act.

The carriage moved quickly across the cobblestone streets, and I watched out the window as the city passed by in what seemed to me now a meaningless blur of hustle and bustle. Thremedon was my home; I'd known it all my life, and yet for all I recognized it now it might have been any central metropolis, teeming with its own people, its own traditions, and completely severed from my heart.

The servant sent to greet me bowed low, and I fought the urge to do the same back to him, as it would have damaged my standing considerably. I would never grow accustomed to being the sort of man to whom other men bowed. Perhaps it was something to be born into and not learned at all. That, more than anything, told me how much things had changed, the small worming ways in which Rook had got into my mind, because there was a time when I would have said that there was nothing that couldn't be taught. Now I wasn't so sure.

Then I had to concentrate on following, keeping the servant's back in front of me, or else risk getting lost in th'Esar's winding hallways—little better than catacombs, I thought, for all their decoration and fancy curios.

This time I counted them as we passed: two antiquated mirrors, one very large portrait of th'Esar himself, a tapestry, a door with no handle, a window with bars. The farther we moved toward our goal, the dimmer the light became, until we were plunged into the same grasping darkness that I remembered. I could no longer discern the shape of my surroundings and I could do no more than follow after my guide, ever ahead and turning so swiftly and so sharply that at times I felt dizzy.

I found myself thinking that it seemed th'Esar should have a more accessible set of chambers, for it wasn't logical to assume that the noblesse with whom he met daily would accede to being led through the depths of the palace like rats through a maze. No, it seemed more logical that he would only have such a room as the one to which I was being led for his own private dealings, ones he didn't want subject to court gossip and whisperings.

This was his route for spies.

It was a long way to go for a little privacy, I felt, but then th'Esar's secrets were considerably more important than those of most men. Then I thought of the woman who'd been with him on the night of the ball, dark and striking and, most notably, perhaps, incredibly familiar toward th'Esar. Perhaps *some* of the secrets he held were the same as all men's.

It was only when the servant stopped, turning on his heel with a motion eerily similar to his predecessor's, that I realized we'd arrived at our destination.

"Thank you," I said to him, with all sincerity, for I was certain that the dizzying trip to th'Esar's secret meeting room could not be an enjoyable one, and I was equally certain of just how lost I'd have been without the guidance.

He merely nodded, then offered me the briefest of smiles.

I steeled myself and opened the door.

Th'Esar was seated in the same seat he'd been in before, giving me the momentarily jarring sensation that no time had passed at all. Of course, his companion was no longer the woman, but a man I was surprised to recognize as the Provost of the city.

". . . panic in the streets, not to mention the Basquiat, Your Majesty, if you don't mind me saying. The bereaved are gathering, and there isn't anything that starts a riot faster than unhappy people who feel they've been mistreated." He hesitated, as though this last had been too much, and bowed low in the court fashion. "Your pardon."

Th'Esar held up one square, powerful hand. He'd seen me enter.

"I will continue my discussion with you at a later date, Provost," he said. "Do not fear. If the situation is truly as bad as you say, then we will have to think on a way toward solving it."

The Provost nodded like a man careful not to look too disappointed. His hair was the same shade as th'Esar's and his chin very similar.

"Yes, Your Majesty." He turned then, understanding his dismissal when he saw me hovering guiltily in the doorway like a child caught out late. I could do nothing but offer him an apologetic look, and he left the room by moving past me without so much as a glance.

"Now," said th'Esar, switching tack with a voice full of command and purpose, "what news do you have of our Dragon Corps? I trust that in the time we have given you there has been more than one event worthy of our attention."

"Well, there is one matter," I said, immediately forgetting what it was I'd written in my notes—Rook's speech full of curses, as well as half-remembered complaints from Niall and Raphael, dark remarks made by Ghislain, and Adamo's shouting behind closed doors. I forgot it all, and swallowed the sudden fluttering of panic that threatened to break loose from my throat. Th'Esar had this effect on people. It was no wonder his networks for intelligence were so precise and effective. "Rook—that is, the airman Rook, who flies your dragon Havemercy—he says that she's . . . off."

Th'Esar regarded me with a look that bordered dangerously on disapproval. "Off?"

In for a chevronet, in for a tournois, I thought weakly to

myself, and nodded. "Yes, Your Majesty. I overhead him saying that she, it—the dragon, that is—he said *it* isn't flying the
way it ought to."

"Perhaps Airman Rook finds himself incapable of the task
of flying our most prized dragon," replied th'Esar. "We have
heard that he exhibits traits of inconsistency in his behavior
when flying."

I wondered then just how many spies th'Esar had set about
the Airman, and whether I would have to keep a closer eye
now on the men who came to collect the laundry, and the
women who cleaned the rooms; even the young boys who
kept the dragons clean and well oiled. Not that this was my
place, of course. I owed no loyalty to the airmen; I had no reason to inform them of th'Esar's spies, especially not when I
myself could still be counted among them. I couldn't explain
this sudden troublesome loyalty, only knew with a familiar
helplessness that it had everything to do with Rook, the way
it all did—the way it all would until I revealed the truth.

"I—" I paused, marveling weakly at the realization of
what I'd been about to do. Rook had tainted every corner of
my mind to the point where I would defend an imagined slight
on his prowess to th'Esar himself. I felt ill. "As I understand
it, he *is* the best flier among his fellows. If he thinks there's
something wrong with Havemercy—"

"There is nothing wrong with our dragons," th'Esar said,
with a clear note in his voice that this was the final pronouncement on the subject. "You have clearly misunderstood
what it is we asked you to do in the first place."

Disappointment flooded my mouth, hot and bitter. I held
my tongue.

When he'd found I had no more to report other than what
th'Esar clearly regarded as the fanciful misgivings of a man
whose skills he appreciated but whose opinions he had no
use for, I was dismissed promptly and without hesitation.

I'd failed on both sides of the equation. Th'Esar refused
to see the truth—no doubt he had his reasons, yet I was infu-
riated all the same—and, what was more, when Rook demanded an answer, I could no more defend my ineffectiveness

than I could prove to him the sky was green. I'd got nothing but a curt dismissal regarding the matter of the dragons, and I knew that it wouldn't be good enough to take back. I should have pressed th'Esar; I should have made him listen.

Rook would have done it that way. No matter what happened, his voice *would* have been heard if he were the one in charge of speaking his mind. Whatever other shortcomings he had, getting his point across was never a problem.

I left, thinking that the long struggle back through the crooked hallways would wear me out, but I exited the palace fairly brimming with excess energy, as though I'd been caught in a fight and sent home before the knives had even been drawn. My hands were shaking, my cheeks hot. I decided to walk back to the Airman, as the weather was fair, and besides which I'd seen too much of the city from carriage windows of late. Perhaps I would feel more at home in Thremedon if I truly immersed myself in it once more; it was an approach that couldn't hurt.

Before I'd even passed very far from the palace I stopped again. Something was bothering me, and it took a moment to realize that it was the memory of the Provost's curious meeting with th'Esar. What snatches I'd heard of their conversation rose clear into my mind, and I turned my head toward the sun.

The stark, proud lines of the Basquiat stood off in the distance, serene shape belying the true chaos surrounding it if what I'd heard hadn't been an exaggeration.

Perhaps it was a desire to speak with Marius, who was often at the Basquiat late into the day, or perhaps it was that I didn't wish to face Rook with my stubborn and unexpected defense of him still ringing in my ears. For whatever reason, I turned around and headed in the direction of the Basquiat.

I hadn't noticed it before from the window of the carriage, probably because I was so wrapped up in thinking about Rook and of what I would say to th'Esar, but I did now: the people keeping their distance, huddling together in small groups and whispering about a plague, or about th'Esar covering something up. That there was nerve enough for this sort of talk in broad daylight, on the streets no less, told me more than

I thought I wanted to know. When I cut through the Rue d'St. Difference, I saw a woman crying in a hat shop, and when I doubled back for having come too close to Charlotte, I came upon the 'Versity Stretch, as busily populated as I'd ever seen it. It was as though everyone was out of doors instead of in, and when I stopped a girl on the street to ask, she shook her head.

"Most of our professors have gone off sick," she explained. "At least I think that's what they *say* it is. The explanation was actually surprisingly vague."

"Ah," I said.

"Yes," she replied. "Only it's sort of funny that the lot of them would have gone off sick all at once, don't you think? It's got a bit of a stink to it."

I knew—as she was a student of the 'Versity—that if I didn't make my escape now, I'd be there three hours listening to her particular theory on what had happened. Feeling rude but desperate, I quickly thanked her, then went along my way, picking up my pace as I came to the familiar turn of Whitstone Road that would lead me straight to the Basquiat.

If asked, I couldn't have said what I was rushing for, but I thought that it was something more than a student's curiosity or interest in a problem unsolved.

The Basquiat was almost too colorful, although I'd heard that it had come about as a disagreement between the founders, and that in order to please everyone they had simply used each suggestion of color that had been presented. The result was something spectacularly striking, which I suspected was what they'd been after in the first place. The seven domes atop its staggering towers were no two the same. Some were done in swirling patterns, and others had the checkered effect of a chessboard. The largest dome—not the topmost, but the largest—was a hollow onion of pure gold, and beneath it was the open tower magicians used to chart the weather or converse with the falcons. The center tower was a round room with arched windows that stretched from floor to ceiling, and it was here that the members of the Basquiat met. At ground level there were two doors, one large and perfectly centered and the other smaller, framed by a pointed capstone and off to one side.

This was the entrance for nonmembers of the Basquiat, and the one I saw the people crowding around before I'd even managed to get close enough.

No one, I saw, seemed to be using the official door, though when I neared it there *was* someone sitting there on the steps in front of it. His hair looked a little long—it was in his eyes—and he had drawn his knees up to his chest in what appeared to be abject misery. It was hard to place him without his eager smile and tentative kindness, but I thought all at once that I knew him.

"Excuse me, is that . . . Hal?"

His head flew up so fast that I half expected to hear his neck pop, and he blinked at me for a moment before I saw the flicker of recognition pass through his red-rimmed eyes. He looked as though he hadn't slept in days.

"I— It's Thom, isn't it?" His voice caught on something, faltering and wretched.

I felt again the unfamiliar kinship I had when we'd met in the bathroom, or perhaps it was simply that here was a person as miserable as I was, and in him I recognized some likeness of myself.

"It is," I said, and moved to sit next to him on the stair.

"Oh," he said, and sniffed as though he had a cold. "It's good to see you again. I thought I'd offended you at the party. I didn't mean to. If I did, I'm very sorry."

I didn't know where to begin. Should I start by telling him the fault was obviously mine, or that there were clearly more important things on his mind than some foolish fit of temper I'd had at th'Esar's ball? I settled for reaching out to place a hand on his shoulder.

"Have you been here long?" I asked.

He nodded, and I saw his throat work for a moment as though he were trying to keep from crying. "It's Royston," he said at last. "Margrave Royston. I had a letter. It told me that he's here, only I don't know how to— They've said I'm not to see him."

I felt a sweeping rush of sympathy, imagining what I would do if anyone had tried to tell me I had to stay away from Rook, even though I'd tried to tell myself that very thing time and time again. Besides which, it wasn't the same situation at all. For one, this was clearly more serious. Anyone at all could see there was something being kept secret within the walls of the Basquiat. Having no idea what that secret could possibly be made it worse, not to mention the rumors I'd heard, the missing professors, the talk along 'Versity Stretch.

At once, with what wits I had left, I endeavored to think about this logically. "Hal," I said, "what did your letter say?"

He smiled faintly, but there was no spirit, no heart at all, in the expression. "I thought there might be some clue, but it said no more than I told you. The Margrave Royston is here and he is not receiving visitors at this time. When I came here—I came here straightaway; I only received the letter this morning—there were others. It's just as you see it. They're not letting anyone who isn't a magician enter, and we've seen no one at all come out again." He drew a deep breath; I saw his mouth tremble and twist, and I knew he was on the verge of tears. He'd already been crying: his eyes showed me that. "I spoke with a young woman—her father's within, she told me, or so it was written on her letter. She said that he told her once of a different entrance, a secret one, but as secrets go it may be better hidden than what's happening to the magicians being kept inside there. But all I can do is sit here, useless and crying."

"Come," I said gently, resting a hand on his shoulder. "Shall we talk to the young woman you spoke to? It seems she knows more than we."

"She doesn't like to be interrupted," Hal replied. "She's much too busy threatening people. I only got a moment of her time, because she seemed to know what she was talking about—her rights as kin—but then, I'm not kin at all. I'm just—" He bit off without warning and shook his head almost savagely, and I gave his shoulder what I hoped was a reassuring squeeze. It was quite possible that it wasn't anything of the sort, but it seemed to steady him somewhat. "I'm sorry," he said at length. "I'm—I believe the phrase is at my wit's end, and that's exactly how it feels. At the end of my wits; at the end of everything."

"I don't blame you," I said.

"I just— I don't know what to *do,*" Hal whispered helplessly. He turned blue eyes on me, clear and pale and worlds apart from Rook's icy blue. There was no guile at all in Hal's eyes; the only bruise upon their clarity was sadness and fear. "I only know that I *must* do something. He'd . . . he'd do the same for me. Only he knows *everyone.* He'd go to his connections, he'd find a way, whereas I haven't even been here a month. You're the only person I know. It's almost funny that I've run into you. The city is so big, I wouldn't think—"

It was a cruel thing to offer Hal hope when chances were there wasn't any, but I felt a sort of twinge, familiar as it was foreign from my days at the 'Versity, and I gently tuned him out. The beginning of a plan was forming in my mind. It was inspiration; it was a thesis.

"Hal," I said. He must have noticed the change in my voice, the trembling excitement of something we might do, for he looked up at once, his expression a thousand forms of pleading: all of them desperate that I *could* help. "I don't want to promise you anything I can't deliver," I continued, trying to temper that excitement, "but I *am* your connection in the city. I've just been to speak with th'Esar," I said, close and private that no one else would hear us. "Something is happening—something is happening *here.* He wouldn't listen to me because I'm not anyone he needs to listen to, but he'll listen to the Dragon Corps. They're his *Dragon Corps.*"

"Oh," Hal said, quite breathlessly. "You can— I'd forgotten you know them. Can you *do* that?"

I paused for a moment to ask myself the very same question. The answer was no, or at least probably not. But it wasn't just for Hal's sake that I'd be asking them to help; it was also for their own sakes, and the sakes of their dragons. Surely if I phrased it in that way—surely if I told Rook it was the only way they'd listen to him about Havernercy, which wasn't entirely a lie—then at least I could give Hal the reassurance of a little knowledge. Not knowing what had happened to the Margrave was clearly driving him mad with misery, and his was a truly guileless face. I couldn't simply leave him there, sitting on the steps of the Basquiat, the rumors sending him further into the depths of worry and his own traitorous imagination.

"Come," I said, standing and offering him a hand. "We'll find a way."

He took my hand and stood, but then he hesitated, looking back at the Basquiat over his shoulder. "What if something happens?" he asked. "What if they open the doors? What if they start letting people in?"

I thought of the Provost's words of caution, of th'Esar's expression. I thought of the Volstov's iron fist, the curtain that Thremedon drew over the most important of her dealings.

"They won't," I told him. "This is your best recourse."

"My only recourse," Hal replied. He paused for a moment, weighing the matter at hand, then squared his jaw. "Yes, I'll come with you. It's— Royston would do it, were it the other way around."

I gave his shoulder another squeeze, then we left the Basquiat behind. Hal didn't look back.

Once we were out on Whitstone Road I flagged a hansom and told the driver there was an extra tournois in it if he'd get us to the Airman faster than if we were flying a dragon.

"Sir has a way with words," the driver said.

It was the most uncomfortable, jostling ride I'd ever experienced, for the driver was a man of his word, and when we arrived not half an hour later, I was covered all over in bruises. And, I suspected, Hal was as well.

"Should I," Hal asked, hesitating at the door, "wait out here?"

I thought of how cruel the airmen could be when faced with a stranger. I'd had theories on why once—their distrust of the rest of the world which, I'd argued, they needed in order to foster a disproportionate trust among one another. It was their mechanism: the corps against the rest of the world. It was what allowed them to be so deadly and so fierce. I'd sought to condemn this behavior once, but now I was less sure if they weren't in some ways, at least, partially justified—especially in light of what was happening right now in the rest of the city.

The last thing Hal needed was to be mistreated at their hands, for in order to be pilots of such precision and merci- lessness, most of them had severed their ties to any empathy with which they'd been born. The system required this of them, but nevertheless it was a fact of life inside the Airman's walls.

At the same time, it would be perhaps just as cruel to leave Hal out here to wait as we discussed things within. It would place him in much the same position he'd been in earlier, sit- ting outside alone in front of the Basquiat, enduring an inter- minable wait.

"You'd best come," I decided. "Stay close, and say nothing. If you're lucky, they'll barely acknowledge you—and I'll need all the information you have to hand about what's happening at the Basquiat. It may be what convinces them to act."

"If something is happening to the magicians," said Hal as- tutely, "then the Dragon Corps may be next."

Best not to phrase it like that, I thought, but they were smart enough to deduce that for themselves, and the unspo- ken threat might indeed inspire them to rally together and ap- proach th'Esar with their complaints.

I was pleased to note that I did know a little about Rook by this point, a specialized sort of knowledge. At the very least, I understood enough about him to be certain of this: that he wouldn't fight a war for anyone so long as he felt vital pieces of information were being kept from him by those in charge.

When I thought of Rook in the air, piloting a dragon that he said was "off," I wanted to be ill.

The Airman was quiet, for it was early yet, and no man was yet awake and arguing over the coffee or the tea. I bid Hal sit down on the edge of my couch, told him I'd gather the others despite how dangerous a game it was to wake them, then started for Rook's room.

It was my only recourse.

I was not even halfway down the hall when his door opened and he stepped out. "You're fucking loud," he snapped at me. "There's men trying to sleep here."

That was his way of asking me how I'd fared. I drew close to him, for I knew how angry he'd be if anyone overheard us. "Th'Esar refused to listen," I began, but he cut me off with an angry sound.

"I knew it," he said. "I knew you'd be fucking useless."

"Listen," I said to him. "Please—listen to me for only a moment."

He folded his arms over his chest and gave me exactly the sort of look—impersonal, uncaring, almost amused by how useless I was—that so shattered me. You're my brother, I wanted to say, but my tongue and throat blocked the words, and I couldn't.

"Fine," he said at last. "Spit it out."

"There's something happening in the city," I said, wincing that I could phrase *those* words easily enough, but not the others. "Something very important. I'm not sure entirely what the details are, but there are magicians being kept quarantined in the Basquiat, and their families told of their whereabouts but denied permission to see them. The Basquiat is locked up tighter than—" I flushed for a moment. "Tighter than th'Esar's safe," I finished, changing tack halfway through the metaphor. "Some are believing foul play. Some sort of cover-up."

Rook snorted. "Magicians," he said. "Fucking magicians, *always* fucking magicians. They don't have anything to do with us."

I licked my lips and shook my head. "That's untrue and you know it," I said. "Magicians built your dragon—all the dragons. It's their magic upon which the dragons run."

Rook mulled it over for a while, toying idly with a loose thread at his sleeve. His chest was still bandaged—a direct result, I was beginning to think, of whatever game it was th'Esar was currently playing with the corps. I felt like a common shadow puppet, and I knew that if Rook were to feel this way too, he would be spurred to some kind of action. It was my job—my duty as his brother—to make sure he acted effectively, in a way from which he might benefit.

At length, Rook said, "So you're thinking this problem with Have—"

"Is related to whatever's happening with the magicians," I concluded.

"So you're thinking," Rook said again, "that if we figure out what's going on with the magicians, then we'll figure out what to do about Have."

"Something of the sort," I confirmed. "Exactly."

He looked me up and down, not entirely appreciative, but at least as though he considered me actually *there,* which was a step up from where we'd been a few moments before.

"You're too fucking smart for your own good," he said. "You know that?"

I shrugged. "Th'Esar wouldn't listen to me. He has no reason to."

"But he'll listen to us," Rook said. "We're the fucking Dragon Corps. I'll go get the boys."

A shiver ran down my spine, unbidden and fleeting. I felt as I imagined the Ke-Han magicians must have felt when using their skills with the weather: as though I'd unleashed into the world something impossibly feral and beyond my control.

I hoped that I was doing the right thing. I would have liked to believe that I was doing it for Hal, to aid his cause as best I could, but the curious stirrings of unexpected loyalty I'd felt toward the Dragon Corps in th'Esar's presence hadn't diminished since I was dismissed.

I knew that it was my brother's doing, this strange unprecedented suicide I'd committed, for if ever th'Esar found out I'd betrayed him, it would be my head.

In some ways I considered it my own small way of apologizing for the things I couldn't say—and it was then that I realized I was stupider and crazier than Rook had ever been.

CHAPTER TWELVE

❦❦

HAL

The Airman was quieter than I'd expected, and there was no decoration on the walls. It was perhaps a strange thing to notice, and yet, since my arrival in town, I'd felt continually overwhelmed by what I'd privately come to view as the city's insatiable desire for opulence. This was true of Miranda at least, the most elevated of the maidens and the one I'd explored most extensively at Royston's behest.

Thinking of Royston enshrouded me in a quiet, solitary despair. It was as though I was cut off from all the world—or as though, by losing Royston, I had somehow lost my touchstone to the city. I was cut adrift.

I missed him terribly, and if I allowed myself to think of it, I would surely start to cry again.

Instead, I focused on my more immediate surroundings. I was not so unaware of them that I couldn't recall Royston telling me everything he knew about the dragons and their unusual pilots. He said that very few civilians ever got to see the inside of the Airman because the corps wouldn't allow it. The way he'd described them was something like a very primitive, very xenophobic tribe of warriors who held themselves so high in their own esteem that they became quite separate from the common people.

So I was both curious and anxious about meeting these airmen, who were in many ways the heroes of the country and yet whom no one seemed to like very much at all when you came right down to it. Royston had been speaking at length with their Chief Sergeant on the night of the ball before I'd slipped away, and I assumed that the rest must—they *must*—have friends of a sort somewhere or other. But it was still rather an interesting paradox and one I felt very lucky to view for myself.

I heard a shout from down the hall, and someone went storming past the open door of the common room; I recognized him as the man with a harem of women surrounding him the night of the ball. He had long, blue-streaked blond hair tied back in intricate braids and a purposeful look about him, as though anyone who got in his way would be very sorry, indeed. I found myself quite glad that he didn't spare me so much as a second glance but went on barreling along to bang on a door much farther down.

"Ghislain," I heard him say, "you'd better wake the fuck up, seeing as how we're hauling ass to the palace. Right fucking *now*."

I couldn't hear a reply, but there must have been one because the next thing I heard was a bark of laughter, and an enormous crashing sound, as though the braided airman had kicked the door down.

It was while I was listening to this that Thom reappeared, observing the scene in the hall with an inscrutable expression. I stood immediately, eager to find out what had been decided, though admittedly I'd been unable to stop my heart from leaping wildly up into my throat at the airman's mention of the palace.

"Rook is . . . quite forcefully decisive," said Thom rather apologetically as he approached me. There was something about his face that made me wonder, however much it was none of my business, what sort of connection had been forged between these two seemingly so different men.

An enormous man came tramping into the hallway, looking as though he'd just rolled out of bed; he was followed closely behind by the airman Thom had identified as Rook.

"Rallying the troops, are we?" The enormous man's voice was like falling rock. "I wondered how long it would take you to crack."

"It ain't *me* that's cracked," said Rook, but he didn't elaborate further than that.

Ghislain—for that, I remembered, had been what Rook called him before kicking down his door—appeared to take this as explanation enough, for he nodded and set off down the hall in the opposite direction, where I could see doors set sporadically, small and cramped into the walls.

I stood unnoticed with Thom in the doorway, and while I watched I couldn't help but feel a sense of admiration at the seamless way the members of the corps worked without having to pause for any kind of apparent communication. Between the two of them, Ghislain and Rook set about rousing the remaining airmen with a synchronicity that clearly mirrored what they exhibited in the air. Surely it was showing my country manner all too plainly to stare at them so, but I found I couldn't quite help myself.

"I managed to convince him," said Thom, as though he needed to hear the words in order to believe it. "Rook is rather like the ringleader. Once you've got him convinced, the others will follow."

"Did it take a very long time to figure that out?" I asked, remembering what he'd been charged with and how he'd been made to live like a foreigner among the Dragon Corps.

"Not as long as you'd expect, no." He offered me a smile, familiar, as though we were friends. "Not *that,* anyway."

I didn't feel adequately equipped to guess after his meaning, but he'd been kind to me of his own volition, without any reason for it, and I was grateful. "Well, you can't learn everything all at once."

"I suppose not," he said, raising his voice to be heard over an indignant cry demanding to know what kind of rat bastard entered someone's room unannounced.

"You can't," I said, sure of myself in at least this. Royston had said as much to me when we'd first come to the city, and I was glad to have some opportunity to share my newfound wisdom. It was nice not to be the most uncertain person in the room for once.

"Well," he said, and went rather quiet and pink.

"Who's this?" A young man—young because he seemed

closer in age to Thom than the others, and somehow less
hard—came up to where we stood waiting in the hall. He had
a wide-awake look about him, as though he was the only one
of all the twelve remaining airmen who hadn't been sleeping
when Rook and Ghislain began their systematic rousing of
the corps. He wore the high-collared blue uniform I recognized vaguely from the ball, though there were a few differ-
ences. There was a burn mark on his shoulder for starters,
and both epaulettes were missing.

"Oh," said Thom, turning about at once. "You're awake.
That's good. Rook—I believe—is going to ask th'Esar what
is happening to the dragons."

"Is he?" asked the airman. "We're all going? Because
Anastasia's been—" He looked at me again, with fleeting
mistrust before lowering his voice. "Anyway, she's acting a
little strange."

I wasn't at all interested in learning the secrets of the
Dragon Corps, but I saw this privacy as a reflection of my own
intrusion, as though I'd been noticed and caught out at last for
not belonging here.

Thom nodded, looking concerned. "I believe they intend to
find an answer, or more likely they intend to demand one." He
laughed weakly, as though the very idea of anyone demanding an answer from th'Esar was a distressing one, indeed.

I didn't care about the imposition. However foolish it was
of me, I resented any man who would tell me where Royston
was, then declare I wasn't allowed to go to him.

There was a pause, punctuated by the sound of men tumbling from their beds and the pacing of booted feet against
the floor.

"I'm Hal," I said, awkwardly. It was only then that I remembered what Thom had told me about keeping silent, and
that perhaps that was the only reason why he'd kept from introducing me until now.

"Are you?" The airman gave me an appraising look. He
didn't respond in kind, with his own name. "I suppose you're
a friend of Thom's?"

"Yes," I said, hoping I wasn't assuming too much. Thom didn't speak out immediately to correct me, though, and I felt marginally better about my own impulsive answer.

The airman didn't introduce himself, though. Instead, he only looked at Thom as though expecting to hear more of an explanation as to why he'd brought a stranger with him inside the Airman. It was much akin to either the most exclusive of small country villages or, the thought entered my head unbidden, a prison, wherein everyone knew one another's business, and distrusted all outside matters. Perhaps one day, if I didn't say anything to offend him again, I would be able to ask Thom how he'd managed to live under such conditions all this time.

My room at the chatelain's house had been small, but there had at least been a bed, and not a couch.

"Balfour," someone hollered from down the length of the wide corridor. "Good, you're up."

When I turned, I rather thought I'd been plunged into a roman, or that my life had taken some strange fantastical change. Ranged together in the hall were twelve men in matching uniforms but of such dissimilar appearance as to be completely—individually and separately—the most striking people I'd ever had the opportunity to see up close. When I'd first met the Margrave Royston, I'd been captivated by some impalpable quality he possessed, the innate ability to capture the attentions of a room without speaking so much as a word. Each of these men here had the same power—and when they stood together the effect left me breathless. I'd seen them at the ball, but now I was in their midst.

"Who's the kid?"

Rather abruptly, I was torn out of the reverie, as I remembered the talk of the coarse manners of the airmen. Twelve pairs of eyes pinned me into place, and from behind me I was certain Balfour was doing the same. I cleared my throat, mouth suddenly dry.

"He isn't—" Thom hesitated, then changed whatever it was he'd been about to say. "He's a friend of mine."

The handsome one I'd seen at the ball—Rook—gave me a

look that was equal parts amusement and malevolence. He seemed about to say something when the redhead standing next to him elbowed him sharply in the ribs and indicated something over our heads.

I turned, helpless in my curiosity, and not wanting to stand out against any uniform motion that might underscore my position as an outsider. Standing opposite us was the fourteenth and final member of the Dragon Corps. He stood with his arms crossed, and his bearing was that of a man who knew full well that crossing his arms would be discouragement enough against any kind of insurrection. I recognized the Chief Sergeant of the airmen from Royston's table at the night of the ball although he now had a beard and there were exhausted bags under his eyes.

I realized all at once that this was a coup. I was partially the cause of it, and I felt my cheeks and ears grow hot.

"And just where do you all think you're going?" The Chief Sergeant didn't appear pleased.

The men were momentarily very quiet, reminding me somewhat of a large passel of children who'd been caught worrying the chickens. Then Airman Rook stepped forward, crossing his arms just as neatly over his own chest, and I moved quickly out of the way, so that I wasn't caught in their gaze as it met, straight and fierce as a path of fire.

"We're going to see th'Esar," Rook said. There wasn't any room for a *please* or *may I* in his tone.

"Oh?" the Chief Sergeant asked. "Is that so? I don't believe I signed the necessary paperwork for that."

"You can take that paperwork . . ." Rook began.

Thom cleared his throat and stepped forward to join him. "You may already be aware of this," he said, more gently, in what I assumed was an attempt to placate the Chief Sergeant, "but we are on the verge of something quite terrible. Inside the Basquiat at this very moment is some untold collection of magicians who are being kept there indefinitely for a reason it seems no one but th'Esar himself and those closest to him are privy to. Family and friends crowd outside the building, yet no one is being admitted entrance. Likewise, I believe that most—if not all—of your men are experiencing some manner of difficulty with their dragons."

"So we're thinking," Rook cut in, "that if there's something wrong with the magicians, and magicians made our girls, then knowing what's wrong with the magicians might maybe explain what's wrong with our girls."

Thom colored just slightly—I believed I was the only one who'd caught the change—when the airman Rook used the word "we." It was another interesting detail, but one I was ultimately too miserable to make very much of.

"So you're going to meet with the Esar," the Chief Sergeant said, "because you fancy yourselves a group of bastion-blessed *diplomats*."

There was another long silence, as everyone was left to consider the Chief Sergeant's words, rumbling and dark and strong as a physical blow.

Rook tossed his braids over one shoulder; I felt reminded of the stamping and posturing of a thoroughbred horse. "Th'Esar doesn't give us some fucking answers," he said, "then we ain't gonna give him a fucking Dragon Corps."

"The way we see it," Thom translated quietly, "is that it's impossible for him to expect the men to fly under such conditions. If he won't listen to the reason of one man, then he must surely listen to the reason of his fourteen airmen, without whom his war might never be won."

"I see," said the Chief Sergeant. "And what, if you care to enlighten me, brought this pretty piece of inspiration on?"

I swallowed thickly as I heard Thom clear his throat again as he glanced toward me. Then, as surely as if Thom had pointed in my direction, fourteen pairs of eyes were drawn to me and fixed me soundly in place. More than anything, I wished I could have disappeared, quickly as a shadow, hiding myself along the wall or at their feet.

"This," Thom said into the uncomfortable quiet, "is Hal."

The Chief Sergeant cocked his head and looked at me. "I know you," he said, unexpectedly, and I breathed an infinitesimal sigh of relief. "You're Royston's . . . apprentice. Aren't you?"

I nodded faintly, trying to work up the courage to speak. "His assistant," I confirmed, when I could at last find the words. "He introduced us at the ball."

"I remember," the Chief Sergeant said gruffly. "Said a few other things about you, too. Like how you're clever as a whip and sharp as tacking."

This time, when I blushed, it was under such intense scrutiny that I wished more than anything for a Talent that might allow me to disappear entirely. This, however, would give me no aid in finding Royston.

"I received a letter," I informed the Chief Sergeant miserably. "It said the Margrave Royston had returned from the front and was at this very moment inside the Basquiat, and that—per his request—I was to be informed of his whereabouts. But I wasn't to be allowed admittance. I've been waiting outside the Basquiat all morning—you should see the crowds; family and friends, and no one knows anything—" I broke off, fists clenched so tightly at my sides that I could barely feel my palms where my nails bit into them. Thom reached out and put his arm around me, and over the sound of someone's uncomfortable giggling behind us, I thought I heard the Chief Sergeant sigh.

"Royston's a friend," the Chief Sergeant said slowly, "and the corps is my business. *I* take care of you lot. Have you forgotten it?"

The silence that followed his question seemed to indicate that, even if they had forgotten it before, everyone was certainly reminded of the fact and once again quite impressed by it.

"So?" Rook asked darkly, the only man not even slightly impressed by the sheer force of will in the Chief Sergeant's words. "*You* take care of us. What're you gonna fucking *do* about it?"

"The Esar won't listen to you if you storm his door like angry children," the Chief Sergeant countered smoothly. "Why in bastion's name don't I have thirteen reports filed from you about the problems you've been having up in the air? Is it because you're all too fucking proud to see straight?"

"It sort of . . . built up on us, sir," said Balfour quietly. His head was bowed, his shoulders slumped with shame, and I saw him toying with his gloves, tugging the fingertips loose from his fingers.

"Didn't seem as how we knew we were all experiencing the same thing," Ghislain added.

"Fuck you all at your mother's tit," the Chief Sergeant snarled. "Don't a single one of you move until I get back here in five."

"What happens in five?" an impossibly pale man asked from the back. The man next to him burst once more into uncomfortable giggles.

"We call us some carriages," the Chief Sergeant said. "Gets us to the palace much quicker than walking, doesn't it?"

ROOK

So there we were—all fourteen of us and the professor, and the tagalong he'd managed to pick up out front of the Basquiat—waiting in th'Esar's foyer nice as punch for His Majesty to grace us all with his imperial sun-blessed presence. I thought that if it'd do any of us a lick of good, I'd have gone for the throat right there, but like the professor said, more than anything we needed to know what the fuck was going on before we did anything. Most people are stupid 'cause they allow themselves to stay stupid, and I didn't manage to get out of Molly by staying stupid for long.

So anyway; there we were, no matter what we were all thinking about, sitting in chairs or standing and ranging around because the waiting was starting to piss us off, like me for example, and Ace too, because we both knew how bad things must be if our girls weren't listening to us proper. We were all sort of mad at ourselves, too, even though Adamo'd been a little over the top earlier because of whatever soft spot he had for that Mary Margrave of his, because this was halfway our own fault and we knew it. We hadn't been looking after our girls properly, and fuck the damn paperwork; we should have brought it up to Adamo the first time it happened instead of letting it get so bad while we tried to ignore it.

Meanwhile, the professor had one arm around his taga-long's shoulders and I could see Compagnon watching them all sidelong and trying not to giggle, which, if I hadn't been so pissed myself, would've set me to giggling, too. Instead, I was just mad, and if teasing Balfour wasn't going to make me feel better, then there wasn't *nothing* that was going to work. I wanted to get something done, I wanted to march right into th'Esar's fancy meeting hall and give him a piece of my mind, and maybe doing that'd distract me long enough from the guilt worrying at me, like maybe if I'd done something for Have sooner, then things wouldn't have got to this state at all.

"Shit," Ace said to me, drawing me aside all private-like. "They're just doing this to make us sweat."

"We'll make 'em sweat before it's through," I promised. "I figure we gotta have a plan for it. Like when we're flying."

"Oh?" Ace asked.

"Yeah," I said. "But I'm no fucking good at plans."

Basically, there was one idiot in this entire room who knew people better than the rest of us, or did in theory any-way, and who could work these things out on the back of his hand or Balfour's gloves if you gave him the pen for it. He was sitting there saying into his tagalong's ear whatever soothing horseshit he had stored up from a lifetime of horse-shit memorization.

"All right," I said, whistling sharp, and he looked up quick as that, which made me more pleased than I'd like to admit. "Yeah," I confirmed, "you. Leave your boyfriend alone and get the fuck over here. Th'Esar's making us wait, so we might as well use it against him, right?"

Everyone was watching me now, which meant I was the only one who saw the professor's tagalong go red as a tomato all the way to the tops of his ears. It was like a circus sideshow.

"Ah," the professor said, giving his tagalong a squeeze be-fore he stood. "How do you propose we do that?"

"We gotta go to him like a team," I said, spitting his own words straight back at him. "Right? We gotta use our strengths and his weaknesses against him. It's your own theory."

"Well," said the professor, looking at me with his doe eyes, like I'd given him a present and making me *real* uncomfortable, "in a manner of speaking, I suppose it is a . . . bastardization."

"Fuck you," I said. "Who the fuck're you calling a bastard?"

"I believe," said Jeannot smoothly, "that he's calling your *ideas* the bastards."

"Shit," I said, 'cause that much was more than halfway true. "Well, that's all right, then."

"Well?" Thom spread his hands before him. "What did you have in mind?"

"I figure it this way," I said. "We've got a man here who—Esar or fucking not—needs a whole lot of convincing. We've gotta mix it so there's no way he *can't* tell us what we need to know."

"You want to bargain with him," said the professor. "You want to *bargain* with th'Esar."

"Exactly," I said. "Blackmail him. Whatever it's called. But we've all got to do it together, because if *one* of us calls foul and the rest don't back him up, we're all screwed cheap as a Hapenny. You get that?" Compagnon started giggling, but all the boys were with me, even Adamo, whom I'd never thought of as *one of the boys* and still didn't. The tagalong was watching us as if it were the best fucking theatre he'd ever seen, which in a way I guess it was. "All right," I went on, turning to the professor. "So how do we do it? How do we make him do what we want?"

"Well," the professor said, real slow like I hate, but I could see he was thinking it over properly, and I forced myself to be a little patient. "I suppose the best bargaining tool you have is what you do for him. What you've already done."

"So we threaten to take it away," I said.

"In a manner of speaking," the professor agreed. "Yes. Only— I don't think you can phrase it as such, in as many words. You have to be more subtle—"

And then, before we'd had time to talk it out good and proper, the door in the far corner swung open and one of th'Esar's worm-mouthed servants made himself known to us with a stiff bow and a whining, "His Esteemed Majesty the Esar is waiting for you in his royal conference room."

"Right," Adamo growled out. "Step to it, men."

We all fell into line for the first time in our lives. There wasn't one in our number who wanted us to lose face in front of th'Esar, not when we knew we were cornered. What he hadn't counted on was how every man fought like a dog when his back was pressed up against a wall like ours were right now, and we were fighting for more than just ourselves, too. We had our girls to think about.

I hated the royal conference room, 'cause it was a bitch to get to, and worse than that it made me feel all turned around, like I was flying sideways and didn't know which way was up. Raphael'd said once that he read a book that explained why everything was built all winding and confused as shit in the palace. Actually, the way Raphael put it was "a very subtle intimidation tactic," but what that meant in real talk was that it made everyone except th'Esar feel out of place, and when people felt out of place they made dumb mistakes like getting *nervous,* and that was right where th'Esar wanted to put people. Nervous people needed a leader; nervous people did exactly as they were told. 'Course that wasn't taking into account how nervous often preceded panicky, and there wasn't nothing you could keep panicky people from doing once they got it into their heads to do it.

Get enough people together like that and it wouldn't matter *what* th'Esar said: They'd tear the Basquiat down to the ground to get at what they wanted. Part of that was caring, I guessed, from what the tagalong had said about it being all family and loved ones down there—and I knew I didn't need to ask which *he* was, since we were talking about that Mary Margrave—and even me with no heart to speak of knew it plain as day that people aren't ever crazier than when they've got *caring* mucking up their brains on top of everything else.

The professor was walking up by me and Ace, like he'd

taken my appeal as free license to do as he pleased. Or maybe
he just thought he'd have a better chance of talking th'Esar
down like he had Adamo if he were standing close by. But he
knew his stuff, however pointless it'd been in the past, and I
thought maybe for the first time I could see my way around to
looking at his viewpoint as not *entirely* cracked.

Much as I hated to admit it—and I wouldn't ever admit it
out loud—some of what he'd said was even going to come in
useful, this trick the professor had of manipulating folk just
by learning things about them. Of course it'd backfired soon
as I realized how well it worked for keeping the professor in
line, too, though I doubt that'd been what he meant to accomplish when he started teaching us. Wasn't the first time
anyone had underestimated my cleverness though he was
probably the first to get out without a scratch on him.

Then the servant stopped, and a second door swung open,
and I had more important things to think about.

We filed into the receiving room, Adamo first 'cause he was
the most impressive out of all of us, even the professor—who
when it came down to it was only a 'Versity student. And, if
we were saying all the what-came-down-to-whats, when it
came down to it, we were *Adamo's* airmen, and not th'Esar's.

There wasn't room on the dais for fourteen men and two
more besides, but some of us were scrawnier than others, and
we crowded in like schoolboys at the back room of a burlesque
show, jostling and elbowing for the glimpse of a creamy thigh
or better. 'Course, looking at th'Esar was none so exciting as
Lady Greylace, even though his clothes cost likely near as
much as hers. I thought it was a little funny, looking around,
that th'Esar was built powerful, like a sensible sort of man and
not the sort who'd match his clothes to the cream of the walls
with their fancy gold trim, but there we were.

Then again, I supposed that was the sort of thing that happened when your parents were your cousins, and things'd
been that way for generations.

Th'Esar sat in his chair—not quite a throne, but still fancy
enough that I was betting no one else'd make the mistake of
sitting in it. He was toying with the signet ring on his finger

like he was just waiting for us to make the first move when even the dumbest kid down in Molly knew that you didn't speak to th'Esar before *he* spoke to *you*.

Finally, after Ace had crossed and uncrossed his arms so many times that I was near to considering just throttling him right there, th'Esar cleared his throat.

"To what do we owe the pleasure of this . . . unique visit?" he asked, like he didn't know what to call it and like he didn't know *exactly* the reason why we were here in the first place. I felt my blood start to heat like boiling water, threatening to bubble over everywhere at once.

Someone put a hand on my arm and I knew that it wasn't Ace, so it must've been the professor. For some fucking strange reason, instead of hitting th'Esar then and there, I checked myself. Threatening th'Esar wouldn't be any way of helping our girls, as much fun as it might have been, and I knew the others wouldn't have appreciated my rash behavior any. Not that I was doing it for them, or the professor's stupid hand on my arm; I was doing it for Have, and I'd break any man's face in that said different.

"Your Majesty," said Adamo, only his voice had changed, got real fine like he was some 'Versity professor dictating instead of a man used to barking orders at them who listened about half as often as not. "We're here about our dragons."

"What about them?" said th'Esar, still studying that damn ring of his, although anyone with eyes could tell that he was listening good and proper now, his back gone rigid and his pale eyes sharp.

Adamo paused, like he was wondering how best to put it, and it was then that I knew without a doubt that Proudmouth had been flying as off as all the rest, and that he was a damn hypocrite for not filing his *own* report to his *own* damn self. "They aren't flying properly," Adamo said at last.

"We have considered the idea that they may be in need of maintenance," th'Esar allowed, the fucking bastard.

"*We've* considered," I said, speaking loud and hot before anyone could stop me, "that it might have something to do with all those magicians locked away in the Basquiat."

It was then that th'Esar looked at me, and I guess it was supposed to be an intimidating look, but anyone could have told him that I didn't intimidate, so he was just wasting his energy and all our time. Still, I thought I could feel it working on some of the others, 'cause they stood up straighter, and there was some sparking, snapping thread of nervous energy running through the lot like we were all of us joined into a lit fuse.

I half expected Compagnon to start giggling with the strain of it at any moment, though he was probably considering what Adamo would do to him if he did, and that was the only thing shutting him up even now.

"What do you know of the magicians in the Basquiat, Airman Rook?" Th'Esar asked his question like he really thought I knew something more than what anyone with a brain could know; that there was some serious shit going down and a crowd big enough to choke the streets surrounding.

"I know them magicians are the ones that made our dragons," I said, since he'd *addressed* me and all, so I guessed Adamo and the professor would just have to get their fainting over with later. "If there's something that's happened to 'em, then I guess it's not such a stretch to think that maybe it's got something to do with the way our girls ain't doing what they're supposed to anymore."

Next to me, the professor winced, like using bad grammar in front of th'Esar was an unimaginable crime. I didn't care. I wasn't like Adamo, couldn't turn it on and off like a switch. Even if I could've, I wouldn't've, because as far as I was concerned th'Esar was a man the same as anyone, and just because his great-great-granddaddy had seen to conquering a nation didn't give him any more rights than the rest of us, 'specially me, and *especially* when he'd had the nerve to tell us our dragons weren't doing what we said they were.

I'd've liked to see him try and fly one.

He waited a long moment, examining each of our faces like we were a room of criminals and if he could get just one of us to crack, he'd have us all. "You are *all* experiencing this?" he began at last, and it was the first time I'd heard him sound anything other than smug and infuriating. "This . . . wrongness with our dragons?"

I didn't like the way he said "our," but I let it slide when the professor tightened his fingers on my arm.

"Yes, Your Majesty," said Adamo, speaking for all of us. After a moment everyone set to nodding, like they'd all been waiting for their neighbor to go first. It was like not knowing what had happened to the girls had cut off our balls and we had to behave neat as students in case th'Esar had any information that would lead to fixing them.

A strange look passed over th'Esar's face. He might've been worried, for all I knew, though it sure looked all wrong on him. He probably wasn't much used to it.

For a second I thought he was going to kick us all out of the room. He put a hand over his face for composure, and when he removed it his expression was back to normal, the way it looked in all his portraits.

"We have faith in your ability to weather out this disobedience as best you can," he said at last. "In addition, we will have someone sent to inspect the mechanics of the dragons should they continue to give you trouble."

"My men," said Adamo, straightening up—and he wasn't that tall to begin with, but he could look fucking *impressive* when he wanted to, "won't fly under these conditions."

I felt something unfamiliar, pervasive, and kind of warm in my chest, though whether it'd come from the others or something else I didn't know. It was a little like being proud, I'd've guessed if I'd been forced to name it, though I'd never had it directed at anyone besides Havemercy when she'd done really fine.

"Is that so?" asked th'Esar, though somewhere deep in the back of his expression I could tell something was shaken loose. "We regret that it has come to this."

"We're fighting your war," said Adamo, and I didn't need to look at the professor's face to know he'd gone stupid with shock; he must've been figuring it was all over for us now that he'd lost his one sane ally in all this. "I think we've got a right to know what's going on, and I say we ain't—aren't—leaving the ground until we do."

The threat settled into the middle of the room like a flag torn from the pole. For a moment things were impossibly silent, like maybe we were all holding our breath and waiting to see whether th'Esar would snap and order us all executed for treason, or whether he'd smarten up quick and remember who it was'd been winning this war all along.

It was th'Esar that looked away first, head bent to examine the ring on his finger again, but we all knew what it meant.

Just because a man was th'Esar didn't mean he didn't give signs of surrender the same as all the rest.

"If any of you sees fit to spread this about the city," he began, "we *will* see to it that the only place you'll ever fly again is off of the cliffs at Howl's End, do you understand? If there is word of this anywhere—if our Provost thinks the people have been given so much as an inkling—we will hold the lot of you personally responsible, and we will not hear otherwise on the subject."

I thought I understood what he was saying, and it was pretty clever, because anyone could claim accidents happened, but here he was telling us right up front that even if accidents happened, it would still be our fault. That had us fucked, good and proper. Yet as much as I hated it, if he could see a way toward fixing Havemercy, then I guessed I'd have to stand it.

Leastways, I had to stand it until she was fixed, then I could think of a way to repay th'Esar for all his kindness.

Some of the others were grumbling quietly, but I knew they were all just as stuck as I was, keen to get the information th'Esar had even if it meant he'd caught us in his net.

"We understand," said Adamo, in a tone of voice that held dark things for those of us who didn't.

Th'Esar paused for a moment. "Who is that?" he asked finally, looking toward the tagalong. "He isn't one of our corps."

"Margrave Royston's assistant, Your Majesty," Adamo answered, so smooth it was like he'd been expecting it all along. He was smarter than his smashed-up face let him look. "If he leaves this room, then so do we."

There could've been a standoff there and then, only we'd already postured long enough, and it seemed th'Esar'd grown tired of it. Good; better not to waste all our time and get the fuck on with it.

"There is a sickness," said th'Esar. "It began shortly after you were called upon to resume your services to our realm, and it began with some of our oldest and most treasured families of great Talent. With the information that we have been able to gather to this date, we can state that the illness manifests with similarly minor symptoms across the board. All the cases began with headaches, small fevers, and an aching of the joints. This later progressed to dizziness among the subjects we observed, leading to a general state of disorientation and nausea. It is after an afflicted person's attempt to *use* his or her Talent that the illness hits hardest, often disabling the patients in question almost immediately."

It was a lot of talk to explain something that th'Esar had been keeping a secret all this time, and parts of it sounded real nasty in particular, like keeping the magicians under observation as some kind of medical experiment instead of invalids needing proper care. Considering how th'Esar did things, I wasn't much surprised.

I took that to mean that whatever was going on with this magicians' plague, it'd begun just after the air raids started up again. That was a long fucking time to keep us in the dark about things, though it explained why he'd been so keen on calling back them that'd wronged him bad enough to be exiled in the first place. He needed them pretty bad, since all his good little soldiers had been hit with this "sickness." I felt anger snap through me clean like a whip, knew that I couldn't release it 'til we'd heard the whole story—but th'Esar was going to have to see a way toward explaining why he'd kept his own counsel about something as fucking serious as whatever plague had hit the city while we fought to defend his own precious self.

No one spoke, and so he continued.

"We do not know the cause, only that it has thus far afflicted only our magicians. As you can imagine," he added, suddenly sharp again, like he had any right to be intimidating when he was such a liar it made the rest of us look like the purest saints of Regina, "it has been a crippling blow to our efforts in the war."

Abruptly—the way it felt when Have turned a perfect arc or we dove with the wind singing around us—everything fell into place. Why the Ke-Han had been rolling over, getting us real nice and sure of our victory. The Ke-Han'd had another move planned all along, the way Adamo always did in chess, and right when you thought you were about to take the king, he'd come in from behind and destroy everything you'd worked for. The raids had all been one hell of a distraction, and if Have'd been flying right, I'd've left the room to get on her right then and teach the hordes a thing or two about how much I hated feeling like I'd been tricked. They'd done us over *real* nice.

"There's magic in the dragons." That was the professor this time, and I don't think he realized right away that he was addressing the fucking Esar because he'd got that tone in his voice, like when he argued with me even when he knew it was suicide, and hadn't said "Your Majesty" even once. "That's why they aren't working. You knew there was something wrong with the magicians, it's the *simplest* connection to make between them and the dragons. It's obvious. Whatever's attacked the magicians is also affecting the—" His voice caught on something, like maybe the realization that he was as good as telling th'Esar he'd fucked up bad. "It's affecting the dragons," he said quickly, with a trace of whatever iron it was he had in him that had kept him standing after the ride with Havemercy.

Maybe he was also realizing what it meant to be standing with us when th'Esar had marked him out real private as his own spy. That part of my plan, at least, had gone over without a hitch. It was easy to see what side the professor was really on, and whatever satisfaction I felt over it was just because I'd planned things exactly that way.

"We had hoped that it would not come to this," said th'Esar, neither acknowledging nor discounting what the professor had said. I thought he might faint with relief, but he went on standing. He was stubborn like that. "The corps is our best hope in the war to come, and with the magicians—disabled, as it were—perhaps the corps is our *only* hope."

Big fucking surprise there, I thought, but I only sneered a little.

"Your Majesty," Adamo started again, real placating like. "I'm afraid I don't understand what sort of a help we can be with things going wrong the way they are all over."

Th'Esar lifted his head, serene as you please, like he hadn't spent the last months lying to us, like we wouldn't have all got killed for no proper reason if we'd been a bit unluckier and not so good at our jobs.

"We are greatly in need of time," he said. "Time to figure out what we can do to counteract this ailment, that we might beat our enemies across the border for good."

"You want us to keep them occupied," said Adamo, and it wasn't a question so much as something he'd only just figured out.

"Yes, Chief Sergeant. That is exactly what we are asking of you."

"Flying our dragons the way they are now," said Adamo, careful and clear, "is simple madness. If it isn't suicide yet, it soon will be." He left out the part I knew he wanted to add: that it was something th'Esar couldn't ask us to do, 'cause nothing got a man riled up like telling him what he couldn't do, and Adamo knew it. There was no sense in provoking him—he was a man already on the edge of something too big for him to handle and something he had to handle nonetheless.

Much as I hated th'Esar right then, I didn't fancy being in his boots, either, and not just 'cause of the color of them.

"Your Majesty," Jeannot spoke up, stepping past Ace and Ghislain and making his way to the front to stand by me, "allow me to presume so much as to see if I am completely clear as to your royal plan."

There was something snide in the way he said it, but it was perfectly politic. Jeannot was fucking clever, make no mistake. Th'Esar nodded and waved his hand in a gesture that seemed to indicate he was done wasting words on us and just wanted us to get all our cards on the table at once. Maybe then he'd sweep us from underneath. Maybe not.

"The reason we weren't informed of the present situation was that we would continue to keep the Ke-Han busy at the pass," Jeannot explained, neat and simple as you'd like, "during which period the corps could buy vital time for some . . . cure to be discovered."

Th'Esar's mouth went a little white and his cheeks a little red, since his complexion was the sort that betrayed too much emotion—not enough of the old Ramanthe in him any way you cut it. "In a manner of speaking," he said at length, "that was indeed our plan. We hope, Airman Jeannot, that you are not insinuating your displeasure for this plan?"

"I hope I'm not *insinuating* anything at all, Your Majesty," Jeannot replied, and melted back into the crowd, having made his point loud and clear enough even for the deaf, dumb, *and* blind.

We were all silent for a while, mulling that one over, since it was pretty obvious to all of us by now that we'd been used as bait, flying targets, a forlorn fucking hope they called it in romans or in melodramatic theatre, and I was so mad right then seven shades of red had come down over my eyes. It was only the professor's fingers digging into my elbow that kept me locked into place, and even that wasn't going to be enough real soon.

"I take it that no cure has yet been found," the tagalong suddenly said. We all must've forgotten he was even there because suddenly *everyone* in the room was looking at him, even me, and we could all see clear as day that he was crying.

"The illness is a peculiar one," th'Esar said, not out of pity for him, just stating the facts. "It seems to have affected first and most seriously those of purest Talent, and has worked onward from there to those with Talents more and more diluted."

"So basically," I said, "for the first time, you're lucky if you're a mutt."

The left corner of th'Esar's mouth twisted, sort of like a

mirroring of my own sneer. "I suppose that is one way of phrasing it," he conceded at last.

"Your Majesty will beg my pardon," Adamo said, in a voice that didn't sound as how that was what he wanted th'Esar to be begging for in particular. "But I can't let my men fly under such circumstances. At this point—with the rate of deterioration—flying any one of the dragons out to the Cobalts and back would be enough of a risk, much less trying to use them for battle."

"We have no other recourse," th'Esar replied.

"Then we're going to be overrun by the Ke-Han," Adamo said, squaring his jaw. "Without anything but the Cobalts standing between us and them."

Now there was real trouble. To be honest? I thought th'Esar was going to sentence Adamo to death right away, and his face turned purple like a dragon'd set his head on fire. It was ludicrous enough to be funny, only there wasn't a single man jack of us who could see their way around to laughing—not even Compagnon. We weren't the only poor fucks who were screwed seven ways, both up *and* down. Everyone in Volstov was going to be smoking opium and having twelve wives pretty soon, that is if the Ke-Han didn't just decide to fucking kill us all. It was only a matter of time—which was why th'Esar'd been so careful with it—before the Ke-Han rode on over here across the plains and took what they'd been wanting since it had belonged to the Ramanthines, because we didn't have a way to defend it.

It was a sobering thought. It made a man feel helpless, and if there was one thing I hated more than anything else, it was knowing someone'd tied my hands behind my back. But no matter which way I turned the problem to the light, I couldn't see my way clear toward solving it. The whole thing blew like a Hapenny whore.

"Are you refusing to do your duty, Chief Sergeant Adamo?" th'Esar asked.

Adamo didn't back down for even a second. "The way I see my duty, Your Majesty, is this," he said. "We signed up to die for our country. In the past, some of us have done exactly that. But part of our code is to protect our dragons before anything else—and if we fly them as you wish us to, there's no doubt in my mind that they will be destroyed. If that's what you're thinking is best for our country—to let them fall into the Ke-Han's hands, to let the Ke-Han have at what they want so badly—then I'm ready, as a soldier and as a man loyal to my country, to hear your reasoning."

Th'Esar made another one of those bird-wing motions with his hands. "We are working tirelessly even now to find a cure for the illness," he said. "Yet we must have time to think—to incorporate into our actions this troubling new knowledge you have brought before us. It changes a great many things." Adamo nodded once, curt, like the fucking perfect soldier he was. "We will call for you this evening, once we have considered the evidence before us, and, hopefully, have come to an arrangement that is more agreeable for all of us. But understand this, Chief Sergeant Adamo—if *I* say that the dragons must be sacrificed, then they must be sacrificed."

There was this terrible silence, and I felt it deep down as my bones and blood and even further. Right then, if I'd been allowed to keep my knives on me before stepping foot inside the palace, I would've split His Majesty apart before he had a chance to spew out platitudes and horseshit as fucked up as all that. He might've paid for her, but Have was *mine,* and I'd've staked my life on how the other boys felt pretty damn close to the way I did.

Adamo just nodded; and then he bowed, stiff and formal, like we'd all been dismissed without us noticing, and turned to leave.

"Your Majesty," the professor said, clearing his throat, and I had to give him points for how brave he was—even though it didn't matter much for how stupid he was at the same time as that. "There is one other matter, if I may presume to address it."

Th'Esar lifted an eyebrow. "You've presumed many things today," he said, leaning forward in his chair. Then, against all fucking odds, he nodded. "Be quick. Our time is quite precious, as you are well aware."

The professor swallowed and came forward. "As for the situation with the magicians being kept in confinement at the Basquiat," he said, "since this young apprentice has already learned of this private matter—and as the reason for the magicians' confinement is not, in fact, due to the quarantine of disease but rather to prevent the spread of panic alone—then I should think there is little reason at present for this young man to be kept from his mentor. It may also prove somewhat useful—though of course Your Highness is far better versed in these matters than I could ever hope to be—to allow a fresh young mind to work on the problem in tandem with a man I believe to be one of Your Majesty's most talented magicians."

"The Margrave Royston," th'Esar said. He obviously thought it was worse than being bled to death, being given a good idea he hadn't thought of himself, but he wasn't a fool, and I could see right away he liked it. "Very well," he said after a long pause. "The young man shall be taken to the Basquiat. The rest of you, however, must return to the Airman and await our summons."

Things happened after that sort of all at once: Adamo barking out orders, and the tagalong thanking the professor as though he was some kind of saint or something, and then there were servants being let in, some to show *us* out and the rest, I figured, there to show the tagalong the secret way of getting inside the Basquiat. I almost wanted to go with him, to get some answer about how to fix Have, but that wouldn't've done anyone a lick of good. Besides that, I was too busy watching the strange look that came over the professor and made him glow all over, almost like he'd stepped into a shaft of sunlight—only we were deep inside the palace, and so he couldn't have done.

I guess it must have been pride or maybe even happiness, but in any case it wasn't the sort of expression I'd ever seen the professor wear before that minute. Not during all his time at the Airman. Not even once.

CHAPTER THIRTEEN

ROYSTON

I didn't know how long I'd been there, but at least I did recognize *where* I was: inside the Basquiat, her golden dome arced and splendid above me, and I wasn't alone. All around me were the refugees of the epidemic—faces I recognized and faces I did not, all in various stages of misery.

At times I was worse than others, but during periods when my fever was less pronounced, I could piece together something of what I'd been told and what I'd come to understand on my own. Somehow—and even suffering as I was, I *knew* this was the key—the Well had been poisoned. We were all afflicted by it, every last one of us, from those with the purest Talent in their veins to the most bastardized; from Berhane and Daguerre and even Caius himself to Amer from the Bacque, who dealt in tricks and potions (all performed for a fee) at the farthest end of the Crescents.

It was something akin to a nightmare.

Such a disease was unprecedented. It undid us from the inside out, working first at the core of our Talents, until we could no longer hear the sound of it in our own bodies. Then, as Talent and blood were bound so inextricably together, it began to work as any disease on what held us together as men and women, raging through us as swiftly as any plague that had ever struck at the heart of the city.

During my stay—however long it was—I know that there were some who died, though when I asked who they were, no one would answer me.

I had to leave; I had to be somewhere quiet, where the punctuation of Daguerre's moans would no longer shatter my thoughts like so much glass, and I could think this through to the end. There was something we were all missing—I *refused* to die—but Daguerre was always moaning, and Marcelline weeping against her pillow, and there were two young girls who curled together and shook so violently that their cot rattled against the marble floor. Because we were underneath the golden dome, everything was louder than it would have been in another room—louder and more pronounced, every noise we made echoing across this grand triumph of architecture above us. I could no more think than I could stand.

I tried to devise a system of counting the hours, counting the days—I tried to ask an attendant how long it had been since I was brought to this place—but for all I knew it could have been minutes or it could have been weeks. Time had become interminable, untrustworthy. I thought I would go mad.

And then Hal came to me.

At first I thought I was imagining things, hallucinating his face above my bed. It could have been the fever reaching an advanced stage, the signal that my end was nearer than I wished to admit. But when he sat upon the edge of my cot, it shifted, and his hands were cool upon my brow, his fingers brushing through my hair.

"Hal," I said.

His eyes were red, as though he'd been crying. "They aren't letting anyone in," he said, soft and close as though it had been a year, and not weeks or days at all.

If I'd been able, I would have got up immediately to find out who was in charge that I might dispense with them in an appropriate fashion. Whatever the Esar was thinking, it was madness to hold us all here in one place without any indication as to when this policy would cease. Surely it was recipe for a riot. I couldn't imagine what the Esar thought he would accomplish by handling things in this fashion.

I fought to sit up. My motor skills were infuriatingly limited, but Hal had been crying. "It isn't as bad as it may seem," I said, which apparently was not at all the right thing to say, for as soon as I spoke, Hal's shaky composure crumbled as swiftly as the blue rock of the Cobalts and he buried his face, wet with weeping, against my neck. His nose was very cold. "Hal," I said again, whereupon he made a high, keening sound in the back of his throat, like someone at the very end of his resolve. I put my arms about him instead and said nothing at all. I wished then that I'd not been so unrelentingly stubborn as to set what rules I had made for us in the carriage. There were so many opportunities lost to us, the awkwardness of the night after the ball, when Hal had started up the stairs to the bedroom after me, and countless days when I found my favorite chair made just a little too small by Hal's joining me in it.

He'd as good as made his decision, and I had been too blind to acknowledge it, too caught up in suspicion and headaches. And now that I knew it, I could barely summon the strength to lift my arms around him. It was a cruel joke of some kind or another, but I would not give in to regret just yet.

"They wouldn't let me in," he mumbled, repeating the words as though they were a poison that needed to be bled from the hurt he'd received by not being able to see me, of all things. Yet not even the most selfish part of me could be touched at the effect my departure had had on him, for it went against everything I held dear to know that Hal should ever be hurt unnecessarily.

I did feel a curious sort of pride, though, mingled with my sympathy and frustration at the situation. Hal had found some way in to see me, and judging by the number of invalids, there were many more people yet waiting for news. I'd known Hal was clever, and I'd known he'd be suited to the city despite his misgivings. To me, this was irrefutable proof that my beliefs hadn't been unfounded, nor clouded by whatever other feelings I harbored for him.

"Well, it isn't exactly a very pleasant place to be," I said, curling my fingers in his hair even as I spoke. He fit so neatly against me that it made my chest tighten for a moment, and I found it difficult to breathe. I'd never experienced such a symptom previously with the illness that had so thoroughly possessed me, so I had to assume it was Hal who caused it— a symptom of that other, quieter illness, which had nevertheless snatched my senses away as completely as the fever.

"Royston," Hal said against my neck, like a plea or a prayer and not at all like my name.

I could have told him, "I believe the Well's been poisoned and us along with it," or, "You should leave, before anyone tries to make you, and I am forced to remonstrate with them," but I paused for too long, and the fleeting urge to be sensible withered and dropped from my mind like old fruit.

Instead, I kissed the top of his head, breathing in the familiar soap-smelling cleanness of him. It soothed me in a deep and satisfying way, a cool sensation filtering all the way down to my core and cutting right through the heat in my fevered brain. "It's all right," I said, not entirely sure that it was. Yet I felt very much as though it might be, it *could* be, which was more hope than I'd possessed in all the time that had passed since being brought here. "Sometime soon you shall have to tell me the story of your daring break-in. I'm sure with your aptitude, it was much like something out of a roman."

He laughed at that, quiet and diffident, and finally lifted his face to mine.

"I'm glad you came," I said at last, because it was true, even if some part of me couldn't bear to be seen in such a weakened state. It was the more frivolous side of me, vain and foolish, and I paid it little heed. There was no place for such preening idiocy in this room full of killing fever.

"You're sick," Hal said, carrying on even as his voice snagged on something low and unhappy. "That's what they told me. Everyone here is sick."

"Something like that," I said, then, because I had resolved to be as honest with Hal as I possibly could, I continued. "I believe—though it is my own personal speculation, and nothing more—that what has struck us has something to do with the Well."

I saw him struggle to understand, or perhaps to prioritize what I was telling him over his own feelings, which were plain as invitation on his face. "Then it's something to do with the magic," he said at last. "As a whole, and not just magicians?"

"I suppose it is," I said after a moment, though admittedly I hadn't been thinking of it in terms beyond my knowledge of what the poison was doing to me and my fellows, burning us from the inside out. In some ways, my worldview had shrunk to this room of the Basquiat, cramped and close with friends and strangers alike, and though I'd thought often of Hal, it was almost as though I'd lost the ability to think beyond the confines of it.

I supposed it was my own selfishness come full circle again that I could think of nothing but the ways in which a situation affected me and my immediate surroundings.

"Then it's true what the airmen were talking of," Hal said, then shook his head slightly, as though he'd caught himself in a misstep. "They're how I got in, the Dragon Corps and their— Well, Thom. His name is Thom."

The student Marius had often spoken of with the kind of pride reserved for a father had been named Thom, I thought, my fevered mind making the connection unbidden. Marius was here the same as I was, though he hadn't opened his eyes since the room had been flooded with sunlight this morning.

"Do you mean to tell me," I said very slowly, both out of a desire to be very clear and because my head felt inconveniently fogged all of a sudden, "that you went to the *Dragon Corps* first to find a way into the Basquiat?"

"Well, no," answered Hal, flushing to the tips of his ears. "Thom found me waiting on the steps here, and he thought it might be a good idea—more helpful—to get the airmen involved, because the Esar was more likely to listen to them. And they—" He froze, looking around us suddenly as though expecting to see every face turned with interest toward our conversation. Finding no interest, he nevertheless leaned close, breath warm against my ear. "They're worried because there's something wrong with the dragons, do you see? Because of the magic in them as well. They aren't flying properly—your friend, the Chief Sergeant, he said he refused to let them fly under the circumstances, that the dragons had become too unpredictable."

"Bastion," I swore, loudly enough that Marcelline looked over at me in surprise. She was drawn and pale, but at that moment I could think of nothing but my own blind stupidity, that

I could *ever* have thought something as deadly as this could be affecting only the magicians who walked and breathed, and not the creations into which they poured their Talents. I'd never worked on a dragon myself—it was too specialized an endeavor—but I'd known some of the men who had, old and powerful. Such men had been some of the very first to fall ill. None of *them* had made the immediate connection either, which hardly comforted me, as some of those men were now dead.

I had to take control of my thoughts. I recalled the very earliest days of harnessing my Talent, all the while doing my best to ignore the sickening vacuum that existed now in its place. Working against the cluttered state of my mind was a task I could accomplish: I simply needed to concentrate. Hal's hands were on my shoulders, kneading with absent, fretful motions. I closed my eyes, allowing the reality of his presence to calm me as it always did.

"In any case, I suppose what we did was storm the palace," Hal went on, still so close that I couldn't see his face. I thought perhaps that I'd misheard him, or that this was another trick of the fever turning words into what they weren't, for if I knew anything I surely knew Hal, and the idea of his storming anything, let alone a palace, was so out of the realm of possibility that I felt it must be my delirium. How much could have happened since I'd been brought here that such a thing could change?

"Pardon?" I asked finally.

"Well, it wasn't a real storming, not entirely, because the Esar let us in, but I got the feeling that we'd have gone even if he hadn't. They were that serious about it. And I can't think of much that would have stopped them." I could feel his skin growing hot against my cheek, blushing at what he'd done or what he'd been caught up in by outside forces.

"Hal," I said, and traced my knuckles down the curved length of his spine. I felt a smile playing about my lips; it was the first I'd worn in days. "You haven't been here a month and you're already storming the palace?"

He drew back, eyes bright with something that stood out

starkly against my bleak surroundings of illness and misery, and it filled me like a cup to the brim. "I was worried about you," he said.

I kissed him.

I might have blamed it on the fever, though I felt considerably more lucid now than I had since the onset in the Cobalts. And I might have blamed it on what Hal had done, for certainly the devotion apparent in it was a gesture that would touch even the most callous of hearts. Yet more than that—and I knew it as surely as I had felt my Talent drained away—was the fact that I loved him, and that people were dying, and though there were things I regretted, I wouldn't allow Hal to become one of them.

His hands went still against my shoulders, then quickly slipped up behind my head, as if he were afraid I'd change my mind too soon and he'd miss his chance. I held him close, hands low to where his back narrowed, hoping to soothe his fears.

I knew it was foolish. If I could have chosen, I certainly wouldn't have opted for a setting such as this, surrounded by the sick and likely dying, myself so infuriatingly weak that it was all I could do to go on holding Hal when he pressed close to me.

The kiss was too eager, Hal's inexperience too evident, and my fever cut it short before its time. Yet when it ended, Hal's hands were curled tight at the back of my collar, and his shirt bunched up underneath my own hands, and there was no one here to tell us to stop.

We were, after all, very far from the countryside.

He said something so quiet that I almost missed it, but then he said it again and it was my name, broken and soft and nearly unfamiliar.

His fingers trembled; I could feel them against my cheek as he stroked the overgrown roughness at my jaw, the gray at my temple.

"Hal," I whispered against his mouth, and he shivered as though a current had passed between us.

"Find somewhere private and leave us in peace," Alcibiades muttered from a cot somewhere to my left. Hal colored all at once—I could feel it as well as I could see it—and we parted, though I promised myself that one day I'd repay Alcibiades for the sentiment. Yet as embarrassed as I was, I knew he was right. "Hal," I said, carefully. "This isn't—"

"I know," he agreed, though he refused to relinquish his part in our embrace and, as I admit it was the only thing that presently held me up, I was grateful he insisted upon being so tenacious. "I'm so glad. I thought, when I heard from the Esar that the magicians—"

"I don't intend to die," I told him firmly. "And as you can see, I am certainly not *yet* dead."

He nodded mutely, and I saw him struggle visibly with the worry that plagued him until I wished there were anything at all I could do to reassure him. There was however nothing but dissembling and false promises, and I refused to lie to Hal.

"When this is over," I said, avoiding the terrible word *if,* "I hope you'll allow me to kiss you properly, in a place that is neither a carriage nor a sickbed."

He flushed and bowed his head. "Royston," he said, "I don't think the Esar knows what to do."

"No," I agreed. "I don't think he does either."

"Then," Hal asked, "then what are we to do?"

For the moment, all I could think was that I wanted to lie down and surrender—if only for a little while—to sleep. I fought the urge, however tempting, knotting my fingers in the sleeves of Hal's shirt to keep myself upright. "We must do what only we can do," I replied, taking my time with the words; it was the only way I knew to keep them crisp and certain and indeed anything other than wearily slurred. "We must put our minds to this. I don't suppose we might call a man to fetch some of my books?"

Hal almost laughed at that, but there was something tearful behind the sound. "Between us both," he promised, "we'll remember."

It wasn't the most original plan I'd ever come up with, but it was the only one we had.

"Come," I said, "let's see if we can't arrange these pillows more comfortably."

In the bed next to mine, Alcibiades coughed something that sounded as if it might be derogatory. Let him scoff, I told myself; I was determined to save his life, along with mine, before the Ke-Han descended upon us all and none of our grand gestures in the hot, dark room mattered any longer to anyone.

THOM

It was quiet in the Airman, the sort of quiet I imagined descended upon soldiers before a battle, or upon the desert before a sandstorm. It was an unnatural, tentative quiet, and there was nothing in it I could use to distract myself from how badly my hands were shaking.

"Fucking stop that," Rook said. "You're like as not to make somebody nervous if you keep on *fucking* doing that."

There was no one in the common room but him and me. Earlier, Evariste had passed through once on his way to make coffee, then once on his way back with a cup in his hand and the smell of the burnt grounds thick on the air. Other than that, we were completely alone. I didn't think that Rook was capable of being nervous—I believe he'd forgotten how it was to feel anything of the sort—but nevertheless I clasped my hands together and put them between my knees.

There was the silence again.

It was better to know our fate, I was certain, than to be acutely, painfully unaware. Knowledge was the key; whether it was a knowledge you'd been seeking or something else entirely, it made no difference. You had to work with what knowledge you were given. Only if you weren't given anything, you had to wait—and the waiting was interminable.

I flexed my hands between the bony press of my knees. I reminded myself of what we'd accomplished that afternoon and kept my own private relief as a small flame against the darkness. At least Rook and the other airmen wouldn't be flying unarmed with the truth about their dragons. It was cold comfort, but it was nevertheless something.

"So," Rook said, "what do you know about the magicians, anyway? I mean, that *fucking* Well. What do you know about it?"

The question nearly startled a sound out of me, and for a moment I found myself so distracted by my own tangled thoughts I didn't even answer him. What I knew about the magicians was limited by my area of studies, but I knew *magicians* in particular, Marius being the most immediate example, and the handful of professors I'd had who'd been blessed, or perhaps cursed, with Talents of their own. I wondered where Marius was now; I could have used his guidance.

"Not very much," I admitted.

"Fuck," Rook said, but there was less malevolence in it than usual. "I thought you knew everything, 'Versity boy."

I rubbed wearily at my eyes. "Yes," I said, "well. Not everything."

Rook gave me a look that seemed to intimate I'd suddenly grown a pair of horns, or perhaps a tail. "Don't start gettin' women's *moods* on me," Rook said. "I've got enough fucking trouble right now without it being your time of the month."

"Hardly," I said. "I'm simply feeling somewhat sobered by the day's events."

"*Simply feeling somewhat sobered by the day's events,*" Rook parroted back at me, giving each word a sneer. There was that malevolence I'd been missing. I'd spoken too soon about the change I'd imagined in him. It seemed I was much better at imagining changes than I was at effecting them. "Bastion. You ever listen to yourself? It's like you really *are* useless."

I recalled my earlier triumph with Hal, and felt heartened, however momentarily. "Not entirely that, either," I said.

"No," Rook agreed, throwing me off somewhat. "Guess not, though it sure took you long enough to make yourself useful." He chose that moment to stop pacing the length of the common room and sit down hard next to me on the opposite end of the couch, crossing his legs wide, and moving lazy as a cat. There was a certain tension beneath his movements, though, noticeable only when he came close, and even then it was rare. In some ways though, I had been training myself to do exactly that, notice the subtle changes, the slight variations in his nonchalance. I was only just now growing aware of how dedicated I was to the study of him, my long-lost brother.

It was a troublesome propensity of mine, and one I had no right to cultivate under these peculiar circumstances. I felt childish, and exhausted with the day's efforts. I wanted to curl up on my couch and go straight to sleep, but to do that would have meant asking Rook to leave, and I could no more command him than I could th'Esar himself.

I pressed the heels of my hands against my forehead instead, staving off the advent of a headache. "I barely studied the Well," I said softly. "I wish now that I had, but it never interested me."

"Idiot," Rook said.

"Indeed," I replied.

"S'not what I'd've studied," he added, after a pause. "If I'd ever lost my fucking mind and decided *school* was what I wanted to do with most of my life."

"You would have done quite well," I told him. If not for his cleverness, I added to myself, then certainly for his ability to intimidate others into giving him exactly what he wanted.

"Fucking right I would've," he said. "But I chose Have. *Shit.*" He tore off and shook his head, his face angry and harsh in the fading sunlight, his blue eyes narrowed and his wide mouth tight. All his features, I decided then, seemed each to be taken from many different men's faces; they were a strange and startling assortment, and the ferocity behind his every expression was what made him so painfully handsome.

"I'm sorry," I said, as if I were talking to John and not Rook. "For your dragon, that is. It may be that th'Esar and those close to him will divine a solution—"

"Or it may be that th'Esar and those close to him may never *divine* a way to unstick their heads from being shoved so far up their own rumps they can barely see the light of day," Rook offered.

"That," I agreed, "is also a possibility."

"You did a pretty decent job in there," he said then, as though every word of it were painful to him. "Not like you taught us a fucking thing, but you were all right."

I felt a strange suffusion of warmth—pleasure, I supposed, at being complimented as though I were a stray dog who'd done right for the first time in his flea-ridden existence. I couldn't help my starved gratitude from showing plainly on my face; as soon as Rook saw it his mouth curled down at the corners and he looked sharply away.

"Th'Esar—the Esar—had no right to keep what he knew from you," I said, choosing my words with the utmost care. "He might have killed all of you for pride. It is treason to say so, but he has behaved more like a fool than a leader."

"If he's fucked my girl," Rook said, "I'll pay him back for it."

"That mightn't be too wise," I cautioned.

"You're not my fucking mother," Rook said, "so don't act like you are."

I turned away from him, feeling the blow more deeply for the hope he'd given me. Perhaps that had been his plan all along. Even with the feverishness with which I applied myself to studying him, I could no more predict him than I could predict the outcome of this war. But the hurt and my own shame coursed through me all the same, hot chasing cold in my blood. I had no room to judge him, nor room to love him, either.

I bowed my head.

That was when he took my chin in his hand, simple as reaching across the table for a slice of toast at lunch, and looked at me, really looked, while I fought the urge to run as far and fast as I could in the other direction. He was looking at my eyes. Something turned over in my stomach, uncomfortable and real, like the first moment of falling or the first time he'd taken a dive on Havemercy when I was up in the air with him. He let his hand drop after a moment, but he went on looking like I was a puzzle, something he couldn't quite figure out. I couldn't find it in my heart to drop my gaze a second time. I was fixed like an insect, caught in a box of my own making. Pinned. Trapped.

"Don't fucking know why you did it," he said. "Don't even know if it'll help."

I realized all at once this was his way of thanking me, whether he acknowledged it or not. My heart turned to glass in my chest, and I knew that at its next beat it was bound to shatter.

"John," I said.

His face changed in an instant, more quickly than the turns he'd taken on Havemercy. There were shards of glass in my veins, and he shoved me away from him.

"What the fuck did you just call me?" he said. His voice was low and deceptively smooth; I felt certain it would whip around, fast as a dragon's tail, to strike me the moment my back was turned.

"John," I said, the words drawn out of me by some force too powerful for me to stop, too powerful for me to name. I suppose it was the truth at last, at the wrong moment, at the most ruinous one. This was disaster, rolling like an avalanche. I couldn't stop speaking. "Your name is John—*was* John—you told me to stay where I was, and I—"

"Who put you up to this?" Rook said. "Who fucking told you to say that?"

They weren't questions; they were too terrifying to be questions. I knew he'd beat the answers out of me as soon as demand them, but I could admit no feeling that would allow me to be afraid of him.

"I'm your brother," I said.

"Fuck you," said Rook. "My brother's dead."

"I went to live with the whores on Tuesday Street," I said, frozen helpless in place for all I couldn't keep my tongue still. "They took me in, they called me Thom. I . . . there was a man; he told me you were dead. I thought that you must have gone back inside to look for me, and that was why—"

"Shut up," he said.

I wished that I could.

"I never thought I'd see you again." It wasn't the way I'd

meant to do it. In fact it went against everything I'd planned, right down to my best of intentions in the very beginning. It was too late now, too late to cushion the blow for him as I'd wished it could have been for me.

He lunged forward then, and I thought he *was* going to hit me. Of course, he had every right to do so if he wished, as I'd hurt him in far worse ways. No matter what faults Rook possessed—and they were many; I was not so blinded by my guilt to believe otherwise—I knew that what I'd done was worse. I'd betrayed him; he was my brother and for a long time—*such* a long time—I'd known it.

Instead, he only took my face in one hand again, and pushed my hair back at the right temple where it hid a small white scar, a relic of running too fast on legs too short when I'd been younger and heedless of anyone's remonstrations to be careful.

"You were always fucking running near the stairs," he said at last. Something squeezed tight in my chest, so that I had to exhale a nervous sound of release.

"I'm sorry," I said quietly, and he dropped his hands from me as quickly as he'd moved before, though there wasn't any real urgency behind his movements. Rather, it was more as if he was so disgusted that I didn't matter to him one way or the other and *especially* not because I had some silly scar proving we shared the same blood.

He didn't say anything after that, only sat still and stony as a mountain. My hands were starting to hurt, and I realized I'd been squeezing them between my knees since he'd told me to do something about their shaking. I felt a sudden and desperate wish for things to go back to the way they'd been, even before knowing I had a brother, because if I hadn't known, then I wouldn't ever have hurt him in this fashion. Even if all the parts of him that *could* hurt had disappeared along with the boy who had been John, that knowledge didn't preclude my own guilt, and it certainly didn't change what I'd done to him.

I put my head in my hands. "I'm sorry," I said again, though it sounded tinny and meaningless even to my own ears. "I meant to tell you sooner."

I felt a change come over the room, in the small space between us, as though I'd somehow gleaned the same ability the
airmen boasted, to be able to taste danger in the air or smell the
stronger emotions. My mouth was impossibly dry.

"How long," he said, calmer than I'd ever heard him and all
the more terrifying because of it, "have you known?" He was
adding up the details in his head, searching for the possible
moment of revelation; his eyes held none of the callous distance to which I'd grown accustomed, but they were focused
on the wall behind me, and not my face. Even then I wished
he'd look at me, though the desire spoke only to the depths of
a place in me I wished never to accept as mine.

I should have been straightforward from the start. Or, barring that, I should have gone on lying. Anything at all seemed
better than this: this awful careening path I'd taken that tore
up everything I'd carefully sown.

"Since you told me," I whispered, as though by softening
my voice I could somehow soften the impact of the blow.
"That night, when you were hurt, and I— I'm *Hilary.*" For all
my restraint and the careful compartments in which I'd tried
to keep my feelings, I couldn't prevent the desperation from
crawling into my voice.

I didn't deserve to ask anything of Rook, and I wanted
everything from him. It had been the same when we were
boys, I thought. A familiarity, deep and irrational as blood,
and I wanted to tear at my hair for what it had done to me.
What I had done to him in return. John, Rook. My own
brother, who was meant to make everything right.

He moved at that last and I flinched, though there was no
need. He didn't even look at me. I began to think it might have
been better if he *had* struck me, or at least reacted in some way
that might have alleviated my guilt, however briefly. Instead,
he got up, unfolding his legs very slowly, but with no ambigu-
ity that could leave anyone to mistake it for hesitance. No, it
was a deliberate pulling away, piece by piece, to sever all ties,
and I felt it with a wrench, as though I'd somehow lost something more than a brother whom I'd never truly had to begin

with. It was worse than being struck, worse than my bones breaking. But Rook, of course, was clever enough to know that.

I watched him go, helpless, with no right to call him back and no reason to believe his reluctance to do violence went beyond this silent exit. If I tried to stop him, I thought, it would most certainly push him into something regrettable.

He paused in the doorway, so fierce and unhappy that I felt it underneath my skin. How my brother had come to be such a person with his wild braids and quick jeering I couldn't understand. Whenever I studied his face I found not even a hint of the John I remembered. Of course, twenty-one years was a very long time, and perhaps the things I remembered were remembered all wrong. Perhaps in my brother had always been this man, just as in me there had always been someone who would grow up to develop the ability to manipulate others and a questionable code of what was right and wrong.

"You don't talk to me," said Rook, and for one wild moment I thought it was a complaint before the honest hand of reality came up to slap me in the face. This was the way things would be from now on. Our new rules, just when I'd made peace and felt comfortable enough to leave a handful of the old ones by the wayside. "I don't talk to you, and this? It never happened. Far as I'm concerned, my brother died when he was three. You go long enough believing something like that's true, then it becomes true, you see what I'm saying?"

I didn't. I couldn't. After all, I'd spent *my* whole life believing him to be dead, only to have it proved wrong, and the contradiction hadn't made me any less glad to discover him alive and—in most ways—well.

"It isn't true, though," I said, unable to keep from pushing my luck, as though I was compelled by some greater force to see this to its bitter conclusion with no holds barred, nothing held back. "You can't just— We *are* brothers."

"I think it's a little rich, gettin' a lecture from *you* on what a man can and can't do to his own brother," said Rook flatly. There was no malice, or spite, or even the rare tolerance I'd come to cherish in his voice. There was only nothing, empty and clean the way I imagined his chest to be, a hollow echoing where his heart should be.

"My brother is dead," said Rook again, as though I hadn't heard him properly in the first place. I half expected him to follow up the statement with a threat detailing what would happen to me if I brought it up again, or at the very least something to forbid my coming near him in the future, but he merely turned away from me and walked out the door as though I'd ceased to exist altogether.

After that, I didn't see him at all. When I mentioned it as casually as I could to Adamo, he said that Rook had signed up for all the extra shifts he could to give th'Esar the time he needed to work things out.

I tried to slide a wall of glass between my thoughts and my heart, just as my brother had done for some reason I hadn't understood, and now would never know. With him flying the way he was, and under such dire conditions, it seemed likely I should prepare myself for the possibility that I might never see him again.

While this wasn't the worst I'd ever felt, it was certainly close.

It seemed that in the second meeting th'Esar had called, some manner of tentative truce had been called between him and the Chief Sergeant. The solution wasn't an ideal one by any means, but the way Adamo had explained it sounded as though what they'd agreed upon was a kind of unofficial system of volunteering, the way the crush shifts worked only now it was *every* shift, and anyone who thought their dragon was good enough to fly that night could sign up and batter back the Ke-Han to the best of his abilities.

Much as I hated to admit it—and I did hate it these days though I'd always considered myself a loyal citizen—th'Esar was a shrewd thinker. In a group such as the Dragon Corps, tightly knit and yet infused with a sense of honor and pride that would rival His Majesty's, asking for volunteers was a clever system to employ. In some ways, it became a competition, indicating you were a coward if you didn't volunteer straightaway. It was the same mentality that had kept them quiet about their dragons in the first place, and yet for once, I made no notes for my own private documentation.

If I were to be completely truthful, I'd have expected more of a split within the group, with the more pragmatic men electing to stay out of the mess entirely, at least until their dragons were rehabilitated, and the wilder risk-takers signing up for all the shifts. Instead, though there were certainly some who took longer to sign up, I found myself seeing everyone taking to the halls in much the same manner, soot-soaked and cutting in line for the shower, or falling asleep right in their chairs in the common room due to having been up all the previous night.

I asked Ghislain about it, as, beyond the vague sense of unease I got around him, he'd nevertheless struck me as one of the more sensible men bunking in the Airman.

"You never played sports as a kid, did you?" He tugged at the blackened towel around his neck, waiting outside the shower room.

I didn't see what sports had to do with anything, and said so.

He only smiled, sharp and always startlingly bright. "Do anything as a team?"

"No. Well, study projects, sometimes. With a group," I amended. The closest thing I'd had to a team, I supposed, had been the whores who'd taken me in, but that had all been very long ago, and anyway I didn't think it was what Ghislain was talking about.

"Well," he said, "and this is only my own way of thinking, mind, but when you're doing something you love—really love—you can't let the way others play the game get in the way of that, if you follow. It don't matter if your coach is hassling you, or whether you don't like how some of your teammates indulge in the sport. When you're out there, you've got a goal to accomplish, and you can't see to letting all that mishmash weigh you down."

In some ways, I felt as though I would never stop learning

the lesson. What I'd set out to accomplish with the Dragon Corps had been foolish beyond recourse. I would never understand them the way they understood one another. No matter which way I turned, it seemed that I was to be reminded of my failings as a teacher. And Rook's conspicuous absence reminded me of my failings in all other areas of life.

The nights were the worst. I lay on my couch listening to the far-off sounds of explosions, imagined or real, and all that stood between the Ke-Han and Rook was a dragon who wasn't even flying properly. I couldn't pinpoint exactly what it was I thought I stood to lose with Rook's death; I'd lost him this time just as surely as I'd lost my brother in the fire twenty-one years ago. Yet every night I listened just the same, terrified that every explosion would be the last, or that I wouldn't hear the telltale sound of boots in the hallway, denoting another night's return, whole if not entirely safe.

I couldn't have said why I indulged in such a torture night after night. It certainly wasn't my business to look after Rook, and there was no reason now to wait up for him as there once had been. The only thing I could come up with, staring at the ceiling in the darkened common room while my brother raced off to risk his life or give th'Esar's men more time to win the war, was that I had a duty, however misplaced, and that it was mine and no one else's.

Perhaps I'd given up the right to look after Rook when I hadn't called him brother straightaway, but if I didn't do it, I didn't know who would, and that thought kept me up much later than the explosions ever did.

CHAPTER FOURTEEN

❦❦

HAL

Two men died, and three women, making five in total since I'd come. This was why I refused to leave Royston; it was as if I thought that, by remaining at his side, I could ward off death simply with how fiercely I loved him. This was insane, but the room seemed to evoke that after a time in all its inhabitants, the close air laden with fever, the sickly smell of epidemic, of sweat, of unclean bodies tossing and turning without relief.

On the first day, Royston was so certain that *we* would be the ones to break the riddle of the fever and find its cure that I could do nothing but believe him.

"You must find those who are still capable of using their minds against this," Royston told me, holding one of my hands with both of his. "I would suggest trying Alcibiades— he's the blond man who keeps grunting at us—as well as Marius, if you can coax him into opening his eyes. You remember, I spoke with him at the party? And then there's . . . ah, Marcelline, the redhead. Over there, do you see her?"

I lifted a cup of water to his lips, and he drank greedily. "Yes," I told him. "I do. I'll try my best."

I had no trouble in coaxing Marius to come, though he insisted first on checking the condition of a pale woman with blond hair. She was the same woman with the fluttering fan that Royston had been flirting with at the ball, though I hardly recognized her now. Alcibiades and Marcelline agreed to come, as well as a small young man who overhead my conversation and told me his name was Caius. I'd known all along that Caius Greylace was a real person, of course, and not a character from a roman like so many of the others I'd read about, but it was strange to see him living and breathing in front of me. It was almost like encountering Tycho the Brave under the golden dome of the Basquiat. The fever seemed to have struck one of his eyes—the left one—which was gray and filmy as death, but the other was so crystal clear an emerald color that it unnerved me; he reminded me of an old statue with one of its jewel eyes missing.

"The rest are bemoaning their fate," he told me in a high, easy voice. "I don't think you'll find much help among them, only I did manage a game of High Kings with Berhane earlier this morning. You may ask after her." He paused, noting my confusion, and added helpfully, "The blonde. With the curls. She may, however, vomit on you; it's what she did when I won."

I gathered Berhane as well, as per Caius's suggestion, though she required my aid in helping her over to Royston's cot, where our small group of the bedraggled and feverish was gathered.

"Ah," Caius said, making way for the fifth and final addition. "Come sit here by me, darling; if you feel the need to exile your lunch in the same manner in which you exiled breakfast, feel free to do it once more in my hair."

"Have you seen your hair lately?" Alcibiades asked wearily. "This isn't the place for vanity."

"Don't tell Berhane that," Marius said in a quiet voice, holding out a hand to steady hers while she settled. "She considers it still the highest of priorities."

Somewhere far off in the corner of the room, the same young woman began yet another fit of coughing, and as I took my seat at Royston's bedside we were all momentarily sobered by the sound. It strengthened Royston's resolve, however, and he even sat up with minimal aid from me.

"First," he said. "Caius. What do we know?"

Caius pushed limp, pale blond hair back from his eerie eyes. "What do I know, you mean," he said.

Berhane pursed her lips, leaning her head against Marius's shoulder. "Rumors are rampant," she said. "I don't know if a single one of us here knows a damn thing about what's happening. You're closer to the Esar than all of us—or were, in any case."

"Before I began to go blind," Caius said, without a hint of anything more than cheerful acceptance. "Yes, that is true. I was working on devising some sort of cure, in fact, before the fever took me."

"Well?" Royston demanded. "Caius, now isn't the time for tangents, and of the two of us—I believe, though I cannot be sure—I'm the better equipped for knocking sense into you than you are for escaping."

Caius sighed. "Very well," he said. "It was a snake."

"A snake," said Alcibiades.

"That's preposterous," Marcelline added.

"I saw it with my own eyes," Caius insisted. "A snake. Black as onyx, with eyes like two opals, sparkling and changing color in the light. It was dead, but there it was, curled at the bottom of the Well. The Sisters fished it out, but by then it was too late—the color of the water was turning black as though someone had dumped a pot of ink into it. The only curiosity was that the inky color hadn't yet finished dispersing, as if the whole thing were paused in time and the clouds of murky black unfurling with very slow precision."

"A snake did that," said Alcibiades.

"I'm telling you what I saw," Caius said. "The Esar sent for a group of us. By that point, the Wildgrave and a few others had already taken ill."

"He said that he had a fever," Marius interjected. He sounded more angry than shocked.

"This was the time of the ball," Royston said grimly. When Caius nodded, I saw pleasure at having been right mingle in Royston's expression with displeasure at what being right meant. I offered him water another time, but he shook his head slightly.

"This was the time of the ball, indeed," Caius confirmed. "The ball was something of a ruse—I suspected more than a few would realize it. You may have noticed the incongruous *lack* of our esteemed Majesty at his own party. Grievous poor manners, and I told him as much, but he needed the time to show us what had happened. Then, of course, we set to torturing the Brothers and Sisters of Regina to find out which of the guards was responsible for this. We suspected foul play—naturally, for it could be nothing other—but we had no idea what *sort* it was, or why a snake, however clearly of magical origin, could *poison* the Well simply by crawling into it and dying there." Caius paused for a moment, and without thinking I offered the glass of water to him. Unlike Royston, he took it gratefully, and I steadied his hands against the glass with my own as he drank deeply from it. "Ah. That's better," he said, voice indeed sounding much less dry and harsh. "Where was I? Mm, the Brothers and Sisters, and how we tortured them for answers. Yes. As you might suspect, we went through a number before we came to one who knew anything at all."

I winced, and turned away. Royston covered my hand on his coverlet with his own, and I tried to force the image from my head. This was a problem that needed solving, and there was no time to let my emotions get the better of me. Yet I became this involved even in my romans, so telling myself it was "only a story" did little good to erase the injustice of the innocent Brothers and Sisters undergoing such an ordeal.

"Go on," Royston said quietly.

Caius nodded. "It *was* one of the Brothers," he continued. "He'd been bribed into it—at *quite* the exorbitant price, I'll have you know; he would have been a rich man when this was all over if I weren't so very good at my job. They must have offered to take the stitches out of his lips and everything! In any case, the Ke-Han had reached him, and we're damned to bastion and back if we know *how* they did it, but he stole a sample for them. We can only assume it was the analysis of that sample that the Ke-Han employed in formulating their poison. When they had it perfected, they gave it tangible form in the guise of a snake—it's a powerful thing, or was before it served its purpose and died there. And, when last I spoke of the matter, common theory was that it was the work of a great many Ke-Han magicians, since their Talents lie more in the natural realm than the subversion of nature. The snake, we have also surmised, was merely for the sake of function; it must have slipped in entirely unnoticed. That, too, was exceedingly clever. I should like to congratulate the man who thought of it."

"Before you torture him to death, you mean," Alcibiades said.

"Credit where credit is due," Caius replied smoothly.

"All this time, then," Royston said, steering the conversation smoothly back to its purpose, "you can assure us that the men working on the problem have been attempting to devise an antidote to the poison the snake released into the waters of the Well?"

"Exactly that," Caius confirmed. "They've taken samples from the Well, in much the same way as the Ke-Han did to fashion the poison in the first place. We've been seeking to combat this trouble from the same standpoint taken to begin it. I wonder if that's the proper tack to choose, but I'm no longer, as you may see, on the team of scientists still working to find a cure."

"And they've tested the snake," Royston asked.

"Of course they have," Caius replied.

"And they've found no cure," Marius said in a dull voice.

Caius said nothing at all, though he did gesture around the room. The woman began her coughing again, and our group seemed all too suddenly distracted by the sound.

"How long have they been working to find it?" Berhane asked, wincing even as she did so.

"I would say it's been a month," Caius answered. "Perhaps a little more than that. I am uncertain as to how long it had been before I was called to the scene, but I assume it was a few days to a little more than a week, and no more."

"Seeing as how they wanted you for all the torturing," Alcibiades said.

Caius's smile gleamed. "Something to that effect."

"We must read up on everything we know about the Ke-Han magic," Royston interjected.

"With what romans?" Marcelline asked. "Whom shall we

send to fetch the relevant material? Who will be granted access back inside?"

I feared at that moment Royston would ask me to do the job, and that I would have to refuse him—for Marcelline was right, and once I left, I'd have no such luck returning.

"My dear Marcelline," Royston said, closing his eyes and leaning somewhat heavily against my side. "We are in the Basquiat. Hal has two good legs, two good hands, and two good eyes, in case these facts have all escaped you, and there are in fact fifteen libraries within this building at our disposal."

"He won't be granted access to any of *them*, either," Marcelline pointed out, but her dark eyes had been gifted with sudden light.

"Then he'll just have to be devious," Caius replied. "He's small. He seems clever. He should be able to manage."

I didn't know whether to be touched at their faith in me or overwhelmed by the task now set upon my shoulders. Royston breathed against my side, rasping occasionally but a warm weight that hardened my resolve all the same. There was no time for hesitation, or my own uncertainty in the face of a foreign and somewhat terrifying authority.

Thom had faced down the Esar for me, after all. I could certainly fetch some romans.

Royston gave me directions to the nearest of the libraries, then the most thorough, and *also* the one that was likeliest to have a collection of all accounts of known poisons and their antidotes, until he had to stop halfway through at the perplexed look on my face and call for paper so that he could dictate as I wrote it all down. I was cheered by the smallest of things. That Royston's voice was yet strong enough to pitch to a yell in order to be heard when many of the others were arguing lit a tiny spark near my heart. It stayed there, glowing and ebbing with Royston's progress, and I found it harder than I'd thought it might be to actually leave the room with the golden dome to find the romans.

"Hal," Royston said, and though his eyes were closed, he

was smiling at me. "We can't do anything more without ro-mans, do you understand?"

"Forget this mysterious bastion-forsaken *snake* plague," said Alcibiades. He didn't sit up very often anymore, but his opinions were as strident as ever. "*You* two are what's going to make me ill."

I held very tightly to Royston's hand, then forced myself to release it, stepping gingerly around the cots strewn hap-hazardly across the floor. The quicker I left, I reasoned, the quicker I could return, then give the romans to minds that would understand them, unravel this mystery, and take Roys-ton home with me.

The first library I went to—the one Royston had told me had the most extensive collection of publications on known poi-sons and antidotes—was a room at the bottom of a spiraling staircase. The walls were fitted with high windows covered in metal filigree, and there was row upon row of impossibly tall stacks that seemed to reach from the floor to the very high ceiling. Hidden in the shadows against the left-hand wall there was a wheeled ladder, and scattered thoughtfully here and there were low, squat chairs with gold feet and small round end tables supporting stained-glass lamps. It was a room clearly designed for the access and reading of romans, and for one full minute I could do nothing but stand there in admira-tion and longing.

After a moment of wide-mouthed wonder I thought of Roys-ton, and also of Alcibiades in the cot next to his; of Berhane, who could barely manage to move, of Marius, who looked gaunt as a skeleton, and Marcelline and her red-rimmed eyes, and of Caius, who had tortured people to come to the bottom of this mystery and was nevertheless going blind. I couldn't take the time to savor the view before me, I told myself rather an-grily. There were people depending on my work here.

Thankfully, the scrap of paper I held in my hand suggested the best place to begin, denoting organization of the romans as set by binding color, then by faded golden number on the spine.

When I wanted to reach the higher stacks I had to first pile the romans neatly on one of the little round tables, then make my ascent, clutching tightly to the paper list and all the while praying I didn't fall off and break my neck or anything similarly embarrassing and ruinous.

It was when I descended for the third time, having at last settled into something of a functioning routine, that I noticed I was no longer alone.

A woman sat in one of the low chairs, posture-perfect with her legs neatly crossed, making her seat seem more like a throne than a cushioned reading chair. Her dark hair was twisted back from her face in the same fashion as worn by the women in portraits of the old Ramanthine nobility. Her dress was a deep, bloody crimson, and the hem brushed delicately against the floor as she tapped her foot. That was the only delicate thing about her, I thought, and though it was a strange thought to have, I'd never been quite so intimidated by anyone in my life, not even the Esar.

She was reading the topmost roman I'd left stacked on the table, one finger idly tracing the line of the words, as if she hadn't seen me yet. When I stepped off the bottom rung of the ladder her head lifted immediately, and I felt as though her black eyes would bore a hole right through my head and out the back if I couldn't escape the force of her gaze.

"You aren't a magician," she said. Her voice was like the wine Royston had bought in Bottle Alley, the same color as her dress.

"No," I said, knowing full well that I had no skill at lying, and that even if I wanted to try, now was certainly not the time to start. "I'm not."

"You are the Margrave Royston's— Hal," she said, pausing to tuck away a curl that had fallen loose from her chignon.

I felt the blush before it came, staining my cheeks and throat, but she only smiled, full-lipped and amused, as though I'd done something particularly entertaining.

"Surely Royston must have explained to you the rules of the Basquiat and its libraries," she went on. "There is information here that cannot be read by anyone other than sworn magicians."

I drew a breath, thinking once again of that room with all the sick people lying jumbled together on their cots, and how I might very well be their best and only hope at this point to solve anything. I could see, too—and thought I might never forget—the looks of frustration in the magicians' eyes at being able to do nothing. If I could help in any way, I knew that I had to at least try.

"We—that is, Royston and I, and some others; I'm not sure of their titles—we believe that there might be an answer in one of these romans as to what's making everyone sick," I said at last, in a voice as assertive as I could make it.

She regarded me for a moment longer, and I had the most curious sensation of something soft sweeping in the corners of my mind.

"Berhane is a friend of mine," she said at last. "And little Caius will need something to occupy his mind now that he is no longer the Esar's lapdog."

"I— Oh," I said. Then, I nearly jumped, for I'd realized all at once what her Talent was—or rather, what it had to be. I hadn't seen the badge on her chest that would have declared her status as a *velikaia,* but now, I no longer needed to. She'd taken what information she'd needed from my mind with more precision than I'd removed the romans from their stacks, which meant that she was also a magician, though she didn't seem nearly as sick as the others.

She closed the roman and set it to rest on top of the pile with the others, and I saw then that her hands were shaking. As soon as she followed my gaze, she placed them in her lap as if there were nothing at all the matter, and I wondered just how much control she was exerting over her *own* mind in order to override whatever effect the illness was having upon her body. I wondered why she wasn't upstairs with everyone else.

"I remain in the library because the Esar keeps us here as though it is a prison, and not our own palace. A palace truly fit for magicians, and Margraves, and *velikaia,*" she told me. "I find my comfort among the books."

Then she smiled again, and her teeth were impossibly white against the dark of her face.

"'Hang the rules,' I believe, is the expression Royston would use under these circumstances," she said, and I felt hope bloom wild like a sunflower within my chest. "Though you'd best be more clever about keeping yourself from view in the future."

"Thank you," I whispered, holding the romans I'd brought down with me off the ladder tight against my chest.

"And you might start with this volume," she added. With one of her large, graceful hands she indicated a volume about halfway down from the top. "It contains a few treatises on magical illness, though, sadly, not illness that attacks magic itself."

"*Thank* you," I said again, too overwhelmed to do anything but go on expressing my gratitude to her repeatedly.

It was only when I reached the door, stack of romans threatening to topple unsteadily one way or the other at any moment, that I realized I'd missed one very important detail. I turned around precariously, and though I knew it was rudeness unimaginable to shout within the confines of the library, I called back to her.

"What is your name?" I was certain there was a more proper way to address a *velikaia*—I was certain Royston might even have mentioned it to me—but countless nights without sleep had driven all but the most basic knowledge from my mind. I hoped she would forgive me.

"You may call me Antoinette," she answered, and though I'd heard her quite clearly, she didn't seem to have raised her voice at all.

When I came back to the sickroom, Royston was sleeping, and I was careful to put my load of romans down before arranging the covers carefully around him where he'd thrown them off in a fit of tossing.

"My," Caius remarked from his bed, waving an idle, white hand. His cot was aligned now with Royston's; he must have moved it while I was gone on my errand. "You would have made an excellent student of the 'Versity. Or a pack mule, possibly, as both are prone to carrying disproportionately heavy loads."

The unsettling thing about Caius—or perhaps the most unsettling, as there seemed to be a consistently growing supply—was that at times I was sure he could be no more than a few years above me in age, *if* that.

"Antoinette suggested we start with this one," I said, holding it up from the rest.

A sly look passed over his sharp-featured face. Next to him, Berhane stirred in her own bed and fought to sit up, hair clinging limply to the side of her face.

"Antoinette is here?"

"Well," I amended, "not *here,* but in the Basquiat. I saw her in the library, I thought she was going to tell me to leave. Only then . . . she didn't."

Marcelline coughed the way she'd begun to that morning, and Marius began to stir in his bed, fighting his way free from the blankets to help Berhane into a more comfortable position on the little cot. It was then that I noticed the beds had been rearranged, and that our little group had moved to form a misshapen sort of circle to one side of the room. I felt the beginnings of hope fill my heart with warmth. We were going to solve this.

We had to.

"Pass us the romans then," said Marcelline, once she'd had a glass of water and could speak properly.

They felt heavier as I passed them out, and I was worried that some of the magicians might not be able to hold them up properly, but of course I had underestimated them, and even Berhane balanced her own text neatly against her lap with hands that didn't have the strength to hold it properly.

I sat on the edge of Royston's bed as lightly as I could so as not to wake him, but soon enough I heard the sigh and felt the stirrings that meant I'd done so anyway.

"Hal?" His voice was rough with sleep, and something deeper that I knew was the sickness rooted deep within him.

I moved immediately to sit next to him, adjusting his pillows so that he could sit up and remaining close in case he felt the need to lean against me once more.

"Shall we begin, at the behest of our dear colleague, with nature and the known magical plagues?" Caius's one bright eye nearly sparkled. I tucked in close to Royston, and held his book open for the two of us. In some ways it was so like our earliest days in the country that I felt the change all the more keenly.

This was how our days passed.

On the second day, as Berhane could no longer read, we began our work afresh—sometime, I judged, in the very late morning—and I read loud enough for both her and Royston to hear. I noticed that Marius was more distracted by her condition than he would have liked, and he kept asking for theories to be repeated over, weariness and apology beaten into every line of his face. By evening, she'd fallen into fitful sleeping, and before I fell asleep, curled in at Royston's overwarm side, he whispered softly against my temple, "We cannot strain her by letting her join us tomorrow."

On the third day, both Berhane and Alcibiades were no longer capable of reading with us, the former asleep and the other intermittently—but very rarely—offering sharp yet weary criticism. We'd still come no closer to a solution by the time Royston rested a shaking hand upon my arm and admitted to me that he could no longer understand the words I was speaking as a language he knew.

"Well," said Marius, soft so as not to disturb Berhane. "I didn't want to be the first one to admit it."

"Hal and I will continue," Caius said, his voice never losing its keen edge.

"Hal must also—occasionally—rest," Royston suggested. I wrung out the damp flannel I kept in a basin of cool water by the foot of his cot and draped it over his forehead.

Very quickly after that, his breathing evened out, and I knew he was sleeping.

"Doesn't it trouble you, as well?" I asked Caius, softly, so as not to wake the others.

He shrugged, barely more than a disconcertingly pale shadow in the dark room. All the lamps were being kept at half-light, perhaps to avoid troubling the magicians whenever they wished to sleep, but the effect was such that, after all the squinting I'd been doing, I felt as though I, too, were going to go blind.

"At certain hours it's worse than others," he said. "However, I *am* uncertain of how much more time I'll have to work on the problem at hand. I thought it might be best to make the most of it—'it' being that short period of blessed wakefulness, while I still have *one* eye."

I took up a book we'd not yet started and flipped it open, even as I moved to sit by the foot of Caius's bed. It was the best position to take, I thought; this way, I could read a little more loudly and leave Royston undisturbed as he slept.

"Shall we, then?" I suggested.

Caius frowned. "Poisons and antidotes," he said, as though it were troubling him. "Poisons, poisons—we're getting nowhere."

I bowed my head. "It's true," I admitted at length, though it pained me greatly to do so. I'd had such high hopes when we'd begun, but we'd effectively lost both Berhane and Alcibiades in the past two days, and we were no closer to understanding what was happening than we had been at the beginning.

"We must lay it all out, from start to finish," Caius said. "What we don't know is ruining us."

We were at the task for most of the night, until Royston began to cough very near morning and I returned to tend to him. When Royston was sleeping peacefully once more, so was Caius.

On the fourth day, Marius became delirious with fever, and Marcelline could no longer help us due to ceaseless coughing; then there were only the three of us.

What we didn't know was ruining us, I told myself, and while Royston and Caius slept, I repeated the list Caius and I had made—half chart, half questions—over and over again, until I saw it every time I closed my eyes and tried to sleep.

The Ke-Han had taken a sample of the magic waters from the Well; they had invented a poison to work against it, presumably also of magic; it was this magic that worked as a fever through Royston's veins, this magic that brought a flush to Alcibiades' cheeks, and this magic that was beginning to blind Caius's good eye.

We had to undo the poison, but we had no idea how to proceed, as it took so many forms.

On the fifth day, Royston could no longer control his vomiting. He apologized profusely, which seemed to me a waste of energy, and then slept once more for much of the day. I continued to read on my own while Caius watched me. Under any other circumstances this would have daunted me, but I refused to be distracted.

At last I reached the same point Royston had just the other day: the words no longer seemed to be ones I recognized, though they had been not a moment before. I rubbed wearily at my eyes, my own head pounding and aching between the temples and behind my eyes. I could barely see at all.

"You'll drive yourself mad that way," Caius said, and punctuated the statement with a crystalline laugh.

I sighed wearily, and for a long time I didn't speak at all. Then I asked him, "Caius, what *is* your Talent?"

He smiled his snake-thin smile and breathed in deeply, almost reverently. "Ah," he said. "My Talent lies in visions."

"Visions?" I asked.

"It's particularly useful when the Esar requires information from certain unwilling parties," Caius explained.

"Oh," I said. "So the . . . torture you mentioned earlier, that was—"

"Not physical," Caius confirmed. "No. You are curious, perhaps, as to why the Esar banished me in the first place?" I nodded mutely, and whether or not he could see me, he took my silence as agreement. "I was too young for such a gift," he continued, quiet, reminiscent. "I misused it. I drove a man mad for . . . private reasons."

"And you couldn't cure him afterward?" I asked, horrified by the ease of his admission.

"No," Caius replied. "Though, if I die before he does, the general consensus is that he will return to the state he was in before I tore his mind apart. He would be very pleased to see me in such distress—would be, that is, if he were more than a drooling, wild-eyed mongrel."

I rubbed at my eyes again, too weary to offer him a reply. He didn't seek one, either, and I left it at that.

On the sixth day, Berhane died.

It happened before I woke, but the murmuring of distant voices broke into my dreamless sleep and I sat up quickly, my heart pounding fit to burst. There were men gathered above her cot who covered her with a simple gray coverlet and carried her from the room.

"I did write to her," Marius said, his voice still tinged with delirium and fever. He turned away from us and pulled the blankets up over his head.

"She had such lovely hair," Caius whispered, and for the first time, I thought I detected the shifting of emotions in his voice.

I turned my face against Royston's shoulder and cried. If he was taken from me in the same manner, I was certain I'd never forgive myself. I returned to reading, but it was no longer any use. I could barely concentrate—the words danced before my eyes, tantalizing but impossible to catch—and the sound of Royston's rough, ragged breathing interrupted every thought I might once have had. At last I could manage it no more, and I admit that I surrendered, closing the book, pulling my knees to my chest, and crying myself to sleep.

It was then that the idea struck.

Inspiration woke me with the same jolting, electric shock that the sounds of Berhane being taken away had done earlier that morning.

"Royston," I said, grasping his hand and shaking him. "Royston. Royston, please, wake up!"

He groaned with tired resistance and struggled to pull his hand from mine. I let him go, but only to grab his shoulder instead, shaking him harder. At last his face twisted into consciousness, and his eyes moved beneath their lids. A moment later he opened them blearily, staring at me for a long time without recognition.

"It's Hal," I said, on the verge of crying again. "Please, Royston, I need you to listen. I think I've had an idea about the poison, Royston. *Please,* listen to me—"

His eyes snapped into focus, though I saw it was with considerable effort that he managed to follow my words from the first to the last. "Tell me," he said. His throat sounded rough enough as to pain even me; I could barely imagine what it must have felt like to him.

I ordered my thoughts into as much coherency as I could manage, and yet I still spoke them one after the other, jumbled and tumbling from my lips without any structure at all. "The Well," I said, "Royston, it's not— We can't *cure* the magic from the Well, there's been no cure found yet, but Caius said that the man who went mad will be cured if *Caius* dies—and what about the story of Tycho the Brave, who couldn't cure his lady of the curse, so he killed the magician who'd placed the curse in the first place? The chatelain had a copy of that roman, and we read it together— Never mind, it's just a story, only Caius *said*— And wouldn't that be the same—wouldn't it—if the magicians who made the poison were killed? It's possible," I concluded, helplessly and breathlessly both. "It's— It sounded better when I first thought of it, but *wouldn't* it be possible?"

Royston stared at me, uncomprehending. When he grasped it, understanding rose on his face like the dawn. I could see it, almost as though it had a particular color, come sudden into his eyes. "The Ke-Han magicians have a round, flat tower in the center of their great city," he said, his voice trembling. But not, I thought, on the edge of fever. Rather, it was the edge of excitement. "It's too far in to have ever been destroyed by our dragons; besides which, the Ke-Han magicians control the very air around the dome. That is where they operate. They concentrate their magic, which is what makes them so powerful—able to move the very rivers from their beds, roil the winds against our dragons and the oceans against their shores. But it also makes them . . . a giant blue target."

I pressed my hand against my chest—as if somehow that could stop the wild, frantic pace of its beating.

"But how?" I asked. "How can we do it?" Looking all around me, I could see that it was hopeless. Without magic, we could never hope to get close enough to kill the Ke-Han magicians, much less every last one of them.

It was a shot in the dark, wild and desperate. I was *certain* it was the right answer. I was also certain it couldn't be done.

"If the dragons are still flying," Royston said.

"But how?" I repeated. "How can we even let the Esar know what *we* know?"

"Ah," Royston said. "Leave that to me."

That was when he started screaming.

CHAPTER FIFTEEN

ROOK

Fighting every night on a dragon who couldn't even see her way past her own fucking wings and sometimes wouldn't've been able to fly her way out of a wedding veil didn't have too many fucking benefits, but there was *one,* and it was the one I was looking for: I didn't have to think about nobody or nothing. It was just me, Have, the way she jerked and bumped beneath me, the way sometimes she fought me when I tried to steer her, and the belching of flames and smoke when I did my best to aim and fire, her whole metal body shaking between my legs and me just hanging on for dear life.

Like I'd told the professor—my fucking brother; fucking *Hilary*—there wasn't any time to be thinking when you were up in the air. It was even more true now that Have'd gone out of her mind, and the only thing keeping me from plummeting to the ground—or worse, getting caught alive by the Ke-Han—was how tight I could hold on to her with both my thighs.

I developed a sort of trick for staying on her that involved wrapping the reins around both my wrists, underneath the gloves. This could fuck me or save me, depending on how things shook down. Like, for example, if Have got hit by a blast of wind which the madness didn't make her even more determined to fight and she went down because of it, then I was going down with her without any way to wrangle myself to safety. And that would be it, lights out for good and forever. But if she did another one of the crazy flips she'd done the first time—which almost sent me flying to my death, and the only thing saving me sheer pissed-off determination, and me nearly tearing off my own two legs by the time she'd righted herself—then I'd be pretty glad for the reins holding me to her back. After all, two broken wrists were the sort of thing you had to barter to avoid a broken neck. It was just that simple.

Anyway, I didn't have any choice. I had to take these chances, since now more than ever the only thing keeping the Ke-Han from kicking down th'Esar's door was us, the Dragon Corps, and we were *really* fighting like dogs.

If I didn't die—like, if these stunts didn't kill me—I was going to wipe the smug look off every last Ke-Han face. I just didn't know how I was going to go about doing that, or if I'd ever get the chance to see it done.

It'd only been a week—maybe less, now that all the days were blending together in one mess of almost dying and almost dying again—and already we were on the edge of being no more fucking use to anybody. Compagnon had done a run with Spiridon that put her out of commission, we guessed probably for good, and all of the swifts but Balfour's Anastasia could barely lift their own heads for flying. We were fucked at both ends, and pretty soon we were gonna crack right in half with the pressure of it.

That didn't stop me from flying out, though—'cause like I said, somebody had to do it, and besides which, it kept me from having the time to think about *anything*.

So I was out on my lonesome, just me and Have since it was all the corps could spare, flying low along the mountains all night long and blasting down fire whenever we thought the Ke-Han might've forgotten about our being there.

The thing was, it was just a game of tag at this point: We had to keep letting 'em know we were still okay for flying, because if they weren't clear of us, they couldn't leave the cover of the mountains. The main *problem* with this plan was that they could hold out a hell of a lot longer than we could, since the only girls we consistently had up in the air were my Have, of course, and the other two Jacquelines, those being Jeannot on Al Atan and Ace on Thoushalt. As for the rest, there was Adamo on Proudmouth, Ghislain's Compassus, then, when they could wing it, Evariste and Niall on Illarion and Erdeni, in that order. All the other girls were fucking *out*. It pissed the others off, especially Ivory, who I'd never have pegged for it, but that was how it'd broken down, and that was how we had to abide by it.

It pissed me off, too. There wasn't none of this that didn't make me redder than Ke-Han wine with rage, but all I could do was keep picking them off one by one, *if* I got lucky.

Oh, and I had to get out well before sunup, too, since Have got confused by the light now, on top of everything else. The way we'd learned *that* was a real son-of-a, nearly taking the whole Airman down with us.

But that night was quiet, just me and the whole Ke-Han army hiding like rats in the mountain and Have occasionally spitting.

Then, she said, "We aren't alone."

"Yeah," I said, "right, sure. Whatever you say, darlin'."

"No," she told me. "I'm not mad. Don't use that tone with me or I'll snap your neck, you foul-mouthed whoreson."

"Leave my mother the fuck outta this," I said. "She didn't do a thing to you, and you know it."

"She birthed you, didn't she?" Have asked, real snide, just like old times. It *wasn't* like old times, though, and I had to keep reminding myself of it.

"Yeah, guess so," I said. "So who's with us, then?"

"All of them," Have said. "Everyone's coming."

Maybe this was a sign—maybe she really was losing it, and this was where my luck ran out. I'd been drawing too much on it lately anyway, and I guess I should've been expecting it.

Then, there was a sound like a swift coming up on my left. I twisted, assuming the Ke-Han'd taken the time in the Cobalts to figure out how to get their catapults to actually work—only I saw the glint of fading moonlight off metal wings.

"Shit," I said.

It was Balfour, riding Anastasia.

Have was right; I should've known to trust my girl. Behind me I could see the winking of the other airmen and their rides, like the stars had come down from the heavens to dance with us, to interfere in the lives of mortal men just like they did in the old stories.

"Shit," I said again.

"We have a target," Balfour called out to me, voice almost swallowed up by the wind. He made a fast circuit around me, doubling back.

"The fucking *coordinates*," I shouted back at him.

"We're taking out the magicians," Balfour howled. "We've got to hit them—at once!"

There might've been more to what he'd said, but I didn't need to hear it. Every man jack of us knew that the magicians of the Ke-Han stayed all together in their blue dome. I hoped to the sky that they hadn't decided to break that tradition and start working with their army rather than from back at home.

We'd never been able to get close enough to the city before—but then again, the entire Ke-Han army hadn't been holed up in the mountains waiting to invade Volstov before, either. Having enough fuel to get there and back didn't matter for shit, now. Worrying about the Ke-Han winds didn't matter for shit, now. We had a chance, however small it was, and we had to take it.

It was like spitting below you in the pitch-dark, but we had barely an hour of nighttime left, and if we were going to get this done—and all the boys'd come out to play, so you'd better believe we were sure as fuck going to try—then we had to fly out now.

One thing I knew for sure: We could make it back to their big blue city before their warriors could, even on horseback.

"We can do this," Have said in a queer voice.

I spurred her in the flanks. "That's my girl," I said.

And then we were flying, me and Have in the front, but all fourteen of us more or less flying *together*.

Right away some of the others started dropping altitude, like they were having real trouble flying in a straight line, and some of the girls were bucking in the air no better than wild horses, but the sky was pretty big even with all of us in it, and I guessed there was room for everyone. It was only instinct that set me against moving as so large a group. We'd make a damn big target for any lucky son-of-a who happened to look into the sky at the right time. Flying solo had its own risks, but it never made me feel itchy in quite the same way as this, like Have and I were getting crowded in on either side. Even though the corps was a team, official-like and all that, everyone with a brain knew that Havemercy and I worked best when it was just the two of us alone together. We just rose above that, was all, and though it was a weird time to think of him, fucking Hilary, he'd never seemed able to get that straight from the first, either.

It wasn't like I wouldn't help any one of the boys who needed helping, but my job was to do that by taking down every last man of the Ke-Han that I could, and that came first.

We were all taught to look after our own selves before anyone else, and if it went against what everyone else did, well, we weren't nothing like anyone else, anyway.

The wind whistled past my ears as Have picked up speed, like we were racing against the others rather than with, the way we did some nights coming home, punchy with adrenaline and no way to bleed it off but to act like we were ten years younger and stupider to boot. Now there wasn't anything we were racing against except time, and it had all become deadly serious.

I caught sight of Jeannot having a real problem with keeping Al Atan from speeding off ahead of the rest; he was keeping her reined in nice and tight just to hold whatever sad-bastard formation we were clinging to with so many limping, crazed machines underneath us. I'd never had cause to think of Have as a machine before, but then she'd never fought me like this before. Thinking of her as a person only made it seem just like watching somebody's mind unravel like they said Caius Greylace made happen once, and *that* was something I didn't like any which way.

Right then, Have was humming a little tune under her breath, sweet and strange, and a little eerie, too. To our right, Vachir gave a screech, like the kind she wouldn't ever have made if she'd been in her right mind and knowing what we had ahead of us, how important the element of surprise was. I couldn't quite make out Merritt astride her, but I knew he had to be shit-panicked at that, wondering whether she was going to do it all the way there and warn the Ke-Han where we were and just how fast we were coming. But she didn't make another sound after that, though, and I'm sure we all felt a little relieved about that.

So long as I was feeling things, a little bit of pride didn't hurt either, since we were each one flying at best with a half-cracked dragon, and not one of us was falling to anything worse than a little dip here, or an exceptionally strong tug on the reins there. As far as I saw it, so long as everyone could keep from crashing into the Cobalts, it'd be all right. There was a shaky moment there when it seemed like Raphael would have a scrape of it with his Natalia, but then she pulled up real sharp in a wrench that'd probably have broken her neck if she'd had bones to break, and after that it was air silence from that end same as from Vachir's.

We'd never flown in such a group before, except in the real bad times—and even then it wasn't all of us, maybe seven or ten at a time. Th'Esar just didn't like the idea of losing all his dragons at once, if it came to that. There were always a few of us kept in reserve; it was good strategizing, pure and simple.

Only it seemed like there wouldn't be any need for strategy if the Ke-Han were just going to waltz into the capital and take over. We'd been pushed into making a move, and now we just had to fight it out or die trying. That sort of thing suited me just fine, I guess, seeing as how it was better than just waiting around.

It was still dark out, and a good thing that it was, but it wasn't so dark that you couldn't see the color of the mountains beneath us, blue and deep like the fucking ocean, only the ocean had some sparkle to her, cheerful, like maybe if you crashed then it'd still work out all right. Not so with the range. They were dead blue, steel blue, capped white on the top and no more beautiful than a great jagged stretch of deception.

Lapis was carved out like a bowl by the edge of the Ke-Han River on one side, and on the other tucked into something like a valley—which was going to make the flying real difficult—and the big domed haven for the Ke-Han magicians smack in the middle, like the big blue target on a dart board. Its obviousness had always made my skin prick just a little, but I wasn't a complete idiot, and there'd been no way before now to make it work without running out of fuel entirely or being dashed to bits against the Cobalts for trying until the sunrise. Taking down the Ke-Han wasn't worth losing Have, only now it was sort of like I'd lost her already. I couldn't really think about that.

The whole city was laid out in circles, which I guess was the shape the Ke-Han worshipped, only because of us, half the wall, the outer-most circle, was torn down.

The way I looked at it, the magician dome would make a pretty target if we all could see to flying that far. Ivory in particular seemed to be taking it rough, with Cassiopeia making hollow, smoke-filled sounds like she'd forgot the proper way to breathe fire, and Magoughin's Chastity undulating in the air like some kind of sea serpent, only we sure as fuck weren't flying through water.

The only problem I could see was that Lapis doused her lights at night—the Ke-Han weren't dumb any way you sliced 'em—and without fire to depend on as any kind of a reliable resource, we were pretty fucked as far as seeing our target ahead of time went.

The color blue wasn't so easy to see in the nighttime. It just blended into so many shadows, and I didn't much like our chances.

At least there was always the possibility that some idiot had helpfully repaired the guard towers, fitted with wide, silver bowls of fire that were just cozy as beacons lighting our way.

We came up over the crest of the mountains, Adamo nearest me. Proudmouth didn't seem to be having it as bad as all the rest, though I had an idea that had a lot to do with Adamo himself, and how when he told a thing what to do, it sure as bastion had better do it. And sure enough, the city was black as the night around us—which would be getting lighter in an hour or maybe less—and I didn't know whether that was a blessing, like they didn't know we were coming, or whether it was another one of their fucking traps.

But at this point, did it really matter whether it was a trap or not? We'd come so far, taken the dragons out past all reasonable endurance.

We were going to finish it, or finish ourselves; one or the other. Like I said, decisions seemed real easy when there wasn't any of that horseshit sitting-on-the-fence kind of waffling.

We knew what we had to do, and we were going to do it. Only two sides of the coin.

All that mattered now was what we knew, and what we knew was that somewhere in the lapis city there was a big blue saucer that had a bull's-eye on it.

"The sun's going to be coming up," said Have, like she could smell it.

"We've got a while yet, girl," I answered, though privately I wished there'd been more time for us.

Adamo rose up in front, wheeled around halfway like he wanted to say something to the lot of us, only he thought that'd make things seem too morbid.

"Bastion *fuck*!" I called to him, loud and heckling over the rush of wind. "You got a speech to make you'd better do it now!"

He paused, like he really *was* thinking about it, and shit, I thought maybe he had every reason to after all.

It'd be dawn soon, and with first light there was no telling *what* the dragons might do, the condition they were in now. Might be some of them weren't so sensitive as my girl about it, *or* might be we'd all drop like stones from the sky and that would be that. It was a pretty ballsy gamble all around, especially for th'Esar to make with his beloved dragons. I thought about what he'd told us about how if *he said so,* then the dragons were as good as sacrificed. He'd meant *us* that day too, though I'd been so mad and caught up about Have that I hadn't quite caught it proper.

Knowing it now didn't make me as angry as I thought I'd be, but my shoulders hurt, and my wrists were starting to ache where they were tied up, and I was just exhausted.

"Don't do anything stupid!" Adamo barked at us finally, then turned Proudmouth so that her tail flicked wide of the lot of us. Then, she dove in a steep descent toward the city.

We all followed, fourteen beauties glistening in the night just a little too swiftly to be clouds. I almost thought it was a shame nobody was looking out their windows this time of early morning, 'cause they would have had quite a sight to see.

The wall was crumbling in all but a few places when we flew over it, and I felt a savage sense of triumph that we'd accomplished *something* at least that hadn't been just another part in the Ke-Han's giant ruse.

It was a pretty neat reminder of what happened when you messed with Volstov, when you thought you could take on the Dragon Corps.

We followed the path of the river, fat and gleaming in the fading moonlight as it bordered the city and fed toward the ocean. It wouldn't lead us to the magicians' flat, round tower, but when you only ever saw a city from the air, you got to picking out focal points that would help you triangulate your own position in relation to whatever was visible around you. We'd never got so far into the city as to be able to take out the magicians, but the tower itself was pretty hard to miss, so we were sitting pretty in terms of finding the thing in the dark.

As far as our luck stretched, that was about it, because next second a blast of wind hit us all so fierce that I thought for one minute it was going to send every man jack of us spinning off in different directions as easy as dandelion seed.

"Goodness," said Have. Or rather, she screeched, else I'd never have heard her over the hurricane threatening to tear the skin off my bones. "It's too windy to have tea with the Emperor today. More's the pity."

"Damn it, Have," I said through my teeth, trying to wrench her back into a straight line. It wasn't easy, with her fighting me and the wind at the same time, twisting frantically like a pinned animal. Only she was a pinned animal with enough metal and crazed, dying magic in her to kill me without a second thought. First rule: Never go against your dragon's nature.

But I *wasn't* dropping out just so the rest of the boys could be heroes and get statues built of them, Ghislain's twice as big as all the others.

Just as quick as it had started, the wind changed direction, like it was *pulling,* and I thought about how wind could tear houses down, rip trees up from the ground, all that kind of reassuring stuff you start to think about when you're caught in it and ain't got no proper recourse but to wear it out lest it wears *you* out first. I pushed Have up so that we were near to vertical, and twisting over and over like she'd used to do when I bragged I'd never get airsick, one swift tight barrel roll after another.

I could hear some of the boys shouting, and occasionally felt the buffet of air that meant someone had passed too damn close to us. But for all purposes, my mind had shrunk to hold no more than me and Have. It was what I knew, what I was good at, and it was the only way any of us was going to survive this.

"You're going to make us both sick," said Havemercy. "And there won't be time for cakes at all."

I didn't know whether she was trying to be funny or if this was just the end of the road for us.

I didn't figure much that I even cared.

Instead of answering, I gritted my teeth and pulled her out of the climb, facing the wind head-on again. We'd come no closer to the tower in all this time, and I saw then that the magicians' plan was pretty standard, but it'd serve them just fine, 'cause they just assumed they needed to keep us off until morning, which was all they'd ever done before. By morning, we'd have to either back off or have found a way past the gale. What they didn't know—that there wasn't any backing off— was no fucking comfort if we couldn't get near enough to their tower to take them down. Fighting this wind wasn't going to do us any favors with saving fuel, either, and it was going to hit the swifts first since they were built the smallest.

Even if we could get near, there was no telling how well we'd be able to use fire to our advantage in razing it to the ground. At this rate, we'd be better off to wait for the first of us to fall from the skies and hope he aimed for the Ke-Han tower.

The thought didn't cheer me any.

"We're never going to get *near* them like this!" Jeannot screamed over the wind. The only way I could tell it was him was by seeing Al Atan, twisting crimson and gold like a contortionist's trick in the air; I couldn't see any of the others, which meant I couldn't hear them, either.

Then there was this sound.

I'd've sworn by all of bastion that it was the worst sound I ever heard in my life, like metal scales being peeled away from metal bone. I knew that wasn't the way our girls were built, but still, it was like someone was being ripped apart, starting at the wings. Have groaned something awful, which I only knew 'cause she started shaking underneath me and then I saw where the original noise was coming from.

Compagnon was riding Spiridon *through the fucking storm.*

I don't know how he did it. Must've been that he figured if he got high enough above the winds and just barreled down through them, he might make it, and that was what was happening. He'd only get one shot with it, and I realized right away what that shot meant. If he got through, he'd be too low too fast, and he wouldn't be able to come 'round again, but it would sure as fuck *work*—whatever that meant.

It was like everyone was holding his breath. Waiting. Watching. That sound tore through us all; even the wind seemed to die down. And there was Spiridon, like someone'd loaded her into a catapult, slamming right through the gales like they meant no more to her than smoke.

Something moved past me on my right, and I thought it was debris or something caught up in the wind before I saw the flash of copper and silver, and I realized it was Thoushalt, with Al Atan swift on her tail. Both our other Jacquelines at once rising up on either side of Spiridon, more beautiful than anything but Have, and Adamo shouting himself hoarse from somewhere behind me, like there was any control left to be had now.

I saw them break past the wall of wind—saw Thoushalt

switch her tack without warning, which must've meant Ace had seen the blue dome. He had better eyes than the other two. It was why he came second on the board. Spiridon came after her, and Al Atan pulled even, like it'd been their secret plan all along. Have screamed and I couldn't hear anything above that, though I'd like to think, just then, the boys were screaming too, only theirs sounding like triumph.

Then Al Atan started *howling* fire, just seconds before the three of them hit the dome right smack in the middle. A split hair of a second past that, the winds dropped, and so did the rest of us. Into the moment's silence spilled the sound of the explosion that followed just on the heels of our boys' descent.

No way man or metal could survive that.

That was about the time all dragons started their wailing, and they twisted free of us, following Ace, or Compagnon or Jeannot and their girls down upon the buildings below.

Like hell, I thought, were they going to get all the glory for themselves.

"Ready," Have said, just like old times. Just like she could read my mind, and like hers wasn't even more scrambled than breakfast.

The wind howled in our ears as we descended, shooting straight down to the remains of the dome, where flames were belching and walls were collapsing, and somewhere beneath the louder noises I thought I could hear the Ke-Han wizards screaming, or burning, or both. The air stank. We flew straight in, everything so hot I could almost feel my skin peeling. It was just like flying straight into the sun.

Can't say for sure what anyone in the lapis city was thinking right about then. The fire gods were wreaking vengeance on their heads, circling haphazard and reckless over the round roofs, raining smoke and burning gasoline down onto the wreckage. The dome was shattered—burning—and, because this was where the sun rose, I saw dawn begin to stain the sky, pink as a lady's thighs.

I screamed as Have brought us down too close—not for fear but for the pulsing heat of it. We poured fire into the crack in the magicians' dome; beside us, Compassus turned a flip too smooth for her size to tear away a piece of its wall with her tail. Proudmouth was there too, doing the same thing on the other side, and just behind the bigs were the fire-belchers on *either* side, coming up along the holes Compassus and Proudmouth had torn for them and spewing fire straight inside.

The whole building had gone from Ke-Han blue to Volstov red in no more than a minute. Maybe less.

Then something came whistling past me and Have, something pretty damn big, and we almost didn't duck it soon enough. Catapults, I figured, lobbing huge rocks at us to bring us down. The Ke-Han weren't stupid—they'd proven that much already—and of course they had a defense plan. Normally they weren't a problem, but caught limping the way we were, even trebuchets were a real threat.

They all started coming like the mountains themselves were exploding toward us. Like as not, they were going to hit some of us, and the rocks they were slinging were big enough to take us down.

I saw one of the boulders go hurtling toward Proudmouth's back—she couldn't see it, not to mention she was too big to get out of the way quick enough—but we needed the bigs for sheer force. I was too far away to get between the speeding rock and Proudmouth's back legs when Luvander streaked into place on Yesfir, got caught smack in the side, and went down all at once, rock and man and dragon together.

It was panic in the skies because the skies had been brought down too low. All I knew was that I couldn't pay attention to the others and set to ducking the catapult fire even as Have twisted and struggled against my commands.

All I could hear, all I could *smell,* was fire.

I brought my girl away from it, from where we were making a real mess of the dome, vomiting fire on everything that moved and ripping out chunks of whatever was left of the walls with Have's tail. What we *really* needed now was to take down those whoresons manning the catapults.

They were positioned on the outer reaches of the city, which wasn't hard to figure, that being the most strategic place to have them. Have took down a pagoda with her tail as we raced too low overhead, and we had to duck a fucking *shower* of debris as it rained down on us from above, one of the catapults spotting our progress. We twisted around the one that'd fired on us—Have wasn't big enough to smash through it like one of the crushers might've—but then she threw herself at the tower of wood and knocked it off center. I felt one of my molars crack against the impact, but the catapult went down.

That's my girl, I thought. There was no one in the whole world like her.

We headed for another of the catapults, and Have nearly tore her wing in half to get the second down same as she'd done for the first. There was blood in my mouth and smoke streaking my goggles so bad I could hardly see—but I *could* hear, and there was a crash nearby, too close to be any of the fighting going down in the center of the city, where most of the action was taking place. I brushed the smoke from the lenses of my goggles and saw Chastity and Magoughin to the left of me, doing a better job with the catapults than I ever could.

I whooped it up, though I didn't think Magoughin could hear me, and set my girl to the next one.

We had about half of them down when Chastity arched sudden and painful, and I saw the catapult she was wrangling go down on top of her.

We were out two Jacquelines, *two* of our fucking bigs, and one of the swifts, and who knew what else since I'd stopped paying attention. I was so fierce and shaking with rage that Have must have picked up on it, which I guessed was why she turned about quick as a gasp and had us headed back into the city, where our boys were making their last stand.

It was a fucking nightmare, everything on fire no matter where you looked, and scraps of torn-up metal shimmering on the ground as the flames heated it shapeless.

I couldn't think about that kind of stuff, couldn't listen to the screech and groan of what dragons had already been brought down when I was flying, but the sound of it was what brought Havemercy up short, and that was when the boulder got us by the tail, sent us into a spin, and brought us down.

The impact broke some ribs, I was fucking sure of it. It

was a good thing we landed the way we did, or else it would've broken both my legs, and I needed those for running and otherwise putting myself to good use before I was through. It was tough work to untangle my wrists from the harnesses, especially while Have was twisting her head back and forth like she was in agony, and in the end I had to cut myself free with one of my knives.

Growing up the way I did, I *always* kept my knives with me, even when I was flying. There were two of them, prettier than the ones I'd had when I was a kid and dirt poor on top of that, and their blades were real sharp. They'd come in handy now, since there were plenty of Ke-Han warriors on the scene—some trying to douse the fire, some aiming arrows at the men still left flying.

I could see Compassus sweeping low, her shadow like an omen as it passed above us—I heard Ghislain screaming, then I saw him *actually picking Luvander up;* was he out of his mind? Anastasia was practically falling out of the air—I didn't know where the *fuck* Adamo was; there were too few shadows overhead. Even Have was down for good.

I twisted myself around with a snarl and a grin, knives held for fighting the way I knew almost as well as I knew flying. I couldn't take on a whole city by myself—sooner or later, they'd bring me down—but before me was the dawn. It was the same dawn that would rise over the mountains between me and Volstov, the same dawn that would bring the news of what had happened here to Thremedon.

Inside that city, my city—somewhere—sleeping or not sleeping, crying or not crying—doing bastion only knew what with himself—was *my brother.* I knew sure as that same dawn that I loved him, same way as how the blood was flowing too fast for lying to myself. I was fighting now, and I was fighting for him alongside of revenge.

A Ke-Han warrior came at me with one of them long, flat Ke-Han blades, and I met him head-on, screaming his own war cry right back in his face.

CHAPTER SIXTEEN

ROYSTON

Hal was holding my pocket watch with white fingers and staring at it when I lost consciousness, so in fact I knew the exact moment it happened, down to the very second.

It was three past seven in the morning when I collapsed, and forty-eight past when I came around afterward, Hal looming above me, one hand against my chest while the other still clung to my pocket watch.

"What time is it?" I demanded.

In retrospect, it wasn't the most sensible thing to say, but there must have been something in the sound of my voice that gave Hal hope, for his whole face lit up.

"Forty-eight past seven," he replied, not letting me go.

"How long was I out?" I asked.

"Forty-five minutes exactly," Hal replied. "Royston, you sound—"

"As though fever has no longer made water out of my brain?" I offered. I blinked my eyes a few times to clear them completely and took stock of my surroundings. I wasn't in a room I recognized—it was far too ornate to be my own home, the ceiling decorated like a midday sky blushed with pale cloud wisps—and I appeared to be lying upon all of Volstov's most uncomfortable couch. I had no idea how I'd come to be here, much less where "here" was, though I was sure knowledge of the latter might inform me as to the former. "Hal," I added, momentarily tentative. "Where in bastion's name am I?"

"Oh," Hal said. "This is one of the Esar's sitting rooms."

I thought about it. No, I decided at last; I needed more help than that. "And—why exactly am I here?" I asked.

Worry damped down the light in Hal's eyes. "Have you forgotten everything?" he asked, and I saw his fingers tremble.

"Hardly *everything*," I replied, covering his shaking hand with one of my own. I was stiff and sore all over, the reason for which I was certain I knew—only I couldn't quite remember it. "I'm aware of my own name. And yours, as you may have noticed."

"Yes," Hal said. There were dark circles under his eyes. "Yes, of course. Only we were waiting here—the Esar said we might—and you were very ill, then you collapsed completely this morning. I'm—I haven't slept."

"Forgive me," I said, and meant it sincerely.

"For making me think I would lose you?" Hal asked, fingers tightening against the front of my shirt. "No. I don't think so." He drew in a steadying breath. "To answer your question," he went on, voice calmer, "we've been here since yesterday afternoon, when you demanded an audience with the Esar and—I assume because you were so loud about it—you secured us one."

I began to remember, or thought I did. It was still somewhat difficult to decipher. "Ah yes," I said, more confident than I felt. "And then we . . ."

"And then we explained our theory to him," Hal said. "Or, I did. And whenever he threatened not to listen, you began to scream again."

"How clever of me," I replied.

"I thought so," Hal agreed. "At least, it seemed to work."

"And then?" I prompted.

"And then," Hal continued, "when the Esar had listened to our full solution, he called for the Dragon Corps. They all flew out, even though they were suffering something the same as the magicians. I hope—" Hal broke off, and looked up at the ceiling. "Only they haven't returned," he finished gravely. "None of them. They've been gone a long time."

"Bastion," I swore, memory flooding back to me all at once. "But if I'm better—"

"Then presumably it means they managed to take down

the Ke-Han magicians," Hal replied. "All of them. If our theory was correct."

I passed a hand over my eyes and swallowed, the full impact of our actions settling as a deadweight tied to my heart. "We've been very busy," I said. "You haven't slept."

"If I look even half as tired as I feel," Hal admitted, "then it must be a very unpleasant sight to get well to."

"You look terrible," I said, ruthlessly honest. "That doesn't mean I wouldn't prefer seeing you to anything else."

I would have expected him to be too tired even to blush, but the familiar pink color touched his cheeks, and I felt properly aware of him for the first in a long time.

"Well," he said. "I feel as though I'm liable to collapse at any moment, just so that you know." Then, presumably having used up the last of his stamina to explain the situation, he leaned his head against my chest where I knew he would fall asleep if I let him. "I *am* glad you're all right. I thought maybe—when the others started fading away so quickly—I could barely keep track of how many had died, were still dying—"

"You need to sleep," I told him, and wrapped my arms close about him even while knowing perfectly well that this would not be the place for managing sleep. The Esar's couches might have been designed for a great many things, but neither rest nor comfort was one of them.

There were other forms of comfort though, and Hal had been awake and worried for a very long time.

"I know," he said, voice heavy and warm. I could practically hear the drowsiness in his voice rising up to claim him. "I will. It's just— We were so busy."

"And we've accomplished something quite unheard of," I reassured him. "You've not even been in Thremedon a quarter of the year and already you're saving the city."

He made a self-deprecating noise in his throat, but didn't protest any louder than that, and so I knew he was likely settling to sleep. Despite the unforgiving architecture of the couch, and the entrenched stiffness in my joints, I thought that I could be quite pleased to lie here and enjoy Hal's repose.

Then the door opened. The Provost wasn't a man prone to kicking down doors—as, after all, he had people to do that for him—and only directly involved himself in matters that required a touch of finesse, or those that were critically important to the security of the city. This—judging by what Hal had told me—had to be the latter.

"Margrave Royston," he said, sounding decidedly more flustered than he had the last time we'd spoken. "By decree of His Majesty the Esar, I am to inform you that your company is to be deployed within the hour, and he expects you to be punctual."

For a moment, I had to admit I was dumbfounded. Against me, Hal stirred, then sat up, rubbing sleep from his eyes with a sheer stubbornness he rarely displayed.

I felt sure that the groaning in my muscles wasn't only in my head. As I sat up, it seemed impossible that the sound wasn't loud enough to echo off the Esar's outlandishly decorated walls.

"Talk sense, Dmitri," I said, perhaps more curt than one could afford to be with the Provost of the city, but then I'd never had much good common sense to speak of.

The Provost folded his arms as though he were dealing with an obstinate child, and when he spoke again his voice had lost its gilded edge. "The army's moving out. *Today.* The Ke-Han city's in flames over there, and no one knows what's happened to the dragons, but we've got to leave now if we want to get there in time enough to make a difference. If we want to hit them hard enough that maybe this time they really won't get back up again. And," he added, after a pause, "we've got to get the dragons out."

"No," said Hal. He spoke quietly, as if he'd only been thinking it and hadn't really meant to utter it aloud. "You can't— You've only just got well again. What if— *No.*"

"Hal," I said. "Everyone who's well again will be heading out to fight. I cannot linger."

His eyes were more gray than blue as he considered this,

then he leaned up to kiss me with a suddenness that made
something in my chest burst open like the seedpods William
had collected in the country. I took his face in mine and—
though this wasn't to be any kind of a farewell—took my leave
from a loved one the way countless soldiers had throughout
history. Hal murmured in surprise, at my sudden capitulation
no doubt, and he lifted his fingers to touch my throat.

We were interrupted by the sound of the Provost scuffing
his boots uncomfortably against the carpet, and Hal pulled
away with his cheeks burning fiercely. I myself felt no remorse over our actions. It was as though all the most sensible
parts of me had been burned out by the fever.

I couldn't bring myself to regret it.

"Well," I said. "It would seem you've made your informed
decision."

"I don't want you to go," said Hal, and even though he
couldn't bring himself to smile, his expression was lit with a
fire that flared beneath his evident exhaustion.

"I must," I said, feeling suddenly wretched that there was
no real comfort that I could offer him.

"If I've heard correctly," said the Provost suddenly, buoyed
by impatience or discomfort or both, "there isn't much *left* of
the lapis city. Not to say that them as are there won't be fighting hard as first-time convicts, but," he paused, as though examining the wisdom of his reassurance, then seemed to think
the better of it. "Well, you never know."

I felt an odd sense of gratitude at the effort he'd made,
however misplaced. The city had indeed been turned on its
head if I was feeling a grudging sort of appreciation for the
Provost. I nodded and stood.

"Go to the house," I said, in a tone that I hoped conveyed
something beyond simple concern. "Sleep. If I find you looking this tired when I return, I shall be very cross."

He stood then and put his arms about me so tightly that I
thought my ribs would surely crack under the strain. "When
you return, then," he said, voice echoing with none of the
tremor that shook his thin frame. "You'll have to wake me up."

"Of course," I said, then, "Hal, I have to go."

He released me, rubbing his sleeve over his eyes in a habit that he had not yet outgrown from either his childhood or his time in the country.

"Hurry then," he said, in a tone that made me wish to do anything *but* leave. "The quicker you're done with the Ke-Han, the quicker you can come home."

I knew that I would never leave if I didn't manage it that instant. I clenched my hand where it would have reached for one last touch and instead turned away from Hal, striding out the door the Provost held open for me.

I heard him fall in line behind me, silent as he'd been the day he'd come for our chat at Our Lady of a Thousand Fans, which now seemed a lifetime ago. I was nearly certain he was thinking of that day, as well.

Or perhaps that wasn't it at all. He was a hard man to read.

"There've been wagons and the like taking soldiers through the streets all day," he said. "They're dropping them off at the foothills and sending everyone through as quick as they come."

"Surely it will take more time than we've got to cross the mountains," I said, as he drew even with me. He shook his head.

"They're not using the usual routes— You'll be going straight across. They're using the tunnels, see? Does fuck-all for the element of surprise, so I guess that's why they aren't the preferred option, but with the dragons bringing the city down around them, I guess the Ke-Han have figured out what's what, and there isn't any need to attempt to sneak up on them *now*. What men do they even have left to hit us? It'd be a suicide run, and they know it."

It was the most the Provost had ever said to me all in one go that wasn't a decree read off of a piece of paper.

"Ah," I said, and nodded.

"There'll be a carriage for you outside," he went on. "As I understand it, further instructions will be given at the foothills, but from the sound of things it's not going to be anything more complicated than keep going until either *you* can't or *they* can't."

I quashed the perverse impulse to ask whether the Esar had a preference either way.

We exited the building, the sudden light threatening to set off a headache in my temples before the shock of it passed and my thoughts cleared. It was still early enough for the skies to be gray, though I knew that if there were any dragons still in the air, it would place them in a dreadfully vulnerable position. If news had returned, then surely so had at least some of the dragons, I told myself, but one could never be entirely certain.

Palace Walk was eerily empty as we strode down the center of it, without any of the usual gossiping noblesse accompanied by their servants, or those who had business with the Esar marching hopefully up to the palace doors.

"Will you be joining us on the field?" I asked, with perhaps less kindness in my voice than I'd intended. We weren't close enough to indulge in the verbal sparring I made a habit of, and I realized it too late. Fortunately, as Dmitri himself had said, I was greatly needed for the war and therefore couldn't be tossed into jail for insolence.

He shot me a rueful smile, instead. "Once I've finished collecting everyone that's meant to be there."

The hansom waiting out front was all black, which I felt was grimly apt, and the horses waiting tossed their heads as though they were impatient to deliver me to the fiery scene of battle. The Provost stopped short, nodded to the driver, then turned off in another direction completely, presumably to uproot another man from his home to send him off to join our last stand.

I didn't wait for the steps to descend but rather opened the small door and hauled myself up and in.

It wasn't empty, a fact I barely had time to register and adjust for before I sat on Alcibiades' lap. He wore an expression of extreme irritation, though his eyebrows shot up when he saw me.

"If you aren't the luckiest whoreson this side of the Cobalts," he snorted, then set to examining the side door as if I wasn't there at all.

I tried to match his annoyance as best I could, but I felt nothing but a curious kind of relief at seeing a familiar face, a companion of mine who'd managed to survive the plague. I hadn't had a chance to speak with Hal about what had happened to the others after Berhane's passing, though it wasn't until I'd seen Alcibiades that I knew I'd feared the worst.

Next to me—where I'd taken my seat on the bench opposite—someone stirred, though I hadn't noticed him, a pale cutout in the dark of our carriage. I recognized the fall of his blond hair, though, and the same lazy elegance he'd exhibited while napping during his occasional attendance at meetings of the Basquiat.

"I told you not to speak until we'd reached the mountains," said Caius, though he didn't open his eyes, and he sounded a little dreamy still, as though he were half-asleep.

"What a warm welcome this is," I said, pulling aside the little window curtain so that I could watch the city as it passed quickly around us. "I'm quite happy to see the rest of you alive as well."

"Don't worry," said Caius, with a yawn like a cat's. "I'm sure it won't last long."

Alcibiades shrugged broad shoulders, though he too was looking out the window now that I'd exposed it. "I'm just looking forward to getting this over with one way or the other," he said.

"Soldier's talk," Caius retorted. "Any academic will tell you that nothing exists in such extremes except for stories in romans for children."

"The same romans that led to Hal's discovering our cure, do you mean?" I watched the spires of the Basquiat off in the distance and knew I would never be able to look at them again without remembering our confinement.

Alcibiades snorted again, and Caius merely made a censorious sound in his throat as though he thought he had better things to argue. The coach fell silent as we withdrew into whatever more private thoughts we were each of us entertaining.

I had never considered myself to be anything like the more

patriotic soldiers who would fight and die simply because our Esar told them to. I'd always believed it was the province of the intellectual to scoff at such mindless obedience. I thought that there were better solutions to a conflict than an endless war, despite my Talent's natural proclivity for it, and though I was a loyal citizen of the realm and did my duty as it was commanded, I'd never been stirred by anything deeper than that. For me, there was only the threat of treason and the desire to do a job well enough that I might return once more to the comforts of the Basquiat and Tabernacle Bar.

With every bump and sharp swing of the carriage as it turned corners it had never been built to turn, I saw more of the city I'd come to as a haven from my country upbringing. She had taken me in as her own after I'd spent the long years of my childhood feeling as though there mightn't be any place to which I truly belonged.

Thremedon was my home, and it held everything I had ever loved or had ever been given cause to love me.

I thought of Hal, rubbing his eyes with such force he was sure to damage them, forcing himself to stay awake through one more chapter, one more page, until finally he'd solved it. We were all of us fighting in our own ways, and to protect the things we loved seemed to me the best reason I'd ever been given.

I wondered then if the lapis city would still be burning when we came to it at last, if our forces at the front would still be fighting. It was a scene I both did and did not wish to see, but I felt a supreme and wholly strange gratitude to be living at this time, for whatever horrors it held, whatever tragedy, it was a history I could call my own.

ROOK

As far as I could understand them, the Ke-Han who were holding me prisoner kept asking me why Havemercy wasn't flying. Despite the barriers between us being able to communicate properly—like how we didn't speak the same language, and also happened to fucking hate one another on principle alone—my reply of "Fuck you" seemed to come over loud and clear. We understood one another just fine as far as the basics were concerned.

So at bottom what it shook down to was that they tried a lot of things to get me to talk. But I was better than that.

"You brought her down," I told my favorite guard, who must've kept requesting sessions for torture with me 'cause the feeling was mutual. He was missing an eye, which he obviously thought made him look real tough. "You fucking solve *that* problem on your fucking own!"

He didn't like taking no for an answer. Not a single one of the Ke-Han sons-of-a did, but I wasn't yessing anytime soon, and they weren't getting *anything* out of me. We were equal parts stubborn; the only problem *I* saw was that they were the ones holding the whip.

And the Ke-Han were pretty imaginative. They kept me like a rat in the dark, starving me, dripping water somewhere just to drive me wild. No matter what they did, though, I wasn't spilling anything. I knew that if they had any of the other boys, they'd be doing the same thing: just taking what was being laid down and suffering in private when no one could see them silently screaming.

It was kind of a bitter thing to hope, and one that made my stomach turn jack-flips inside of me, but I was praying at that point to anyone who'd listen that Have was in pieces somewhere. She'd've preferred it, rather than give these whoresons something to use. But even as I tried to think of her being gone for good, I also realized what a fucking genius she'd been—seeing through me and Thom and sensing we were of the same blood.

Worst of all, I didn't know if it'd work or not. Could be I'd sit here in this hole in the ground with the rats eating my toes or whatever the *fuck* it was they thought they were doing, with my girl destroyed, while meanwhile the Ke-Han rallied their forces and burned every last building in Thremedon to the ground, just as a thank-you. So that was pretty bad, even worse than the nightly visits from my one-eyed friend.

I don't know how long it went on. Like I said, I lost track of time, and I'd have better luck asking the rats than my captors.

And then one day—no fucking warning or *nothing*—this trapdoor above my head opened up, which wasn't the usual route they took when they were coming to visit me special and ask me their questions again, and I was hauled out into the sunlight, people talking in the Ke-Han babble all around me and the sun so bright I had to close my eyes against it. I was shivering, this close to puking all over someone, and what I really wanted to do was spit on somebody—only I didn't think I had any saliva left in my entire mouth, so that little show of defiance was out of the question.

I was shaking too much to be mad.

They wrapped a blindfold around my face—which I should've thanked them for, 'cause at least I didn't have to deal with the sun directly—and shoved me along some path that felt like I was walking on shards of glass the entire time. I figured it for rubble, but it could have been some brand-new kind of torture for all I knew. I was close to throwing myself down on it and hoping I hit something particularly sharp by the time they finally let me stop, and by then I was walking on something smoother but too hot, like sand under the sun at noontime.

They'd taken my boots at some point, probably days ago, so the whole ordeal was a real pisser.

I stood there for a little while, Ke-Hans whispering close by and some not so close by, and as far as disorienting me completely went, this was a pretty good trick. Finally, I felt someone's fingers at the back of my head, and when they took off the blindfold and I got a chance to get my bearings, I realized I was standing in what *used* to be the magicians' dome. I was surrounded by a group of men and women, all of them Ke-Han, and most of them looking pretty much the way I felt, all shelled out with no home anymore.

For some reason, they'd all gathered together like a bunch of toys in the torn-up shell of the dome. If this was some ritual killing, I just wanted them to get it over with.

In front of me was a man who dressed so fine and held

himself so straight I knew who he was without even needing to be introduced. No matter *what* a man was, Volstovic or Ke-Han or Arlemagne or *anything,* there was no mistaking royalty.

I'd come pretty far in life for the Ke-Han warlord himself to be requesting an audience with me.

I probably should have bowed or something, but if I'd tried it I'd've gone completely off-balance, what with my hands being tied behind my back, and the rest of me being dizzy in the first place.

The warlord had his hands folded behind his back and for a long time he didn't even acknowledge me; he was just surveying the damage, drinking it all in, like some sort of sick game he was playing with himself. When he turned around, there was a cat's kind of anger in his eyes, wild and fierce and narrow. I lifted up my chin. It was the only show of defiance I had left.

"You wear your hair the way we wear ours," he told me, and though his accent was rough and his words stilted, at least it was a language I fucking recognized.

"Yeah?" I asked. I was dizzy and half out of my mind; there was blood under my fingernails, and this cut Have'd scored across my chest when her wing snapped was festering. I could smell it, rotten and sick, especially in open air. "Looks better on me, though."

The warlord smiled, the expression thin and sharp. I wondered for a moment why he didn't just kill me for my insolence, because it was clear as the mustache on his face that he wanted to, but instead he lifted one hand with his palm facing out and complete silence descended over all of us. There wasn't even a whisper or the sound of somebody *breathing* too loud on the air—that's how quiet everyone was, and just 'cause their warlord had shown them the palm of his hand.

"It is because of the terms of the treaty," he said, "that I refrain from killing you."

"Treaty," I said. The sun was getting to be too much. "What fucking treaty?"

"The one we have just signed," he replied. "I believe it was an hour ago."

With a bow, one that was stiff and curt because bowing to

nobodies was something he'd never had to do before, he nodded to his left, and I saw that it wasn't just the Ke-Han who were gathered around in a circle watching me like I was the main attraction at carnivale. There were a group of people I didn't recognize but who sure as fuck weren't Ke-Han standing there, most of them inspecting a pile of scrap metal I could only assume was the last of our girls, but a few must've broken away from the rest at my arrival, and at this signal from the warlord, they came forward.

"Shit," I said, when they got close enough for me to see. "I know who you are."

"Is that so?" the man asked, motioning for the man with him—and he was one I didn't recognize at all—to untie my hands. I winced the second he touched me and swore in the Old Ramanthe.

"Yeah," I said, pain coloring my voice enough so I cursed again to chase it out. "You're the one they exiled for fucking the Arlemagne prince."

"Ah," said the Mary Margrave, not even blinking. "Indeed, you are correct in that regard. It is thrilling to see you still possessed of all your wits."

"Well," I said. "Some of 'em. Maybe."

"You have suffered less than the rest," the Margrave told me. "None of the others we hoped to find here in confinement is still living."

I felt this strange thing happen inside my stomach. I really would've been sick, and all over too, except there was nothing for me to get rid of inside my stomach. Instead, I guess I must've groaned, or moaned, or something. It sounded real pathetic, even to me, but then I barely heard it.

"Nobody else?" I asked. "Fucking *none* of 'em?"

"Four made it back to Thremedon," the Margrave said. "You are the fifth and final survivor—all that remains, I am sad to say, of the Esar's Dragon Corps."

I licked my lips like I thought that would do anything toward making them feel any less dry. "We ain't th'Esar's Dragon Corps no more," I said, sounding just like the real kid from the streets I was.

If there was a treaty, there wasn't a war anymore. And if there wasn't a war, there wasn't any Dragon Corps; it was simple as that. With only five of us still living, and most of our girls no more than junk metal by now, then there wasn't anything left of us—literal or figurative, in body or in soul.

I could smell it about to happen before it did, could feel my vision waver as I lost all feeling in my hands.

"Airman Rook," the Margrave said, but if there was anything more he said, I didn't hear it, seeing as how I blacked out right then and there and didn't even feel it when I hit the ground.

When I woke up, I guessed I was somewhere else; in any case I wasn't standing, and the Margrave wasn't there. I thought I saw my brother—real this time, and not some dead hallucination—and he called me by two different names, Rook and John both, 'til I didn't know who I was, and it didn't really even seem to matter over the hurt rooted deep down like it was a permanent part of me.

He told me to sleep, and I wanted to tell him he was my fucking little brother, which meant he couldn't tell me what to do, but then the blackness reached up again with nimble fingers and pulled me down into the quiet where there wasn't nobody, not even me.

HAL

I wasn't made for this sort of excitement. As much as I enjoyed the stories found within my favorite romans, of daring escapes and heroic battles and discoveries made in the eleventh hour, I found living them a far less attractive proposition than reading about them, and the strain of it had left me ill and exhausted more often than not. I didn't have the constitution for large, sweeping events; or, at least, that had been what I'd told Royston in the days after his return, when we had time to spare for speaking.

He'd been busy, as part of the delegation formed by the Esar at the last minute to negotiate the terms of our peace treaty with the Ke-Han. He'd even have to leave yet again, however briefly, to see that the conditions were being carried out.

Royston had explained the terms of the provisional treaty to me thusly: that all surviving dragons were to be retired, but that the pieces found past the Xi'an border were to be returned to Volstov. That the Kiril Islands were to be returned to Volstov, that the Ke-Han people would allow Volstovic occupation while they rebuilt their city, and that an established border would be fixed along the Cobalt Mountains. All in all it was fairly simple—at least, simple enough that I understood it all—and not even Royston could find anything about it to argue against.

When I had gone to visit Thom at the Airman, he told me in a terrible sort of voice that only four members of the corps had made it back from their final flight, and that the rest of the airmen had most likely been captured and tortured, or killed.

A funereal atmosphere hung over the whole building like a shroud, the airmen reduced to less than half their number, and I could see it on the faces of those who remained that not one of them was daring to imagine any of their fellows could escape if they'd lived long enough to be imprisoned.

The airman Rook hadn't been among the men who'd made it back, and for that brief, dark window of time when we'd all thought him dead, I'd spent many a day trying to alleviate the weight of Thom's misery. It had given me a distraction from my own fears, for even then no one had been speaking of our certain victory with the assurance they'd exhibited during the time of the ball. Rather, everyone skirted around the issue, as though they were afraid they'd tempted fate quite enough for one lifetime, and now they were waiting to see on whose side she truly fell before they all began to congratulate themselves.

The day I'd received my letter from Royston had been the day the Airman received word as well about Airman Rook, who was alive, and the status of the other airmen, who were not. It was a month after the battle. Thom had come to meet me soon after, rather than stay and show his relief in the face of the Dragon Corps' staggering loss.

"As much time as I've spent with them," Thom had said, voice hooked low on some rougher emotion, "it isn't something I would presume to . . . intrude on."

I understood, then, that he felt as strongly about Airman Rook as I did about Royston. I couldn't say I particularly understood the reasoning behind it, but then if I were being perfectly fair, I supposed it wasn't exactly the sort of thing you could explain to anyone with reason alone. People are connected in many different ways, and I was only beginning to learn a few of them.

Things happened very quickly after that.

I'd half expected th'Esar to organize another ball, since winning the war seemed a much better reason to me than covering up an insidious plague, but after he'd returned, Royston told me that wasn't the way that things worked. Apparently signing a treaty had all sorts of complicated connotations, such as how you couldn't really celebrate your win too much because that would be too close to parading under the Ke-Han's noses, and that wasn't the way to foster proper peace between two nations.

"But we *are* at peace," I said, staring out of one of Royston's many round windows at the city, cloaked that afternoon with the grayest rain.

"Yes," Royston said. I felt his rough cheek against my ear, and I smiled. "I never thought *I'd* be there to see it, but indeed, it would seem we are."

Even the city herself seemed to acknowledge it. It was a beautiful sight stretched out before us, all of Thremedon smiling privately to herself beneath the clouds.

Then the invitations to the ceremony arrived, thick and ornate as everything else from the palace. That it was called a ceremony, Royston assured me, didn't mean it was going to be anything particularly terrifying, even though he spent the better part of the day searching for his favorite cuff links and moving about as though he couldn't sit still, which he only ever did when he was very nervous.

"If you're going to tell me not to worry about something," I said, perched on the window seat of our drawing room with a roman in my lap, "then the least you could do is have the courtesy to pretend you're not doing the exact same thing."

He paused in the middle of the room, then came to sit on the couch beside the window, leaning his head against my hip. I thought it couldn't be very comfortable, but the flush of warmth low in my stomach prevented me from actually suggesting another position might be more favorable.

"I'm sorry," he said. "It would seem I set a very poor example on top of everything else."

I smoothed the gray at his temple with my fingers. "We could always stay home and read," I suggested. It was not an entirely practical suggestion, and one he was bound to refuse, but I thought it was important I offer it nonetheless.

Royston laughed then, hoarse as though he still hadn't completely returned to his old health. "Hal," he said, "I believe it is my duty to prepare you for the very real possibility that one day you may be reading a history of these very events we have so unexpectedly managed to survive and find yourself a character in it."

"Oh," I felt my cheeks go warm. "Surely not."

"Nonsense," he said. "If it hadn't been for you, this all would have ended in the Basquiat—and I include myself in that assessment."

I crawled down off the window seat to sit beside him instead, putting my arms about his shoulders and resting my face right against the break of his high collar where I could see his throat. "I did it for you," I said quietly. "No one else needs to know."

"Ah," said Royston. "Well, it's a pity that I made mention of it to the Esar, then."

"What?" I blinked, sure that I'd misheard him, or that this was one of his dry jokes that I'd not yet entirely got the hang of and, sometimes, suspected I never might. "Are you— You aren't serious?"

"I certainly am," he said, fingers making idle patterns against my shoulder blades so that I sighed. Somehow, his touches calmed me, despite the more and more alarming information he imparted. "I believe he made some mention of offering you a position of honor at the 'Versity."

"What?" I said again, feeling as though I'd missed some vital detail, or that perhaps I'd fallen asleep again the way I'd done for a time after the war had ended, dropping off without warning as if my body had just decided to catch up where it could whenever it felt like it, so that Royston would find me curled up in strange places and find himself inspired to move me to the bed.

"Well, I'm sure it will all be sorted out at the ceremony," he said, and kissed my forehead. "That is, if I can find my blasted cuff links."

CHAPTER SEVENTEEN

THOM

The ceremony was set in a long reception room at the palace that had plush red carpeting running down the center of it and chairs on either side where the noblesse sat. Behind them, the higher-ranking officers of the Volstovic army stood. At the very end of the room stood th'Esar himself, and seated next to him was th'Esarina, resplendent in crystal and pure white.

This was ceremonial dress—it had been for generations—and none but a rare few were allowed to see it.

At any other time, I might have felt out of place, but there was no room in my heart or my head for anything except the man standing not quite mended at the back of the room with his fellow airmen.

They were a much smaller group than they'd been before.

As th'Esar read the names, first of the magicians who had given their lives in the final battle, as well as those who had fought and lived, I found my gaze drawn irresistibly to what remained of the Dragon Corps, dressed that afternoon all in black instead of their customary royal blue with the gold epaulettes of their dress uniforms. Balfour held his new hands folded awkwardly in front of him, still not entirely comfortable with the prosthetics the magicians had created for him. Once, I would have been fascinated to know that there were magicians who could employ the same technology they'd invented for the dragons to make prosthetics for a man who'd lost his own hands, but I felt no pleasure now to see the science in action. They shone silver and alien, and a little too big for him, but most poignant of all, I thought, was the fact that he had no gloves that would fit them. Ghislain stood still as a shadow at his side, his arms crossed over his chest. Adamo stood by himself, pointedly ignoring the moment when Luvander slipped in late to stand with the rest of them. He wore a bandage over one eye, and inclined his head toward Ghislain to ask what he'd missed, their mouths moving in near-silent whispers. Every now and then, Ghislain would nudge Rook with his shoulder, to get his opinion, and Rook would scowl the same way each time, knowing full well Ghislain hadn't forgotten where he was injured and where he wasn't.

Rook hadn't spoken to me since we'd set foot in the palace, not even to snap at me for following him watchfully, as though I was afraid his ankle would give out on him at any second. Rather, he ignored me completely and limped to the room where the ceremony was being held, melting in with the other airmen as soon as he arrived and not once looking back.

I told myself it didn't matter. Acknowledgment was more than I could ask for and I should have been thankful he'd lived at all. It was much more than many people in my situation had been left with.

By rights, being neither a hero nor a soldier, I had no place among those attending, but Rook had made some bitter remark about *family,* and in the end no one seemed to have noticed me enough to object to my presence. Th'Esar himself even had some misguided impression that I'd done something instrumental in all this mess; that I'd aided Hal or put Hal in position to solve the riddle on his own with barely a second to spare. I wasn't sure if this was true or not, but as always, there was no arguing with th'Esar. You did as you were told, and kept quiet about it.

That left me here, in this somber, private room, watching Rook, as always, from afar.

I noticed as some of the magicians passed me by that they were dressed all in black, just as the airmen, so that despite the finery of the noblesse and th'Esar and Esarina themselves, the ceremony was ultimately a dark one. The war had ended, and a provisional treaty had been signed, which was more progress than we'd previously made in my lifetime—in several lifetimes—but it had still come at an unimaginable cost. There were so few magicians remaining to us, and no more than the barest remnants of the Dragon Corps, not to mention their dragons. I'd overheard Adamo speaking to the Margrave Royston about it—of the fourteen girls, there were only five who still resembled themselves. Havemercy wasn't one of them.

When I thought of her in pieces on the other side of the mountains, I felt a distant sadness overtake me. She wasn't my dragon, and it was often said that, because they were made of metal and machinery, the dragons had no souls at all for us to mourn their passing. But when I recalled Havemercy's affinity for the dirty jokes Magoughin told, and the sharp, fond way she'd spoken to my brother, I couldn't help but wish she'd made it through in one piece. If not for her own sake, I added more privately, then for my brother's.

We were given medals individually; that was the ceremony's purpose. Mine was a small silver star for services rendered to the crown. Each of the airmen received a golden shield except for Rook, who received two, one of them inlaid with rubies, and the magicians were each given a crescent of ivory. There was no celebrating.

Hal himself was honored separately, and I saw how uncomfortable it made him. There was no precedent for what sort of war medal he should receive, and so th'Esar had chosen to hang about his neck a silver key, which I thought fitting and which made Hal blush to the tips of his ears when he knelt to be decorated with it.

And then, after a period that seemed both as swift as mere minutes and as endless as days, it was done.

Marius caught my sleeve as we began to file out of the room, his hands shakier than usual, but his eyes as clear as they'd ever been before the disease had almost taken him. The sight of his familiar face so overwhelmed me that I was speechless while he fingered my silver star, a rueful smile playing across his lips.

"I told you you'd manage it," he said at last, clapping me

on the shoulder. His voice was still rough from his ordeal in the Basquiat. "There was a time when I assumed I'd been talking out my ass, but I'm glad you've proved me wrong."

I ducked my head to hide the bitter turn my laugh took. "You were right about it," I said. "It was an opportunity I could never forgive myself for passing over to another."

"There was no other," Marius said. "I know you don't entirely ascribe to my side of the philosophical border, Thom, but these things do happen for their own reasons—and not just because I'm a stubborn old man who was bored with hearing men argue foolishly over what was to be done over a trifling offense."

"Impatience or fate," I murmured, too weary to be properly wry. "I wonder which it was?"

"I'd say a combination of both," Marius offered. "Compromise is all the rage these days." He paused, then added, "Will I see you back in the 'Versity come spring? We've a dearth of keen minds since you left. Though in all fairness, I'm not supposed to say as much out loud to any of my students."

"You'll have Hal soon enough," I pointed out. "Famous throughout all of Volstov."

"And rightly so," Marius said. "We all ought to go on missions to the countryside, same as Royston."

I smiled somewhat more honestly at that. Who knew what friends Marius had lost during this time? I shook his hand in mine, letting the grip linger, and his sharp eyes softened.

"Well," he said. "Whatever you choose, Thom, I hope it serves you as well as you have served."

There was nothing I could say to that, and we parted ways soon after, Marius in the company of a red-haired woman named Marcelline, and I alone, wishing I were the sort of man Marius believed I was.

After that afternoon, Rook had something of a relapse, and because he was too feverish to protest, I tended to him. Adamo didn't object—in fact, there was something in the set of his jaw that seemed to indicate he rather endorsed my stubbornness—but I was too busy tending to Rook to think about it. There were burns along his left side, and there had been some question as to whether or not he'd be able to fight off the infection that had crept into the raw, open wound over his chest. On his back—when I had occasion to see it—was a complicated web of precise, deep cuts, already healed over, that would one day be a map of scars. Those were no battle wounds; he'd suffered them at the hands of the Ke-Han, and every night as I tried to sleep I saw them before me like a tangled maze, out of which I might never find my way.

It was foolish of the other airmen to have let Rook attend the ceremony—though in truth he'd insisted on it—and now he was suffering the effects of that rashness.

"You might not even have the chance to see them unveil your own statue," I told him one night a few days later, believing him to be asleep.

He grunted, and opened one eye. It was piercing blue, not touched by any fever, and my heart dropped all at once.

"Don't fucking lecture me," he said. "You got no right to it."

He was right, and I turned my face away from him, seeing to the basin of cool water and the wet cloth I'd been using to bring down his fever during the nights, when his temperature inevitably rose.

"No," I said. "That's true."

I could feel his eyes on me a long time after that, even after he'd closed them, and his breathing had evened out into the regular patterns of sleep.

On the fourth morning he was well enough to stand, and though I saw how bitterly he hated to do it, at midday he allowed me to help him to the window, out of which we could see the unveiling. The other airmen were in attendance, and so the Airman itself was once again pervaded by that eerie silence when she was left all to herself. It was all the more eerie for the knowledge that it would never hold the same boisterous noise as once it had, and that the men I'd come to know and even, if only a little, to understand would never return to leave their boots lying in the entranceway, or play their confusing game of darts against the common-room wall, whose paint still bore the pocks and marks of the game. Perhaps it always would.

I hoped, strangely, that no one would ever paint over that smaller tribute to the men who'd lived and died for all of us. In the most complicated of ways, I truly missed them, even if I'd never been their friend at all.

"That big one," Rook said, startling me out of my reverie. "That one me?"

I turned to him, barely daring to hope—but his face was turned away from mine, caught in a shaft of sunlight, and so beautiful and still as to be a statue himself, though I doubted they'd included on his statue the small scar at the corner of his eye, tearing through his right eyebrow, or the sharp, unhappy line of his mouth.

I longed to embrace him—to be embraced by him in turn. My brother needed me, and could no more reach out for me than he could rebuild his Havemercy. We were on opposite sides of the window from each other.

"I'm not sure," I replied, careful with my words. "Perhaps, when they return, the others will tell us."

"Maybe," Rook agreed, nodding once, and seemed to believe that was final.

I suppose it was.

When he was again well enough to walk on his own and had no more need of me, I still sought to do the littler tasks for him, bringing him his meals when he preferred them and otherwise hovering around his doorway like a moth beside a lamp, just in case he might still require my assistance in some matter. This was how I caught him at packing soon after the unveiling of the statues.

This was also the first time he ever truly invited me inside his room.

"Stop fucking lingering," he said, rolling up a pair of trousers into a ball and shoving them into a canvas rucksack. "Either get in or get out, but being in between like that can be fucking annoying."

I chose the former option—how could I not—and slipped inside, closing the door quietly behind me.

"You seem to be leaving," I said. It was the only thing I could think of, and I knew it was I who needed to speak first.

"Yeah," Rook agreed. "Looks like, doesn't it?"

I clasped my hands behind me and dug my nails deep into my palms to find some surer footing. "Is there," I began, "do you have—any particular destination in mind?"

"Not good to stay someplace where everyone knows what you look like down to the bump in your fucking nose," he said. "Ghislain told me the statue's pretty fucking spot on, so I'm taking my corps money and going somewhere else."

"Oh," I said. "So you're going to—travel."

"That's what going somewhere else means," he said.

I couldn't let him leave; not without saying what I should have said before anything else. "John," I told him, all in a rush, "I'm sorry."

He went still for a moment, and I thought he was going to yell. He struggled with something very tight in his jaw, but he seemed suddenly to overcome it, and all he said was, "Yeah. I got that from all the fucking crying."

"For what I did to you," I said. "*Not* for how it turned out for me."

"Look," Rook told me then, "ain't it better just to say we don't *have* any brothers anymore? Twenty-one years, for fuck's sake. Can't you just let it drop?"

"No," I replied. The conviction in my voice frightened even me.

"We did some mean fucking things to each other," Rook said. "And there were times when we pretty near almost did more. I wanted to break your fucking jaw sometimes, or worse."

I swallowed. "Yes," I said.

"You lied to me," he said, and from the roughness of his voice I almost thought he might have meant, *And I lied to you, too.*

I stared at his poster of Lady Greylace, wondering if he'd take it with him, some small memory from home—but Rook wasn't the sort of man who indulged in any sentiment, much less nostalgia, the most cloyingly sweet of all. I closed my eyes, pinching the bridge of my nose with my fingers.

"I did," I said.

Beyond that, I didn't know what else I felt. I wanted something from him—John, Rook, my brother and the man he'd become—but it was such a jumble of emotions I could barely untangle one from the other, not unlike the maze of torture carved into his back.

"Yeah," he said. "So that's that, and I'm going."

We were quiet for a long time, standing on opposite ends of the room together. I was unsure of how to mend myself, but men were resilient creatures, and somehow we might both manage it, given enough time. Rook was going to see the world. I was going back to my studies at the 'Versity. We might yet find each other again, even if it took another twenty-one years.

I could barely swallow my own excuses, but I forced myself to do so.

"Perhaps," I said, my voice shaking despite my best efforts, "you might send me a card in the post."

"Care of," he said. "Maybe."

"When are you leaving?" I asked.

"Tomorrow morning," he said. "Got myself a ride and everything."

I made my excuses and took my leave of him before I did or said anything rash. If Rook was going, then there was no more reason for me to stay in the Airman. I had to rearrange the pillow on the couch, dig the last of my notes from underneath the cushions. I was missing a few socks—part of one of the earlier pranks, no doubt, and one which I'd never got around to realizing until now—and then I sat down all at once as my legs gave way beneath me and cried at last in the common room for all the times I hadn't.

No one came in; no one saw me. It was as private as I'd ever managed to be in the Airman, now that I no longer required such privacy.

Because I was so tired—because I'd been unable to sleep properly for weeks—I must have drifted off, and when I woke it was early morning, my whole body stiff from the uncomfortable position I'd been curled into all night long.

I combed my hair with my fingers. My suitcase was already packed; I was already wearing my shoes. I paused only for a moment by Rook's door, but it was quiet inside and no light spilled out from underneath it, and I knew immediately he was already gone.

That was it, then, I told myself, and squared my shoulders against the change. I would have to write Chief Sergeant Adamo, now ex–Chief Sergeant Adamo, a letter of thanks; and shorter ones for each of the other airmen, Ghislain and Luvander and Balfour. It was a small gesture, and one by which they'd like as not be baffled, but I was certain I needed to bow to the formality of the moment, as if by treating my time with the Dragon Corps as a chapter in my life I could just as easily *end* it as one.

Except for Rook—John—who was sitting on the stairs when I opened the door. I nearly fell over him before I caught my balance.

The sun was rising from the direction of the Cobalt Mountains, rising properly now, and the whole sky was alight without any hint of the grayish color of predawn.

"So, Hilary," Rook said, "where're we going?"

I closed my eyes and let the sunlight wash over me. "I've always wanted to see the hanging gardens of Eklesias," I said.

Rook stood up and shifted his sack more comfortably over his right shoulder. "I don't even know where the fuck that is," he said.

ROYSTON

Things had changed, and they also hadn't. For some time since the unveiling, there was talk of tearing the Airman down now that it no longer served a purpose, and popular opinion had long been that the building was a blight on the architecture of Thremedon, flat and too modern and entirely out of place. Yet no one ever quite got down to doing anything about it, and it went on standing solid and gray as a mausoleum, a testament to the Dragon Corps in its own way.

The view from the Rue d'St. Difference was different now

that there were statues lining the crossing between lower Miranda and upper Charlotte. I couldn't walk my usual route home from the Basquiat without seeing all fourteen of them, which I supposed was the intention when it was decided they should be erected there. Nevertheless, it was still jarring to see the faces of men I'd known magnified and elevated to the status of war heroes.

In that respect, I was exactly like Hal: not *entirely* prepared to deal with the realities of living in a time when the statues were freshly built rather than hundreds of years old.

On the days when Adamo wasn't giving guest lectures at the 'Versity, "like some fucking professor" as he so adeptly phrased it, we would meet occasionally for lunch, and it was during these times that I took full advantage of the opportunity to compare him to his larger bronzed counterpart.

"He's taller than you," I said, signaling our waitress in the hopes of speeding up the service of our coffees. If there had been a statue of *me* set along the Mirandaedge, I was sure this wouldn't have been a problem, yet Adamo refused to use his fame toward such petty ends as obtaining a decent and expeditious cappuccino. How very like him. "And handsomer, certainly."

"You're sure you didn't lose *your* eyesight in that plague?" Adamo drank his coffee any way it was served, and particularly if it was black, which forced me on occasion to wonder why we were even friends at all.

"That was quick," I said. "Perhaps your time at the 'Versity hasn't been wasted after all."

He shrugged easily, though there was still darkness in his eyes when he turned to look at the line of statues all along the Rue. "After dealing with my boys," he said, "talking to a bunch of students who're actually *interested* in what you've got to teach 'em isn't really much of a challenge."

"Oh, don't be so sour just because you've found your true calling so late in life," I told him, and laughed when he brought his teaspoon down hard against my knuckles. "Bastion, look at the hat on that one."

Just as the Ke-Han in their lapis city, we were rebuilding.

It was a slow enough process even *without* the daunting task of restoring destroyed buildings to their former glory— something the Ke-Han alone must suffer—but there were some days when I believed us up to the task, and some when I suspected I would never see my city fully recovered. Between the loss of the airmen and what colleagues I'd bid farewell to beneath the golden dome, it seemed as though there was no replacing what we'd lost. There were days when I could no longer look at the Basquiat without remembering, and it had once been my favorite sight in all the city.

At my suggestion, Hal and I went on long walks around the city, and I pointed out the best places to go for a quick meal in between daily lectures, or where he might drop in to a private library if he needed to study in *real* peace and quiet.

"And I just follow Whitstone Road to get to you?" he asked on one such walk, when we stood side by side in front of the 'Versity fountain, sun dappling the water so that it arced like molten gold in all directions.

"That will take you to the Basquiat," I confirmed, and slipped an arm about his shoulders for no other reason than that I wanted to and could.

He fished for something under his shirt at the neck, and drew out the silver key the Esar had given him with a glad look of triumph. "This time, they can't keep me out."

"I would use my Talent to explode anyone who had the gall to try," I confirmed, and he kissed me then in front of the spray, so that by the time we were finished we were most unfortunately damp.

For the first time I could remember, there were empty seats in the Basquiat, but there were familiar faces too, and more than I'd dared to count on. The handy trick about doing a service for royalty was that they couldn't turn around and banish you once again after they'd made a public acknowledgment and handed out the medals.

Among the magicians I'd known before the plague, Caius remained, and though I was sure Alcibiades would rather have spat on us than join our numbers, I did see him about the city every now and again, mostly with groups of men who I assumed had been soldiers once. There was talk of erecting some sort of a monument for those magicians who had died during the plague, and when after a few weeks it became evident that no one was particularly keen on reentering the room at the top of the golden-domed tower, it was cordoned off. One of the magicians with a Talent for sculpting stone carved an uncanny likeness of their faces around the walls, and though I'd visited it with Hal when it had first been opened to the public, I found I couldn't bring myself to go again after that.

What had started as a plan to acclimatize Hal to the winding streets of Miranda unofficially became his habit of walking me to and from the Basquiat every day, pointing out everything I'd showed him with the kind of tenacious memory and eagerness to learn that I knew would serve him well at the 'Versity. I'd been right to bring him to the city, and not only because he'd saved all of our lives in the process.

Hal belonged in Thremedon; he belonged with *me*.

I'd never before been a man prone to permanence. In that respect, I was much the same as the city herself, for even with all her familiar landmarks she was constantly shifting just below the surface. For the most part, her appearance remained the same, but she was always changing just enough to keep me on my toes. I, too, felt myself in constant flux, adapting to her whims and pleasures. For Thremedon, it would not have been a problem to remain ever so in this permanent state of mutability, but I was a man, and there were some things that for me must necessarily remain constant if I were ever to remain this content.

One afternoon, barely half a week before the spring term began at the 'Versity, I returned home to my private tower to find Hal waiting for me on the top step. In one hand he held a long roll of fine paper—I recognized it immediately for a list of required texts—and an envelope in the other, its 'Versity seal broken. His cheeks were flushed from the brisk nip of late winter air.

"It's *so* long!" he exclaimed, as soon as he saw me. "How am I ever to find all these books? I thought I'd start early, but I'll never be done!"

I drew close to him, giving the list a brief glance. "You'll find," I said gently, "if you look at the titles a second time, while better composed, that you are familiar with at least half of them. If you wait a moment while I fetch my wallet, we shall visit the shops together, and I'm sure by the end of the day we'll have them all."

"Thank you," Hal said simply.

There was a wealth of feelings in his words, which extended far beyond the moment. I found it necessary just then to turn my face away from his, and in doing so I found myself faced with all of Thremedon descending before me toward the water, the uneven rooftops catching the clean sunlight through crisp, bracing air. This was my city, beautiful and dangerous and twisting and coy, and I knew in that moment that I had at last come home to her.

Because the hardest part of war
is figuring out what to do after . . .

With much sacrifice,
the armies of Volstov,
led by their mechanical dragons,
have brought the Ke-Han to their knees.

But dragons have no place
at the negotiating table . . .
and they can't fight the intrigue
that threatens the fragile peace.

✠

SHADOW MAGIC

✠

by

Jaida Jones and Danielle Bennett

The follow-up to *Havemercy*

A Spectra paperback

In stores now

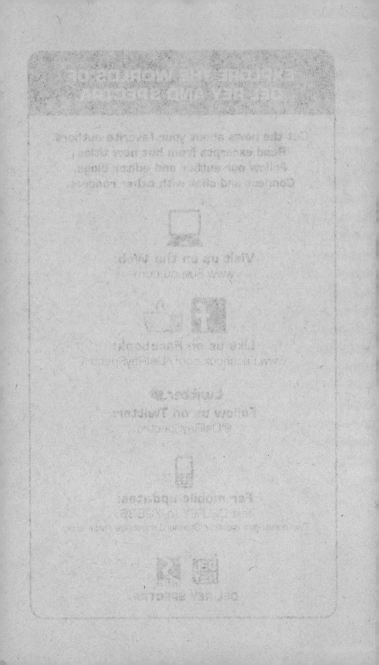